UNEXPLODED

By the same author

The Changeling
The Wave Theory of Angels
Fifteen Modern Tales of Attraction

UNEXPLODED

Alison MacLeod

HAMISH HAMILTON
an imprint of
PENGUIN BOOKS

HAMISH HAMILTON

Published by the Penguin Group
Penguin Books Ltd, 80 Strand, London WC2R 0RL, England
Penguin Group (USA) Inc., 375 Hudson Street, New York, New York 10014, USA
Penguin Group (Canada), 90 Eglinton Avenue East, Suite 700, Toronto, Ontario, Canada M4P 2Y3
(a division of Pearson Penguin Canada Inc.)
Penguin Ireland, 25 St Stephen's Green, Dublin 2, Ireland (a division of Penguin Books Ltd)
Penguin Group (Australia), 707 Collins Street, Melbourne, Victoria 3008, Australia
(a division of Pearson Australia Group Pty Ltd)
Penguin Books India Pvt Ltd, 11 Community Centre, Panchsheel Park, New Delhi – 110 017, India
Penguin Group (NZ), 67 Apollo Drive, Rosedale, Auckland 0632, New Zealand
(a division of Pearson New Zealand Ltd)
Penguin Books (South Africa) (Pty) Ltd, Block D, Rosebank Office Park,
181 Jan Smuts Avenue, Parktown North, Gauteng 2193, South Africa

Penguin Books Ltd, Registered Offices: 80 Strand, London WC2R 0RL, England

www.penguin.com

First published 2013
001

Copyright © Alison MacLeod, 2013

The moral right of the author has been asserted

Set in 12.5/16pt Fournier MT Std
Typeset by Jouve (UK), Milton Keynes
Printed in Great Britain by Clays Ltd, St Ives plc

A CIP catalogue record for this book is available from the British Library

ISBN: 978–0–241–14263–9

www.greenpenguin.co.uk

For my mother, Freda, with love, as ever

SPRING

I

The talk that May afternoon was of the rockfall at the undercliff. A fisherman's dory had been buried, along with his dog, and the collapse had taken part of the sea wall with it. The news, though negligible compared with the reports from across the Channel, was repeated and wondered at in town, as if the nerves of the population ran like thin fuses through the cliff-line's strata of chalk and flint.

She stepped from the dim cave of the house-goods shop into a dazzle of sea light, and, turning left rather than right, walked briskly north up Ship Street, away from the prom where onlookers still gathered in the hope of seeing another boat safely returned. The music from the empty rides on the Pier receded. She shifted the weight of purchases in her arms. At no point did she turn back to take in the spectacle on the beach, for she didn't want to see what the man in the shop had described, the ghostly flotilla of little boats, some pocked by gunfire, listing oddly around the old carousel.

She crossed Church Street and hurried through the grounds of the Pavilion, past its dream of domes and minarets. There was no time to stop in the gardens or to take tea at one of the sunlit tables. She had to be home before Philip. It's what everyone said these days: routine was the thing.

At The Level, the town's public common, she lowered her basket and let herself rest for a few minutes in the meagre shade of an elm.

On the green ahead, a group of old men played a ruminative game of bowls, for the schools had not yet emptied, and even the benches around the boating pond were empty except for a young mother and her runaway toddler.

Locally, The Level was known as such for the simple reason that little else in Brighton *was* level. Most of the town swooped recklessly skyward, as if it were a dizzying ride that had been plucked from a pier and dropped carelessly on to the coast. On three sides of the town centre, hills climbed north towards the wheat fields of Sussex and the hump of Ditchling's ancient beacon, east towards the rail terminus and the deep, untamed valley of Devil's Dyke, and west towards Race Hill, the racecourse, and the town's perennial Gypsy encampments. For all its effort at gentility down the centuries, Brighton had never managed to escape the wild excesses of its highs and lows.

Like The Level, Park Crescent and its gated acres of garden lay in the flat bowl of the town. But that hot, simmering spring, the bowl was less a bowl than a crucible in which the events of the year to come – their vagaries and intensities – would catalyse into the hard, unyielding metal of the inevitable.

Along Brighton's seafront the five-mile ribbon of the promenade ran east towards the ravelled line of the coastal cliffs and west to the elegant mansions of Hove – among them, Evelyn's childhood home on Brunswick Square. Twelve years before, her parents had disapproved of her move from Hove to Brighton. It had been another measure of Geoffrey's unsuitability. Her new husband was not a man of independent means. Her parents did not know of his family. His mother, they'd learned from local sources, had not been 'of sound mind'. Geoffrey did not drink enough to pass muster in her father's club. Even the very comfortable townhouse on Park Crescent had failed to impress them. It hardly mattered that its Regency park had reminded her of the gardens of Brunswick Square, where she'd played and read for long hours as a girl. It wouldn't do to choose a house on a whim, her mother had said. There were slums near Park Crescent. The slaughterhouse was too close. The racecourse was also too close, with its blight of criminality. Even the beach at Brighton had been spoiled by tawdry pleasure-seekers. A Brighton address would be their ruin.

They moved into Number 7 on the 1st of May 1928 and shocked her mother by dispensing with a live-in maid. Instead, Tillie came to them each morning from her own house on Magdalene Street, or, rather, she had come until the week before, when her husband was called up.

In the shop that afternoon, Evelyn had clutched Tillie's list and gathered the items as if each were a talisman against uncertainty, and if the uncertainty was great, the weight of her basket was greater still. On her journey home, she balanced an oversized box of soap flakes, a storm lamp, parcels of candles, boxes of matches, a bottle of witch hazel, first-aid provisions, bars of carbolic soap, emergency lavatory paper and a bottle of cod liver oil. As she walked, she stopped several times to shake the blood back into her right arm, though she never let go of the plait of onions that she gripped to her ribcage with her left.

When the King had surprised the country with his unprecedented call for a day of national prayer, it was warning enough. Whatever the BBC said, the situation could only be dire. Still, she'd procrastinated, pushing Tillie's list deep into a pocket and avoiding the town centre for most of that week – the seafront in particular, for she couldn't bear to see the boats lurching on to the beach and toppling with the wounded and the frightened.

Fear was an infection – airborne, seaborne – rolling in off the Channel, and although no one spoke of it, no one was immune to it. Fifty miles of water was a slim moat to an enemy that had taken five countries in two months, and Brighton, regrettably, had for centuries been hailed as an excellent place to land.

At home again, in the kitchen that had until only the week before been Tillie's domain, Evelyn lowered her basket, pulled off each glove, unbuckled her jacket, and gobbled water from her hand at the sink. It was hot for late May, ridiculously hot, but she felt relieved by the success of her expedition, and now, as she heaved open the kitchen windows, time slowed. Her breath deepened. The scent of lilac spilled in from the terrace. Only when the front door slammed and Philip charged up the stairs to his room – singing out his hello – did she turn at last to reassemble the day.

Her prize onions lay where she'd dropped them, on a kitchen chair, looped like three feet of baubles on a piece of parcel string. She'd forgotten the ticket in her purse and had experienced a childish rush of pleasure and embarrassment that morning as Mrs Chavasse waved her forward to the front of the WI hall to collect her winnings. When would anyone have French onions again?

She slipped out of her jacket and into Tillie's apron. At the table, the arc of her nail cut cleanly through the first onion, and its skins fell away, crackling like static. Soon the rhythm of the knife on the chopping board lulled her beyond thought. She couldn't know that this was the last beat of a pure, untrammelled present; a final moment of uncomplicated absorption.

When she sensed someone in the room, she turned, expecting to see Philip, happily clutching his cornet of sweets. He and Tubby, Tillie's boy, still made their Saturday pilgrimages to Billet's, laying out their pocket money in a row of grubby coins, and although Philip always tried to make his sweets last the week, he usually succeeded only as far as Wednesday. But today, as she turned, it wasn't Philip she discovered but Geoffrey in an odd sort of profile: his broad, pin-striped back rested heavily against the door jamb; his chin was doubled on his chest. She hadn't heard him come in.

Go back, she wanted to say. *Go back to our routine. Don't you see? There is nothing so beautiful and so necessary.*

Her eyes stung and welled. She glanced at the clock on the win-dowsill. Not even four o'clock.

'I came direct from the station,' he said, bending to kiss her neck.

London, she reminded herself. Wednesday afternoons were Lon-don. Monday afternoons were the Camp.

She smiled up at him but she didn't want the words. She didn't want anyone trespassing on a peace of mind that was already, like fresh snowfall, pocked with the chaos of prints. 'Philip's upstairs,' she said, reaching for the chops in the Frigidaire. 'He'll need help with his multiplications. Would you mind, darling?' Her husband's jacket smelled of platform waiting rooms and the stale brake dust of trains. *Go back, go back.*

Another new recipe. They rose from the pages of *Good House-keeping* like orisons of calm.

Place 1 lb. of onions in salted water.

'Did you get that tooth looked at?' she heard herself say.

Boil till softened.

'There wasn't the time.'

'But you're back early . . .'

Keep the water. Mix the breadcrumbs and seasoning with the whisked egg. Put chops in the Pyrex.

'Seymour-Williams wanted a word.'

She looked up – his voice was flat, like something dead under a tyre – as she reached for the next onion. On and on she chopped, producing far more than the recipe required. Her eyes streamed, but she heard her voice grow oddly sing-song, as if her effort at cheer would encircle them like a charm. 'I hope it wasn't that business about what's-his-name again . . . the prodigal ledger clerk. How did he think he would get away with it? A bit of me admires the man's gumption but does he lack *all* imagination? How many embezzlers risk prison for a future in *sandbags*?' She pulled a po-face but Geoffrey didn't laugh.

He was removing his collar studs and unlooping his tie. 'No . . . I'm afraid it was another matter altogether.'

Change was creeping under the door and through the windows of their home, persistent as gas. (*Be observant. Do not touch door handles or other pieces of metal if spots appear.*) It was gathering over the house in spite of the purity of the day's rinsed blue sky. It was spiralling down the flue. At night as they slept, it would settle over their hearts.

She pushed the mound of onions into a pot, placed the pot under the dome on the range, and washed her hands at the sink. From the corner of her eye she watched him draw back his chair and lower his head, as if there were a one-minute silence she knew nothing of or a solemn loss she was failing to observe.

No one, he said, could countenance it, but given the evacuation from France, Head Office had had no choice but to agree a plan. If the country were invaded by daylight, each branch would bury a portion of its cash holdings, transfer another portion to a designated location, and burn the rest. Much of Lloyds' assets, indeed much of the country's assets, had already been shipped in gold to Canada, and no one, he admitted, could even say whether the transfer was legal. If word got out, there would almost certainly be a run on the banks.

Evelyn felt the hard knot in her chest relax. So this was it. Nothing that had actually *happened*.

But he didn't release her hand. His fingers were cold next to hers. She noticed a piece of dead coke on the floor in the corner, a bit that Rosa, their Spanish char, had missed that morning, and she had to stop herself from rising to sweep it up. She made herself focus. She turned up the corners of her mouth to show she was listening.

'All of this means that I'll be required to take the remaining cash and bonds from the vault to –'

Her eyes widened. 'Not here. We couldn't possibly have it here.'

'No, not here,' he said, and he knotted his fingers in hers. 'I'll take it to the station. From there, we'll travel with it on military passes.'

'Travel?' She laughed. She'd make him laugh it off too, in spite of Lloyds, in spite of Seymour-Williams. 'Geoffrey, no one will be travelling during an invasion, least of all the family of the man who is Head of the Invasion Committee . . . Surely we're duty-bound *either* to stay and be invaded like good citizens *or* to return the case of sherry the Committee is bound to foist upon you this Christmas, firstly as a token of their thanks, and secondly, because sherry is *such* excellent value now that Franco has broken Spain.'

But he didn't return her smile. She doubted he'd heard a word she'd said. 'Seymour-Williams wants my choice of four men by Friday.'

She inhaled sharply – 'But it will be chaos. Philip is too young' – and she felt some frail certainty crack, clean as a wishbone within. 'We can't leave . . .' Somewhere a joist or ceiling beam creaked, as if the house itself were shifting. Only then did she understand what it was that he wouldn't say: '*You'll* leave? You'll leave us?'

He closed his eyes and pressed his hand to his jaw to quieten the riot of nerves in his mouth.

9

'. . . You will.'

'No,' he said, 'only if –'

'For the day? The week?'

The toothache was leeching the colour from his face; his forehead was clammy. 'It's precautionary stuff, Evvie, worst-case scenario. That's all. I daresay they have to have a plan, people at the ready.' He opened his eyes and forced a smile, a digression, a stab at the casual. 'The Bank of England is stockpiling Molotov cocktails. Can you believe it? The clerks, evidently, stink of gasoline.'

But it was too late for laughter. His timing was all wrong. 'For how long, Geoffrey?'

In the flesh of his neck beneath his ear, she watched his pulse jump. 'Indefinitely, I'm told.'

She bowed her head to hide the heat of her face. The tea towel in her lap was stained. Blood among its cabbage roses. She checked her hands and nails, panicking, as if it were her blood and not drippings from the chops. She was no good with all this. She felt queasy whenever she crossed the threshold of Hatchett's, the sweet stink of suet and blood catching at the back of her throat; the flies stranded and buzzing on strips of sticky paper by the overhead light; rabbits, pigeons and guinea fowl suspended on hooks like charms on a ghastly bracelet. Her mother was right. She'd make a mess of things in the kitchen. She hadn't been raised for the kitchen. At her finishing school, she'd been lectured on the importance of overlarge centrepieces and *l'art de recevoir*, not in how to joint a bird or gut a rabbit. She wouldn't cope without Tillie, but Tillie could hardly cope with her own family now that she was on her own. Evelyn was lucky. Everyone said so. Geoffrey wasn't going anywhere. 'Reserved occupation'. Until now, she had been lucky. Ashamed of her good fortune. But lucky.

Through Mrs Dalrymple's open window next door, the BBC's afternoon organ music boomed out suddenly, ludicrously. An acrid sharpness bit the air. Burning. Something was burning.

She pushed back her chair, walked slowly across the room to the range, and lifted the smoking pot off the heat. 'That's it, then.' She'd forgotten the water. She'd forgotten to add water to the pot. How stupid. Her prize onions were a black mulch.

He was on his feet, opening the back door. 'Evvie, never mind it now. Let's just get some air.'

'No . . . Really. It's fine. It will clear in a moment.' She couldn't move from where she stood. 'I'll bring you a brandy for your tooth. Why don't you relax in the sitting room?'

But he held the door, waiting.

Outside, the perfection of the day – a flat, Gilbert & Sullivan sky of endless blue – irritated her. In the Park, two rows of Girl Guides were being led through a frenzy of jumping-jacks by smiling older girls. Where had they come from? Why was everyone exercising German-fashion these days? Didn't young women read furtively any more or smoke or fall in love with unsuitable men? Had there ever been a time when everyone wasn't so cheerfully public-spirited, when privacy hadn't been selfish? (*Make a note of the thoughts you get. Test them. Are they honest? Unselfish? Neighbourly? Clean? If not, what can you do about it?*)

What had happened to all the reprobates in town? Where were the malingerers, the mobsters and the pimps in their camel-hair coats and glacé shoes? What had happened to the artists in their run-down digs and the happy adulterers dancing in the open air on the Aquarium's deck? Where were the pretty boys and the men who walked the prom, their white socks flashing their code beneath the hems of their trousers? Had even the peep-show girls and the dandies joined the war effort? Had Fear made good citizens of everyone?

Not that she didn't want to be steady and decent and true, to follow Geoffrey's lead. She'd married him for his intelligent kindness, for his sense of fairness, for his loyalty to people. On Tillie's envelope each week, he'd never failed to write, 'With our very sincere gratitude', and he meant it. He didn't regard one's servants as a different class of human. She'd married him because he was a banker who had little regard for the trappings of wealth or class; because he'd been, in this respect, so entirely different from her parents, with their reverence for 'old money'.

The year before, he'd defied even her dowager mother. 'But some boys,' her mother had exclaimed, 'are sent away to board as young as the age of four! Philip is *seven*. Think of the opportunities already lost, Geoffrey. Think of Philip, of my grandson, not of yourselves.' The local Grammar would do, he had told her. He wanted Philip to grow up as he himself had, on the coast with the sea air in his lungs. He wanted the boy to understand that life was not one large, eternal club. Whatever advantages his son had been born to, he would not grow up with the sense of entitlement Geoffrey had witnessed among so many of his peers at Oxford. Her mother had turned to her then. 'Careful, darling,' she'd warned with her vinegary smile, 'or you'll be acquiring doilies and an aspidistra next.'

Her parents had disapproved of Geoffrey within minutes of meeting him, and while the force of her mother's feeling had dulled with the years and with the death of Evelyn's father, it had never disappeared, for Geoffrey was everything they were not: reasonable, thoughtful, fair.

Yet who was he today? When had he ever taken a major decision without consulting her? She turned to him, studying his face as if reading his lips, as though he were speaking to her through a thick pane of glass. He was pointing to a patch of earth. 'Just there,' he was saying. He hadn't coaxed her on to the terrace simply for fresh air. There was something else. That's what he was telling her as he pointed to a spot beneath the lilac bush.

'Whatever do you mean?' she said. Tears, real tears, not onion tears, pricked at her eyes. He was going to leave them. They had never been apart as a family, not even for a night, yet now he was capable of abandoning them.

From the branches of the old beech tree, rooks lifted into the sky, drifting like blown ash. Over the red-brick walls of the private park, a tram scooted by on Union Road while, from the high hill of Elm Grove, came the wail of an ambulance.

'I've buried it. Not too far down . . .'

'I don't understand . . .' She had to shake herself.

'Two hundred pounds –'

'*Money?*'

'A precaution.' Each syllable was a labour. 'Two hundred pounds and . . .'

A girl in a bright cardboard crown ran past them on the park path at the bottom of the terrace steps, her brown plaits flying.

'Geoffrey . . . ?'

He looked away. 'A keepsake . . . That photo you liked of the three of us on the Pier last summer.'

13

2

She gave up on sleep and slipped out of bed, reaching for Geoffrey's cardigan on the bedstead and pulling it over her slip. In the kitchen, she felt for the torch on the shelf and shoved her feet into the pair of old plimsolls by the door. When she turned the key and opened the door, it was to a vast moon, full-faced and bright, and the suddenness of it, the promiscuity of it in the blackout, made her pause, unnerved by its light and the beat of blood in her neck.

She eased the door shut, walked across their terrace and down the steps on to the Park's perimeter path. There was no need of the torch after all, and she abandoned it to the bottom step.

In the silvered darkness, the laurel gleamed. The beeches tossed flickering shadows on to the lawn. She had never been in the Park so late, and it wasn't as if she could have explained to anyone – to Geoffrey, say – what she was doing out there.

Perhaps she had wanted to see, to smell, the night flowers once more. Was that it? Along the winding path, the fairy lilies were out, and the white campion. Moonflowers trailed their sweetness. Was it too early for the towers of white phlox and their honeyed scent? Night flowers served no purpose. They were unwarranted gifts – small, delicate triumphs that exceeded purpose, that sang of useless variety. A late frost could wither them, and in even the mildest of years, they were more ephemeral than the moths that hovered over them, yearning for nectar. What were flowers to a war? What was anything?

At the end of the summer, seeds and shoots would be gathered, the bulbs and tubers lifted, the beds turned, and the lawns of the private Regency park ploughed into vegetable plots. Even the moat at the Tower of London had been given over to root veg and greens. Soon, everyone said, common garden flowers would be a luxury, and as she walked into the leafy tunnel along the Park's winding path, the night air left her dizzy and haunted, as if its scent were already a memory; as though she were already a former, bygone self; a woman who, regarded with hindsight by an older, more knowing self, seemed an innocent, a dreamer, a fool.

At the boundary wall, near the gardener's hut, the night rumbled faintly – a car edging its way along Union Road. Its lidded visors reduced the headlamps to two cautious shafts of light, and she darted away like a trespasser, or, worse, a mad woman in her underclothes trawling the night for meaning.

Let them land on the beach, she thought. *Anything, anything other than this waiting*. Everything had changed that week. The Home for Crippled Children was to be moved deep into the countryside. Hitler, it was rumoured, did not approve of crippled children. On the Crescent, three more families had left for America. The synagogue on Middle Street had taken down its sign. Her grocer no longer seemed able to add up in his head. At St Peter's, the vicar urged his congregation – in the words of Timothy, Chapter 6, Verse 12 – to 'Fight the good fight of faith' and 'lay hold on eternal life', but she'd seen his eyes glaze over strangely.

More pragmatically, the BBC had started issuing daily guidance for those suffering from 'faintness of heart', a convenient catch-all of a phrase that seemed to address breathing difficulties in the unseasonable heat as well as inadmissible feelings of panic and cowardice.

The night was cut by a tang of earth – fresh topsoil somewhere ahead – and the thought of all the new green life, of its blind need to push up, made her inexpressibly sad. *Sleep, sleep*, she wanted to say. *Not now, not yet.*

Sometimes, on calm days or still nights, the huge sash-window frames of the house shook unexpectedly – depth-charges in the Channel, Geoffrey said – while on the beach, oil from destroyed ships was washing in with the tide and clotting like blood between the pebbles. Neither of them could speak of it. Bright-eyed young men, beautiful, foolish and frightened young men, were being blown to pieces – literally, she thought, *to pieces* – as she sat in her Wednesday-morning knitting circle making socks for feet that would be lost to amputations, and mittens for hands that would never cup a waist or a breast again.

And every day, closer. An amphibious landing. A physical invasion.

There had been occasional hours that week when she'd managed to escape her thoughts. You could fill yourself up with fear. You could clasp it to you – out of a sense of concern, duty, preparedness – but, as the day passed, you somehow forgot to hold on, or you tired of holding on, and, guiltily perhaps, privately, you let the fear go, as if dropping the baton in an interminable relay race.

So fear was overtaken simply by the ringing of the telephone, or by Philip shouting he'd found a bicycle tyre at the scrapyard, or by her own voice automatically reminding him he wasn't to play at the scrapyard with Tubby Dunn. Fear yielded to the starching of Geoffrey's collars and cuffs; to the pleasure of May blossom and the horse chestnuts, plump and lustrous again with spring. Fear was forgotten over a book or a weak cup of tea at the Pavilion Tea Room; over the address labels she stitched to each item of Philip's clothing in case, in the chaos to come, the unthinkable happened and they were separated. It was lost to sterile dressings and antiseptic in her First Aid class. It dissolved in sleep but gathered once more into a grim ballast as she opened her eyes to each new day.

That ballast had first settled in the pit of her in her girlhood days when, behind the Regency bow-front and the Corinthian columns of Brunswick Square, her father's mood would, routinely but without warning, turn from impatience or irritation to cold fury. Sometimes she'd watch his entire face change, as if his physical form were suddenly inhabited by another man, a stranger, while his eyes, wildly flaring, seemed hardly able to recognize her.

Her mother had had little choice but to swiftly dismiss the servants for the day and to send her out into the gardens with books her governess left her to discover in the attic nursery. Behind the gate, in the lee of a box-hedge, she read to herself from *Tales from Shakespeare*, *Aesop's Fables* or Kipling's *Just So Stories*, murmuring each story aloud as if the words on the page were antidotes against those being uttered behind the bow-front of her home. Later, she would work her way, indiscriminately, through much of nineteenth-century literature, from Sir Walter Scott to Walter Pater to Mrs Gaskell to Dante Gabriel Rossetti, relying on the lending library in Hove because her mother assured her that book-buying was an affectation of the middle classes. Only the Lawrence Family Bible and *Burke's Peerage* were allowed to reside permanently at Brunswick Square.

To imagine wasn't to escape but to go deeper; to see through to the secret life of the world. Alone in the gardens, her hands went numb in winter and her face burned in the summer, but better that exile than having to listen to her mother's efforts at appeasement; to the way she parroted her husband's every view in order to calm him. Together, they happily despised communists, liberals, pacifists, agitators, suffragettes, servants, Jews, Catholics, the Americans and the French, the 'great unwashed' and the Corporation. But while her mother's compliance occasionally defused his temper, she could never quieten him for long.

The tumours succeeded where she had not. The doctors blamed a lifetime's dedication to chewing tobacco, but her parents disagreed even after her father's throat had closed up with the growths. He had three months waiting to die in rigid silence, unable to do much more than chew and spit into the brass spittoon that sat permanently by his chair and, finally, by his bed.

With her marriage to Geoffrey, Evelyn had escaped Brunswick Square, and by the time of her father's death two years after, the panic of those domestic disturbances had settled into the dark sediment of memory. If anything, she could take pleasure in the knowledge that her marriage was nothing like her parents' union. From the beginning, she'd loved Geoffrey for his steadiness, for the evenness of his temperament, for the calm of his touch and his wide, cool hands. She had, in every sense, got away.

Only now, the war, the world itself, all of it was tipping into the unpredictable, and Geoffrey seemed neither steady nor even. What had he told her only that afternoon about the tin? If she and Philip had to leave without him – leave to go *where?* – he had said she was to find the tin and stitch the notes into the lining of a skirt or coat.

She didn't want two hundred pounds. She didn't want precautions. She wanted him to go back to being the person he was.

For years they had strolled into the Park each night after Philip had got off to sleep. Sometimes they chatted with wandering neighbours but they spoke little to one another. It was enough to feel the pressure of the other's arm, to be held in the Crescent's charmed half-moon of a space and slip into its steady Regency calm. They'd pause to look up at the lion and lioness on their plinths on either side of the Park's gates, their stone heads eternally turned in opposite directions. The male looked outward over Union Road and across The Level, towards the line of blue sea a mile to the south, while the lioness gazed back over the Park's lawns and the gabled slate rooftops of the houses. But now, suddenly, after twelve years of marriage, he'd broken their bond. He'd told her he would abandon them. *He* had become the unpredictable, the unknown dangerous quantity, and here she was, wandering alone in a garden once more, wanting, with the bleak passion of a child, for life to simply return to itself.

She picked her way through the abandoned hoops of a croquet game, crossed the north lawn and seated herself wearily on a bench. At the edge of the Park an owl, white-faced and impassive, lurched out of nowhere into flight, and her heart stammered in her chest. A barn owl, she was sure. It flew in the direction of The Level, its pale undersides flashing, its blunt, unlikely body ploughing a seam in the dark.

Night birds and foxes, creatures of the countryside, were coming into the town and discovering, in its alleyways and parks, in its bins and allotments, the shelter of the blackout. In the meantime, household pets and even the donkeys from the seafront lay in stiff, rotting heaps at the back of Brighton's veterinary surgeries; animals were too difficult to control in air raids, apparently. The world was back to front, helter-skelter – absurd. The Queen took lessons with a revolver after her morning tea. *The Times* urged golfers to keep a rifle in their golf bags. Old women were stockpiling garden forks and shears. At Devil's Dyke, a German fighter plane had come down in a churchyard, its fuselage riddled with bullet holes, its wings folded back like a wounded bird's. Sunday ramblers had picnicked proudly beside it.

She'd laugh if she weren't so uneasy, if she had anything like the composure she'd once credited herself with. Only recently had she come to accept that her former sense of calm, of well-being, was little more than the ruse of privilege; the straight back of deportment lessons.

Men were still arriving, broken, in Brighton. The trains at the station heaved with the injured, the dazed and the defeated. Everything was coming too close.

The night before last she and Geoffrey had lain awake together, rigid as they listened to the massive, stuttering drone of the first German bombers circling the skies of the town. Zoom-za zoom-za zoom-za. (*Do* not *run away from the plane. If you have to run, run* towards *the plane, not* from *it.*) They came in low over Lewes Road, then banked above the Park before rising and flying north in the direction of the station. 'Getting their bearings,' Geoffrey had murmured. And she thought, *I'll hold my hands up. I'll do whatever I'm told. I'll let them at me. I'll be a disgrace.*

She'd been putting it off, but now she'd do it: a rucksack for each of them; a pair of boots; a change of clothes; extra socks; waterproofs; a comb each; toothbrushes; compressed food; brandy; gas-burn ointment; plasters; ration books; the bank book; ID cards; gas masks.

But where would they go? Towards London? (*If you run away, you will be machine-gunned from the air as civilians were in Holland and Belgium.*) Towards Ditchling and into the Downs?

Everyone said it was unimaginable, but she could imagine it: flint-eyed soldiers lining the London Road; officers, impeccable in their dress uniforms, in the boxes at the Theatre Royal; their elegant wives taking tea at Boots, amused by the quaintness of the ritual; loudspeakers at street corners; Jews – had she ever known a Jew? – writers, artists and intellectuals disappearing in the night; public executions at the Town Hall; neighbours denouncing one another; at Brighton Grammar, a rank of new teachers. Philip would bring home a fresh history textbook, and she would forbid herself to say anything as she turned its crisp, deceitful pages. There would be fitness regimes and biological assessments and betrayals and humiliations. Would she, Geoffrey and Philip be able to *be* one thing and behave as another? And where, never mind who, would Geoffrey be?

She crossed the Park, arrived at their terrace, and was bending for the torch on the bottom stair when the thought returned to her. He had hesitated when telling her the contents of the tin.

A picture of them on the Pier. Why think twice? What did he want to spare her knowing? Had he buried a pistol with the notes and the picture? The Enfield revolver he kept in the safe in his office? She'd give it back. She didn't want it. Is that what had been unsettling her all night?

She switched on the torch and ran its light over the terrace to the border opposite. The patch of turned earth was by the lilac bush. The garden spade stood upright in the soil, its handle glinting. Geoffrey had told her they must leave it there; it must remain a marker, obvious but nondescript.

He'd looked away. When he'd answered her, he'd looked away.

The ground was dry with the weeks of unseasonable heat, and the topsoil more unyielding than she would have expected. She had to cut at its surface with the edge of the spade until she hit the moister, looser earth beneath. Woodlice scuttled, surprised. She glanced up at the moon's full, inscrutable face. What if Mrs Dalrymple from next door was walking about in the middle of the night, as she often did?

The old lady had informed the air-raid warden that she couldn't abide the long, heavy shutters of the house; they made her feel like she was being closed into her grave. She relied on a candle, as she had in her childhood. But now, if Mrs Dalrymple spotted her in the moonlight, she'd possibly shout, as she often did, and wake the Crescent. She'd cornered Philip only last week. 'Philip Beaumont, do not grow up. Men are execrable buggers!' Then she gave him a handful of shillings, three aluminium pots for the scrap-metal drive, and permission to play with Clarence, her pet tortoise. Her blue language was the last trace left of her old East End voice. When the Beaumonts had first arrived, she had confided in Evelyn that, before she'd married 'so disastrously well', she had worked in a London garment factory making underwear for the ladies of the British Raj. 'Lace knickers,' she said with an air of genteel distraction, 'so they could get the air on their fannies.'

Evelyn had liked her immediately.

A sudden metallic clunk made her forget Mrs Dalrymple. She raised the tin. McDougalls Self-Raising Flour. The lid was difficult to prise off. Had Geoffrey hammered it shut? Her nails couldn't manage it, and the spade was too large. She slipped back into the shuttered gloom of the kitchen. The cutlery tray lay on the sideboard. A butter knife popped the lid.

Twenty ten-pound notes.

No revolver. And no photo either, unless it was tucked inside the Lloyds' envelope.

She slid her nail under the flap and stared.

At the bottom, two small green capsules gleamed like bullets.

3

He woke and, before he could remember what the hot-water bottle was doing on the pillow next to his face, the thought intruded. Thursday, the 30th of May. A day that was meant simply to slip into Friday, into the ease of late spring, and be forgotten. Would it?

The bedspread and sheet lay snagged at the bottom of the bed, rejected by at least one of them in the mugginess of the night. In the dark of the room, he could just make out, next to the vase of lilac blossom on the bedside table, the glass of water Evelyn had poured for him before bed. She'd added a few drops of peroxide from Tillie's brown bottle in the scullery, and had made him gargle with it before sleep. Then she'd passed him a paracetamol, wrapped a towel around the hot-water bottle and laid it against his throbbing face. The procedure seemed to have worked. The swelling in his cheek had gone down. The abscess must have burst in the night. A bit of penicillin, and he'd be human again.

Last night, the tooth had been their excuse to speak no more of it – of the Bank and his news. Now she slept on, her back to him, her right arm twisted awkwardly below her head. The last time she'd spent a night like that, she'd woken with an acute case of tennis elbow, and, day after day, he'd had to help bathe her and dress her in what had become a series of oddly tender rituals.

The memory did nothing to discourage the erection he'd woken with. Nor did the whiff of peroxide from the glass or even the faint taste of pus in his mouth. He rose, toed his way blindly to the washstand, poured fresh water from the ewer into the basin, splashed his face and rinsed his mouth. The room was already hot for half past six. Soon, he would open the shutters and blast the room with sunshine. It seemed in the worst possible taste somehow, the weather for a summer fete at a time of mute, collective dread.

He unbuttoned his pyjama top and climbed back into bed, forcing himself to turn away from her, towards the clock, as if the steady progress of the luminescent minute hand would dispel this morning's need, more urgent than usual. After their upset yesterday, he'd removed himself to the sitting room with a glass of brandy. His mind had clamoured suddenly for the deep escapism of sleep, but he'd dozed only fitfully, waking every few minutes to the bombardment of brass-band hymns from the Salvation Army citadel across the street.

Dinner was overcooked chops, green beans and day-old bread. The onion fiasco had spoiled her *Good Housekeeping* hopes. Philip had chattered, mercifully. *Tarzan Finds a Son* was playing at the Regent, and could he go? Orson's big brother, Hal, had seen Tarzan when he'd dived off the board at the SS *Brighton*, which was *before* Johnny Weissmuller was Tarzan, but *after* he'd swum to fame at the Olympics. Now Hal was twenty years old and serving in France, but Orson said Hal said that Tarzan was still his hero because only the fittest survived in the jungle.

After dinner, Philip had played with his yo-yo in the Park while Evelyn did the washing-up. At half past eight, she called him in, got him washed and to bed. Geoffrey listened to her overhead, walking slowly from room to room, closing each set of shutters for the blackout, sealing the three of them off, as if theirs were suddenly a house of mourning. When she joined him again, the excuse of her novel and the nightly, pre-news broadcast of the national anthems of all the Allied nations relieved them both, once more, of the pressure of conversation.

She disappeared before the end of the news, busying herself with the peroxide and hot-water bottle before running a late-night bath. She said she could still smell the scorched onions in her hair; that he should get himself to bed anyway; his bottle was ready. He nodded and said, 'Yes, why not? You relax, it's been a long day' – even though neither could remember the last time they hadn't retired for the night together. If he was honest with himself, wasn't he relieved that she had decided to spare him her tears?

Now, irrationally perhaps, he longed to bridge the distance between them. Her slip had climbed up over her thighs in her sleep. He fingered the ends of her newly washed hair, a dark tangle that smelled of her DuBerry's shampoo. He moved closer to the arc of her back, to her vertebrae, a Braille for his fingers. Yet to wake her would mean watching the new, painful memory of yesterday cross her face, and the prospect of it unsettled him as much as his longing impelled him.

He kissed the nape of her neck, slightly salty now after the warmth of the night and the heaviness of her hair upon it. Beneath his palm, the skin on her elbow was rough; the hair on her arm, fine and soft. He ran his hand over the curve of her hip, fuller in the last few years. His testicles ached pleasurably. 'Evvie.'

'Hmm . . .'

It was not entirely disingenuous. 'Your arm. You're sleeping on your arm again.'

'It's fine . . .'

'Just shift a little . . .' He drew her close, wrapping her feet in his. The muscles in his calves tightened. His heart drummed in his ear.

Why, he asked himself, from the deep comfort of their bed, *had* he agreed to the Bank's request? He hadn't admitted to her that no one at Head Office had exerted pressure. On the contrary, they'd suggested he take a bit of time, mull it over, but he'd told them no – of course – someone had to be prepared. He was the branch manager. It simply made sense.

Sometimes, privately, he felt unnerved by the depth of his feeling for her. It was at odds with the moderate person he usually was. He loved her too much – needed her too much – and perhaps he was never quite sure where one feeling ended and the other began.

Had he agreed so readily to Seymour-Williams's request simply to prove to himself that he could? Had he wanted somehow to cauterize his heart?

If so, he was making a kind of progress, not only in the guarantee he'd given at Head Office the day before, but also in the grim business of the pills. He'd cancelled the appointment twice, prevaricating, but, at last, he'd made the necessary arrangements with Dr Moore. He'd acted rationally. He hadn't allowed any personal weakness to stop him from taking the difficult decision that other men had taken, discreetly, for their families.

After the unconventional unhappiness of his childhood home – the secrets, the dissembling, the mournful visits to his mother in her room at Graylingwell – he had never aspired to anything more than a conventional family life. He'd wanted only an affectionate home, a shared sense of purpose, and the respect and love of his wife and son. The simple things in life were actually rather extraordinary – he'd never believed otherwise – and if he provided the life, the four walls of it, Evelyn animated their home. She was the thinker, the natural wit, the discerning eye. Next to her, he was a primitive; a blunt mass;

straightforward, diligent, and clear in his judgements only because he lacked the patience for complication.

He felt a surge of being, not only in their most intimate moments, but also in seemingly unremarkable exchanges: when his palm brushed hers in the space between them on the train; when she glanced at him over the top of her book; when her voice called from the top of the stairs. It was as if her hand or glance or the shape of his name on her lips released him into life.

'My muse,' he'd once called her, warmly if a little self-consciously, and she'd looked up, quizzical, surprised, but delighted, as if, in that evanescent moment, he'd seen through to the beating heart of her.

He glanced behind him at the clock. Twenty minutes to seven. And again the thought, fast and sharp as the nick of a blade: *what might the day bring?*

'Evvie?' His thoughts were snapping in all directions. ''Morning . . .'

She turned towards him at last.

'My tooth is better.'

'That's good . . .' Wifely. Perfunctory. Only at the cusp of waking.

He kissed a spot behind her ear, and she pressed her back and buttocks to him, sleepily, instinctively. Nothing, no memory of yesterday, intruded. He turned, briefly, groping for the bedside drawer – the ringing jingle of the old brass handle, the sweet, sudden scent of mahogany, his fingers grappling, then the brown paper bag and the square of waxed paper and cellophane. He concentrated on the wrapper, making a small tear with his teeth and lifting the thing free. He blew into it twice, to check it was sound, cautious as always.

'What time is it?' Her voice was thin, anxious. She'd remembered.

He moved to her, hauling her gently on to his chest. She was still light-boned, small, almost breastless, and the heat of her thighs on his made him strain towards her.

'No rubber,' she said through the murky darkness.

'Yes, it's there. I've got it on already.'

'Not today.'

'What do you mean?'

'Leave it off.'

He reached out an arm and found the switch, but as his hand came away, he knocked the small white marble base; light flooded their bed, their faces, their eyes, and the heavy gold fringe of the shade trembled.

'No more,' she said.

He rolled her on to her side, then leaned towards her on one elbow. 'No more what?'

'Rubbers.'

'I don't under –'

'Just no more.'

He could feel the latex wrinkling around him. He heaved himself over her, supporting his weight on his splayed hands. He closed his eyes, and rocked against her, trying to revive himself, to move past the moment. He bent low and kissed the line of her collarbone, then her shoulder, already brown with the heat of spring. He was still conscious of his infected mouth; he must keep it away from her lips. When he opened his eyes, she was staring at him, coldly, her eyes straining.

'Evvie?'

'I won't have it.'

'What won't you have?'

She looked at him, embarrassed, angry. *'Precautions.'*

Yesterday. It was still yesterday. The shock of his news. She squeezed her thumb and index finger to the corner of her eyes to stem the tears. The dirt under her nails distracted him briefly. How had she got dirt under her nails? She'd bathed before bed.

He didn't expect her to reach down and slide the rubber off him. He didn't expect her to guide him into her. He felt both strangely relieved – she wanted him, she wanted him after all – and disturbed, by her insistence, by the anger still sharp in her face, by the tears standing in her startled eyes. He tried not to think. He'd withdraw on time.

Through the shutters and the window open behind, he could hear the sounds of the new day on the Crescent and beyond: the treble of a blackbird; the heavy hoof of the pig-man's horse in Union Road; his clamorous tipping-out of the swill-bin; Mrs Dalrymple meowing to her tortoise on her front step. The waves of pleasure and tension rose and dipped. He raised her hip in his hand and pressed her to him. A moment more, he thought, he'd allow himself just a moment more – when he withered inside her.

4

Evelyn Lawrence met Geoffrey Beaumont at the Royal Pavilion Midsummer Ball of 1926. She had turned eighteen that year and had spotted her gown in the arcade of glass display cases at Plummer's Department Store: a simple sleeveless design in white chiffon with a drop-waist sash and an organza flower at the hip. Her mother had studied the gown through the glass display as if she were viewing a breed of monkey at the London Zoo. The handkerchief hemline was questionable; the fabric flimsy. Did Evelyn *want* to be showy?

Her cousin James was on his hols from Cambridge where he was reading Medicine, and had gladly agreed to escort her. But after his third glass of Veuve Clicquot, as they strolled between dances in the Pavilion Gardens, he'd confessed to her that he'd persuaded a beautiful girl to join him for a cigarette and a discussion of whether art was possible after a world war, or – he grinned at Evelyn – was everything doomed to idle expressionism?

Evelyn glanced back. The girl, a redhead in pale green silk, waited on a galleried balcony.

'I take it the question is hers, not yours?'

'I only need a line, Evvie . . .'

'You have too many already, James!'

'She's clever. She's clever like you.'

'You see!'

'You once told me that finishing school would have finished you off were it not for the art classes.'

'History of Art classes. If she knows her art, she'll finish you off.'

'It is my sincere hope.'

'James!'

'Evvie, dear heart, listen. If I fail in my cause, I'll have no choice but to confess to your parents that you are so winsome, I'll need to marry you myself, and to hell with even-featured, physically impressive children who don't drool. I think they'll come round to the idea once they realize your dowry won't even have to *leave* the family.'

She shook her head, smiling. 'My first proposal . . . Somehow, I'd imagined it all so differently.'

'I'll tell your mother it all began with that sudden shower as we stepped from the cab, when, yes, Aunt Maude, it was as you'd feared: Evvie's flimsy gown clung to her, and I couldn't help but observe –'

'With your anatomical eye . . .'

'With my anatomical eye – of course – that her breasts are of a size and shape otherwise seen only in the delicacy of champagne glasses' – he glanced for corroboration at the empty coupé in his hand – 'and *that's* when I knew, dear Aunt, that's when I knew I had to have her.'

'One line . . .'

'You are the bestest.'

'You are unstoppable. Ask her if she regards Max Beckmann as an idle expressionist.'

'Beckmann?'

Her smile was sly. 'See you shortly.'

The Pavilion's oriental domes and minarets were floodlit and golden, as beautiful and unlikely as ever. High overhead, gulls floated spectral against the inky sky, while partygoers strolled across the lawns, their laughter rippling strangely. From the ballroom, the slow-slow-quick-quick tempo of a foxtrot spilled into the night, and, somewhere, a woman declared drunkenly that she'd lost a shoe.

As the lawns emptied, Evelyn began to wonder just how late it was . . . Had James forgotten her? Ahead, in the dim light of a red paper Chinese lantern, she could see loops of smoke rising from a cigarette, although she had to edge closer before she could make out its owner. 'Sorry to trouble you.' She tried to sound breezy. 'Would you have the time?'

As he stepped into the light, smoke escaped his nostrils. 'Certainly.' He pushed back a starched shirt cuff. 'It's twenty minutes past ten.' He was tall, long-limbed. She couldn't help but observe that the sleeves of his tailcoat were actually too short. 'The only thing worse than *borrowing* one's tailcoat,' she heard her mother declare, 'is *buying* one's furniture.' For her mother, it went without saying that one inherited one's worldly goods – and that one owned a good tailcoat.

On his breath she could smell whisky, no doubt from a flask hidden in the pocket on the underside of his tails. He reached into his jacket and offered her a cigarette from a case but she shook her head. She never managed not to cough, she explained, privately regretting that she sounded like a child. She met his eye, and looked away again, as if to examine the paper bloom of the lantern. He invited her to join him on a nearby bench but she declined, unable to say that a damp bench would mark her gown. Across the lawn, the lanterns were dissolving into the mist that had crept up from the front. 'You can smell the sea,' he said.

In the narrow pool of light, his eyes were a rich brown, warm as autumn chestnuts, but was there also, she wondered, something guarded about them? Did he labour under a certain reserve? And now, was he simply too polite to walk away and rejoin his party?

'Yes,' she said abruptly, remembering the sea. 'There's a definite tang in the air.'

He pointed to the Pavilion's central dome and offered some fact about its construction. As he did, she noticed that the underarm seam of his jacket was split, and had to suppress a smile.

A stray couple walked past. The man was singing a tune – ''Deed I Do' – and tapping out the renegade beat on his top hat as his partner's hips sashayed to the rhythm. Their figures disappeared before his voice did, but, when it too was gone, the night seemed quieter, emptier – as strange as a theatre after closing, when the boxes, the bright plaster cherubs and even the chandelier's dazzle have been absorbed into the ubiquitous dark.

Each suddenly felt odd, like an exile, between worlds. He dropped his cigarette to the ground and crushed it with the toe of his shoe. 'Would you like me to escort you inside?'

'I'm keeping you.'

His eyes widened. 'Not at all. I only thought –'

'Yes,' she said, getting hold of herself. 'Yes, I really should locate my cousin.'

They introduced themselves, belatedly. She liked his smile, even though his strong teeth seemed slightly overlarge for his mouth. His expression was reserved yet honest and direct. It was a *good* face, she decided.

She rocked slightly on her heels while both ransacked their brains for something more. She almost laughed. How, in the middle of provincial Brighton, had she found herself standing with a stranger in the gardens of a pleasure palace? When had they stepped into *The*

Arabian Nights? Her mouth tingled with a sensation she couldn't put words to, while he considered reaching over the rail to break off a bloom for her hair. But 'Look!' she said. 'Lilac, still.' After her words, the gesture, he decided, would have been stagey.

She was about to inquire about his party inside but stopped herself. He did not offer her a sip from his flask. Too familiar. Nor did he offer her his tailcoat for her shoulders, because the night was, after all, warm.

'I hope you're clever with a needle and thread,' she said, taking even herself by surprise. He looked bemused. She laughed and took the liberty of poking her index finger into his armpit. 'It would seem you've expanded tonight.'

'Ah,' he said, a smile playing on his lips. 'How careless of me.'

'And in a debutante's company.'

'It seems I've let myself go.'

'I shouldn't have to see such things.'

'Quite.' He nodded gravely.

'I'm shocked, of course.'

'I can only apologize. Sometimes, I shock myself . . .'

She forgot her performance. 'I don't believe you!' She grinned, then turned her face quickly to the sky.

'Drat.' He reached for his cigarette case. 'There goes any hope I had of intrigue.'

She shrugged. 'If it helps at all, I can't actually *see* you in the dark.'

'That's very kind, thank you.'

'Shall we repair to the light?'

'Yes, I really must get you back.'

'I *would* say that my cousin will be worrying about me, but it's more likely I'll have to remind him who I am.'

'Impossible.'

'Alas, you don't know James.'

'Alas' – his voice in the night was amused and warm – 'I don't imagine you're easily forgotten.'

She turned, snapped a lilac bloom off the bush, and slid it behind her ear. 'Mr Beaumont, I'll beg you to remember that, as a debutante, I am *entirely* forgettable, and my escort will challenge any man who avers otherwise.' Her smile twitched.

At the top of the flight of stone stairs, the anteroom was as stuffy and raucous as a schoolroom. Near the door, a group of perhaps half a dozen young men clutched their capes and canes, and debated loudly and drunkenly the effects of May's General Strike. His party, she assumed. Four of them greeted Geoffrey as he passed, and he returned a few quick words. One of the four also nodded warmly to her. Another among them, a man with a monocle – black eyes, a hairline crack at the rim of his eyepiece – looked intently at Geoffrey but did not nod. Was it a snub?

She would think little more of it, of this stranger, until a year later when she'd turn in her seat at the Savoy Theatre and recognize him immediately in the row behind them. He'd been peering at the programme, monocled again, the edge of its lens still faintly cracked. As he'd chatted with his companion, she'd murmured instructions to Geoffrey to turn around, to look casually, but he'd merely shrugged, seemingly without recollection. After the interval, the pair didn't return, and at the time it had seemed both something and nothing.

But on the night of the ball, although she briefly felt the puzzle of the man with the monocle – the incongruity of him – she moved quickly past. If James happened not to be where he said he'd be, she'd never find him in this crowd, and Geoffrey would feel obliged to wait with her. They would be forced into small talk. Perhaps there had been another girl he'd been interested in before she'd interrupted his evening. Or perhaps he'd simply been enjoying a quiet cigarette and his own company.

He was broad-shouldering a path for her through the crowd. Somewhere in the distance a tray of empty champagne glasses crashed to the floor, loud as the tide on the shingle. A young man was shouting, in her ear it seemed – 'Georgie! Georgie! We're off! For Lord's sake, *Georgie!*' – but they were nearly at the ballroom. She watched an old man in his winged collar bend low, imperiously unsteady, over a glass-topped table until his long, Roman nose met a delicate line of cocaine – and again, '*Georgie!*'

In a moment, they would push through the wide doors and cross the parquet dance floor. She would point to her cousin, alone now, she hoped, on the balcony, and they'd smile their brief goodbyes, shrugging and apparently helpless as the fervour of the crowd and the volume of the ten-man band separated them without the need for formalities.

But as they stepped into the crashing light of the ballroom where the band were playing out the final dizzying throes of a jazz number, the last blast of the night, the crowd surged, and a pair of dancers, ecstatically entwined, backed into her. Geoffrey reached out; Evelyn felt his hand, light on the small of her back, and, in that instant, a charge ran up her spine.

They spent the first night of their honeymoon in an elegant but precarious hotel on Ile St-Louis. The seventeenth-century mansion was slowly subsiding into the Seine and one day, their host had informed them with a Gallic shrug, it would be *de luxe* accommodation for 'the feeshes'. The smell of drains wafted in through the window. Geoffrey's feet hung off the edge of the mattress. Evelyn traced with her toes the cracks that grew like rangy sunflowers up the walls. 'Perhaps I should say . . .'

He propped himself up on an elbow.

'That I'm not . . .'

'That you're not . . . ?'

'Reluctant.'

'Ah.'

'You thought I was going to say I wasn't a –'

'Indeed. I was already composing the note I would pin to your chest when I returned you, Cost, Insurance and Freight, to your mother.'

She plucked a hair from his chest and, half laughing, half wincing, he drew her to him.

After three years of marriage and as many miscarriages, Evelyn's fourth pregnancy felt like a reprieve.

At three months pregnant, they celebrated with a picnic in the Park to which they invited her widow mother and his widower father. She didn't look well with it, her mother declared, and the conversation had dwindled painfully to talk of the diseased branch of the beech tree overhead, bare of leaves in June, and whether or not it should be cut off. By the end of her sixth month, she could no longer walk even as far as the Park. By the seventh, she was confined to her bed. But no matter, Dr Moore, the Beaumonts' old family doctor, assured her brusquely. If she did as she was told, she would carry to full term.

She did, yet what followed in the twenty-four hours of Philip's birth was like nothing she had imagined. She had expected the extremis of the labour. She had expected exhaustion and exaltation. Instead, she'd haemorrhaged. There had been only the sense of her life and her child's life slipping together from the world on a tide of blood.

When it had finally stopped, Dr Moore had taken Geoffrey to one side. The baby's shoulder had been badly lodged, but they'd managed to free it without breaking the arm or collarbone. He was a large baby for so small a woman. She'd lost a great deal of blood and she'd been 'on a very dangerous brink indeed'. Her uterus had almost certainly been compromised. Indeed it was highly unlikely she would carry another child. Even if he were wrong, she would not, he believed, survive another labour, and – here his old watery eyes narrowed beneath their wild Scottish eyebrows – it was Geoffrey's duty to ensure his wife did not fall pregnant again. *Don't be a beast*, those eyes said, and Geoffrey felt a fist punch through to his heart.

As she came to, he pressed his lips softly to her left eyelid, then to the right, and, as she opened her eyes, she smelled something new in his hair, on his jacket – the sweetness of a cigar he'd smoked with a neighbour in the Park outside. In spite of her every intention to brighten, she felt a thorny envy for his ease in the world; for the way the well-worn ritual of a cigar with another man seemed enough to persuade him that all was well that ended well. She was fine, he murmured. The baby was fine.

She nodded because she couldn't trust herself to speak; to say, didn't he know, she'd had to fight not to go under as Dr Moore had barked at her, as though from the top of a well. And she hadn't, she hadn't gone under. She'd been awake through the horror of the haemorrhage even though she'd been unable to open her eyes. She'd heard them telling Geoffrey very firmly to 'leave her now', and she'd wondered to herself, *Is this what dying is?*

'You're on the mend,' he told her. 'And he's already too big for his booties.'

Who was this new, small person in the cradle beside her bed if not the stone that had been tied to her ankle as she fell?

Geoffrey took her hand and stroked her fingers, as if any greater display of feeling might overwhelm them both. Once, he'd imagined that time must suspend itself for life's great transitions; that it must give way, in those seismic shifts, to some fuller apprehension of reality. Yet in the twenty-three hours of Evelyn's labour, time was not overcome. It had turned to mortar. He'd felt himself, everything he was, stiffen at the sounds of his wife's agony, and he'd longed to bolt from the house; to drive through the December night, blasted with cold air. Life had brought him up short. He could neither go up the stairs nor leave the house. It was all he could do to straighten himself for the moment when the midwife would come to him, her face ashen, and lay her hand on his sleeve.

The room still smelled of disinfectant. All that blood.

He rose to open the window. In the watery sunshine of a December morning, as the ordinary sounds of the new day reached them, he pressed his wife's cold, pale palm to his cheek, and she smiled faintly at the odd sensation of his two-day beard. He thought, *Her face has changed; she is someone different today*, and he felt her eyes search his for the answers to her confusion and pain.

He wouldn't understand. It wouldn't even have crossed his mind yet. Suddenly she'd turned into a fragile thing in their bed, a bone-china cup of a woman, a woman who wouldn't mend. Not properly. He would never crush her against him again. The fiercity would go out of his love. He would never be able to forget the sight of the blood-soaked sheets piled high in the scullery sink, and their mattress, wrapped in a tarp and carried away.

She smoothed her bed jacket. He moved to the hearth and stoked the coal in the grate. In that moment, each felt a loneliness so profound they had to battle inwardly not to resent one another.

They recovered, slowly. They named Philip for Geoffrey's father, who had died just months before the birth of his first grandson. They loved one another again, and their love grew, something neither of them, privately, had expected following the trauma of her labour.

Sometimes, in entirely random moments, Evelyn would see her son and have to blink back the memories of the red storm of his delivery. She never forgot, though other women had assured her she would, and occasionally, in those long gazes, something seemed to pass between Philip and her: a flickering of mutual confusion, guilt and apology. Even as an infant, hungry for a feed, he'd struggled to latch on, and she'd wondered, without any hope of knowing, whether the blind panic of his birth had created some unsteadiness, not just in her, but within him too. He was physically robust like his father, but there was something else – a worry, a need, a vulnerability in him – that she could never put right, perhaps because she had put it there herself.

Once, in those early days, she'd asked Geoffrey if she seemed to him naturally maternal. 'Of course!' he'd exclaimed, but Geoffrey was no judge of these things. He'd grown up on painful visits to a mother he hardly knew. *Naturally* she seemed maternal to him. Any woman at home with her children seemed maternal to him. By his standards, even her own mother, remote and lofty on Brunswick Square, was motherly.

Whatever the truth of it, of her, Dr Moore's judgement had ruled out any other pregnancy. For a time, a part of her had wanted to prove the old doctor wrong, and to have with Geoffrey the large family they'd always assumed was their future. Another part of her was relieved to have been officially dismissed from duty. Geoffrey had said there was no question. He wouldn't risk it.

So they switched off the bedside lamp. They grew accustomed to nightwear. They'd learned to heed Dr Moore's advice, relying on rubbers, withdrawals and wordless apologies.

The mark was still there, of course, the small patch on the ceiling in the sitting room, brown beneath a coat of ivory paint, where the blood had spilled to the bedroom floor and seeped through a crack in the floorboards. Sometimes Evelyn would watch her husband in his wingback chair after dinner, his head on the antimacassar, his face tipped up as he blew ribbons of smoke over their heads, his gaze seemingly trained on that guilty spot. Or was it her nerves making something of nothing? 'Be careful, darling,' her mother had once said to her not long after Philip's birth, 'or we'll be packing you off to the Nerve Doctor.' The Nerve Doctor had long been the bogey of her mother's cautionary tales. Composure and restraint were not merely required, but assumed.

The first day she'd been able to sit up in bed, a week before Christmas 1931, Geoffrey had arrived home from the Bank, smiling unsteadily, with something hidden beneath his snowy overcoat. 'Guess,' he said. He looked so hearty and well, he seemed to her then like another variety of human.

'Flowers,' she said, trying to brighten.

'Guess again.'

'A partridge in a pear tree.'

'What about one slightly out-of-tune canary?' He pulled his overcoat back to reveal a small gilt cage. 'I was rather taken with this chap,' he said. A bird blinked back at her.

It would sing to the baby, he said, and it was so ridiculous, so bird-brained, one couldn't help but laugh at the little thing. He sat down carefully on the edge of their bed, awkward next to her, conscious suddenly of his own bulk.

The canary started to sing from his perch. Philip cooed dreamily in his cradle and sneezed. 'Do you like him?' Geoffrey asked.

Hot tears came into her eyes.

She named him Dickie.

Sometimes, they would leave the cage door open so Dickie could fly about the kitchen and stretch his wings, often with Philip, as he grew, stumbling after him. But one day, one of the many cats that prowled the Park stole into the house and gobbled up poor Dickie, leaving behind only telltale yellow feathers at the bottom of his cage. They'd had to tell Philip that his friend had flown away through an open window and that 'any time now' (Geoffrey had consulted his wristwatch) Dickie would be arriving in New York.

'But what will Dickie *do* in Noowook?' asked Philip from behind his bib, blancmange trembling on his lip.

'What will he *do*?!' boomed Geoffrey merrily.

Philip nodded, his eyes huge and grave. Geoffrey glanced at Evelyn. He had only just arrived home. 'Why, see the sights, of course!' he said, gathering his son into his arms and lifting him towards the ceiling. 'That Dickie will be living the high life in no time, you mark my words. He'll miss you. Lord knows, it will be hard for him without a good friend like you.' He pressed Philip against his chest and stroked his head. 'But don't you think New York is a better place for Dickie than that old cage?'

Philip buried his gooey face in his father's tweed. '*I* don't know . . .' Tears were imminent. Geoffrey looked across the table to Evelyn.

'Dickie will *love* New York,' she declared. 'He'll visit the top of the Empire State Building, and he'll perch on the head of the Statue

42

of Liberty. In fact, I wouldn't be a bit surprised if dear old Dickie finds himself dining with the Rockefellers themselves tonight.'

Geoffrey turned to her. '*Not* the Rockefellers,' he said under his breath. Then he passed Philip into her arms as their son started to howl.

She'd forgotten. Jewish banking dynasties, the Rockefellers and the Rothschilds of the world, were, he'd explained, the scourge of international finance. On this point he had agreed with her father, an accord that had unsettled her, but then, many of the women at the WI espoused the same view. When she'd laughed at 'that man' Oswald Mosley rallying his amateur, well-bred army of 'blackshirts', Geoffrey had pointed out that many of the best people in Sussex were giving their sons to Mosley.

'Who are these "best people", darling?'

He'd glanced up over his paper. 'People looking out for the national good, I suppose.'

'Well, Mosley won't have my son.'

'Philip is three.' He'd smiled his wry smile – 'I don't expect the shirt will fit.' And she'd had to laugh.

5

The air that late-May morning was already scorched. At the corner of the Crescent, Geoffrey and Philip crossed Union Road and passed The Level, where the lawns were yellowing and the boating pond was reduced to sun-baked mud. Philip's Hercules bike rattled between them, and Geoffrey was relieved by the noise that masked the mood he couldn't shake.

Earlier that morning – after he'd fallen away from her – Evelyn had slipped to the lavatory without a word, without a laughing 'oops' between them. Neither had made eye contact yet, but they'd both felt it: unhappiness settling into their silence like a dirge.

He'd told her not to trouble with breakfast for him; if he and Philip got away a bit early, he'd manage a bathe in the sea before work and would grab something from the muffin man on the way to the Bank.

Now father and son crossed Ditchling Road and navigated the commotion of the new Open Market, where the Baker Street slum and the slaughterhouse had, until recently, clung like a stain. Geoffrey had led a small, influential group who had petitioned the Corporation to rehouse the inhabitants and transform the area, and Evvie, he knew, was fiercely proud, even though he'd told her that, ultimately, it was only selfishness on his part. He could no longer bear the glimpses of misery each morning: the glassless windows; the women staring suspiciously from their dark thresholds; the babies, floppy in their mothers' arms; and the children playing near open drains. Men without work idled against the slaughterhouse wall, the gutters running with blood, as the rag-and-bone men circled the streets, gripping the reins of their nags.

Geoffrey and Philip emerged on the market's far side, on the London Road, and stopped at the forge to peer in through the stable door. This was their daily ritual, before Geoffrey turned south for the town centre and Philip humped his bicycle west up the hill to the Grammar.

Dawkins, the farrier, was easing the shoe off a Co-op delivery horse. Its large feathery hoof rested between the man's knees on his leather apron, a vast energy somehow made still in this place of fire and steam.

The dray snorted as the old shoe came away. Dawkins rubbed the matted foreleg and lowered a new shoe into the hungry furnace until it emerged white hot. He lifted the horse's leg again and tried it roughly for size. Through the fuming cloud came the sharp stink of burning hoof, and they saw the dray's yellowy eyes roll.

At the anvil, the farrier pounded the shoe into shape, then moved to the barrel of cold water and plunged it in. Steam hissed, Philip's face exploded into a grin, the tang of cooling metal rose into the air, and Dawkins reached for the first nail.

'What if it's too long?' Philip whispered.

'I expect the horse will let him know.' Geoffrey winked. He was putting on a good show of paternal steadiness, but, privately, as he watched Dawkins hammer the nail into the huge hoof, he envied the farrier his ease, his apparent rightness in the world. Already at eight o'clock, he himself was hot; sweaty with a mute shame he couldn't reason away. His collar felt tight. His testicles felt leaden. The scene earlier with Evvie – the strange failure of his body – had left him jangling.

The dip in the sea before work had merely been his excuse to escape the house and the unease between them. Now he needed it, the relief, the punishment, of cold water.

The old beach chalet was lit by cracks of light as thin, as impermanent, as hope. He groped, clearing cobwebs and dead flies as he stepped over remnants of the previous summer: two deckchairs, a beach pail that clattered with shells, a threadbare towel. He stumbled out of his suit and arranged his clothing on the pegs. Beneath his bare feet, the planks creaked, and the smell of his childhood summers – the sweetness of balsam wood baking in the sun – recalled, instantly and too keenly, an ancient freedom from himself, from self-consciousness, from everything but the imperatives of running and diving.

As he stepped outside, he had that sensation of nakedness, of exposure, that he experienced each year before his first swim, as if he were some classification of mollusc emerging pale and soft from its shell into the open air. But the morning sky, east towards Saltdean and west as far as Shoreham, was a trumpet-blast of blue, and, against all expectation, he felt the heaviness of the morning lift as he squinted into the light. There, alone and briefly unaccountable to anyone, the relief was immense. His neck unstiffened. The knot of shame in his stomach loosened, and his twelve-year-old self seemed to flicker to life within him. He could almost see himself running again, gangly-legged, with friends, across the gated green lawns of Hove down to the lagoon.

This morning, Brighton beach would do – it was a shorter journey back to the Bank – and, at the age of thirty-six, he walked across the pebbles. Soon the beach would be closed for the war but today,

46

the scene was as ever – or it was if he let himself forget the strange emptiness of the piers and the promenade.

On the seafront behind, hunched carriage drivers waited between the Palace Pier and the West Pier, their restless horses jingling with promise for any visitor foolhardy enough to risk a seaside town marked for invasion. High overhead, cirrus cloud drifted like the ragged end of a dying man's last thought. The Italian ice-cream man sat on the kerb next to his three-wheeled bicycle reading his paper, no doubt hoping against hope that Mussolini would not enter the war. Further down the prom, a fishwife hollered 'Winkles! Sixpence a pint!' to no one.

The King's Road was bright, still, and as empty as a place of contagion. Not so much as a chip carton blew down the prom. No summer holidaymakers raced against the breeze on bicycles or laughed behind the wheels of sporty motors. The excursion boats no longer ferried pleasure-seekers from the end of the Palace Pier to Dieppe. Hotel porters and bellboys, jellied-eel and cockle sellers, shopkeepers and carriage drivers seemed suspended in the heavy translucence of aspic.

But on the beach itself, one could still imagine that nothing had changed. The tide was in, and the surf dragged the shingle in a perpetually casual show of force. An old man in a beach slip bobbed in the waves ahead like a white-headed seal. A mother and three children in newspaper sailors' caps played in the shallows, the youngest screaming at the crashing arrival of each new wave. A stray mongrel sprinted back and forth, tussling with a dead cuttlefish in its mouth. Three teenaged girls in beach pyjamas planted their tuppenny deckchairs on the pebbles.

The fishermen were already tipping out the second catch of the day, and their children hopped between boats or clambered out from below them. Earlier that week, these same men, men of the old fishing families – the Gunns and the Rolfs, the Leaches and the Howells – had been hauling the desperate and the wounded into their boats while bullets strafed the sea around them like skipping stones. Men who had never ventured further than the Isle of Wight had steered their way to Dunkirk by the glow of fire on the horizon.

Now they were at their dees again, as if all the smoke of France had been only a brutal trick of the light, as if the beach weren't soon to close. The children helped out before school each day, with the older boys spearing twenty or thirty herring on a stick before laying them out in gleaming rows, ready to be smoked.

An ancient man, wearing a blue woollen cap even in the day's heat, looked up from the net he was mending to spit cord from his mouth. 'On your way,' he called to the children, 'or the Schoolboard Man will be here to lock up the lot of you!' They scattered like pigeons at gunfire, chasing each other across the beach, the boys threatening the girls with scale-smeared hands.

Two women sunbathed on vast white hotel towels. One looked up dreamily, vaguely irritated by the children's noise. On spotting Geoffrey, she adjusted the knot of her haltered swimming costume and turned her face.

It was a curious sort of freedom to be divested of his pinstripes. For this rare quarter-hour, he was not one of the town's leading bankers. He did not approve, decline and seal fates. He had not agreed to serve as Superintendent at the new internment Camp, nor did he head the town's Invasion Committee. The man who entered the sea was not that reliable citizen, and, for a few moments more, he imagined himself walking free of his identity, unpeeling his responsibilities and abandoning them like clothing at the water's edge.

He had not told his wife of twelve years he might abandon her and their son if the worst came to pass. She had not looked up at him this morning, her eyes narrowing with mistrust.

When the first wave hit, he felt as if he'd been cut in two. His lungs snapped. His bones ached to the marrow. The heat of the day was misleading. It was only the end of May, after all, and this, the open Channel. Yet it was the stranglehold of the cold water, its over-whelming of all thought, that drove him deeper.

He flung himself below an oncoming wave and his heart kicked in his chest. The cold punched his ears. His forehead throbbed. Some-thing brushed his leg and was gone. A yellow-and-brown tin of KLIM powdered milk rolled in the seaweed at the bottom. He sur-faced at last into the sunshine, spitting salt water, eyes burning.

When he looked around, he was briefly disoriented. The sea was blinding; the horizon seemed to have dissolved. The reliable buoy of the old man was gone, and the currents had pulled him thirty or forty yards. His fellow swimmer was heaving himself up the beach, his elderly girth now covered in a towelling robe.

A few of the fishermen looked past the old man to him, their eyes narrowing over their tins of tobacco. Water was something you tried to stay out of, their eyes said. Whoever you are, you're a grown man and you're bad luck, throwing yourself at the sea like that.

Somewhere in the Channel a boat blew its siren. At the end of the Pier, the anglers cast their lines and floats into the swell. He climbed the steep shelf of the beach as the automated music from the carousel started up in the distance, a dismal, tinny accompaniment to his exer-tions. He looked to the men at the dees, and looked away again only to see the two women sunbathers staring warily too, as if, in his stum-bling preoccupation, he might at any moment intrude upon their privacy. He blinked in the strong light, trying to spot his chalet in the long, monotonous row, and in that moment he felt lost, out of step, in a place as familiar to him as his own childhood.

They'd got it wrong, the fishermen. He wasn't bad luck. It was worse than that. '*Precautions*,' she'd whispered hoarsely. No precautions. She'd eased the rubber off and her eyes had dared him. It wasn't just that another pregnancy could kill her. That was *his* fear, more than it was hers. Her stubbornness about the rubber was code for what she wouldn't bring herself to say: that it was he, her husband – not the enemy – who had suddenly put her and Philip at risk. If the enemy landed, he'd leave them. It was a betrayal. An abandonment. What, her eyes had demanded, was the point of precautions *now*?

Whatever her own private logic, it was between them, unspeakable, an oily dark thing, and it hardly mattered what actually came to pass. It hardly mattered if German barges appeared at this very moment, an ominous semaphore on the horizon, or if he and Evvie lay next to each other, safe in their bed for the next forty years. He had told her it was possible he would leave.

6

That morning, as his father turned south for the Bank, Philip cycled up the London Road, past the Co-op Department Store and Goodall's Greengrocer; past the Cat and Dog's Meat Shop, Jessop the Barber's, the watch-repair shop, and the boot mender's, the open door of which released the delicious smell of new leather. Behind him, a milkman's barrow jingled with empties. At the tram stop, two Gypsies waved fistfuls of wildflowers. He bumped over the kerb, crossed the tram-rail and glided past Dr Baldwin's surgery and Mrs Dowley of Dowley's Fish 'n' Chips, bending over, tipping yesterday's chip fat down the drain and showing, by accident, the backs of her fat, fish-white legs. Then the gas fitter's flashed past, the radio-set shop and the tinsmith's window, where the morning light bounced off milk pails and cake tins.

At the corner, he made a sharp, wheel-juddering turn and heaved himself up the hill of the Old Shoreham Road. He stood tall on the pedals and wobbled up and up, through the colossal, catacombed darkness of the railway viaduct bridge. High above him, pigeons sat on the narrow ledges of the iron girders, immobile as toy ducks lined up in the shooting gallery on the Pier.

Orson's brother, Hal, had been known as a damnfineshot. His hands, Orson claimed, always smelled of gunpowder. From the time he was just twelve years old, Hal had won every prize at the shooting gallery. Next he was made Squadron Leader in the school militia. Now he was a Second Lieutenant overseeing three rifle sections and two dozen men in France. Orson said there was nothing Hal couldn't do. Philip wished he had an older brother. He wished it all the time. Orson had Hal. Tubby had Frank and Alf. He had no one.

The underworld of the bridge spewed him into the light, and he aimed one hand at the sky. 'Eh-eh-eh-eh-eh!' he shouted, and enemy aircraft fell from the sky.

At the Grammar, he leaped from his bike. Orson was waiting. 'You won't believe it,' he said in his own lugubrious way.

Philip turned, but the school was still there.

'*Behind* us,' Orson sighed.

Philip walked around to the other side of the sheds.

It didn't seem possible.

Overnight, a city of tents had risen from the playing fields.

Never before had those fields been so crammed with life and yet so hushed. The two boys kept to the sidelines. The tent-dwellers stared at the sky like old men in a dole queue. They gnawed at buns and gulped water. They rubbed their hands across their whiskers. But they weren't old.

The first few faces did not look outwardly hostile, but something in their expressions, in the glaze of their eyes, made Philip's stomach tighten. One man had no arms, only bandaged stumps, like the pollarded trees that poked up stiffly over the playing fields from the road beyond. A swarthy, shirtless man with a red-and-white towel wrapped around his head was striding towards them. Orson stumbled into a run but the man caught Philip by the shoulder. 'Cannae you read?' He pointed at a white placard nailed to the boundary fence.

Philip swallowed and looked past him to the two men at the nearest tent. One gargled at the other: 'Oi, Jimbo, gimme back me ruddy crutch!' They seemed to speak English but not as he knew it. *Were* they English? Hal had a smart uniform. That's what Orson said. Many of these men were only half dressed. In the distance, three were washing from the same bowl. The broadest had a pirate's patch over one eye.

'Whass your name, lad?'

He tried to stop his leg from trembling. 'Philip.'

The man bent down and laid a heavy hand on his shoulder. 'Philip, this is noo place. It's noo place at all. Now go find your mate an' get yourselves to your lessons.'

Philip's voice wobbled in his throat. 'Are you prisoners of war or war heroes?'

'I'll be honest with you.' With slow, careful fingers, the man shifted the towel on his head. 'I'm not so sure myself this morning.' And now Philip could see. The towel wasn't a towel. It was a loose white dressing.

The man swatted at a fly but it landed again and again. Between the bandages, blood oozed, thick and dark as blackcurrant jam.

The wireless buzzed as the juice went through it. 'Germany calling. Germany calling. Germany calling. Station Bremen 1, Station Bremen 2 and Station DJB on the ninety-metre band. You are about to hear a talk in English.'

'Not tonight, Geoffrey . . .'

Philip looked up from his sketchpad on the floor. His mother was peering over her Mrs Woolf. She didn't like Lord Haw-Haw. She didn't like him hearing Lord Haw-Haw. Children weren't supposed to. That's what she'd said before. But his father only raised two fingers, which meant *quiet, please*, and the tip of his cigarette burned red.

'The last week has been supremely eventful in the history of the world. It has witnessed the first great climax of the German campaign, and, as to the result, there is now no doubt whatsoever. In disorder and despair, the British Expeditionary Force has sought to save itself by withdrawing from the Continent, but the very attempt has produced British casualties of a shocking magnitude.'

Philip leaped up from the floor, his eyes bright. 'I saw them! I did! They're up at the Grammar!'

His mother raised a finger to her lips.

He settled on the carpet once more. He considered his Spitfire and sighed. Why couldn't he draw better? To trace was to fail.

Evelyn closed her book and leaned her head back. Geoffrey stared at the ceiling, blowing smoke as high as the picture rail.

'Along a strip of land six miles deep, the British are still trying to cover the retreat of their forces across the Channel. On Wednesday, sixty British ships were hit by bombs and thirty-one were sunk, and today comes the news of still further British losses. The number of British and French prisoners taken is at present beyond computation.'

Evelyn crossed and recrossed her ankles. On the street outside, a woman's heels clicked past, and somewhere on the Crescent, a door slammed heavily shut.

'As you listened to the British radio a week ago, did you get the impression that there was going to be any withdrawal at all? Did you think that the necessity for a rearguard action was being contemplated by the dictator of Britain? Is it not a slightly novel experience to see the British people being treated as congenital imbeciles? And now, as the bloody and battered fragments of what was once the British Expeditionary Force drift back to the shores of England, the likelihood of invasion grows by the hour.'

Evelyn turned sharply. 'Geoffrey, I think we've heard enough.' But she knew her words were pointless. Who could turn off Lord Haw-Haw? Who in the country did not feel compelled to listen for the facts the BBC would not report?

'Is it not a little amusing to think of the trumpetings with which Churchill became Prime Minister of Britain. *He* was the man to frighten Hitler! *He* was the providential leader who was going to lead Britain to victory. Look at him today, unclean and miserable figure that he is. When Germany threw off the shackles of Jewish gold, this darling of Jewish finance resolved upon her destruction. But thanks to *God* and the *Führer*, it is not Germany that is confronted with destruction today!'

Another voice spoke: 'That is the end of our talk. Our next regular transmission of news will take place at 11:15.'

'Philip, my love, it's late . . .' His mother's hand was ruffling his hair. He hauled himself to his feet, clutching his pencil and sketch-pad. Then he approached his father's chair and waited for him to bend so he could offer his hug goodnight. Sometimes his father reciprocated with a whisker-rub. Not tonight. 'Father?'

Geoffrey looked up and blinked himself back into the moment.

'Doesn't Mr Churchill wash?'

'Of course he washes, Philip.'

'Lord Haw-Haw said he was unclean.'

'Lord Haw-Haw made a mistake.'

'Is Mr Churchill a Jew?'

His mother started to lead him up the stairs. 'See, Geoffrey. He really should have been in bed long ago.'

'He's not an infant, Evvie.' The hinge in his jaw flexed. 'No, Philip. Mr Churchill is not a Jew.'

'Mr Feldman our baker is a Jew.'

'Yes . . .' Geoffrey nodded gravely. 'Mr Feldman our baker is a Jew.'

'Does *he* have much gold?'

'Not much, I shouldn't think.'

'Well, that's all right, then, isn't it?'

Geoffrey motioned him on his way. 'Yes, nothing to worry about there, old bean.'

7

That spring, the news spread like Spanish flu through the Grammar: Hitler had chosen the Royal Pavilion for his English HQ.

Although no boy could say which boy had actually heard the broadcast, word had it that Lord Haw-Haw had made the announcement himself. It was the most thrilling news of the war so far.

Like its neighbour Park Crescent, Hanover Crescent was an elegant anomaly in the jumble of Brighton housing. Its Georgian townhouses were compositions of pilasters, pediments, arches, bow-fronts and balconies. Its position overlooking The Level declared it a place of privilege and privacy, and Orson's house, Philip discovered, was even quieter than his own because Orson's brother, Hal, was off being a hero in the war, and Ivy the housekeeper never seemed to speak, and Orson's parents were old and so rarely seen in his house that Orson sometimes seemed like an orphan.

That day after school, he asked Philip if he wanted to know a secret.

Orson was nearly two years older than Philip. While most boys from the Grammar walked home every afternoon to Hove, these two both descended the hill to Brighton, and Orson seemed not to mind if they walked together, with Philip pushing his bicycle, even though he was only eight. But that spring day, out of the blue, something happened. Orson said, 'Come over to mine.'

*

Upstairs in Orson's room, Orson was on the rug on all fours with his head under the bed where even Ivy wasn't allowed to look, he said. As he eased the secret out from under the bed, Philip's jaw went slack.

Orson said he'd made it himself from a second-hand inductor, a crystal detector, and plates he'd stolen from his deaf grandmother's set. 'It even picks up Radio Bremen.'

'Lord Haw-Haw . . .' said Philip.

Orson nodded. 'Lord Haw-Haw.'

An oatmeal box held the inductor in place. A bit of gauge wire made the connection. In metalwork class, he'd soldered earphone connections to the base. Then he'd strung aerial wire along the picture rail in his bedroom and down the outside wall, where he fixed it to a pipe he'd found at the bottom of Hal's wardrobe. He'd dug a hole in the ground, packed it with soot, as the science master advised, then plunged the pipe in, earthing his connection. The case was plywood and parcel string. A semicircle of paper marked the positions of the stations. The tuner was a knob from the dead-specimens cabinet.

Orson had defied the quiet of his house.

Sometimes Philip wished he was also two years older and ten years smarter, but that afternoon, he felt only grateful that Orson had entrusted his secret to him. Besides, Orson could always be counted on to have something no one else had: a pen that wrote in invisible ink, a stink bomb for Assembly, a code-cracking book, tin cans on a long string, and now, best of all, a home-made secret wireless through which Lord Haw-Haw would speak.

'With rare honesty, the English Prime Minister revealed his true goals to the world when he declared a war of destruction on Germany.

Even neutral observers were surprised at how brutally he rejected the Führer's peace offer. No one in the past months, years and decades has worked harder at unleashing a European war, with the goal of destroying Germany, than England!'

Philip sighed and slipped out from beneath the headset they shared, an earphone apiece. They'd already listened for almost two hours but Lord Haw-Haw had said nothing, not a single word more, about Brighton.

'I have to go now, Orson . . .' Outside, the sky above The Level had bunched into a fist of dark cloud. Lightning flashed like faulty electrics.

'Not yet.' Orson reached for Philip's satchel and pulled out the cornet of sweets. 'Because today our subject is "Hitler at the Royal Pavilion".' He popped a bull's-eye into his mouth.

The air was sticky. It needed to rain. 'No, really. I'm off.'

'I'll begin.' On a shelf above the bed, a German helmet gleamed. Hal had brought it home for him, Orson said; his trophy of war. Now, he lowered it on to his head and seemed to meditate on the line of his school tie against the roll of his belly. In the corridor outside, Orson's mother crept past. The thought of her out there made Philip nervous and he sat down again.

Orson adjusted the helmet's chinstrap. 'After Hitler does all his work at his Pavilion HQ, he likes to take a break and paint outdoors. He carries an easel into the garden and sticks his thumb in the air and makes his eyes into slits. Sometimes he puts on a smock and a beret.'

Philip reached for a humbug in the cornet and sucked ruefully. 'What does he paint? Flowers?'

'Not *flowers*.'

'People?'

'He never paints people, you donkey. He's not interested in *people*.

He paints the Pavilion because that's what he can see, and because he has liked it ever since he saw it on a postcard.'

'Who in Brighton sent him a postcard?'

'Oswald Mosley, of course.'

'Who?'

'Hitler's friend in England, and Lord Haw-Haw's too. Hal has a phonograph of his speeches. On the postcard, it says: "Heil-o Hitler, Fine rally. Good turnout. Brighton is the business."' He passed Philip the helmet. 'Your turn.'

Philip excavated a clot of humbug from his back tooth and put the helmet on. 'Hitler likes to go to the Pavilion Tea Room on sunny days. He likes England better than anywhere now because he has discovered warm scones with clotted cream and jam. Except he has to be careful to wipe his moustache when he's finished or people will laugh and he will have to lose his temper and kill a few to set an example. As he eats, he smiles to himself because the other people at the tables have no idea that they're sitting next to Hitler.'

'Why not? He's on all the newsreels. You have to at least make it believable, Beaumont.'

Beyond the room, the wind took hold of the elms.

8

The weekly Camp inspection, Geoffrey now understood, would never fail to be anything other than grim. Each Monday, he signed off the misery of men bewildered by circumstance and imprisoned out of view on top of a coastal cliff. The Camp had opened in early May, claiming the town's racecourse, and although it was already his fifth inspection, he'd never grow accustomed.

In the old stables, new arrivals were housed like livestock, while those who had arrived in the early weeks were crammed into hot, airless barracks, the windows of which were painted over and covered in grilles. Buckets served for toilets, and standpipes for the ablutions of hundreds. The mission was cement. Day in, day out, under the tireless eyes of their guards, the prisoners produced cement. The dust of smashed limestone got everywhere – in their hair, their nostrils, their teeth, their food. No one was exempt from labour, except those ill enough to be confined to the flimsy hut that passed for an infirmary.

The Army ran the show, but the Home Department had required someone well regarded in the area to put his name to it all, to turn a blind eye, and Geoffrey had won the dubious honour. He could hardly speak of it, not to his colleagues at the Bank, not to Evelyn – least of all to Evelyn once he discovered the newest arrival.

'Mr Beaumont!'

That afternoon, he'd flinched at the sight of his old tailor hunched on a metal bed in the regulation boiler suit. He'd wanted to turn, to run, to pretend he hadn't heard his own name. His brain was reeling, but the old man had smiled, and he had no choice but to pause in his progress through the barracks. 'Now, tell me, how is *Mrs B*eaumont?'

To hear him, Geoffrey could almost imagine they were simply passing the time at the bottom of Trafalgar Street. He couldn't meet Mr Pirazzini's eye. He felt too tall, too . . . well. Blood pounded in his ears and, as if from a distance, he heard himself reply. 'Yes, she's very well . . . Thank you.' What a sickening charade.

After the first arrests, most of the German and Austrian tailors' shops on Trafalgar Street had been looted, but Pirazzini and his wife endured in their premises until that morning, when Mussolini declared war on Britain, and the police arrived.

The tailor's advanced age had guaranteed him a bed in the barracks at least, a bed no wider than he was, a bed that was screwed to the floor.

'Please. Give her my best, will you?'

Geoffrey nodded. *Impossible*, he thought.

The old man had never failed to ask after Evelyn, not since the day nearly nine years ago when he'd spotted her, six months pregnant, carrying too many boxes and bags home from town. She had been a stranger to him then, but he'd insisted she come into the shop and take a seat with his wife before he went out again to find her a cab. He'd paid the driver before she realized, and the next day, through a mouthful of pins, he had refused Geoffrey's efforts at repayment. 'No, no,' he'd muttered impatiently. 'The wheel goes round. The wheel goes round.' His mottled hands had sketched circles on the air, his left ring finger lost, presumably, to an accident with the shears or a sewing machine.

Stooped behind the Singer, his wife had smiled, lifted her foot from the pedal and said, with an accent that was still heavily Italian, 'Please, Mr Beaumont. My husband is he-goat, and life is short, no?' Behind his back, she imitated Mr Pirazzini's circling finger, but in a punning motion, beside her ear. *Loco*, that finger said, but her eyes were tender.

She was probably on the Isle of Wight. In the women's camp. No letters between spouses.

He'd laughed that day all those years ago and had put away his wallet. 'Well then, will I at least be able to persuade you to accept my custom?'

Mrs Pirazzini returned to the sleeve beneath her needle. Mr Pirazzini spat the pins into his four-fingered hand. 'Mr Beaumont, do you not know? A tailor, like an undertaker, always accepts the custom of a tall man.'

So he invented something about a pair of new flannel trousers that needed cuffs. Mr Pirazzini shrugged obligingly. He'd had no idea then that the old man was booked weeks, even months, ahead; that he had clients who drove down from London.

The wheel goes round, the wheel goes round. Now, in the barracks, the old man waved the shiny stump of his finger over the endless row of beds. 'Mr Beaumont, shall we agree on one thing? You will not pity me my accommodation, and I will not pity you the drape of that jacket.'

Enemy aliens. It was necessary, said Churchill, to 'collar the lot'.

A dirty pall of smoke hung over the Crescent. On the pavement below, in the middle of their quiet street, she watched men in face-shields and asbestos gloves huddled over tools and generators. Then a stocky man raised a gloved hand, a fury of sparks erupted into the street, and a section of the wrought-iron spears of her fence collapsed, ringing out as it hit the pavement. It was the same all over Brighton that June. The metal drive. What more could they take? (*Either you sacrifice your selfishness for the nation – or you sacrifice the nation to your selfishness.*)

Inside, the house was as close, as airless, as a forcing jar. Two large flies flung themselves at the hot glass panes. She lowered herself on to the bed in the spare room to wait until the queasiness passed. When it didn't she turned the eiderdown back and pressed her face to the cool sheets. And she saw them again in her mind's eye: the two bright green capsules buried in her terrace garden like toxic seeds. Almost three weeks had passed, and, still, she couldn't stop seeing them.

For eight years they had rearranged their lives around the threat of any possible pregnancy. She'd never so much as asked Dr Moore about another child because that small mark still stained the ceiling in the sitting room like a blood blister beneath the skin. Wasn't it her body that had let them down? After Philip's birth, their great openness had given way to solicitude and caution. She'd learned to feign pleasure and he'd learned to believe; they separated nervously afterwards, and quickly, as Dr Moore's prophylactics leaflet had advised. Middle age had descended upon them too early – a delicacy, a self-consciousness better suited to late or second marriages. But now, he had done the unthinkable. He had resigned himself to the loss of her.

He must have sat, one long leg crossed over the other, in the high-ceilinged surgery. Through the window behind him, he would have been able to see the swathe of Hove Park and the lawns where he had run as a boy. Dr Moore would have folded his hands benignly against the maroon leather of his desk. Perhaps Geoffrey had avoided his old doctor's gaze, but little by little, in the course of that clipped conversation, they would have navigated past the hard edges of the unspeakable.

Two cyanide pills. The only responsible thing.

And what had she done? Had she run up the stairs last night, clenching them in her palm, and shaken him from sleep? Had she accused him over breakfast and washed the vile things down the sink?

No. She had tucked the flap of the Lloyds envelope back into place as if it were an RSVP for a dull party to which she had resigned herself. She'd laid the envelope flat at the bottom of the tin and covered it with the sheaf of twenty-pound notes. She'd pushed the tin back into its hollow, piled the earth into place, and flattened the surface with the back of the spade. Then she'd brushed herself down, returned the spade to the soil, stepped back into the kitchen and turned the key.

The kitchen was strange, its edges moonlit and exaggerated, its surfaces bulging as if under some internal pressure of their own. The cutlery had flashed like spilled mercury in the tray on the sideboard. The coal in the scuttle had gleamed. She'd wiped her feet and slipped off her damp plimsolls.

In their room Geoffrey slept deeply, on his back. She hooked his cardigan over the bed knob and eased herself back into bed. The raw smell of earth was on her hands; washing at the sink would have set the pipes of the house groaning. She clutched one goose-pimpled arm in the other and listened to the steadiness of her husband's breath. As she lay, eyes open to the dark, she grew conscious of a wider, looser scent. Next to him – next to his smell of heat and hair oil and Imperial Leather – she smelled of the outdoors, of the night air. Hadn't she taken something of the night, of its feral silence, inside with her? It was hers now, even more than it was his: the secret of that tin.

Because she hadn't been able to crush the things under the heel of her shoe. Because she couldn't be sure that, some fearful day, she wouldn't not be grateful for them.

The world seemed to twist into a less physical, less solid, version of itself, as if any of its elements – the moon, the Park, the sturdy arc of the Crescent – could suddenly slip from its position, like a flimsy bit of scenery in a Sunday School tableau. If *she* slipped – and she was already slipping – if her grip on life was anything less than firm, how would she trust herself? And if Geoffrey were to leave, how could she be trusted to keep Philip safe? (*Do you show your children that you are calm and undisturbed? It isn't enough to pretend to be calm – you must actually be so.*)

In her mind's eye, she could see the white, uneven grin of his teeth and the red of his lips. His ears were pink, translucent, and the tiny hairs on his lobes caught the light. She could almost feel his childish hands in her own, the ink-stained fingers, the dimpled knuckles. She saw again the curving fringe of his lashes as he slept and the soft brown V of hair at the nape of his neck. His cheek was velvet against her palm; the sleepy warm smell of him delicious. Sometimes, as he nodded off, she traced the delicate blue veins at his temples. *All of this I made*, she thought. Yet would she swallow death one day? Would she feed it to her child on a spoon piled high with jam?

She'd be no good, no good at all. Her brain always seized up; when she panicked, she froze. Who was she to stand up to any enemy person? Even her father's rants and taunts used to strike her dumb. He'd never hit her or her mother, but the threat of violence had pervaded the atmosphere of her childhood, and in her girlhood room, as the syllables of his rage burbled up through the air vents in the floor, she used to pray before sleep that it would stop, that *everything* would just stop.

She doubted she was either canny or tough enough to manage on her own – the civilian reports out of Holland and Belgium had been so desperate – and again, the memory of those capsules flashed like foul treasure in her mind.

In the spare room, she lay stiffly at the very edge of the bed.

The flies continued to cast themselves at the hot pane.

It was not within her power not to love Geoffrey, but for this – this fear of herself that was now hers to carry – she could not forgive him.

9

For the first time, he could not say the old words. After everything he'd known and seen, he gave up the habit here of all places, in the tranquillized quiet of a makeshift infirmary on the remote edge of a seaside town.

He didn't open his eyes. He could hardly bear to see the four walls of his failure. It was enough to smell the bleached lino again and the wood of the cheap hut baking in the heat of June. He reached to his back and ran his fingers over the bandaged lump where his left arm met his shoulder. The bullet was as long and wide as his little finger and burned as if someone were pressing a cigarette to his flesh.

Years ago, of course, Otto had ceased to believe in the prayer's potency, but he'd murmured it each morning anyway for its mundane comfort; for the memory of his mother beside him in his narrow bed, stroking his head as he slipped into sleep. Each night for weeks, she had taught him the strange words – the only Hebrew he would ever learn – and he'd fallen asleep to the scent of her hair on his pillow.

'Modeh ani lifanecha melech chai v'kayam shehechezarta bi nishmahti b'chemlah, rabah emunatecha.'

Now, his stomach lurched at the impossible coincidence of the words rising in the space of the infirmary. He managed to turn. The mumbled prayer belonged to the old man in the bed next to his, the only other wretch ill enough to be abandoned to that airless hut.

For four days they had woken side by side on their metal camp beds in the overcrowded barracks without exchanging a word, for Otto had refused conversation, and it was assumed he spoke little English. Relative silence was the only permissible form of privacy. Today, once again, they were side by side, this time in the room that passed for an infirmary, and his neighbour's ears, Otto realized, were far better than his lungs. The old man – a Jew, evidently – must have overheard his murmured recitation each morning and recognized it. 'Modeh ani lifanecha melech chai v'kayam shehechezarta bi nish-mahti b'chemlah, rabah emunatecha.'

'I give thanks to God for restoring my soul to my body.'

This morning, the old man was saying the words for him.

He would have laughed mirthlessly were it not for the pain in his lungs. Didn't his neighbour know? In places like this, small acts of kindness were cruel as razor wire. Nor did he need his pity. Yesterday had not, in fact, been a day of despair. The light had been extraordinary; the horizon opalescent where it met the sea; the open air a balm. After months in the barracks, he could hardly believe he now found himself standing on a beach on the very edge of England.

He sucked at the stale air. His wound still burned. But at least all was finally still, apart from the buzzing and ringing in his right ear – the phantom whizz of the bullet. Stillness, of course, is not the same thing as peace. The quiet was strained, brittle, like that quarter of an hour each morning at Sachsenhausen, before the pretty nurse with the doe eyes arrived with the injection. Who, who, they'd wonder, would it be this time?

That sickbay had always been stuffed full with the infected, the tormented and the broken, while this room was strangely empty except for their two bodies, each pitiful beneath the cheap regulation blanket. From time to time, the old man's bronchial gasping turned to a retching that echoed in the rafters above them, but otherwise: silence.

At the door, a dull-eyed guard, a new face – new to Otto in any case – rubbed and scraped at the mud that caked his boots; perhaps one of the men who had been digging the latrine-and-shower block yesterday when the pipes burst. Otto watched him, fascinated by the comparative ordinariness of this man's morning; by his frowning attention to the insult of the mud. Yet now more than ever, Otto wished he could turn off his artist's habit of seeing in detail; of dividing every figure, every body, into its component geometry. The guard was all blunt lozenges, with a face that looked as if it had been flattened in the birth canal. His pale blue eyes protruded, oversized and glaucous. His hands were square mitts. Only his forehead was recognizably human: unexpectedly high, vulnerable, and smooth as a child's.

The man looked up and Otto closed his eyes. At Sachsenhausen, the mere affront of eye contact could mean that the nurse would arrive with her doe eyes and the injection. She'd stroke the soft underside of an arm for the vein – a woman's touch, oh God, the tenderness – before the eyes of her patient rolled back and his body went limp.

The guard raised his left boot and rested it on his right thigh. The hobbed soles winked in the dull light of the hut.

Otto would never forget the orchestrated clatter of the hobnailed boots on the cobbled streets of Berlin. He'd never forget the torment of the forty kilometres he later marched and ran each day on the boot-testing track at Sachsenhausen. The memories still terrorized him each night in his dreams: the twenty-kilo pack; the sunstroke;

70

the frostbite; the studded, broken ground; the boots always too large or too small; the crippled, bleeding feet in the communal baths; the men who dropped and were trampled, while others ran to the perimeter, to end their lives on the electric fence.

Was this man one of the Nazi naval prisoners who had, it was rumoured, been promoted to guard duties in this place? It was hard to say. Everyone – whether enemy alien or prisoner of war – wore the grey boiler suits donated by the local munitions factory, for most of the interns had arrived with only the clothes on their backs – dinner jackets, rumpled shirts, pyjamas. Those who'd been picked up at home had been informed there was no need to pack a case; they would be home again in a day or two after their papers and tribunal records were checked. Otto had known better. Three years before, he'd been given the same assurances before he was placed in the van that drove him away from Berlin for the last time.

He was thirty-five and yet a part of him wanted to sob like a child – though why now? He had suffered far worse than this, and here, once more, he was learning how not to feel. Already he was becoming less than human. Already he stank – of stale sweat, salt water and piss. And worse than this wretchedness, worse even than the sheet-soaking terrors of his dreams, was the knowledge he'd woken to that morning.

He was not dead after all.

They'd hauled him from the sea. Pumped his chest. Stopped the bleeding.

His mother's prayer had worked, it seemed. His soul – damned and degenerate – had been restored to his body despite him.

Tubby Dunn's mother was Tillie, who had been, until that May, the Beaumonts' housekeeper. The Dunns lived just streets away from the Crescent – streets and a world away, in a tall, pinched house on Magdalene Street in the great shadow of St Joseph's Church. The Dunns, Philip knew, were Romans, and Romans, he'd been told, were Romans because they didn't have a picture of the King in their church. Tubby's real name was Norman, after his uncle who had died in the Great War, but at home he was known as Tubby because however much he ate, his shoulder blades stuck out like bent coat hangers, his eyes were big in the bone of their sockets, and because the Dunn brothers liked a joke.

Learning didn't come easily to Tubby. Alf, his brother, told Philip it was because when Tubby was a baby, he slept in the bottom of a chest of drawers and that, one day, their Auntie Vi's husband shut the drawer without thinking, and Tubby nearly suffocated in his sleep before their mother realized.

Alf was thirteen and Frank, the eldest of the Dunn boys, was fifteen. Plus there was Peg, their little sister who was always crying. Tubby's father, Mr Dunn, worked as a street-lamp fitter until the blackout came and the Corporation turned off all the lights. He was a hunched man with black eyebrows and deep grooves like tramlines in his forehead. For a time, he had work painting all the bulbs in train carriages blue; then his papers came, and Tubby heard his mother crying in the lav at the end of the garden.

Washday for Tillie didn't end on Mondays now that she took laundry in. The windows of the house were always misted up, the kitchen was tropical, and sometimes when Philip watched her bending over the heaps of ironing, the pure smell of the starch and the hiss of the iron made him feel like she was caught in a battle she would never win. The pile of laundry was always as high as before.

He'd smile hopefully at her over his piece of bread and scrape, and she'd smile back, brushing steam and long strands of red hair from her cheeks, and in those moments, her face seemed to shine just for him, and he loved her as much as his own mother. She was different, of course; different because she was always the same, always just herself, and that meant he could be just himself too when he sat in her kitchen, and he didn't worry about not being enough for his mother who only had him to love.

On Saturday mornings, he never minded walking with Tubby from shop to shop to collect enough cardboard and rubbish for Tillie to burn in her copper all week. Afterwards, they doubled up on Philip's bike for the weekly ride to Billet's for sweets or they goose-stepped their way to Dowley's to share a fourpenny piece of fish and a penn'orth of chips. But that Saturday, Tubby was distracted. 'I'll be going now, Phil. Frank said I 'ave to meet him and Alf.'

Philip wished Tubby could give him even just one brother. 'Can't I come?'

The Palace Pier was quiet for a sunny Saturday in June. The rides were empty, and the penny arcade didn't jingle and ring. Old people snoozed on benches. Children hung their heads over the white railings, grinning as if they were about to set sail. Couples ambled to the

73

end for the view, imagining it – the ships materializing on the horizon, the glamorous flash of cannon-fire – for don't our fears also conceal our wishes?

Philip looked longingly at the sea, but no one had said anything about swimming. Instead Frank marched them on to the damp shingle beneath the Pier. They stared up through the shadows to its rusty iron girders. Feet drummed overhead. Someone's lemon ice dripped through the slats of the deck like wee. A pigeon lay rotting a few feet away. Alf said to Frank, 'You first, then.'

'You.'

'You're older.'

'You're milky.'

'No,' said Alf. 'You got the bigger bellows.'

'Bigger goolies, you mean.'

Alf went for Frank's groin. 'That's what the totsies say an' all.'

Frank wrestled him to the ground. 'You callin' Lorraine a totsie?'

Tubby looked on, mesmerized. Philip wished he hadn't come. Then Frank released Alf from the headlock, opened his mouth, and let out a powerful hum. Alf and Tubby started to vibrate too, in key, and before Philip could ask, the Dunn brothers exploded into song. Alf did the melody, Frank the low notes, and Tubby the harmonies, with Frank waving a hand at Philip, meaning, *Sing, why don't you?*

It was gloomy as a crypt under the Pier, no matter how jaunty the tune. Philip didn't know the song. He knew only the national anthems from the BBC at night and the hymns from church. He smiled at the brothers, blushing at his failure. He wished he was a Dunn brother with a barbershop voice.

It was a tuppence piece that first hit him in the head. Shillings followed, some bright, some grimy green. Revelation rained down through the planks. The Dunn brothers had wooed the audience overhead.

Philip felt that, in the hunt for their wages, he could redeem himself. He was the fastest and had the best eyes in the murk, and all four boys were still clambering on their hands and knees when they heard the sound of the single engine.

Frank popped his head into the sunshine. ''Ere, Alf,' he said, his voice going funny. 'Lamp this.'

Alf got to his feet. Tubby followed Alf. Philip followed Tubby.

A seaplane was skittering down in the shallows of Brighton beach. Somewhere, on the deck overhead, a woman screamed.

'Christ,' breathed Alf. 'This is it.'

'Fuck,' muttered Frank.

The boys gawped from the shadows.

'An' here come the bogies.'

Police from the King's Road pounded towards the surf. Over the boys' heads, on the deck of the Pier, feet thundered for the exit. Ten yards from shore, the hatch of the seaplane shuddered open. Frank took a step back. 'You can get over a hundred geezers in those things.'

Philip wished he had remembered his gas mask. Tubby cowered behind Frank. Philip cowered behind Tubby. At the hatch, a single man appeared.

'Is it Hitler?' Philip's stomach jumped and flopped.

'I need the bog,' whispered Tubby.

'You two,' ordered Frank, 'shut your clappers.'

The invader was dressed in a sober suit. His dark hair lay, freshly combed and flattened, across the high white dome of his head. For a moment, he seemed to contemplate his audience on the beach, as if they were the spectacle and not he. Then he removed his shoes and socks, rolled his trousers up, and slid into the choppy sea.

People from a tea dance at the Old Ship came out and clung to the railings on the prom, the women pressing their hands against their legs to stop their dresses from blowing high. The German negotiated the waves, carrying his shoes at chest height. On the beach, four bobbies clutched their batons. The seaplane lifted off, its floats skimming the waves.

The onlookers — stray sunbathers, children, old couples and arcade attendants in their jackets and epaulettes — stood transfixed at the green railings of the King's Road, watching the lone enemy struggle against the surf to the shallows and hop painfully over the stones. When he arrived on the beach, his jacket and trousers were streaming. He had to bend double to breathe. Nobody moved. Then he straightened, raised one long arm and reached, tentatively, for something in his breast pocket.

'He's got a pistol,' said Alf.

'A grenade more like,' said Frank.

A bobby shouted, fierce as a Legionnaire.

'Get down, you three!' said Frank. '*Now!*'

The bobbies charged.

Wee streamed down Tubby's leg.

Something small and white fluttered in the invader's hand.

On the terrace the sun was already strong. Seed pods exploded in the heat. Dragonflies hovered. Geoffrey glanced at the grainy picture in the *Sunday Times* in which a middle-aged man hovered in the surf, his hand a blur of white. 'Poor devil.'

Evelyn looked up briefly, quizzically, then returned to the Ladies' Page. He read on. The bobbies on the beach had taken Eelco van Kleffens for a German spy, and had assumed his arrival in Brighton was a bungled affair. They had been ready to arrest him on charges of illegal entry when they found themselves obliged instead to find, between them, the Dutch Foreign Minister's train fare to London.

Philip ate his egg. He did not tell his father he had seen the man and the handkerchief with his own eyes. He knew better than to admit to 'roaming' Brighton with Tubby, Alf and Frank.

Gulls wheeled over the Park. Geoffrey reached for a piece of toast and a grilled kipper. The impossible had happened. There was even a photo on the front page. Paris had fallen in just four days, *Paris*, yet here they were, eating Sunday breakfast on the terrace under yet another untroubled blue sky. He fished a midge from his tea, Evelyn buttered a piece of toast, Philip swung his legs idly from his chair, and next door, Mrs Dalrymple cooed to her tortoise.

He tried not to think about the Camp, about the weekly inspection tomorrow. He'd had a call. A Category A alien had tried to take his own life. He'd have to interview the man. The Home Dept. would require a report. He'd have to be sure the man wasn't trouble.

He lowered his paper and reached for the teapot. From underneath the brim of her hat Evelyn raised her face, but only briefly. Would they ever meet each other's eyes unselfconsciously again?

It had been difficult again that morning – earlier. If he had once imagined that she somehow brought him into being each new day, she now had the power, it seemed, to turn him to stone. Neither of them had the words. Below him in their bed, she'd maintained an attitude of willingness, but there was something new etched in her features: a pinched virtue, a shadow of disdain. 'Shhh,' he'd accidentally whispered aloud, 'shhh' – as if to ward off her unhappy thoughts. But it was no good. They had gathered around the bed like a silent jury.

Across the table, she nodded, without expression, at the front-page story. 'They're coming, then.'

He refilled her cup but did not look up. 'It would seem so.'

France had fallen and yet, madly, the Ladies' Page was still dispensing French fashion advice. This week, it was '*L'Air Militaire*' – as if the French had epaulettes and brass buttons on their minds now. She thought about poor, beautiful Paris and the easy days of their honeymoon there, and, for no reason, she remembered how, in 1928, respectable French women, like English women, had worn gloves by day but by evening had abandoned them provocatively. As a bride of twenty, she had thrilled to the sight of bare, elegant arms and glowing skin in the nightclubs and restaurants.

At the bottom of the page, a Ministry of Information notice

warned the *Sunday Times*'s female readership: 'Do you know that if you fail to carry your Identity Card you may be fined anything up to £50 and sent to prison?' Suspicion paraded as national security. She almost said to Geoffrey, *Prison. It's ludicrous*. But she stopped herself. The morning's freedom from conversation was a small, fleeting luxury, for each of them, she imagined. In any case, Geoffrey would no doubt see the sense of such precautions; these days, he saw the sense of every precaution, and she could hardly bear much more good sense. His own sensible precautions, those two pills, waited in the earth just a few feet away, like two gleaming eyes fixed on a future she didn't want to know.

That morning, in the dim light of their room, he had moved again across the sheets towards her. She'd watched his eyes train themselves on a spot somewhere above the headboard. On and on. She'd glanced at the nightstand, at the clock, at the heads of lilac drooping in the stagnant water. 'Shhh,' he'd whispered, 'shhh.' His forearms had trembled, and 'Shhh' he insisted – sharp, half-audible reproaches, though she hadn't made a sound. Then, 'Sorry,' he breathed, smiling weakly as if only just remembering her below him. Sweat lay clammy on his forehead. 'Talking to myself. Mad. Sorry.' He kissed the top of her head and pulled away, his neck blushing as he slipped off the redundant rubber. They seemed neither able to right themselves nor to speak of it.

Now she surveyed her terrace garden. Yellow oxalis, or 'Sleeping Beauty' as she'd known it as a child, was spreading everywhere, strangling the perennials. Without Tillie to help in the house, she no longer had the time to look after the garden, and in the early unseasonable heat the weeds were running riot. She reached down and yanked, then bent to take up the spade.

Geoffrey was halfway out of his chair. 'Evvie . . . ?'

The sight of her with the spade had spooked him. She straightened. She wanted to say, *What were you thinking, planting death in our garden?* But the words were like a code she was required to forget.

She stuck the spade back in the earth, to mark the dread spot by the lilac bush. She collected their plates and ushered Philip upstairs to change.

The day propelled them in and out of St Peter's and through a luncheon for the Local Defence Volunteers. Then it was cricket in the Park for Geoffrey and Philip while she checked on neighbours' houses; numbers 4, 5 and 8 stood empty, their owners having fled overseas. Cricket was followed by tea and stale crumpets at her mother's and a joke from Philip. 'What's the full name of the crumpet factory on Bennet Road?'

His grandmother's lips twitched sceptically but she played along. 'The Sussex Crumpet Factory,' she replied.

'*No,*' laughed Philip, 'the *crumpet* crumpet factory! Do you know why?' She said she truly didn't. 'Because so many *girls* work there!' He rocked in his chair, revelling in the pun. The fact that the crumpet-like qualities of the opposite sex were lost on him at the age of eight and a half seemed immaterial. Mrs Lawrence glared at Evelyn and, later, suggested that it was time for Philip to 'outgrow' the Brothers Dunn.

'Tillie's boys, aren't they?'

'Yes, though, sadly, we don't see much of Tillie now.'

'How do you manage, darling?'

'We miss her.'

'I don't blame you. Whatever must your guests think when *you* open the door to them?'

Sunday dinner was cold ham and new potatoes followed by the evening buzz of the wireless. Evelyn's book lay in her lap. Geoffrey's head leaned wearily against the chair back. Philip drew aeroplanes at her feet. She would have said, *Darling, tomorrow after school, why don't you bring Orson to our house for a change?* but Lord Haw-Haw was suddenly intoning.

She looked up. Geoffrey was already blowing garlands of smoke at the ceiling, his gaze trained on the old mark, and an inertia overcame her. She did not leave the room for air or a stroll in the Park as she had intended. She did not send Philip off to his bath and bed. She merely sat with her book unopened on her lap: *The Years* by Mrs Woolf; Mrs Woolf who had a Jewish husband; a Jewish husband in the Sussex countryside, just beyond Brighton. Were they at this moment listening helplessly too?

Her mother was fond of saying that, if she were a Jew, she would have left for America ages ago. What her mother was actually saying was that all Jews, including those born in England, should do the decent thing and find a country that didn't mind foreigners. Evelyn's father, if still alive, wouldn't have disguised his meaning. Hypocrisy was one of the few faults of which no one could accuse him.

In the end, mercifully, the power of speech was denied him, and his illness drained him of the energy his numerous hatreds needed to sustain themselves. Eight years after his death, her mother madly claimed he'd caught the cancer, not from the toxins of fifty years of chewing tobacco, as the doctors had said, but rather from the germs bred in old wallpaper; in the ancient silk damask that covered the reception rooms at Brunswick Square. The wallpaper theory had been passed knowingly among her mother's affluently uneducated lady friends, including Lady Sykes, who would condescend to be treated only on Harley Street. But what was the tumour in his mouth, Evelyn told herself, but the lump sum of so many vile words spoken?

Years before, by the boat to Dieppe, as her parents saw her off for her stay in France, her father had not, even then, been able to wish her well. She'd been seventeen and looking forward to a new country and the school at Auteuil. 'I shall have you *checked*,' he'd said, 'by my own physician when you return. Don't think I won't.'

Her mother had pretended not to hear.

It had been her misfortune, she'd concluded when still quite young, to be the only child of people for whom contempt was the natural alternative to worry or fear. In Evelyn's most private self, Geoffrey's balance and reason were the evidence she needed that she was altogether different from her parents; that their toxic beliefs had not clung to her like the fabled breath of the old wallpaper.

On the wireless, Lord Haw-Haw was still prophesying doom. The assault of his rhetoric seemed, like her father's old rants, to be coming from everywhere at once: through the stillness of the sitting room, through the high walls of their home, up through the vents and floorboards, and into the marrow of her. 'It is surely time for the English people to reflect that if it is Paris today, it will be London in the very near future. To any Englishman, who still follows these politicians who have led him to the tragedy in which he finds himself, I can only say, "Look thy last on all these lovely things, every hour."'

12

The Superintendent extended his hand across the steel desk of the Camp HQ, but Otto Gottlieb declined to shake it.

'Take a seat, Mr Gottlieb. This shouldn't take long.'

So this, thought Otto, was the reason why his dressing had, after three days, been changed and why he'd been permitted a sponge bath. 'I'd like you to recount for me the events of Friday morning.'

Otto turned to the window. A view, an actual view . . . The sea, all glittering bright. He clapped his hands on his thighs. 'You're quite right, Superintendent. It shouldn't take long at all. I made a full statement to your Head of Patrol on Saturday afternoon.'

'Yes, it's all here.' The Superintendent tapped the file. 'However, I'd be grateful if you could go through it with me again.' He summoned a smile. 'Strictly between us, my Head of Patrol has deplorable handwriting.'

How little, Otto wondered, could he get away with saying?

After the darkness of the van and the cramped drive, he and thirteen other men were released into the open air and had stood blinking at the sight of a beach. They were given a small bar of soap each and fifteen minutes. The sea light had washed over them like a gift.

When the order came, they stripped. Most picked their way across the shingle, but he walked easily into the waves. The soles of his feet had lost most of their nerve endings two years before on the boot track, and now he felt oddly invulnerable. He was the first one in. The tide was strong, sucking at the pebbled shore like a baby's mouth at a breast. Gulls swooped and sailed. The cliffs glowed white, pulsing with a radiance, with a wordless signal, aeons deep.

Behind him, the five guards stood rigid in the surf up to their knees, their rifles pointed at the sky. He dived into the waves and swam, opening his eyes under water. No children's faces. No Room 51. Not here. Finally, not here.

On and on through the limpid sea. He felt as if he could swim for ever, as if, now, today, at last, he had energy to spare.

It had been that simple, he informed the Superintendent. No, he knew nothing about any flashing lights along the coast. He had swum without aim or direction. There had certainly been no plan of any kind, except, eventually, and with the help of a strong current, to tire and let himself go under.

The shot to his shoulder had been an unexpected source of assistance.

No. He had not seen any dinghy on the beach. And no, it hadn't occurred to him that his guards would attempt a rescue. After all, they had just shot him, hadn't they?

'But you heard the warning shot?'

'Yes.'

'And you swam on, unconcerned.'

'There comes a point, Superintendent, when a man *is* no longer concerned.'

'Your tribunal notes say you're an artist.'

'Then it must be so.'

84

'Also – how curious – your passport bears the stamp "Degener-ate". Would you kindly explain?'

'I am a debauched defiler. What more can I say?'

Geoffrey looked up from the file. 'Jewish?'

'It has been said.'

Geoffrey studied the man on the other side of his desk. 'Simply answer the question, please.'

'Secular.'

'Homosexual?'

'No, though at Sachsenhausen, the artists were barracked with the homosexuals, and those men were, on the whole, the best of men.'

'Sachsenhausen? North of Berlin?'

'Yes.'

'You're Category A. You arrived with a sum of money . . .'

'If you read on, you'll see I have already given a full account of the counterfeiting operation – or as full an account as I myself was given.'

'You'll need to sign a statement saying you heard the warning shot and that you persisted in your escape. Your guard had no choice but to fire again.'

'I hope he was commended for his marksmanship.'

Something hot and dark flared in the Superintendent's eyes. 'You're lucky he hit your shoulder.'

Otto smiled. 'I've had luckier days.'

'The Home Department will require you to confirm a good stand-ard of care.'

'Nazi bunk-mates and enforced imprisonment aside.'

'Are you being insolent, Mr Gottlieb?'

'No, Mr Beaumont. Merely accurate.'

Geoffrey stood and moved to the window, as if suddenly indifferent to the company he was required to keep. 'Your English is excellent. We had no idea.'

'I don't believe I ever said my English wasn't excellent.'

'No?'

'No. I have merely avoided conversation. Surely that right at least remains to me?'

'Discretion is an enviable quality – particularly in a spy, for example.'

'Yes, I imagine it's highly desirable, though Jewishness isn't, I understand.'

'Still, it's rare to meet a German, here at the coastal front, with so little trace of an accent . . .'

Otto smiled at the floor. 'I daresay it's also rare to meet a Superintendent who takes so great an interest in his prisoners. My father was a linguist, Mr Beaumont, or was until Jews, including all secular Jews, were relieved of their posts at the universities. Alas, my dear old nanny is the person we must hold to account for my diction. English. And, coincidentally, Sussex born and bred. From a place called Petworth, I seem to recall.'

Geoffrey turned to him, nodding as if amused. 'A small world.'

'Yes.' Otto met his eyes. 'Terribly small.'

13

Saturday, June the 22nd. It was to be the last Royal Pavilion Midsummer Ball until the peace.

The atmosphere was one of rigid good cheer. If the windows of the Pavilion were necessarily blinded, the chandeliers were polished and bright, and if good alcohol was in short supply, there was always the big band to obliterate all thought.

The two couples spilled out on to the north balcony, drinks in hand. 'I can't see a thing!' Sylvia protested, and Tom had to steer her from behind, his hands on her waist, following the glow of Geoffrey's white shirt and tie.

Evelyn laughed, then sighed. Sylvia was always good spectacle. What a relief her and Tom's company was.

Geoffrey hitched up his trousers and let the balcony's low stone balustrade take his weight. He for one was glad of the sudden darkness; glad to be, for a short while, an exile from society. There was no moon, but the night was generous. It seemed to grant them a reprieve from formality; to cloak them in an easy intimacy, as if they were young again and free of the weight of the persons they were yet to become.

With a shy smile, Tom passed Geoffrey an uncharacteristically large flask of whisky. He took a grateful swig, admiring the white of his wife's throat and her slim arms as she motioned across the dark sea of the gardens. The Theatre Royal was at that moment disgorging its crowd into the blackout. Evelyn was remarking on the sight to Sylvia. Dozens of beams from pocket-torches flickered to life, making a sieve of the night.

He took another mouthful from the flask, nodded at Tom's measured account of the latest rumours out of the Traveller's Club, and let his mind idle to the sound of the women's voices and the glimmer of their smiles. They chatted, happily it seemed, and Tom was on excellent form, quiet-spoken but as solid as ever.

Had Evelyn told Sylvia about their difficulties? he wondered. Had Tom already been enlisted to 'have a word', and was that the reason behind the flask? He hoped not. He wanted only the respite of the evening; the chance for him and Evvie to laugh and forget. Surely that was what she wanted too? Surely it wasn't too late for life to return to what it had been just a month ago? Might she relax enough not to turn her back to him in bed later on? For even that he'd be grateful.

Fourteen years ago, she had appeared beneath a Chinese lantern in these gardens, a girl in a thin white gown. She hadn't accepted a cigarette or a seat on the bench beside him but she'd stayed, and her company that night had felt charmed, fleeting. Indeed it had been hard to believe she wouldn't dissolve when they stepped beyond the light of the lantern, but instead, she'd taken form.

He knew what it was to hold her in the night, adjusting himself in sleep to her. He knew the round of her bottom as she nestled against him. He knew the curve of her hip beneath his palm and the dip of her lower back. Her laugh, bigger than she was, still surprised him, if only, perhaps, because he heard it less these days.

Behind the shutters and blackout curtains, the Midsummer Ball was in motion, a decorous secret the building kept to itself. Was it only he who felt that the collective cheer of the night was strained, that the band was too emphatically carefree? Even there, in the fullness of the evening, with the music seducing everyone beyond thought, the laughter, the bare shoulders and the toasts seemed to him a kind of mime they all performed without heart for one another. It was meant to be a final, heady indulgence, a last hurrah, and if it was not quite that, it was at least a relief to see Evvie relaxing in Sylvia and Tom's company, to see her swaying to the music and laughing at Sylvia's round-up of London gossip.

That night years ago, Evelyn had simply asked him the time. She had lost her cousin. She'd been lovely, awkward. He'd never seen such delicate wrists and ankles, and she had so much life, such spark and brightness in her eyes that the honesty of her gaze made their polite conversation seem a nonsense. Then she'd done that outlandish, most undebutante-like of things, poking him in the armpit, sweetly mocking the state of his tailcoat, and in doing so, she'd somehow transformed them both into their real selves. In the pulse of that moment, she'd felt like a familiar, a loved one.

Her unexpected arrival in his evening had also made the earlier ruckus with Leo's friend seem inconsequential . . . As those particular tensions had mounted, it was Tom who had taken him aside to suggest he step outside to clear his head. It was true, he *had* started it, in the gentlemen's smoking room, by asking Leo what he'd been thinking, bringing to the ball that night so contemptible a character. Of course Leo's friend overheard. He had meant him to overhear.

Freddie and Art had pretended to be deep in another conversation, though Geoffrey knew they were of the same mind as he. Fitz had grabbed a drink off a passing tray and downed it before returning to the two debs, and their chaperones, who had been shadowing him all evening. Things got heated. Geoffrey spoke his mind. Perhaps he'd used some regrettable language. A bit of name-calling. He couldn't remember. It had not been his finest hour. He'd had too much to drink.

He probably threw the first punch. He'd never asked Tom to confirm. They didn't remove their jackets. Hence the split seam. He remembered that much. A card table had tipped. A few glasses had crashed. Tom had taken charge of the situation – no wonder he'd ended up in the Diplomatic Service. He'd taken Geoffrey by the arm and led him to the door: 'Of course it's not on. Leo was a fool to bring him. But what's to be done about it? Let's just get through the night, shall we? Go on. Go clear your head.'

Geoffrey had come down from town to Hove the day before the ball to spend time with his father. Fitz, Freddie Vere, Art Stubbs, Tom and, of course, Leo, all of them friends at Oxford, had arrived for dinner on Saturday. No one had expected the chap from Hampstead. No one knew him or his family, though Leo had claimed great things on their behalf. At dinner, conversation had been strained. Freddie had thought it amusing to bring up the subject of a newly translated essay by Marx, 'On the Jewish Question'. But they'd all managed to remain civil for Geoffrey's father's sake, who had been bewildered, thankfully, by the speed of the repartee.

By the time they'd piled into the motors at the end of the ball, the stain of the brawl in the smoking room had almost faded, and everyone, with the exception of Leo and his friend, had driven to London – to Mayfair and the 43 Club. It was past one when they'd arrived, but Mrs Merrick and her deep cleavage still presided over the door. As usual, she welcomed Fitz to the club without charge because he was heir to a peerage, a logic that had always seemed strangely flawed to Geoffrey and the others. But if the cover charge was steep, the girls had poise. A few had been debs. One was the

90

ex-wife of a colonel. He danced that night with a girl called Constance, whose pale silk gown fluttered under the ceiling fans. She was slight and very pretty, in spite of a lazy eye, and her hair was black and lustrous, though shorter than Evelyn's. It was costly – five pounds – to take her back to one of Mrs M's flats. He gave her more than that when he remembered that she would have to pay a pound for the use of the flat. She asked him if he'd brought a French letter, and he'd reached for his wallet again. Then he'd closed his eyes and tried to feel Evelyn in his arms.

In the gardens below, lilac, the last of the season, seemed to haunt the night, and she allowed herself to close her eyes, to store away, for harsher times perhaps, the surfeit of its fragrance. Then she turned again for a view of the ball through the balcony's French doors. At centre stage, a singer sang low into the microphone, her hands imploring, her lips as bright as blood.

Sylvia slipped an arm around her shoulders. 'I don't know about you, but I can't *bear* to be upstaged.'

Evelyn squeezed her hand. 'You? Never.'

When Geoffrey had suggested they invite Tom and Sylvia down from London for the night, she'd felt herself brighten for the first time in weeks. Sylvia was the reminder she needed that the entire world hadn't lost its sense of humour; that it hadn't given in to dread. Sylvia wasn't afraid of anything, not of Hitler or war or of any unsteadiness in herself. Tall, willowy, a natural blonde, she never failed to be noticed, but for all her glamour, she was plain-speaking and soft-hearted with it. She treated Tom's ancient, demented mother with a kindness the old woman had never known, and, in the last year, she had turned their house into a veritable orphanage for five East End children who had lost their parents. As Tom once said, she'd give anyone the faux fur off her back. And relentless tease though Sylvia was, she adored him. Tonight Evelyn had seen her friend's eyes fill up when, after a waltz, Tom had taken her palm and pressed it to his lips.

Admittedly, when Sylvia and Tom had announced their engagement four years before, it had seemed incredible to Evelyn that this was the woman Tom, the discreet diplomat, had finally chosen to be his wife. Even in wartime Sylvia didn't know how *not* to be showy. While Evelyn, Geoffrey and Tom sipped the rough Algerian wine that all guests were doing their best to drink, Sylvia had persuaded the bartender to produce her trademark cocktail, a Sidecar, and as she danced, glass in hand, she jingled with a riot of African bangles and beads. Her lips were plump with maroon lipstick. Her plunging velvet gown clung to her – midnight blue, backless, slinky. It was unlikely she was wearing a single under-garment.

Evelyn's own gown was also backless, though cut high across her collarbones. She'd chosen a mauve silk taffeta but tonight, as she caught a glimpse of herself in a ballroom looking glass, she wondered if the colour did her complexion any favours. She looked sallow, she thought. Middle-aged. Geoffrey had told her she looked lovely – in blue. His colour-blindness always disheartened her somehow; he would never know the full spectrum of colour and he didn't give a jot.

'Turn around! Turn around, Evvie! No, this way . . .' Sylvia had seized her hand. Together, they peeped over their shoulders at their bemused husbands. 'Now, Evvie. Tell the truth. Has Geoffrey had the presence of mind to compliment you on your thrift?' She waved a hand, for Geoffrey's information, across his wife's naked back.

Geoffrey lowered his face and laughed.

'I thought not. Nor has mine.'

Tom cleared his throat. 'The nation thanks you, and I believe I speak for my old friend when I say that we are, of course, helpless with admiration.' Geoffrey raised Tom's flask in solidarity, and they returned to their conversation.

But Sylvia wasn't finished. 'Tom, tell me that you are not *still* talking about that old Etonian lover – oops, I mean, trouser-press – forgive me, I mean *fag* – of yours, James Roedale-Bugger-the-Double-Barrel. Now there's an attention-seeker if ever there was one. For heaven's sake, they'd might as well have let *me* into the Diplomatic Service.' Her cocktail glass was empty again. She winked at Evelyn, stole a sip of her wine, and, tasting it, grimaced.

Tom leaned towards Geoffrey and mumbled into his chest, 'I believe I mentioned him to you once. We only just managed to keep it out of the papers. Apparently, he greatly exceeded his instructions.'

'Apparently! The man was on his way to Germany to tell Hitler we'd be happy to let him do whatever he liked with Europe as long as he left the Empire alone. The man was hopeless even at games at school, yet Lord Halifax lets him loose on an international crisis! Tom, darling, has Geoffrey told you he's the Head of the Invasion Committee for this area *and* Superintendent of the local Camp? He's keeping everyone in Sussex safe from all those alien enemies. Why can't you be a man of action like Geoffrey?'

Tom rolled his eyes for comic effect. 'As a matter of fact, he has mentioned it, my sweet. They're lucky to have him.'

'No doubt, Geoffrey, you'll be glad to hear that I've weighed up the Government's advice and I, too, have taken key decisions.' She smiled, her eyes a-glitter.

Tom took Sylvia's hand in his. 'It's true. My wife has informed me she's having her hair waved for the invasion.'

Sylvia adopted a sober air. 'First impressions and all that.'

Geoffrey nodded thoughtfully. 'I knew you'd never let the side down, Sylvia.'

'You see, Tom? Geoffrey appreciates the effort. And it's either that or walk about with the new Unity Mitford look.'

'Which is what exactly, darling?'

'Why, the turban, *naturellement*.'

Geoffrey, Tom and Evelyn stared blankly.

'So she can hide the shot wound, of course! Silly girl. Mind you, it *is* frightfully bad luck to put a gun to your own head and to, more or less, miss . . . No wonder her beloved Hitler shipped her back to England forthwith. I don't expect she's looking much like the perfect Aryan woman *now*. That's the drawback of brain damage, I'm told. The vacant stare. Most men only appreciate it in the bedroom. '

Tom fished for his handkerchief and made a show of gagging his wife with it. 'My darling, have we told you we really mustn't let you drink?'

She waved him off. 'Evvie, tell him. Tell him you don't mind me. Not very much, anyway.'

Evelyn reached for her hand. 'Mind you? Tonight wouldn't have been the same without you. Thank God someone still has a sense of humour these days. If I have to read even one more Government Information Leaflet, all that endlessly dreary advice, I might just have to gas myself and save the Germans the trouble!'

'Precisely. And if only the Government, with all its advice, would bloody well *advise* the Jews in our part of town how to behave. Did I tell you how —'

'Now, now, darling. This is a ball, not a Council meeting.' Tom's smile tensed. 'Besides, it suddenly occurs to me that I'd like to dance with my wife.'

'But, Tom, you know as well as I do that they're a public nuisance. Lord knows Unity, mad thing that she is, went over the top by declaring herself – what was it? – "a Jew-hater", but anyone with eyes to see knows they *do* push their way to the front of any queue, and they most certainly hoard food. You wait and see. I don't approve of them being hounded out of their own countries – that's not right of course and it's unlucky to land where you're not wanted – but they'll be living the high life off the black market over here when the rest of us are eating our ration books.'

'Evelyn' – Tom had an instinct for damage limitation – 'would *you* care to dance?'

But Sylvia would not be deterred. 'Evvie, you must find the same thing here in Brighton, surely?'

Evelyn looked to Geoffrey for help, then back at Sylvia. 'I don't believe I've ever met a Jew in Brighton.'

'If only we could all say the same' – a thought crossed Sylvia's face – 'although I *suppose* we could say it was a Wandering Jew – or at least an uninvited one – who brought you two darlings together. That's right, isn't it, Tom? Am I remembering correctly? We are in fact unexpectedly indebted to the Jewish race for the great good fortune that is Geoffrey-and-Evelyn.'

Evvie smiled through her confusion. 'I don't understand.'

'You have a Jew to thank, darling girl, for Geoffrey here. Well, indirectly you do. Tom said as much before I met you the first time. I have got the story straight, haven't I, Snookums?'

Tom took the glass out of her hand and shrugged his apology to Geoffrey.

Geoffrey summoned a smile. 'You're absolutely right, Sylvia. I'd almost forgotten.' He turned to Evelyn. 'Leo Hamilton turned up that night with a Jewish chap from north London.'

'The night we met?'

'Yes.' He patted his breast pocket for his cigarette case. 'He was a bit of a troublemaker. A well-heeled troublemaker, but trouble all the same. That's what Sylvia is referring to.

'You mean, the man with the monocle . . . ?'

'I say,' declared Tom, 'you have a remarkable memory, Evelyn. I think he *was* wearing a monocle.'

'Was he?' Geoffrey offered Tom and Sylvia a cigarette, then lit his own and drew deeply on it. 'Leo and I fell out on account of his friend's politics. At first, the chap had seemed to be a man of few words. Not a bad sort. However, as the evening wore on, we discovered he held some rather repugnant views. Regrettably Jewish views. He reverted to type quite quickly, I'm afraid, so, finally, rather than stand there like a hypocrite, I challenged him. Leo wasn't too amused. His friend certainly wasn't. I had no choice but to have it out, so to speak.'

'So to speak?'

Tom plucked at his collar. 'If you hadn't, Geoff, I might have. Leo, I'm afraid, always did have a bit of the Bolshevik in him. As for his friend, Geoff could have run rings in that debate, that was clear, but people were beginning to look –'

'They rowed?'

'Tempers were running a little high. In the end, Evvie, it hardly amounted to more than a scuffle.'

Tom was covering. She turned to Geoffrey. 'You picked a fight?'

'I'd had a bit too much whisky. That's all. You know I'm no good with drink.'

'I thought it best if Geoff stepped outside long enough to cool his head and for Leo to tend to his friend. The Jew chap sulked. I thought it rather telling that, having caused a rift between two old friends, he suddenly had remarkably little to say.'

'By the end of the night, we'd mostly made things up – Leo and I, that is.'

'Indeed,' said Tom.

Evelyn's hand tightened on the balustrade. 'You said you didn't remember. Why?'

He flashed an apologetic smile at Tom and Sylvia. 'What did I say I didn't remember?'

'The man with the monocle.'

'I'm not sure I did.'

'We even saw him the following summer – at the theatre. I asked you then.'

'Did you?'

'You always said you didn't remember.'

'He was a small man with dark hair. I'm sorry but I didn't recall any monocle. He certainly wasn't wearing the thing when –' He cast his cigarette into the night.

'When you hit him? No, I don't expect he was.'

'I believe,' Tom said, 'he'd slipped the monocle into his breast pocket prior to –'

'Your punch.' She stared at her husband.

She was back there, at the Pavilion again, on that night, walking up the stone stairs towards the ballroom. Geoffrey was escorting her back. He had merely been polite, she'd concluded; obliged not to walk away from a young woman who found herself alone outside without an escort or chaperone. Suddenly her embarrassment was acute. She'd wanted only to find James and to be gone. Not far from

97

the door, a group of young men clutched their capes and canes, ready to depart. She could see them still. Tom was there, the same dear old Tom with his bright wedge of a face, and his former full head of auburn hair. Fitz was the portly one with the curly beard. Leo was fair, handsome, with a shy, endearing squint. Clearly they were waiting for Geoffrey to return so they could take their leave. He'd gone outside for a cigarette – to cool his head, as Tom put it just now – but he'd been away nearly half an hour, distracted by her of course. When he appeared at last, she was close behind. His friends were arguing loudly, drunkenly no doubt, about the General Strike. She remembered that. Four of them greeted Geoffrey as he passed, and he returned a few words in passing. Tom noticed her – a new girl with his good friend – and nodded warmly. But Leo's friend, the man with the monocle and the intelligent face, turned and glowered at Geoffrey, who appeared not to notice and carried on. It was only good manners, she told herself then. The man looked at her too as she passed but without seeing, for behind the black-rimmed coin of glass, behind that lens with its hairline crack, a blaze still lit his eye, like the heat of noon through a magnifying glass.

'He had high cheekbones.'

'Did he?'

'And deep-set eyes.'

'Helpful if you're the monocle-wearing sort.'

'Why don't you remember him? You "scuffled", Tom says. You resented the fact you had a Jew in your party, so you rowed with him and then you hit him.'

He sighed. 'I *do* remember him, as I've just said, but not clearly.'

'But Tom says we *met* because of him.'

'We met because you came to ask me the time.'

'You were in a mood. You were smoking in that way of yours.

That's why you were on your own. I can see that now. You'd lost your temper.' And suddenly it came to her. 'The seam of your jacket was split! Under the arm.'

'I didn't like the man's views. I'd had too much to drink. But this is hardly the place. Tom, Sylvia, forgive us.'

She felt her face flush. 'Since when have you needed to approve everyone's views, Geoffrey? Since when has a difference of opinion meant you fight with a man at a ball?'

He struggled not to raise his voice. 'What is it, Evelyn, that you object to, precisely? The unpleasant fact that I found myself in a row the hour before I met you, or that I take issue with Jewish interference in this country's affairs?'

'Listen to yourself!'

'Listen to what, exactly?'

'I may not understand the full political argument, Geoffrey, but I recognize something ugly when I hear it.'

'Are you quite finished?'

Her hand clenched the stem of her glass, and she lowered her voice to a fierce, intimate whisper. 'To think our life together began' – the stars staggered overhead – 'to think it only began because you couldn't stop yourself from *baiting* a man.'

She saw Tom and Sylvia slide through the French doors into the ballroom. Her husband's face was a mask of grim forbearance.

She looked into the night and back again.

SUMMER

14

A hundred yards from the Palace Pier, Geoffrey let himself loiter under the canopy of a derelict oyster stand. The day was overcast, the sea the colour of gunmetal, and the beach abandoned. CLOSED FOR THE WAR BY ORDER OF THE CORPORATION. The signs had been hammered to the railings down the length of the prom.

He fumbled in his jacket pocket for his cigarette case. On the Pier, the rides stood quiet. Only a few defiant anglers tried their luck from the end of the deck. In the tide, mines bobbed at the surface, horned and deadly. Every fishing boat had vanished, as if by some ill-fated sleight of hand.

He tried to focus on the survey for the Committee, on the report he would need to compose to confirm that all was in place for Churchill's visit. He'd been avoiding the task all week.

He cupped the flame of his lighter against the breeze and drew hard on his cigarette. Every beach chalet, including his own, had been strategically manoeuvred and filled with stones. Up and down the shingle, anti-landing-craft spikes lay in heaps, ready to be dug in. Vast coils of razor wire blotted the views east and west, while concrete tank-traps stood five feet high, colonizing the shore. Across the King's Road, the elegant rooftops of the Grand Hotel and the Metropole had been upstaged by the guns on the new naval station.

Without the boats, without the herring dees and the winkle-pickers, the shingle was a bleak vista darkened by the apparatus of war and the rank of oil drums that stretched endlessly towards Hove. Each drum squatted beneath the prom, ready to be rolled down the beach, past the ghosts of erstwhile paddlers, children and old people, into the sea. Each bore ten thousand gallons of petrol, and, for a moment, looking out, he saw it, the impossible: a sea on fire.

Even as he walked the beach, white sheets and pristine table linen were hanging from every window on the Channel Islands. That was the morning's news.

Any day. It could be any day.

That afternoon, there was nothing for it. What choice did he have? He walked back through town in the direction of the Crescent, but at The Level, he crossed the road instead and found the stall almost too easily among the jostle of the Open Market.

The woman looked unexpectedly sensible in a white cambric shirt and a pair of man's corduroy plus fours. Tillie had often told him over breakfast what a marvel she was; how she had cured her son Frank when, at eighteen months, his throat had nearly closed up with strep. Apparently, she had delivered onion poultices three times a day and saved the boy when Dr Baldwin from the London Road, for all he charged, did nothing except wait in readiness to cut a hole in his infant throat. Tillie had sworn by the woman ever since.

From the back of the queue, Geoffrey watched her bend over her scales, add another paper parcel to the balance, and remove a brass weight. She appeared matter-of-fact, unshockable, though she possessed the sort of fair, ruddy complexion that would betray any blush. Her eyes were a pale, sharp blue with exceptionally white whites; her face was unlined; her hands were chapped from a life lived outside. She had the sturdiness, the gravitas, of late-middle age, though whether she was thirty or fifty he couldn't have said. What a sight he must have made, he thought, with his fedora and his attaché case in the queue of pregnant women and miscellaneous others with lice-ridden heads, scabied limbs, and teeth in need of pulling.

The week before, when he had inquired at the surgery in Hove, Dr Moore had tersely mumbled something about two varieties of dysfunction before turning to the window and advising showers over baths. Then, on his Wednesday trip to London, with only minutes until his train home departed, he'd suddenly turned from Victoria and loped back up Buckingham Palace Road and through Green Park to Piccadilly. He turned left into Berkeley Street and on to Bruton, where he slowed his pace. He tried to gather himself but in no time – too soon – he found himself on New Bond Street. He felt sweat prickle beneath his collar. Henrietta Place, Wimpole, Wigmore and, finally – could he do it? – Harley. He hesitated outside a black Regency door with a fantail window, then pressed the bell.

Dr James Lawrence insisted he was delighted by the surprise visit from his favourite cousin's husband. Until that moment, he quipped, he never would have credited a banker with spontaneity, and it was jolly good to be surprised because he had, of course, desperately few things to be surprised by these days, unless you counted the enemy raiders overhead, though even they had become disappointingly predictable. To his mind, the smallest deviations in life's flight path were to be celebrated these days. Wasn't that the middling nature of middle age?

'Evelyn fine?' he asked briskly. 'Philip still at the Grammar?' Geoffrey nodded and reciprocated. They shared a joke about Mrs Lawrence, Geoffrey's formidable mother-in-law and James's aunt. They murmured a glum lament for the British Expeditionary

Force, then rallied and exchanged hopes for the cricket season. They noted the excellence of the weather, or, as James expressed it, 'the rising sap and all that', at which point Geoffrey sallied forth into what already felt like a battle he was losing against himself.

He lowered his voice, conspiratorially, as they walked through to James's office, and made himself say it: 'Out of curiosity, tell me, how do you medical sorts advise a chap when the sap *isn't* rising?' He grinned too hard. It was a clumsy transition – but at least, at last, he'd found the words. Or if not *the* words, words.

His wife's cousin studied him through a fixed but good-humoured smile. The telephone on his desk rang but he didn't answer it. Instead, he clasped his chin and ran his hand ruminatively over his throat. 'When it "isn't rising", you say?' Geoffrey nodded curtly.

Without word or warning, Dr James Lawrence dropped into his chair, clapped his palms together and laughed with gusto. 'Well, naturally, I advise glandular treatment!' He shook his head and laughed again, then sprang to his feet, still grinning, reached for his pipe and pipe-cleaner, closed the blackout, slid a heavy gold pen into his breast pocket, and pushed in his chair. 'I say, what chap in his right mind would turn down a bit of monkey testicle? I myself look forward to the day when I can afford a bit of chimpanzee scrotum or, better still, a baboon bollock or two. Olivia – dear, patient woman that she is – will be relieved to no longer have to check in with me to confirm, very tenderly, whether I've 'quite finished'. Then there's the rather less patient prostitute in Whitechapel who always insists on asking a colleague of mine' – he summoned his best cockney voice – '"Ave you slimed yet, sir?"' He sighed comically. 'Now, Geoff, what do you say? A malt? My club's only around the corner.'

The herbalist's stall was less of an ordeal, but his resolve flagged as he stood in the queue. He felt obliged to let every person who arrived after him go before him, insisting with an easy and benign smile that their needs were greater than his. In his own neighbourhood, just over the road from Park Crescent, he couldn't risk being overheard.

Years before, an old gentleman in the saloon of a seafront pub had confessed he swore by a compound of pulverized roots. Geoffrey had laughed genially at the time. He'd even listened with polite interest to the old man's renewed interest in peep shows, and had been careful to disguise the expression on his face, which said, *Poor bastard*. But the old gent had declared himself a new man.

As he waited and watched, Geoffrey rehearsed his words. It was a case for pragmatism. If only he could remember the name of the root. It hardly mattered that she was a woman. In any case, and most conveniently, she didn't look much like a woman. But the moment he opened his mouth to speak, the words abandoned him.

'No, no,' he'd assured her, 'wrong stall, I now realize. Apologies.' She raised her eyebrows. He felt obliged – foolishly obliged – to explain. His eyes scanned the bottles of herbs on the shelf behind her, and he slipped into the tone of forced jollity one used with servants. 'My mistake! The end of a long day, I'm afraid.' In fact, he announced too loudly, he'd only been looking for – he strained to think – 'fertilizer'.

His cheeks blazed at the accident of a word as the sirens sounded.

She walked up the London Road with her ration book and a new recipe folded in her pocket, like an insurance policy against failure. As she crossed Mr Hatchett's threshold, the stink of raw meat caught her by the throat. The recipe, she explained, was for 'Ragout of Mutton'. In the cold-cabinet lay brains, trotters, tripe, faggots, meat pies, ox-tails and a single calf's liver. She needed a pound of breast of mutton.

Mr Hatchett's skin was pulled tight over the bone of his skull, as if to advertise the fact that there was no excess, no waste, in his business. 'No mutton breast today, Mrs Beaumont,' he pronounced flatly, with a nod to the cabinet. 'Or tomorrow. Or any day in the foreseeable.' His eyes were slate grey, almost lidless. They followed her every step as she walked up and down, assessing the trays of meat, at a loss to determine which piece of flesh she could bear to handle. A rabbit dangled from a steel hook behind his shoulder, staring at her glassily, and the pressure of their collective gaze made her point at last and without confidence to the shiny slab of calf's liver.

Mr Hatchett did not reach for the tray but stood, instead, pulling on the scrawn of an earlobe, and a vision swam up in her mind – an image of him pulling at his scrotum instead of his earlobe – and she had to wince it away. Had she ever cooked calf's liver before? he inquired. It required a degree of skill. If she overcooked it, she might as well serve Mr Beaumont the soles of his shoes this evening. Undercooking posed even greater risks. Could he recommend the beef brain? Two brains would serve a small family. She had only to remove the membrane from each, along with any blood clots she could see on the surface.

He pressed his thin, narrow palms together, resting his chin on his fingers, as if he were Confucius in a red-and-white striped apron. Did Mr Hatchett, she wondered, expect her to prove her worth before she was permitted to buy the liver? She wasn't worthy. She knew it as well as he. But they had to eat. She had to learn to manage. So she lifted her chin, looking past him, and repeated her request. 'The liver, please. If you could parcel it up.' Her words, her tone of voice, her sudden attitude of indifference came together in an apparently offhand display of rank and class, for which she immediately loathed herself.

She couldn't face lunch. She returned home, got the liver into the Frigidaire, closed the door on it, and set out early for the WI. There, in the stifling hall, she struggled through the weekly self-defence class in which women of all ages learned how to box ears with their hands cupped to burst eardrums; to shatter ankles with the help of a good heel; and, in desperate times, to suffocate the enemy with a blow to the windpipe; or – here the group protested – to gouge out his eye successfully with the thumb. Yet even during her embarrassed attack upon a shop mannequin's windpipe, she was distracted by the other cutting she had slipped into her pocket before leaving the house.

Friday, 28th June: Mrs Virginia Woolf will lecture on The Modern English Novel for the Workers' Education Association at five o'clock. The Municipal Technical College, Richmond Terrace, Brighton.

She had snipped the notice out of the *Evening Argus* weeks before and knew it, absurdly, by heart. She couldn't attend – she was neither a worker nor a technical student – but she'd kept the cutting, pressed like a souvenir ticket stub between the pages of her copy of *The Years*, and that day, the 28th of June, she'd dropped it in her pocket as if it were a paper fortune.

Mornings these days were difficult. She'd wake, only to remember the sirens and the dreamlike sprint to Philip's bed; the pulling of clothes over his warm, floppy limbs; the three of them negotiating the stairs down to the basement before stumbling through the scullery and out of its door into the uncanniness of the night.

The coal cellar lay opposite, a dank cupboard beneath the street itself. The crumbling brick walls dripped, and animal droppings lay underfoot. The night before, she'd gathered Philip to her, stroking his hair and singing him back to sleep, while, at street level, the searchlights had slashed the sky, and Geoffrey had run up the external stairs to pound on Mrs Dalrymple's front door.

The old lady had appeared briefly at an upstairs window – 'Would you kindly bugger off, whoever you are!' – and disappeared again. Beneath a full moon, traitorously bright, Geoffrey went on trying to talk her down. A bomber – German – throbbed overhead, while far below, in a stagnant darkness, Evelyn sat perched on top of the sloping coal store with Philip pressed so close to her he must have heard in his dreams the pitching of her heart.

At the hour of his birth, she and Philip had nearly slipped from life together, and perhaps she had never lost the fear or foreboding that she might fail to keep him, not merely safe, but alive. With the drone of the aeroplanes – lower than ever, it seemed – the two of them had huddled, alone and small, like one body again.

The year before, on a shopping trip to London with her mother, she'd made some excuse and found her way to the East End, the Whitechapel Gallery and the vast canvas of Picasso's *Guernica*. The small notice in *The Times* had said the suggested donation was a pair of boots for the Republican cause in Spain but she'd forgotten and had given them instead, with her apologies, a pair of brogues she'd bought for Geoffrey that day. Then she'd walked back and forth, trying to fathom the riotous, monumental geometry of severed limbs and wild faces. One detail above all had stayed with her: the woman at the left of the canvas. Her face was fierce, feral – wolf-like with grief for her child, limp in her arms.

And again, the thought of the two pills flashed.

The large clock on the wall of the WI hall told her she still – just – had time to return home, change her clothing, and go to the lecture. If the details of the lecture were in the paper, surely she had a right to attend, to listen, to escape her own thoughts?

The realization made a small breach in the black dam within her, and the world trickled through. Outside the window, a green finch flashed past, a vivid blur of colour. Afternoon light poured in, golden, voluptuous. It warmed her cheek. It rippled in the loose hair of the young woman in the row in front of her as they practised their kicks.

She assured herself she had only to run to Magdalene Street, ask Tillie if she'd have Philip for dinner, pass her the parcel of liver as a small offering, and thank her sincerely. She could leave a note for Philip on the kitchen table, which he'd find upon his return from Orson's.

She had no illusions. She would find herself out of her depth. She tried to keep up with the new literature, but she read these days largely to convince herself that she still had a private life. In reality, she managed only a few pages at a time. Her concentration was hit-and-miss, and she assumed that the curiosity she'd long prided herself on was, after all, only the slim pretension of youth; a *jeu d'esprit*; the 'precociousness' that her parents had, at best, tolerated.

After all, when it came to it, when life had finally released her 'finished' from the school in Auteuil, when there had been at last a glimpse of freedom, where had her curiosity been? She'd fallen in love with the first man who'd touched her.

As for her cleverness, it was, she suspected, a sham. Good play-acting. A talent for references. A show of sophistication that Geoffrey had been obliged to applaud over the years in order that she might feel different, better, more discerning, than him; better, too, than the women at the WI with their uncomplicated love for the novels of John Galsworthy. Her problem hadn't been, as she'd always told herself, the denial of the university education she'd once craved; the enforced spell at Auteuil instead of entrance into Newnham. Her problem was a quiet sense of superiority that had never been earned or tested; a superiority that had masked her failure to live in all but the most conventional of ways while quietly disdaining convention.

Only at Auteuil had she risked anything. That year, at the age of seventeen, she discovered the knack of truancy and had often travelled the four miles into Paris on the decorous Ligne d'Auteuil.

Initially, her mission had simply been to find a bookshop or library that stocked English novels, for she was homesick and longed for good company, real or fictional. Lost more often than not, she discovered instead backstreet galleries and an art that was nothing like the masterpieces the girls at the school studied in their History of Art. At first, she'd thought modern art ugly and base. On its canvases, reality elongated, multiplied and bent. Where was its purity?

But little by little, she learned how to see all over again. The pure needed the impure. Truth was bigger than the laws of perspective.

It wasn't fixed. It couldn't be had off the peg. Truth had to be imagined.

At La Galerie B. Weill on rue Victor Massé, the owner, Fräulein Berthe Weill, told Evelyn that, some twenty years before, she had used her dowry to pay for the gallery even though her family had promptly disowned her for it. Her hair was combed back very tightly on her scalp and her spectacles were severe on the bridge of her nose, yet her eyes were bright and her gaze direct. Whatever she saw, she *saw*. Her gallery, she said, waving a tiny hand, had been the unrivalled 'Place aux Jeunes' when her artists *were* still *jeune* and unknown: Picasso, Matisse, Derain, Braque, Modigliani, Vlaminck, Valadon . . .

Evelyn nodded. She did not admit, in her schoolgirl French, that she knew none of those names; that her studies in the History of Art would end that term on nineteenth-century society portraiture.

It was on rue d'Astorg that she first saw work by Picasso and was charmed by another gallery owner, another German art dealer in Paris. Herr Kahnweiler flattered her with cups of Earl Grey tea, spontaneous lectures on the paintings that hung on his walls, and invitations to gallery soirées she could never attend. At his encouragement, she even dared present herself on rue de Grenelle at the new Bureau of Surrealist Inquiries where she was interviewed about her dreams in the night and her chance encounters of that day. She mentioned a handsome young ticket collector on the Ligne d'Auteuil who'd asked her to speak to him in English although he couldn't understand a word. He had just wanted to hear it. He'd listened very carefully to words that meant nothing to him. Then, 'You are someone different in English,' he'd said.

'No, I am someone different in *French*!'

But he'd smiled and shaken his head.

Her adventures in Paris lasted for less than a year. In the end, the Headmistress threatened to have her sent back to England 'unfinished' and in shame. Did she want to forego the Season? Did she want to spend her life as the daughter of the house, looking after her parents as they grew old?

She gave up the pleasures of the Ligne d'Auteuil. She never saw Fräulein Weill or Herr Kahnweiler again. She fell in with convention and made her peace with the extravagant absurdities of etiquette. Until her row with Geoffrey on the Pavilion balcony, she had never so much as demurred publicly with anyone's views, let alone her husband's, all of which meant – she glanced at the clock on the wall again – that she was infinitely less entitled to attend a WEA lecture than the bank clerk or bricklayer who risked the contempt of his family or workmates or friends to do so. What risk, she asked herself, what actual risk, had she ever taken?

In *The Years*, North seemed to think her thoughts before she could. 'We're all afraid of each other, he thought; afraid of what? Of criticism; of laughter; of people who think differently . . .' It was as if she were receiving his words direct from another place and time. '"That's what separates us; fear . . ."'

Even in the day's heat, the wide, polished corridors of the Technical College seemed as cool, as forbidding, as a glacial crevasse. Her footsteps rang out as she walked, shoulders back, head high, as if the building itself observed her. In fact, she had no idea where she was going. She'd taken a wrong turn and had lost count of how many flights of stairs she'd climbed. Somewhere a pipe groaned. A horned creature in a plaster coat of arms bared its teeth. She peered through a window slot, anticipating the lean backs of young men bent over machines, but found only shadowy rows of draughtsmen's desks.

She must have misheard the porter at Reception. Up ahead, a single door was open – light seeped over the threshold – but when she reached it, she discovered only a collection of drills and vices, their cables trailing across the floor. The clock on the wall read six minutes past five.

She ran to the end of the corridor, pushed on a door and raced down the staircase like an errant schoolgirl. Her hair started to unroll, arcs of damp spread beneath her arms, and as she descended, she became aware of someone else ascending the flight of steps.

The top of a head, a sunburned scalp through thinning grey hair, came into view in the gaps between the steps. It seemed impossible: Mr Hatchett. Like her, he was in a hurry.

At the entrance to the fourth floor, they each stopped short. 'I believe it's this way,' he said, his face determinedly neutral.

They walked the long corridor in a silence that was broken only by the staccato of their footsteps. She wished she'd worn a hat; she longed now for its brim, for its cover. After several long minutes, he stopped abruptly at a set of double doors, squinted through the slot, and held the door open.

The lecture theatre must have seated at least a hundred. Rows of brilliantined heads gleamed in descending tiers, amphitheatre style, to the front where, unbelievably, the author herself sat in a straight-backed chair in front of a vast chart of the Periodic Table. Together, she and Mrs Woolf were two of no more than four or five women in the room.

Evelyn stared from the entry door high above. Mrs Woolf's face was just visible beneath a wide-brimmed blue felt hat, a hat to which someone had attached a wide white chin-loop of dressmaker's elastic. She wore a red-and-blue plaid blouse with a large bow at the neck, a silver corduroy fitted jacket, and a long navy skirt with white stockings and broad, Roman-style beach sandals. Her feet were crossed at the ankles, there was a sheaf of foolscap on her lap, and she inclined her head slightly as she listened, smiling quizzically at the man who introduced her from the lectern.

The porter Evelyn had first met at Reception explained to her in a loud whisper that if she and her companion wished to be seated together, he was afraid he couldn't oblige. There were no two seats together. Only three or four single seats remained. What would they like to do?

She and Mr Hatchett nearly leaped apart at the question. She glanced at him for the first time, as if to agree which of them was obliged to clarify? He, the male, or she, the person of higher social rank? And in that singular moment, they each felt, briefly, naked.

Mr Hatchett cracked his fingers. Evelyn shook her head in a single, embarrassed syllable as if to say, *No, I am unaccompanied*. She imagined the porter asking to see proof of her WEA membership, or informing her loudly that he would need to check her Identity Card, which she of course had not bothered to bring. She hadn't even remembered to bring her gas mask, unlike Mr Hatchett, whose canister was slung dutifully over his shoulder. But the porter merely nodded and indicated with a finger a seat in the first row on the central aisle. She dashed down the side steps, face burning, and dropped into the heavy wooden chair.

She couldn't have explained why she then felt obliged to turn to locate Mr Hatchett several rows back. He too had taken his seat and now sat, folding his butcher's apron on his lap. He must have felt her gaze upon him, his nerves no doubt sharpened by the tension of their meeting, for he looked up at that moment and his grey, lidless eyes met hers.

She forced the corners of her mouth into a weak smile, a guilty smile – why, after all, had she turned to stare? – but she knew it didn't convince. She saw him stiffen. His Adam's apple rose in the wattle of his thin, shaved throat, and it was he who had the good grace to look away first.

As Mrs Woolf stood to speak, she removed her hat, and, for a moment, appeared unsure whether to rest it in the lap of her host – who had taken the only chair – or on the only other available surface, the floor. Noting the gloom of her host's face, she opted for the floor, but as she bent, she didn't see the handkerchief, a large gentleman's handkerchief, fall from her jacket pocket to the floor.

In the hush of the room, Mrs Woolf looped her spectacles over her ears and began to arrange her papers, as if unaware of the audience that waited patiently, deferentially even. All the while, they used the opportunity to observe unobserved this woman who already seemed to them less a literary spectacle than a person they had collectively dreamed.

Her silver hair matched, elegantly if accidentally, the silver cord of her jacket. The plaid bow at her neck was, at once, both spinsterish and lavish. Her eyes had the oversized, sunken but animated quality of the consumptive, while the fingers of her left hand, Evelyn noted from her vantage point in the front row, were, without exception, ink-stained. Even her lips were faintly marked with blue, as if she'd been pressing her fingers to her mouth, deep in thought as she scribbled on the train from Lewes to Brighton.

Her voice, as it first emerged, was unexpectedly deep; perhaps any threat of female shrillness had been 'elocuted' out of her long ago. 'My title today is "The Leaning Tower". I must confess that it is, at present, but a miscellany of half-formed thoughts on the modern novel. Perhaps with your help I shall develop it into something more sensible.' Evelyn unfastened her clutch and reached for a pen and paper. Mrs Woolf seemed as modest, as unassuming, as she was grand, and her words had their own rolling music.

'Books,' she began, 'descend from books as families descend from families. They resemble their parents, as human children resemble their parents; yet they differ as children differ, and revolt as children revolt. Perhaps it will be easier to understand living writers as we take a quick look at some of their forebears.' She looked up, almost solicitously, from her foolscap as if to assure herself that her audience was not averse to the proposal.

'In 1815 England was at war, as England is now. And it is natural to ask, how did their war – the Napoleonic War – affect the writers of the day? The answer, if you'll allow it, is a strange one. The Napoleonic wars did not affect the great majority of those writers at all. Their vision of human life was not disturbed or changed by war. Nor were they themselves. It is easy to see why that was so. Wars were then remote; wars were carried on by soldiers and sailors, not by private people. Compare that with our state today.

'Today we hear the gunfire in the Channel. We turn on the wireless; we hear an airman telling us how this very afternoon he shot down a raider; his machine caught fire; he plunged into the sea; the light turned green then black. Scott never saw the sailors drowning at Trafalgar; Jane Austen never heard the cannon roar at Waterloo. Neither of them heard Napoleon's voice as we hear Hitler's voice as we sit at home of an evening.'

And Evelyn was again in her own shuttered sitting room, in her chair, as Geoffrey tuned the wireless. Wasn't it the same in every house? The news was as irresistible as it was dreaded.

'Do we strain Wordsworth's famous saying about emotion recollected in tranquillity when we infer that, by tranquillity, he meant that the writer needs to become unconscious before he can create? Yet think of our modern writers. During all the most impressionable years of their lives they were stung into consciousness of things changing, of things falling, of death perhaps about to come. There was no tranquillity in which they could recollect. They told the unpleasant truths, not only the flattering truths. That is why their autobiography is actually so much better than their fiction or poetry. Consider how difficult it is to tell the truth about oneself – the unpleasant truth; to admit that one is petty, vain, mean, frustrated, tortured, unfaithful and unsuccessful. The nineteenth-century writers never told that kind of truth, and that is why so much of the nineteenth-century writing is worthless.'

Evelyn's pen hesitated. She wondered what it must be like to stand before more than a hundred readers and declare a broad swathe of nineteenth-century literature chaff. Surely Mrs Woolf was wrong in this one regard . . . ?

Did her own face betray her? For Mrs Woolf seemed suddenly to train her gaze upon her. Did *she* appear petty, vain or mean? Did Mrs Woolf suppose she was frustrated, tortured or unfaithful? Perhaps she did. Perhaps she was. But Mrs Woolf continued, and indeed she seemed to look at her kindly as she spoke, as if she above all needed to hear: 'If you do not tell the truth about yourself, you cannot tell it about other people.'

And rather than shrink under the older woman's attention, Evelyn stopped scribbling, met her eyes, and straightened in her seat, grateful that she had been noticed at all; grateful that Mrs Woolf seemed to confer upon her those simple, revelatory words.

She was afraid. That was the truth. She would have written it down now like an SOS if she could have, and held it up for Mrs Woolf alone to see. The bleak absurdity of each day was stripping her back. It was making her small, mean and narrow.

Who *was* Geoffrey? Lately she'd felt herself almost gag on the question. One evening as their ritual in front of the wireless began, she'd actually had to rush from the front room to the lavatory to retch, as if there were a single answer she couldn't quite keep down; as if truth lay like an infection in her gut.

He had deceived her about the night they had met; about the dark mood that had possessed him; about his vile behaviour. Worse still, had a part of her always suspected? Had her mind assembled the stray details of that night – the man's hot stare, his Jewishness, the split in Geoffrey's tailcoat – into a truth she had intuited long ago? And if she had sensed it and remained quiet about it, what did that say about her?

Perhaps there were more lies. Over a tipsy lunch in Mayfair before Christmas, Sylvia had intimated that Geoffrey had bedded some well-bred call girl on the night of the ball years ago, on the very night he had apparently fallen in love with her. 'Not that the girl's rounded vowels were her greatest assets,' Sylvia had added, lifting an eyebrow. She had paused in her monologue when she saw Evelyn's face. Her eyes had narrowed through the haze of her cigarette smoke. 'I tell a lie. I'm always mixing that lot up. It was Fitz. Not Geoffrey. It was Fitz. Tom, Freddie and Fitz. The reprobates. There's too much pink in this gin – what on earth *makes* it pink?'

How could he sleep so soundly these nights? He had decided to abandon his family to chance. He'd made a charade of their marriage.

His presence in their bed was both strange and repellently familiar. She hated the shape of his head on the pillow. She hated the slab of the back of his neck. She'd started to notice his smell – milky, as though that were the smell of love when it had soured. She could hardly bear his kiss, his teeth knocking against hers in his solitary passions. Yet he pretended not to know. He insisted on taking her arm when they walked out. He'd play-acted for Tom and Sylvia at the ball on Saturday evening. Later, in the early-morning half-light, he'd looked at her with only mild concern as she lay inert beneath him.

Appearances, appearances. They were a lovely couple. It was often said. But Geoffrey, it seemed, had decided for them both that appearances were enough; that the habit of marriage would suffice. How could she bear it, how could she live the rest of her life miming pleasantries? Other couples did – of course they did – but she couldn't bear to live so alone.

A week before their wedding, she had squeezed his hand as they'd strolled through the Pavilion Gardens. It had been a lover's question: 'If I were to die,' she'd grinned, 'would you marry again?' But he hadn't foresworn the thought. He didn't, in the spirit of the question, in the happiness of the moment, declare 'Never!', whatever the truth of the future might actually be. He hadn't wordlessly insisted on any sacred bond. 'I suppose so,' he'd confessed with a bemused smile.

Need, yes, he *needed* her. He needed a wife. When they had met, he had thought her clever, pretty, different. He had never known a girl like her, a girl still shy in the world but one with ideas, and such spark in her eyes, he'd said. Tenderness. Yes, she was sure he'd felt that. And a deep affection too. But love? He had confused it with need, a need for family and stability. Of course it had affected him: his mother removed from the family home when he was just a small boy. 'Almost unable to eat,' he'd said, only once. She'd wondered that such things were possible.

He'd grown up, he said, on monthly visits to the asylum and brittle hugs from a mother who was painfully, disastrously thin. Her breath was never right, he'd once confessed, and he'd winced immediately for having said it.

He claimed his father never recovered from the loss of her; a loss he and Geoffrey had both experienced long before her actual death, but she suspected that it was *he*, Geoffrey, who had never recovered from his mother's long absence, and that, ultimately, the price of his youthful confusion, of his carefully hidden grief, was Evelyn's to pay. He had married her for the wrong reasons. She'd been too innocent, too trusting, to know otherwise; to believe that a marriage between two willing people could be about anything other than love.

Only now did she understand the terrible gravity of those vows, and the potential of a marriage to spoil a life. After twelve years, he had finally outgrown his old need of her. The war seemed to have inspired in him a certain recklessness, a new and unexpected talent for the unpredictable; a dark sort of autonomy. He had cast off the dependence they had both mistaken for his love and he'd abandoned her to the rituals of their marriage. She found it difficult to fall into line; to be what Geoffrey termed 'sensible', which was the opposite of course of what the French meant by *sensible*. *That,* that allowance for feeling, for sensitivity, was entirely lost these days, vanished, and a failure to numb one's feelings in wartime was as much of an indulgence as overpriced black-market rouge.

On good days, she muddled through. On bad days, she wanted everything – their forced smiles, his habit of clicking his neck, his chemical-animal smell in the loo in the morning – over. She wanted all of it *over*, gone, and . . . she could think only of those two bright green pills that lay buried in the garden.

But Mrs Woolf, the lecture, the privilege of it – *what* was she thinking, letting her thoughts wander? She shook herself back into time. She lifted her face, contrite and open. She listened intently, trying to pick up the thread of the lecture, but something still distracted. It was Mrs Woolf herself. She was somehow . . . disparate. Her eyes were wide, almost too wide, with a small, shrunken pupil. She might have been a soothsayer in silver specs and Roman beach sandals, a woman who, like Cassandra, saw too much; someone for whom fear had necessarily become part of the fabric of everything she beheld. But the fear behind her eyes was at odds with the liveliness, with the *life*, of her voice and the genuine, if weary, courtesy of her smile.

Which was Evelyn to believe: her haunted eyes or the animation of her voice?

'We can begin, practically and prosaically, by reading omnivorously, simultaneously, plays, novels, histories, biographies, the old, the new . . . Literature is no one's private ground; literature is common ground. It is not cut up into nations; there are no wars there. Let us trespass freely and fearlessly and find our own way ourselves. Let us discover how to read and to write, how to preserve and how to create.'

She smiled uneasily and fanned herself with a sheet of foolscap, then fumbled for the handkerchief that was no longer in her pocket. 'I am grateful for your attention and am happy to take questions.'

A silence followed, terrible whole minutes of it, during which the gloomy convenor checked his wristwatch, and even Mrs Woolf, literary celebrity, looked exposed and small before the certitude of the Periodic Table. Then, at last, 'Yes, you, sir?' and everyone in the front rows, including Evelyn, turned in their seats to see Mr Hatchett rise to his feet, his left hand gripping his apron.

16

In Orson's room, Radio Bremen was triumphantly clear. 'I make no apology for saying again that invasion is certainly coming soon, but what I want to impress upon you is that while you must feverishly take every conceivable precaution, nothing that you or the Government can do is really of the slightest use. Don't be deceived by this lull before the storm because Hitler is only waiting for the right moment. Then, when his moment comes, he will strike, and he will strike hard.'

'But not Brighton,' said Philip, shaking himself free of the headset. 'He won't strike Brighton hard.'

'No, because he'll want friendly neighbours,' Orson said.

'But Lord Haw-Haw never says when Hitler's coming and that's just mean.' Philip looked up. Then he clambered on to the bed. 'There's music coming through the wall. I thought you said nobody was allowed in Hal's room.'

'I'm not and Father isn't. And Ivy isn't to go in. But Mother's allowed in of course. I didn't mean Mother. Sometimes she plays music on Hal's old wind-up gramophone, and she tidies up so everything is ready when Hal comes home on leave.' Orson got to his feet and both boys pressed their heads to the wall.

'She must be sad if she likes that music.'

'*No*,' and Orson's voice went high like a girl's. 'She's happy. She likes tidying Hal's room and playing Brahms.'

'The music doesn't sound happy.'

Orson reached up and retrieved the trophy helmet from its shelf above the bed. 'Right. Your go.'

'One day I roll out of bed, open the shutters and find a pigeon on the sill outside. It goes peck-peck, peck-peck-peck. A small yellow tube is tied to its leg. There's a message inside. Guess what it says.'

'Philip Beaumont, you smell.'

'It says, "You are expected today at four o'clock. Speak to no one. *Der Führer.*"'

'Why would Hitler write to you?'

'When I arrive at the Pavilion, a servant shows me through. We walk a very long way. I'm a little nervous. There are carved dragons everywhere. The servant has fat legs and his uniform is too tight. I wonder if Hitler will shoot him one day because he doesn't exercise enough. Then we arrive at a big door and the servant knocks. A dog barks and a voice booms on the other side. "In kommen!"'

'That's not how you say it.'

'At first I can hardly see anything because the chandelier is so bright. Then I see Hitler. He's sitting behind a big desk, bigger than the Headmaster's. On one side is an enormous globe on a wooden stand. He spins it and spins it without looking up once. He's wearing weekend trousers, black braces and . . . and a blue turban. When he turns from the globe at last, his eyes are very wide and blue. I think he's hypnotizing me. "Sitz downen!" he says, and he points to a sofa. I do as he says. His dog is perched by the desk. He throws it a peppermint from his pocket. The dog goes down on all fours with his bottom in the air, and, without meaning to, I go down too. Then he speaks to me. "You vill . . ."'

'You will what?'

'You vill give me all the sweets in Brighton.'

Orson sighed and grabbed the helmet and lowered it on to his head. His eyes blazed blue. 'There is a knock at our front door. It is *not* a dirty carrier pigeon. It is a Secret Service officer. His boots shine like black glass, and he's tapping one boot like it's Morse code. *Open this door immediately. Stop. I hate slowpokes. Stop. I am a very important man. Stop.* My mother sees him and screams. The SS man pulls out his pistol. "Spare her," I say. "*Der Führer* loves all mothers."

'The man shoots our geranium basket instead. Red petals fall everywhere. "Very well," he says, "but you must come with me."

'"Let go of me, Mother," I say, shaking her off, "or I might not be able to save you the next time." I follow the man to a black motor parked at the kerb. The door slams shut. '"Güt," a voice says. "Ein Sunday drive." Then Hitler claps his hands and we're off.

'We take the coast road. We see fishermen's cottages with tin roofs. They have little dirty yards with dirty, barefoot children running about. Geese cross the road, honking at us, but the Führer will not let our driver run them over – he loves animals. He waves from the car like the King to villagers, sheep and shepherds. Then, "Hier!" he orders, and our chauffeur swerves off the road.

'The bodyguard steps from the car, clicks his heels, opens the boot and produces a hamper. There is ginger beer for me and real German beer for Hitler. We stuff ourselves on cooked ham and pretzels. "Save room!" he orders, and out comes Black Forest cake. He tells me he loves Britain. He tells me he has always loved it. Our only mistake, he says, was when we told the King he couldn't tell us what to do any more. Everyone, he says, needs someone to be the boss of them.'

Orson got to his feet, walked to his bedroom door, opened it a crack, and listened. 'Now come with me.'

Hal's room smelled of floor wax and mothballs. The wind-up gramophone sat on a card table by the far wall. Its horn rose like a monstrous flower.

'I was supposed to be home ages ago.'

'Take off your shoes. And don't sit on the bed. You'll make wrinkles.'

Philip considered Hal's bed as he unlaced his shoes. The corners of its blue blanket were tucked tightly beneath the mattress, and the bed looked far too short for a grown-up man.

A faded map of the Empire hung on the wall above. Orson pointed to a shelf of trophies: 'Do you see the one that looks like an old goblet? It's the Troubadour's Cup. Hal won that for reciting "The Charge of the Light Brigade".' Orson made his voice go very low. "Into the jaws of Death/ Into the mouth of Hell/ Rode the six hundred."' He opened the bottom drawer in the chest of drawers. 'This is his air rifle, .22 calibre.' He shook a small box at Philip's ear. 'These are the pellets.'

Between the two tall windows, a desk gleamed. There wasn't a speck of dust. Orson took out Hal's old collection of Tarzan pictures. In the picture on top, Tarzan clutched Jane to his bare chest, and Jane drew her knees up so close you could see an entire cheek of her bottom. She had only a scrap of leather for a skirt. Tarzan wore his trademark loincloth and a thick blade in a leather sheath. 'Look!' Orson pointed to the distinctively shaped handle that poked out near his waist. 'Tarzan has a stiffy!' And they punched each other in delight.

Then the floorboards creaked, and they turned their ears like dogs attuned to a special frequency.

All went quiet again and Orson opened the wardrobe door. 'This is Hal's bat. Essex willow.' He crawled inside. Hangers clattered on the rail. A jacket tumbled from its perch. 'Shoes. Oar. Bicycle pump. Bicycle lamp. Jigsaw box. One-man tent. Croquet mallet.'

'I thought we weren't supposed to touch anything.'

'Mother ignores Hal's jumble.' He retreated deeper. 'Tennis racquet. Girlie playing cards. Tennis ball. Old atlas. Binoculars. Boxing gloves . . .' A milk crate appeared. Philip caught hold of it, and Orson tumbled out after.

'Jumpers?'

'Don't be daft.' Orson reached beneath the woollens and pulled out a heap of things: a tie; a pair of pressed trousers; a black shirt with buttons at the shoulder, like a fencing jacket; an armband with a lightning bolt on it; a gramophone record; a pair of black boots; a lady's stocking half filled with broken glass; and a leather belt with a shiny buckle. 'Watch this.' Orson took the belt, held it vertically, and clicked on the back of the buckle. Out popped a row of sharp steel spikes. Philip had never seen anything like it. He picked up the stocking and held it to the light; the glass bounced in the silken foot.

Orson was at the table, winding up the gramophone.

'What if your mother hears?'

He lowered the needle. 'She's downstairs with Ivy.'

A man's voice crackled to life: '— have striven to arouse in this country the feelings and passions of war with a nation with whom we made peace in 1918. We fought Germany once in our British quarrel. We shall not fight Germany again in a Jewish quarrel!'

'Mosley,' Orson whispered. 'Hal saw him in Worthing three times. The crowds were so big you would have thought it was the King.'

Philip jumped up. 'What was that?'

Orson lifted the arm of the gramophone. Neither moved.

Outside, in the road, someone was whistling. Philip knew the tune . . . It was one the Dunn brothers had sung beneath the Pier that day in May. He ran for the window, grinned, and raised his hand to the glass. Orson reached for his specs. 'Who is it?'

'My friend.'

'You mean, your housekeeper's son? Tell him to go home. He's bloody well going to get us caught in here.'

Philip had never heard Orson swear before. He waved urgent arms at Tubby while Orson struggled with the bolts. 'Tubby!' he whispered at last down to the street. 'What are you doing?'

'You didn't come to ours for your tea. My mum says she's worried witless. She sent Frank off towards the Grammar to look for you, and I said I'd run to your house fast, in case you were on your tod on the front step. When you weren't, I thought you might be here but I didn't know which house so I had to whistle.'

'Why am I having tea at yours?'

'My mum said your mum said. She left you a note. We're having bread and scrape, liver but no onions.' Tubby hugged himself, as if he were standing in the rain.

'What did you say his name is?' Orson slammed the window shut.

Philip hesitated. 'Norman.'

'That's curious . . .' Orson studied Tubby as if he were something flat on a glass slide.

'What is?'

'He looks like a Jew.'

'How do you mean?'

'Bony. In need of a good wash.' Orson pressed his face and specs to the pane. Then he fixed the bolts, closed the shutters, and returned to the crate.

He was putting Hal's things away.

'Tubby – I mean, Norman – is a Roman.'

Orson didn't turn. 'I didn't say he *was* a Jew. I said he *looked* like a Jew.'

'How do you know what Jews look like?'

Orson forced the crate back into the wardrobe, pushed the door shut, and leaned against it. 'Hal told me, of course.'

17

She'd done her evening duty by her absent neighbours. She'd checked their houses. It was an odd sensation, she thought, walking through other people's private lives; disturbing their ghosts; bumping into corners one didn't expect.

She hooked the three sets of keys into place on the key board.

'All clear?' Geoffrey asked with a perfunctory smile.

She nodded and dropped into her chair. He reached for his cigarette. The wireless buzzed to life. Philip pressed his cheek to the broadloom. Beside him lay his crumpled visions of Hawker Demon bombers and his pencil.

He yawned. On Friday evenings, his father sometimes carried him upstairs to bed. He considered his mother's legs, crossed at the ankles. One of her slip-ons had slipped off. In the dim light she read her Mrs Woolf. When she looked up over her page, he closed his eyes quickly.

He heard his father inquire about his mother's day. His mother inquired about his father's. His mother said she'd learned how to take out a man's eye. His father sat down, leaned his head back, and exhaled smoke, dragon-like, from his nostrils.

On the other side of the shutters, a thrush sat speckle-breasted on a chimney pot, rehearsing a single phrase. Bats flitted and dived over the hood of a street lamp. There was the rot of the swill-bin and the whiff of a backed-up drain, and over it all lay the green luxury of June, every leaf etched and bright.

A bicycle bell chimed twice and receded up the street. In the shadow of the Salvation Army's ramparts, two boys bounced a tennis ball at the brick wall. To the west of the Crescent, on the slow-climbing crest that was Ditchling Road, summer lay rapt beneath a snowfall of hawthorn blossom, cow parsley, elderflower and daisies, while to the east, on the Lewes Road, a lone army truck rumbled past on a loose suspension.

The moon rose gravely above the horizon.

Tick tock tick tock tick tock. 'This is the BBC Home Service. Here is the *Nine O'Clock News*.' No one could reassure the nation as assuredly as Alvar Liddell, dressed in his BBC announcer's dinner jacket. All was seemingly shuttered calm. Evelyn turned another page of *The Years* and found Eleanor musing again: 'There must be another life, she thought, sinking back into her chair exasperated.' Evelyn could hear her. Her voice was like Mrs Woolf's, resolute but uninsistent; old and young at the same time. 'There must be another life, here and now, she repeated. This is too short, too broken. We know nothing, even about ourselves.'

Geoffrey rose to adjust the dial, Philip muttered in his sleep, and Eleanor was evaporating into black marks on the page when, as if from another dimension, Evelyn had a sudden, final glimpse; an impression of white hair and tanned cheeks.

How strange it all was. Was she imagining Eleanor or was Eleanor, the 'queer old bird', imagining her?

Of course she wasn't. She was tired, that was all, and lonely. The Pargiters' lives had become more solid than her own.

Geoffrey glanced across to her, and together, falling into habit, feigning marriage, they smiled, weakly, fleetingly, at the sight of their sleepy son, while somewhere on the Crescent, a front door shut, a passing dog yapped, and – *thwack* – the ball bounced off the wall again.

When Geoffrey had arrived home, he'd asked, not unkindly, why she hadn't prepared the evening meal. 'There's only us,' she'd said, as if that explained the departure from routine. 'Philip is at Tillie's.'

He didn't ask why, and to ensure he didn't, she rose immediately from her chair to make him a sandwich.

Now, beneath the glassy calm of the evening, the secrets of the day gathered. While domestic rituals unfolded up and down the Crescent behind windowpanes burnished gold in the setting sun, as Alvar Liddell read the news in crisp, clipped consonants that sedated a nation, it was as if every armchair, picture frame and side table in the Beaumont home drained of colour, slid into shadow, and became something other. A blast wave of the unsaid moved through the four walls, permeating every dovetail joint, every knot of wood, and every bubble and warp of the windowpanes.

Philip had slid guiltily through the front door an hour before. He said yes, Tillie was well, and yes, the liver was good. He did not say that, just that afternoon, he had held a stocking filled with broken glass; that Hal's belt was even better and he'd longed to pop the spikes himself, but then Tubby had turned up outside whistling, and Orson had put Hal's things away, and now he'd probably never have the chance to pop the belt again.

He did not confess that he had not returned home to find his mother's note on the kitchen table; that he had not left Orson's when he should have; that Tubby and Frank had been sent by their mother to find him, and the three of them had only just got in the door when the sirens went. Nor did he say that Tillie had slapped his leg and hugged him so hard that his lungs had hurt.

Although she had assumed she would, Evelyn did not, in the end, tell Geoffrey that she had attended Mrs Woolf's lecture. She did not mention Mr Hatchett or describe Mrs Woolf with her handkerchief and her sandals and her lips that were ink-stained – stained as if she'd been *feeding* herself on words.

After the lecture, as the sirens went, Evelyn retreated to the shelter beneath The Level. There, in the stink of creosote and urine, she'd checked her notepad and murmured the words to herself: 'Literature is no one's private ground; literature is common ground. It is not cut up into nations; there are no wars there. Let us trespass freely and fearlessly . . .'

The woman seated on the bench across from her, corpse-like in the blue light, had mistaken it for 'The Lord's Prayer' and had elbowed her husband to bow his head.

She did not tell Geoffrey that, these days, she was full of fear, but that the contempt she had come to feel for him frightened her most of all.

He reached for another cigarette and snapped the case shut. For his part, he had no intention of telling Evelyn, or anyone for that matter, that he had stopped at the Open Market on the way back from the Bank that afternoon. He could still see the herbalist's face – the brief lifting of her lips, the pinched-off smile – as the word 'fertilizer' came out of his mouth.

The wireless was hissing static. He surfaced only to realize that Evelyn was speaking to him. She had put down her book, the news was over, and she was saying, 'So I've decided.'

He turned dutifully in his chair.

'The hospital.'

'The hospital?'

'I'll volunteer.'

134

'Ah.' He was still at the herbalist's stall, cringing.

'I'll make a few inquiries. About reading. I think it might be restorative for some. Why, just the other day on the BBC, they were saying –'

'At the hospital?'

'I've just said.'

'Is that a good idea?'

'Clearly I think so,' she said with a determined brightness, 'or I wouldn't have mentioned it.' *Let us discover how to read and to write, how to preserve and how to create.* Words made worlds, new worlds.

In the spume of his dreams, Philip sat on the seafront with Hitler, Mosley and Orson. From their deckchairs, they watched the waves and sucked on sticks of Brighton rock. They had taken off their shoes and socks, and Mosley was wriggling his toes. The sun was warm. Hitler frowned at the incoming tide and chewed his moustache. The stick of rock was delicious. When Philip looked at its middle, he saw the same lightning bolt in the circle of blue that he'd seen on Hal's armband. 'Look!' he said, and Orson nodded. Hal, he said, was in the shooting gallery on the Pier, winning every prize. 'Listen,' he said.

'They've started . . .' said Geoffrey. 'They had to clear the entire seafront, as a precaution.'

Together they turned to the shuttered windows and listened to the glass rattle in its frames.

'As I say, I'll make a few inquiries.'

'It's just that you're not particularly good with blood. Your last WI visit to the hospital left you quite upset.'

'Will it go on all night?'

'For much of it, I daresay.'

'The Camp then.'

He looked up. 'The Camp?'

'I'll read to the prisoners. Surely you're not letting them bleed too much?' She folded her hands in her lap.

'It would be awkward.'

'Perhaps they will have requests – their own favourite poems or novels. On the BBC they said that to be read to was –'

'It's a kind thought.' He waited for the next dull boom to fade.

Philip smiled faintly in his sleep. *Boom, boom, boom.* Hal was winning every prize.

'But I'm afraid it wouldn't be permitted.'

Anger burst within her; a small, hot shell. 'Why ever not?' She smiled quizzically. '*Who* would not permit it?'

'The Camp is strictly "men only", Evvie. The regulations don't even allow me to employ female cooks or laundresses. Only the rare visitor is permitted, usually Army or Corporation personnel. Never female, charitable or otherwise. Regulation aside, it wouldn't be safe. It's simply not the place.' He checked his wristwatch, then heaved himself to his feet and gathered Philip from the floor. 'Good lad,' he murmured, cradling their son's sleeping head against his chest.

She had to look away. Sometimes, it was still an effort: to hate him so she would not love him. He'd always been such a good father.

Less than a mile away – another explosion.

'I'll see you upstairs,' he said.

She fanned herself with her book. 'I'll bathe first. Don't wait up.'

'Sure?'

She lifted her chin and smiled again.

At the sound of his footfall on the upstairs landing, she rose, clicked the lamp's switch with her foot, closed the door soundlessly, and stood alone, stooping as if winded. Something gripped the hollow of her stomach – she'd forgotten to eat since that morning – and she felt, too, a pressure under her ribcage, the hot insistence of her clamouring heart.

She walked to the far wall and lay her forehead against its cool plaster, its blank vertical, as if only its solid geometry could keep her standing. In the darkness, a moth flapped its desire in the hot lamp it madly mistook for the moon. She and it. She and it. She and it. On and on it crashed and struggled, as she pressed her cheek and mouth to the cool of the wall. How to cease to feel? *That* was the trick of living.

Something replied.

Boom, boom.

When she straightened at last and managed to turn, the moth lay half dead on the side table beneath the lamp. A common ghost moth. A singed wing. She could smell it. And for one heady, careless moment, uncluttered by any moral imperative, she knew what it was to loathe the world; to feel a flagrant disgust for it and for everything in it, not least her own frailty and longing.

The night exploded again. Boom, boom – boom. On the seafront, they were blowing up the piers.

It was the end, she thought, the end of pleasure.

18

Two weeks later, as husband and wife passed each other on Elm Grove, on opposite sides of the broad, tree-lined street, neither felt any peripheral tug of awareness. She was going uphill, and he, down. He didn't glimpse the curve of a familiar brimmed hat or the particular tilt of a chin; she didn't recognize a certain loping stride. Neither turned suddenly to stare or to call. 'Evvie! Wherever are you going?' 'Geoffrey! Goodness! What on earth . . . ?' Each walked on, in a tangle of private thought.

Less than halfway up the rise, she'd felt her face start to burn in spite of her hat. Her underclothes stuck to her. Her feet blistered. On the steep climb, the July sun hammered the pavement, and pigeons sat still as decoys in the trees.

The racecourse was no longer the destination it had been. 'Closed for the war' meant no buses and no trams, while most cabs now ran on black-market petrol. She wasn't necessarily averse – wasn't everyone simply trying to make a living? – but it would not have been seemly for the wife of a bank manager.

As she neared the top, she was grateful for the sharp, cleansing whiff of sea air – it couldn't be far now – and she navigated her way by the scattered cottages of Bevendean to the east and the streets of Whitehawk to the west. Where had the Gypsy camp gone?

Such heat, such stifling heat even in late afternoon. When the town had receded far enough behind her and not a soul was in sight, she allowed herself at last to stop, unclip her stockings and peel them off. She slipped off her shoes, too, and set her blisters free. The grass was cool, blissful. The sky felt so close. A sparrowhawk swooped.

Only when the tiers of the grandstand appeared, blazing white, did she wipe her face, retuck her blouse, and ease her feet painfully back into her shoes. She had a plan, a good one, and that drew her on. Or rather it did until the palisade came into view.

The wall of razor wire was scrawled like an obscenity against the slope of Race Hill. At the mean opening, she stared up at a guard who couldn't have been more than sixteen; a spotty boy playing at war. No wonder the Gypsies had fled.

She was there to see the Superintendent. Mr Beaumont. 'My husband,' she added, resenting the need to account for herself. Geoffrey should simply have agreed her plan when she'd put it to him. She shouldn't have to rely on the element of surprise.

The boy wore the requisite Local Defence Volunteer armband and carried a rifle with a fixed bayonet – an old, outmoded weapon but deadly enough, no doubt. The tip of his bayonet glinted in the day's expansive light. How mad everything was. A boy with a bayonet was leading her to the racecourse through a corridor of barbed wire. Her book bag knocked at her shins.

It was after four, but the day hadn't cooled, and the trees that lined the street stooped under their own weight. Geoffrey hardly knew this part of town, a warren of streets and tilting houses that clung to its western slope in the hot shadow of the railway terminus.

The area seemed strangely empty for a summer's afternoon. No children drew with chalk on the pavement. Women didn't whisper their troubles over cups of tea and front steps. Delivery boys weren't knocking on doors. It was less a community than, literally, the end of the line for the town's transients. Newspapers and chip wrappers gathered in the drains. Strange cooking smells wafted from open windows and doors. A round-shouldered young man with a battered suitcase passed him, and Geoffrey looked away, pretending to check the address against the note he'd made. Rosa, their Spanish char, lived up this way, but he had no idea where. An older woman crossed the street in his direction, observing him openly. She wore a bright handkerchief on her head and a cheap summer jacket. A refugee, he assumed, and he dipped his head as she passed, embarrassed by the sight of her bare brown feet. Would she look back to see which house he entered?

Number 39 was an unpromising Victorian semi set back from the street: dark, austere, with a peeling front door and a few faded carnations that only drew attention to the riot of weeds. Overhead, above the loose guttering, the roofline rose in concrete crenellations. They looked less like an ornamental feature than teeth, broken and bared. He rolled his sleeves down, slipped on his jacket and buttoned it at the middle, imagining himself climbing the steps to the door, a clean-shaven misfit in a good jacket and tie.

He thought of Evelyn, and a dull ache spread across his chest. The first time she hadn't returned his kiss was weeks ago now. Afterwards, in the refuge of the bath, he'd suffered like a schoolboy, his face pushed into his knees. But there was of course nothing to be said. It was only a kiss not returned. We are broken, he now understood, by everything we cannot say.

Life would hobble on. Indeed, perhaps it was only by accepting the inevitable failures of intimacy that one's married life moved forward and passed into the muted successes upon which anniversary parties, retirement dinners and obituaries ultimately depended.

At the front of Number 39, in a tall, narrow window criss-crossed with blast tape, a handwritten sign had been posted. GENTLEMEN LODGERS ONLY. NO REFUGEES. He thought of Mrs Merrick all those years ago, presiding over the girls of the 43 Club. He recalled his one night of sweetness with Constance – lovely Connie with the lazy eye – and he wondered what had become of her.

He hovered on the top step, contemplating retreat, yet even as he did, he couldn't shake a growing awareness of something within his chest, an electric crackle of possibility, a clarifying jolt to his senses. An odd sort of hopefulness where he had expected shame and queasiness. Some new dynamic had propelled him that afternoon down Race Hill, down Elm Grove, through the town and uphill again past the station. After weeks of deliberation and prevarication, here he stood at Number 39.

The lobby of the Metropole and the women there had been out of the question. Too public, too chandelier-bright.

It was an experiment, he told himself. Would he find himself 'capable' here?

He counted the notes in his wallet, and, as he did so, the memory of his confrontation last month, with the Category A prisoner, returned. He saw again the man's black, sardonic eyes and the faint line of mockery on his lips. The truth was, Geoffrey wouldn't have disciplined his men had they neglected to haul this particular prisoner out of the sea. He was a common cheat who'd arrived in the country with forged bank notes; who'd been living in Brighton on a stash he hadn't turned over to the authorities. He was a drifter without regard for the daily imperatives under which most people laboured; a coward who had bungled even his own suicide. A homosexual, possibly. A Jew, certainly. He called himself an artist, though the art establishment in Berlin had disagreed. The Home

Department had deemed him Category A: a would-be agitator, a subversive.

He pulled hard on the bell.

As Evelyn stepped from the barbed mouth of the tunnel on to what had been, only two months before, the course's pristine finishing line, her bag slid to the ground. Beyond the grandstand itself, the green turf had disappeared beneath a blight of weather-boarded barracks.

Mistaking her shock for admiration, the young sentry drew her attention to the Camp's key features, spread out over more than a mile: a squat cookhouse, a canteen, a fuel store, a laundry, latrines and, in the area that was once, as she recalled, the winners' enclosure, rows of accommodation that housed the permanent patrol unit.

They walked on, passing a row of stable blocks – housing for the new arrivals, he explained. Men in grey boiler suits aired straw mattresses on a patch of grass. Others laboured over vats of cement. 'Gun emplacements,' he said. 'We're the biggest local supplier.' As she passed, their guard shouted something in fierce gutturals, and the men lowered their eyes.

'See the tote building over there?' her escort prattled. 'That's where they used to take the bets, through the slots at the bottom of those little windows. But it's a detention block now, 'cos the windows are *that* small a man would be lucky to get more than a square of toilet paper through – pardon my French. It's as good as airless in there, so if a troublemaker finds himself locked up, he starts behaving, or he does if he wants to breathe again.'

She felt sick, as if she were about to be motioned to the door and asked to cut a blue ribbon. 'Where is the infirmary? Are there patients today?'

He pointed with his bayonet. 'The furthest hut. You can just see the tin roof from here, in the old parade ring. We got one chap – tried to top himself last month.'

He offered to carry her bag. She shook her head. 'He's dying?'

'Should be dead but our lads saved the daft beggar. From what I hear, he's tuppence off the pound.'

'And the others?'

'Just one, 's far as I know. Old geezer. On his way out. And over there, behind the latrines, is our new ablutions block. We had a pipe burst again last week, so it was a right ol' mess, as you can imagine.' He showed her to her husband's 'HQ'. 'Now you make sure you have someone to show you out of here, Mrs Beaumont. Pardon my French, but I wouldn't put anything past this lot. If you ask me, some of 'em need extra bromide in their bread. The I-talians especially.'

In the stuffiness of the office, she stared at her husband's steel desk. The Head of Patrol was no happier to see her than she was to see him. 'I'm sorry to appear awkward, Sergeant, but I think you'll find Mr Beaumont is *somewhere*. It is Monday, after all, and on Mondays, as we both know, he has his inspections.'

The woman smoothed her dress and stubbed out a cigarette in an ashtray the shape of the Eiffel Tower. Geoffrey surveyed the room.

An iron bed and washstand were pushed up against one wall. A gas ring and a kettle occupied a dressing table, under the leg of which someone had shoved a wedge of card. A packet of Player's lay next to the kettle. On a painted shelf, a silver frame, the only thing of value in the room, was turned to the wall. He was curious but his eyes flicked past it. The floorboards were warped and bare save for a bright rag rug. The yellow edge of a child's hoop stuck out from under the bed.

'Fine, yes?' She blotted her lips on a tissue.

He walked to the window and pushed aside the pale muslin curtains. The light of late afternoon tipped like syrup across the chimney pots, the wireless masts and the roof of Brighton Station. On the railway bridge, a train sped by, hissing steam, and the prisoner's words returned to him unexpectedly, their tone amused, ironic, overly familiar.

I daresay it's also rare to meet a Superintendent who takes so great an interest in his prisoners.

He followed the line of the train; felt the pounding of the tracks, the stoked heat of its engine. His hostess, he realized belatedly, was waving a hand, motioning to the room. 'Clean. Yes?'

He blinked and turned, relieved she made no effort to smile in spite of the false cheer of her question. She was tall, in her late twenties or early thirties, with dark hair, slack lips and heavy, pendant breasts. She was not a pretty woman – her eyebrows were too heavy, her face too broad – but she had a full-bodied gravitas, a sombre sensuality, and a voice that did not repel him.

It was enough.

He flexed the tension from his hands. She passed him a matchbox and the pack of Player's, taking one for herself. Then she opened a drawer and produced a bottle of vodka and two tumblers. 'Sorry, Doctor. No tonic.'

'I am not a doctor,' he said, striking a match.

She shrugged, as if to say, *Suit yourself*, and held out her cigarette for a light.

He obliged, lit his own, and exhaled. On the ceiling, a yellowed strip was studded with flies. 'May I ask your name?'

'Leah.'

Her back was beautifully straight. He found it surprising in a woman of her class, and the puzzle of it irked him briefly. 'Where do you come from, Leah?'

'Nowhere,' she said, screwing the vodka lid back on. 'Nowhere you know.' He watched her tap ash into the Eiffel Tower. On her upper arm a livid mark flashed red.

'You've had a bit of an accident.' He nodded to it. It was recent, still blistering, and the shape, all too clear. He didn't need to be a doctor to know that someone had forced her arm down on the gas ring. He looked for a moment too long, wondering at the intensities she had known.

'I put something else on. You won't see. Drink, drink. Is hot today, no? You walked far, I think. You sweat.'

He looked up.

'A man must sweat!' she said.

'Are there other girls, other girls like you, who live here?' He could hear nothing, no signs of life, but he imagined ears at the door.

'Why "other girls"?' Her lip jutted. 'I told you. This' – she nodded at the burn – 'is nothing.' She reached for the dressing gown on the hook of the door but hesitated, realizing the point was not to put more clothing on.

Was she up to this? he wondered. Was he? Or would he feel compelled to pay her out of pity and leave?

'You are worried,' she said. 'Forget.'

'Not worried,' he said. 'Curious.' The Experiment.

He could smell the scent of her hair, loose and unpinned. She dropped the dressing gown on the bed next to him and walked to the window. In the light, the curve of her thighs showed through the thin cotton of her skirt, and he felt a sudden, overwhelming desire to take their flesh between his teeth.

He slipped off his jacket, folded it over the bedstead, and took a seat on the edge of the bed. The vodka slid down his throat. He'd never looked twice at this shape of a woman before, but sitting here, studying her, he realized he liked the substantialness of her. She was heavily female. Only now did it occur to him: he had never been with a woman he hadn't been half afraid of breaking.

He checked his wristwatch, then his nails. He almost made it sound offhand: 'Are you a Jewess?'

At the window, she drew deeply on her cigarette. Someone passed in the street below, and she turned, feigning interest in their progress. Beyond the street, on a platform at the station, a guard blew a whistle, hard and shrill.

'A Jewess?' she said, but her voice betrayed nothing. She bent, letting the sill take her weight, and flicked ash with one hand while rubbing the small of her back with the other, up and down, her long fingers splayed against her haunches. Beautiful fingers.

Then the curtains lifted in a rare, rippling breeze, and she turned to him through the veil of muslin. 'You say . . .' and she held his gaze.

In the distance, something crashed. At the station, a carriage was being shunted into line with a vengeance.

She sat down on the bed beside him.

Look at her, Otto thought, as she seated herself at the foot of the old man's bed. What was the English expression? 'Lady Bountiful'. There she sat, speaking charitably while the tailor rasped his pitiful replies. She'd looked horrified at her first glimpse of him. Unnerved. Reality was not to her liking. Now she seemed more confident. Too confident. She moved from the foot of the bed to the old man's side and took his hand in hers.

Her face puckered at the sight of the bucket beneath the bed, not far from her feet, and she called to the Nazi guard, demanding, as the

Superintendent's wife, that he empty it. She reached for the sponge that floated in a bowl of day-old water and pressed it to the old man's cracked lips. She also required a chair.

'Has the doctor been?'

The guard shrugged.

From his bed, Otto failed to suppress a laugh, and she pivoted, her eyes hot, flashing, as if deciding that, whoever he was, whatever his suffering, he had just forfeited any claim he might have had to her compassion. She smoothed her skirt over her knees but, as she turned back to the old man, her foot knocked the carrier bag by her chair. Books tumbled out across the lino, and not only books. Over the top of them – incongruously, flamboyantly – lay a pair of flesh-toned silk stockings, wrinkled, as if they had been removed in a hurry.

She stooped quickly, pushing them and all but one of the books back into her bag. The guard pretended not to see. Otto laughed again. *Let the Superintendent call in the firing squad*, he thought. *A prisoner has seen Mrs Superintendent's stockings*. In Berlin, he'd painted models in every state of undress. This woman looked – what was the word? – 'corseted'.

'Please, Mr Pirazzini,' she was murmuring, 'you rest. No, I'm fine. Absolutely fine.' As if the crisis were hers. 'Thank you. I shall read to you now. Would you like that? It's a calming piece. I believe you might enjoy it.' She was flustered, embarrassed. The old man closed his eyes obligingly.

She looked behind her, to see if Otto still dared to watch.

Not only did he still watch, he was, she saw, laughing to himself.

She turned her head sharply back. '*The Waves*,' she announced brightly, 'by Mrs Virginia Woolf. "*The sun had not yet risen. The sea was indistinguishable from the sky* . . ."'

Had her husband told her, Otto wondered, about his failed effort to drown himself? Of course he had. *The Waves. Such comedy*, he wanted to declare. *Of all the books in that bag. What a riposte. Ha ha!*

He was diving in again. He could see under water. So clear, so clean, and soundless. No children's faces. No cries. He could have stayed there for ever.

Her voice composed itself into a pleasing music. He could tell she liked the rhythms of the prose. On and on she read. Mr Pirazzini was asleep. Or dead. Did it matter? She was intent on her charity. He had to turn from the sight of her, though tears sprang to his eyes each time he tried to move his shoulder on the pillow. The operation had been postponed again. Staff shortages, too many injured evacuees. The wound festered. Would his arm, his painting arm, ever be steady again?

'Thank you,' he heard her say to the Nazi, as he slid the bucket below the old man's bed. 'Thank you. That's very kind.' Her voice was the silk of the stockings in her bag. The guard's boots passed the end of his bed, to and fro, to and fro. Sweat poured from him. He could no longer distinguish fever from fear. The scar tissue on his back was inflamed, a reaction to too many days inert in bed. During his admission examination, the Army medic had bent to study the crude geometry of hobnails. Then he'd picked up a pen, scribbled a note on a form, ticked a box that said PREVIOUS, and passed Otto the regulation overalls.

Evelyn put him from her mind. She no longer cared that the man had been so desperate that he had, according to the sentry's account, tried to take his own life. He did not seem desperate to her. He seemed highly amused.

She could not hate a total stranger – she would not allow herself to be so irrational – but she despised this man somehow, this enemy alien, and that strength of feeling made her read with a peculiar vivacity, a surge of will, that was carried, in the undulations of those waves of prose, across the room to him.

The Waves, *ha ha. Of course*, Otto thought. *Ha ha*, he laughed, trembling.

Mr Pirazzini opened his eyes and closed them.

She paused mid-line. Behind her, the man was openly laughing now. Her cheeks burned. She wanted to shout, *What on earth could you possibly find to amuse you here? What on earth could you have to laugh about?*

She closed her book. Her heart thudded. The room went quiet, and the heat was suddenly unbearable. She lifted her hair from her neck and then, quickly, self-consciously, let it drop again. She wanted to turn – *Who* are *you? Are you mad?* – but she sat, gripped by a strange gravity, a force field of heat, silence and expectation . . . She didn't even know the sound of his voice.

Mr Pirazzini coughed, and she started in her chair. On and on, he struggled to get his breath. She got to her feet and tried to prop him higher. She called for the guard but nothing helped. Mr Pirazzini's lungs rattled like a pair of dice in a game he could not win.

That airless night, Geoffrey and Evelyn lay together in their blacked-out room, feigning sleep.

He rolled on to his side, stirring at the memory of Leah glimpsed through pale muslin. 'You say,' she murmured again through slick, painted lips.

The relief, at last, had been tremendous.

Beside him, Evelyn cringed again at the memory of the stockings. She could still feel the pressure of Otto Gottlieb's gaze on her back.

All over Brighton that night, people needed air, a breeze. They longed to draw back the blinds, shutters and curtains. The weather needed to break. The war needed to break. The entire town seemed to live on short, staggering breaths.

Then, as if in reply to some reckless act of the collective will or an unspeakable communal wish, something in the atmosphere gave way that July night. Squalls and showers blew in from the west. The lid of summer came off. And in a moment that was, after so many months of waiting, as much longed for (secretly, ashamedly) as it was dreaded, the first bomb was tipped into the early morning of the new day: a fifty-kilogram falling star, gravid, lethal and indifferent.

19

Seven others would follow, whistling terror.

Early in the morning of the 15th of July, the Dornier 17 slipped in under the radar and circled the town.

Most lay clenched in their beds. *Not us. Don't get ideas. On your way now. Bugger off.*

Imagine it.

You are lifted from your bed even before you hear the blast. The walls of your house are sucked in – a full ten inches – before they are pushed back out by a blast wind that is, briefly, of hurricane force. You wake, unable to understand why heaps of gravel and brick dust are being shovelled over you at speed. When you finally look up, your mouth and nostrils are crammed with dust. The skin is flayed from your forearms where you raised your hands to protect your head. Your eardrums have burst, and the pain leaves you staggering as you climb free of the rubble that is your bed.

It's not easy to get your bearings. The dividing walls have fallen. There is a hole of grey sky in the roof. The sense of space is dizzying, and your ears are bleeding. You have to take a running jump to get to the stairway, and downstairs, the floorboards in the hallway are up, as if someone has been shuffling them like a pack of cards.

You stumble outside for air, but even here the day is thick with dust, soot and – you can't make sense of it – a blizzard of feathers.

Throughout the neighbourhood, pillows, bolsters and mattresses have exploded.

There are puffs of smoke. You can't see them, but from high above, they look only like those a child might draw.

You manage to avoid your front garden, which is not a garden at all but a crater. At the kerb, you turn to stare. Your home stands open to the world, a grim, oversized doll's house. How is it possible? The front wall has disappeared. Your private life has been turned inside out. Your mother still smiles from the picture on the side table.

At the back of the house – for your view is brutally clear – the bedroom and kitchen curtains hang in shreds. A cheval mirror, broken on its axis, wobbles like a tooth. In the front room, the furniture lies buried beneath the tons of wet chalk that erupted from the garden. Later, the Regional Officer of the War Damage Commission will approve compensation for your domestic contents, clothing and personal effects to a maximum of £200. He will stamp your C1 form. Payments in most cases, he will note, won't be issued until after the war.

On the pavement, there is blood by your feet. A stray dog is sniffing at it. Someone offers you bandages for your arms, a blanket, shoes, and a cup of tea with extra lumps of sugar. You can't hold the cup for shaking.

Shrapnel still tinkles down the rooftops, though you hear nothing of course and won't ever again. But you can smell the pounded brick dust. You see the lady's corset that dangles from a branch in the tree above you. Glass crunches underfoot. As you make your slow progress, you almost trip over two of your neighbours who are resting on stretchers. Why has no one given them a blanket? 'All right, Iris?' you say. You hear your voice only as a vibration in your throat. 'All right, Ernest?' They don't stir. Concussed, you tell yourself.

But no. In the blast wave of the bomb, in that sudden desert of oxygen, they suffocated.

Others have been thrown through the air. A seventeen-year-old boy wakes on a rooftop five streets away. A man finds his wife stuck rigid and lifeless to a neighbour's shed door, her arms outstretched. Later, in the ruins of his house, on her kitchen worktop, he will stare, mute and bewildered, at the two eggs that sit unbroken in a china bowl.

A fire blazes in the middle of the street. A broken gas main, you are told. It has been reported. Remember, smoking is not permitted. You nod, as if you have actually heard him. Water streams past your feet. Bobbing in the current, you see all manner of things: a toilet seat, a leather comb case, a family photo album, a baby's rattle, a vegetable peeler, a tin of boot polish, a smeared letter, a bicycle tyre and a woman's muddied hand. It still wears a wedding band. The hand upsets you more than the bodies you have passed.

Later, at sunset, as foundations settle, fires burn out and the drains back up, boys from other parts of town will appear. You'll see them searching the craters and the broken ground. They'll dig under roof slates and beams. You'll watch them whoop with joy when they find souvenir pieces of shrapnel, still hot to the touch.

20

The bombings, everyone said, were only a prelude. In a seaside town that boasted neither industry nor ambition, there were direct hits to the playing fields of St Mary's Hall. To Chichester Terrace and Mount Pleasant. To Devonshire Street, Pelham Street School and Tamplin's Brewery. The town centre stank of hops for days.

August the 4th was forecast to be Invasion Day, the anniversary of the day Britain had declared war on Germany in 1914. The passage of time was marked by rumour. Next, it could only be August the 15th, the day Hitler had vowed he'd march through the streets of London. That day, too, came and went, but at last Mr Attlee spoke on the wireless. 'The whole nation awaits zero hour. I want us all to use the waiting time, be it long or short, to the best possible advantage to our cause.' But could the nation imagine it as Brighton could? So literal an invasion. The enemy marching up the beach.

In the town's blackout, illicit roof squatters smoked and star-watched, refusing to be shut in any longer, while in the dance halls of the town, from the Regent Ballroom to the unmentionable Sherry's, revellers danced through the sirens as the bands played louder. Where the nation was stoical, Brighton grew reckless.

Evelyn felt her own bleak sense of abandon. She would not be dissuaded by her husband from returning with her book to the Camp, where Mr Pirazzini lay in his bed, rattling with death but seemingly unwilling to die. He was waiting, Evelyn knew, for Mrs Pirazzini to appear. He had a dying man's faith that decencies, even in a labour camp, would be observed; that Geoffrey would find his wife of fifty years. But Evelyn knew Geoffrey couldn't admit to the old man that there were no reliable records; that the authorities had – in bureaucratic terms – lost his wife and her camp location; that he would inevitably die without her. Everything didn't come right in the end. The wheel didn't go round. Life took care of some and not of others. His faith, like the phrase, had failed him.

Evelyn pressed his papery palm in hers. All she knew how to do was open her book and read to him so that he didn't die in a morbid, miserable hush. Words were protective. They were beats of breath and life. But who was she really reading for, herself or him?

Behind her, a makeshift screen divided her from the prisoner who'd laughed at her efforts during her first visit. Let him laugh now. He was back in the infirmary, to have the bullet extracted from his shoulder. The doctor had come at long last, a heavyset man with thick spectacles and stubby fingers. He stood in the dim light of the painted-over window, sterilizing his scalpel and forceps with the flame of a cigarette lighter.

There were no precedents, no codes of conduct in an internment camp. For Mr Pirazzini's sake, she informed the doctor, she would stay by her friend's bed during the procedure. She would not be moved.

Very well, he nodded, but she was not to concern herself if the prisoner cried out. Since Dunkirk, analgesics were in pitifully short supply. They had given the man two good, stiff shots of whisky on an empty stomach. It would not be a problem if she continued to read aloud as he operated. Indeed, he thought it better for her and her charge if she did so. If she felt obliged to leave the infirmary during the procedure, she should feel free. He could not attend to any faints.

He disappeared behind the screen. The heads of the two guards were just visible over the top. Then the doctor gave the order to hold the prisoner down.

The man protested, delirious and loud. 'Butcher!'

'I have a leather bite, Mr Gottlieb, should we require it.'

'My God, if you amputate, I will –'

'You are overwrought. We wouldn't want you to bite your tongue. Now behave or I shall be forced to use it.'

Evelyn wet Mr Pirazzini's lips with the sponge from the bowl and patted his hand. Even she was aware that the removal of a bullet could damage a limb or kill a man where the bullet had failed. Infections. Damaged arteries.

It was none of her affair.

Mr Pirazzini's eyes fluttered. 'There, there,' she whispered, rubbing his wasted arm. 'It's Evelyn, Mr Pirazzini. I'm here, and this business won't last long.'

A cry filled the room.

She opened her book and stumbled into the first paragraph. '"*The sun rose. Bars of yellow and green fell on the shore, gilding the ribs of the eaten-out boat and making the sea-holly and its mailed leaves gleam blue as steel.*"'

Another cry, deep and guttural. Mr Pirazzini's eyes sprang open.

'Do *not* allow him to move!'

She pulled her chair closer. '"*Light almost pierced the thin swift waves as they raced fan-shaped over the beach. The girl who had shaken her head and made all the jewels, the topaz, the aqua-marine, the water-coloured jewels with sparks of fire in them, dance, now bared her brows and with wide-opened eyes drove a straight pathway over the waves. Their quivering mackerel sparkling was darkened and —*' Was that blood she smelled? She stroked Mr Pirazzini's forehead, but what could she say without reminding him that he was dying, not in his own bed at home, but in a neglected sickbay in a prison camp some-one had conjured at the top of Race Hill?

'*"As they splashed and drew back, they left a black rim of twigs and cork on the shore and straws and sticks of wood, as if some light shallop had foundered . . ."*'

She no longer understood what she read. Her thoughts spun.

Then, 'Nicht – zu – stoppen.' A hoarse whisper.

Don't stop.

'Is everything all right, Doctor?' she called brightly.

'Perfectly,' he replied.

She heard the bullet clink in a basin.

'Mr Gottlieb has finally done the decent thing.'

'I'm sorry?'

'He has passed out. The prisoner has passed out, Mrs Beaumont.'

Nicht zu stoppen.

She had to wipe her eyes with the back of her hand.

21

The following day, after a morning lost to the slow shuffle of food queues on the London Road, she set out again for the infirmary. Geoffrey was, he'd said, turning a blind eye to her visits – breaking the rule regarding female visitors – purely for Mr Pirazzini's sake.

She didn't want his 'blind eye'. She wanted him to *see*. But tacitly, they seemed to have agreed to speak no more of it.

On The Level in the unwavering heat, children skipped rope with a drowsy listlessness. A few spun on the swings or lazily pointed their Woolworths pistols. Union Road was strangely empty of cars. Already the petrol rationing had turned the streets over to bicycles, refuse carts, and barrows laden with leeks and hay. Orgies of blue-bottles buzzed over the dung. A delivery boy rang his bell, swerving past her on the pavement so closely she could smell the sour breeze of his sweat.

When she arrived at last, it was like a fist round her heart.

His bed was empty and stripped. The bowl of water and sponge were gone. Only the empty bucket under his bed remained.

'Dear God,' she whispered.

Death, even when one has grown bored waiting for it, is a bewilderment. A terrible punchline. She sank on to the bare mattress.

Later, when she demanded to know, no one would remember the actual time or manner of death; whether it had been the previous night or early that morning; whether he'd gone peacefully or in confusion; whether there would be or had already been a funeral. Perhaps the minimum rites had taken place already. The guard told her Jews liked to get it 'done and dusted'. But who? she asked, who had been there? The guard had shrugged. All he could say for sure was that the old man's body had been taken to the hospital morgue. The Camp had been unusually efficient. 'The heat,' he said.

The few personal effects Mr Pirazzini had arrived with had been gathered up in a parcel and labelled for return to his wife, although her location remained unknown.

Mr Pirazzini's passing, the death of a good man, was entirely unremarkable. He had been alone. Even Evelyn had not been with him.

How futile everything was. How careless. The world was treacherously random. Mr Pirazzini was gone and no one had noticed.

Tears welled but she couldn't, not here. A sob gripped her, and she had to bend her face to her knees to stifle the next.

'I closed his eyes.'

She straightened instantly. She'd forgotten. She'd completely forgotten.

From the other side of the room, the man's voice again: 'I washed him. With just one good arm, so not very well, I'm afraid, but he wasn't neglected. I covered him in a fresh sheet.'

In her shock, she'd forgotten she wasn't alone, and she felt once more the *intrusion* of Mr Pirazzini's neighbour behind that screen. She'd leave in a moment. She'd get her breath back and leave without a word.

'I requested candles and the assistance of two men to lower him to the floor.'

'Whatever for?'

'Custom. His more than mine, admittedly. I asked the guard to leave us for the night as a mark of respect. When he was suspicious, I asked him how far they thought I could run with a dead man on my back.'

Flippant, even now.

It was as if he'd been waiting to tell her, as if he'd composed the details in readiness for her visit. She didn't want to listen.

'I stayed with him till morning, till the ambulance came.'

The day was so still she could hear a young Army corporal, help-less since Dunkirk, stammering his way through an exercise drill, even from the distance of the Camp's parade square. His commands tugged at her nerves.

'Did you bring your book?' His voice again, but far away now, as if in some remote valley. She was willing him away.

The hut was stifling, and not a single window opened. 'I must see if there's anything I can do . . .'

'Read, if you would – please. From your book.'

Nicht zu stoppen.

'Read from where you left off.'

She could hardly remember what he looked like, who he was, this man in the next bed. She no longer cared. He was an interruption. He was the smell of antiseptic and illness. He was a man who had intended to be dead by now. 'I should inform my husband of –'

'I'd be very grateful if you read.'

She managed to get to her feet, but her face was hot. Her knees were trembling, and the floor seemed to rise up at odd angles. Fresh air. She just needed fresh air.

The wheel goes round, the wheel goes round.

'Please,' trailed his voice. 'You came to read, and I must insist you read.'

160

Insist?

Outside, the drill commands were ever-more fiercely stammered. The corporal's syllables were stabs of anger and fear. He'd be forever at war with himself, she thought, after what he'd seen in battle. Or done.

She had visited some of the BEF men in the Royal Sussex with the ladies of the WI. She'd thought she could manage it, but what comfort had she to offer? What could she possibly say?

One man's hands had shaken so badly she'd thought he was having a fit. But no, he was confessing, and to her, though she'd wanted only to be gone. 'Shall I get a nurse?' she'd tried. But he couldn't stop. He had clutched a dead man's body to shield himself. 'From the gunfire,' he said, 'as I waded out to one of the boats.' He'd known the man. Not well, but they were from the same unit. He'd had a good singing voice. As a boy, the dead man had sung solos in Winchester Cathedral. That's what someone told him later. 'I dragged him by the throat,' he said. 'For hours, till I made it as far as that boat. He was a ruddy colander, Mrs Beaumont, by the time I got mesself aboard.'

'You have to forgive yourself,' she said. 'It was only right that you struggled to survive; it was the *right* thing to do,' and, as she spoke, she felt herself adopt her WI face of composed womanhood. But all along she was thinking, *You poor wretch. That man will never leave you; you'll be hauling the dead weight of him for the rest of your days.*

And there had been another, his head entirely bandaged except for a slit at his eyes and nose. He'd been crying out, over and over, for a 'smoke', barely able to form the word, but the young nurse who'd attended him had finally understood, and when she did, fear got hold of her. 'What can I do? What can anyone do?' she'd hissed to Evelyn, wringing her fingertips. Evelyn had assumed she referred to the bandages. Perhaps, she suggested, the dressing could be snipped across the mouth. She'd find a cigarette. They could take turns holding it to his lips. She would go down immediately and ask someone in the street.

No, the nurse said, as if Evelyn were a halfwit, as if she were making everything worse. Didn't she understand? There was nowhere to put it. A mortar shell. He'd lost part of his face. There was *nowhere* to put it.

She'd walked away. She hadn't had the words. What were the words? He wouldn't have lived the night, that man. Yet Evelyn couldn't care, not any more she couldn't, not with all the senseless – the *nonsensical* – violence always there, never ending, just at the edge of the everyday. Who had allowed life to turn to such chaos? How had everything run rampantly to war when no one was looking?

She was becoming 'sensible', if slowly. (*Tell yourself!* '*I am not interested in the possibilities of defeat – they do not exist!*') It didn't do to go on wondering. It didn't do to ask questions. What were the answers? Who could tell her where to go from here, after the Camp today, after Mr Pirazzini? Who could say where she belonged?

A wave of nausea and heat crashed over her.

Behind the screen, the German prisoner was clearing his throat. Nerves. Today she could hear the nerves behind his assured diction. He was afraid of being alone, or afraid of being left alone with the German guard perhaps. She had her own worries. Her stomach was tight. She couldn't think. The sour sweaty smell in her nostrils was, she realized, her own, and her hair lay smeared in damp streaks across her forehead. Another wave of sticky heat crashed over her. Air. She just needed –

'Your book,' he persisted, 'it might do us both good.'

She got hold of the bucket just in time.

*

Such intimacies between strangers. Every sensation sharpened until he was aware only of her palms fluttering white against the pillow.

Afterwards, when he lifted his weight, bruises appeared like bracelets on the pale undersides of her wrists. He felt a current of something run through to the core of him. Where had he been? 'Lord. Leah, so sorry. What a clod I've been.'

He'd marked her, not as badly as whoever had pressed her arm to the gas ring, but still, it was between them: a surge of something; a charge; a grim, irresistible knowledge. She met his eyes, held his gaze, then slid from beneath him to look, she said, for an earring she'd lost between the sheets.

She usually left her earrings on, and once, her court shoes. She would check her lipstick before and after, sometimes touching up her beauty spot with the stub of a kohl pencil. He enjoyed it. It seemed womanly, not vulgar, as he would have once assumed. Yet when she threw back the sheet and reached for an atomizer on the dressing table, something within him lurched. It was a new acquisition. A gift, no doubt. Silver plate. From whom?

Still naked, she sprayed a fine mist of her scent into the room – to cover, he assumed, the smells of bodies and cigarettes. The window seemed permanently open, and, for a moment, he imagined his explosion of utterances travelling all the way down to the street. How strange it was that he didn't care; that he felt as detached, as unencumbered, as a traveller in a foreign city.

Outside, as if in an adjacent dimension, trains clattered their way in and out of the station. Sometimes, here in Leah's sparse little room, he could hardly hear himself think with the carriages pounding the tracks. It was a good thing. With her, he was reduced to flesh, need, a pulse. It wasn't happiness – if he even knew what that was any longer – but he felt *absorbed*. He felt absorbed by her. She was not beautiful, not lovely, but every detail of her became his each time, and he lost himself in her, he who had made a point in life of not losing himself to anything.

It was only as he reached for his clothes that he noticed the picture on the shelf. It hadn't been turned to the wall.

The man who stared back was his own age, mid-thirties. The face was broad and pitted blue-white by acne and shadow. His neck was too thick for his collar, but his lips were unexpectedly full and soft, and there was a depth in his black eyes that, he imagined, a woman would find hard to turn from.

He nodded to it. 'Ah ha.' But his performance of cheerful disinterest failed. She glanced at the shelf, and something perceptible crossed her face. Then she reached for her dressing gown and offered him a cigarette.

'Suitor or husband?' His face approximated a smile.

She extended her arm for a light, raised the cigarette to her lips and blew a stream of smoke at the ceiling. 'Brother.'

An entirely new feeling came over him, a molten surge. She was lying.

He opened his wallet and riffled through the cash. 'Extra – for the . . .' He nodded with apparent indifference to her bruised wrists. He hoped the overt reference to payment would be the insult he meant it to be. Normally he simply left it without a word on the dressing table.

She tossed the notes into the Eiffel Tower and tied the sash of her dressing gown.

What more could he do or say? He lowered his face, struggling for composure, and pretended to search for his collar studs. How ugly and tantalizing life had become. Six months ago, Leah, this room, the man's dark stare – all of it would have seemed utterly unthinkable.

He washed at the basin and reached for his shirt. His fingers fumbled over the buttons. He didn't merely feel close to her, to this woman whose history was entirely unknown to him; he felt a raw and powerful attachment to her.

She turned the photo towards the wall. A belated concession? A signal that she understood, that she *did* feel something for him, Geoffrey? Or was it simply a habit remembered too late?

She passed him his wristwatch.

He ran a comb through his hair.

'How do you do?' he said from the other side of the makeshift screen.

'How do you do,' she replied flatly.

'I am Otto. Otto Gottlieb.'

She tensed and opened the book in her lap. Above them, flies buzzed in the rafters. Had they followed Death into the infirmary?

'And you?' he inquired.

'Mrs Beaumont.' She pushed her hair, still lank with sweat, off her forehead. 'The Superintendent's wife,' she added, although she knew he knew this well enough already.

He cleared his throat. 'And your *Christian* name – if you will permit a Jew the liberty?'

Did he think himself witty?

'Please, you're quite welcome,' he called, 'to pull your chair to this side of the screen . . .'

Again, the presumption. It was not for him to invite. It was for her to say what she was and was not prepared to do. In any case, she had agreed to read to him only on the condition that she remained where she was. She pulled her chair closer to the screen but she would go no further. Let him think her prim or ridiculous. Perhaps it would allow them at least to forget the spectacle she'd made of herself, just now, over the bucket.

After that wave of wretchedness, she had – *oh, the relief* – found a standpipe down the hill, just below the hut. There was no one anywhere nearby, only the sea, and the cool chugging of water from the tap. She'd been able to rinse her mouth, unbutton her blouse, lower her slip and splash herself clean, although she'd also managed to soak her shoes. She'd rinsed the bucket. If she could just right herself now, she could almost pretend it had never happened.

Of course he would have heard her from his side of the screen. How awful for him. And how awful for her. It was incredible she'd returned to the infirmary for her bag, that she hadn't simply fled.

Yet she knew her agreement to read for him had been no act of charity, however it appeared. The charity, if anyone's, was his. He seemed to understand she wasn't yet steady enough to rejoin the world. She could hear it in his voice, in the note of concern he was trying to disguise. Here, they both knew, she could shelter in a room with painted-over windows in the refuge of someone else's words.

'I am pleased to meet you at last.' He laughed, not unkindly, at – she assumed – the irony of the screen.

'How is your arm?' she ventured, across the distance.

'Mending, I think. A pinched nerve, an unsteadiness, which you'll appreciate isn't ideal for a painter, but things could be worse. Thank you for asking.'

Still he irked her. 'Indeed. It could be worse. I'm told you would have died were it not for the efforts of your guards.'

'True, true,' he said. 'Of course, life might *also* have seemed worth living were it not for the efforts of my guards, but' – and she could hear him rising to some rhetorical flourish – 'you say "tomato" and I say "tomahto".'

She wondered if she preferred him hostile. 'Guards *guard*,' she said. 'It is simply what happens if one is detained.'

'"Detained". I am grateful for your optimism. It sounds as if my employer has merely required me to work late this evening. It is an excellent term.' And he sounded genuinely amused, amused by her. What possibly could account for his good spirits? 'For the duration of your visit,' he continued, 'I shall try to forget that I have been *detained* for over three months without a trial and that, as there is no trial, there can be no prospect of release.'

'But it's simply not a matter for a trial!'

'Mrs Beaumont, I am trying to forget. If you could humour me, I would be most grateful.'

'I don't believe you are "trying to forget". I think you're laughing at me in some way I fail to understand.'

'Very well, then. I enjoy riddles. When is the denial of a man's freedom not a matter for a trial?'

'When? When you are a . . .' She could feel her parents' spite bubbling up within her. The sound, the consonant was forming on her lips, and in the heat of the moment, she didn't know what would emerge: a G or a J. 'When you are a *German*. In other words, when you are a person from an enemy nation. It is nothing personal.'

'How curious. It feels rather personal.'

Again, the flippancy. She opened her mouth to speak, unsure what she was about to say, but she was spared. The guard at the door stepped into the room, glanced at her seated next to the screen, then departed again. Given the hut's tin roof, it was even hotter inside than out. Everything had gone wrong. She didn't ever want to return to this place. Geoffrey was right. Her literary mission, her charitable notions, had merely been –

'The prose,' Otto Gottlieb said, 'it's very musical, isn't it? I'm not sure I make complete sense of it, but nor do I feel that's what the author *wants* me to do. I feel he or she requires something else of me altogether.'

It was kind of him, very kind.

'She,' she said. 'Yes, I agree.' She hesitated, assessing the gamble; whether it was risky to offer any personal account of herself. 'I was fortunate enough earlier this summer to hear the author – Mrs Woolf – speak. Here in Brighton, actually.'

'Ah,' he said. 'How wonderful . . .'

His voice was warm, and so full of unexpected – undeserved – affection that she found herself suddenly at a loss. She pressed the heels of her hands to her eyes. The book fell from her lap and she bent quickly to retrieve it. Yet even in her confusion, she'd felt it: his words, his warmth, thrown to her like a rope.

'Now then,' he said, as if settling back on an imaginary heap of pillows, 'I shall simply listen. I have missed my books such a lot. I used to *scour* – I believe that is a correct usage? – the junk shops when I first arrived in Brighton, and I made some very good finds. It takes patience. You have to work your way past the cracked china, the greasy hymnals and the spectacles of the assorted dead, but I assure you, it is well worth the effort.'

Yes, she thought, smiling, and now, too late, she wanted to take her chair to his side of the screen. Instead, she turned the pages until she found the point at which, the week before, during his grim operation, he had lost consciousness and she had lost her nerve.

'"*In the garden*,"' she began, '"*the birds that had sung erratically and spasmodically in the dawn on that tree, on that bush, now sang together in chorus, shrill and sharp; now together, as if conscious of companionship . . .*"'

22

Trouble roosted between the days of August like the starlings that nestled on the piers at the day's end. They abandoned the town's treetops, chimney pots, domes and towers and occupied those white-decked outcrops that stretched hundreds of feet out to sea. They flickered past the candyfloss booth, the fortune-telling machine and over the frozen electric train. They traced in mid-air the skylines of the ballroom, the orchestra hall, and the vaults of the penny arcade. They settled on the limbs of the rides, on the wild-eyed horses of the carousel, and on the pagoda hats of the little booths. Then, in a single indecipherable instant, as daylight ceded to dusk, twenty thousand birds swelled into one body – a twisting helix, a black tornado of feathers – before descending, minutes later, into a stillness, a shadow over the Pier, a feeling across the back of the neck.

If London looked to the steadiness of Big Ben and the gravitas of St Paul's for a reminder of dignity in strife, Brighton's emotional compass had been the ring-a-ding-ding and the music, the electric lights and the ticket-stub happiness of the Palace and West piers. When the Explosions Unit had arrived that evening back in June, the town prepared to lose its bearings. Even to the casual observer, each pier looked like nothing less than a welcoming dock, an unloading zone for any invading ship, and while both were spared outright destruction, section after strategic section – of decking, piles and girders – was blasted into the sea.

That year, Alf Dunn, Tubby's middle brother, turned fourteen and craved something more than digs in bombed-out houses. As the starlings gathered and the sun slid from the sky, he and a dozen others also descended on the seafront.

It was no casual operation. They had wire-clippers for the razor-wire fencing, rope from a builder's yard, switchblades for cutting it, and mud for camouflage. The tide was rising, but the evening itself was calm, and there was just time to cast a rope bridge from gap to gap, using the stumps of the blasted piles and relying on Tommy Leach's skill with knots.

The trick to a successful traverse, Alf explained, was to lie on top of the rope, bend a knee, hook the foot of that same leg over the rope, and keep the other leg straight for balance. 'See?' he said. 'Your pins don't move. It's your arms and hands that get you from end to end. If you slip under the rope, don't panic. Hook a leg and the opposite arm over, and push down with the other hand to right yourself.'

Tubby and Philip had been allowed to bring up the rear, if only to bear witness and to carry the bucket of camouflage mud. They watched Alf army-crawl his way to the first, second and third landings, wave from the deck, and glide back.

As the moon rose, pock-faced and pale over the darkening sea, the next boy, Vince Hunnisett, crawled on to the first rope bridge, his legs unsteady. 'Don't look down!' Alf called. It was a painfully slow traverse but Vince made it, from deck to deck to deck, and back again. Frankie Boxall was up next. He claimed it was the best blast from a boner he'd ever known.

Boys queued up. Two more boys covered the distance and back, as the ropes juddered and the black sea climbed up the shelf of the beach. It was a relay race against the tide, and it seemed a race they were destined to win until Denny Pilbeam lost his grip, slipped through the third gap and fell into the sea. As he went under, his wail went up, and a vast cloud of starlings rose from the Pier. Bobbies from the King's Road started running their way. 'Scarper!' Alf hollered, then dived into the sea to drag Denny out. Half an hour later, Alf, Denny, Tubby and Philip sat wet, alone and defeated in the basement lock-up of Brighton Town Hall.

The Duty Sergeant was in no hurry. He unlocked four cells and ushered each boy in, silencing their protests and excuses. For a long, lonely time that evening there was only the murky basement, the squelching of their shoes and the smell of the sea. Finally, their respective fathers (and Frank Dunn, aged sixteen) were summoned to claim them.

Geoffrey said only two things to his son on the walk home through the moonlit streets of the North Laine. Firstly, Philip was under no circumstances to tell his mother; she would be sick with fright if she learned the truth. Philip nodded, grateful for the pact. He knew his mother would cry with him if he told her about the cell in the basement and how frightened he'd been without her there to sing to him like she did in the coal cellar. Secondly, and most importantly, Philip was not to see Tubby or the Dunn brothers again. Geoffrey forbade it.

His father had never forbidden him anything before, and Philip knew, without even opening his mouth to plead, that Tubby, whom he'd known almost his entire life, was a goner.

23

Earlier that same evening, as Evelyn turned on to Park Crescent, the low, mournful notes of a brass-band hymn rose up from the Salvation Army's citadel like a plume of smoke from a November bonfire. After the infirmary, she hardly remembered where she'd been. She'd wandered. She'd sat in a high field, staring out to sea. The beauty of the view, of the day, had seemed reckless. At her front door, she stepped inside, cautiously, as if she might have somehow confused her home with another. But no. Geoffrey's keys hung on the key board in the vestibule. He was back before her.

She found him on the terrace, his head thrown back, his face turned skyward. He hadn't heard the back door or her steps across the flagstones. The long lines of his body were stretched out, relaxed. He looked almost boyish.

They kissed lightly on the cheek, looking past one another. 'Philip,' he said. 'At Tillie's, I presume?' He didn't stand to pull her chair from the table. He seemed odd, distracted, not himself.

Neither could have imagined the reality of the moment; their young son in a dim cell in the basement of the Town Hall, with Tubby in the next cell and Alf Dunn in another.

She took a seat and slipped off her shoes. 'Yes, I said he was to be home by dark.' Overhead, gulls swooped past in formation like cut-out paper birds. Nothing seemed true these days.

His tie lay crumpled on the table. She watched his index finger drum the iron scrollwork. She had interrupted a pleasant train of thought. That's what his finger said.

They stared out over the Park, each in their separateness. A gardener was trimming the horseshoe shrubbery, and small children emerged, startled at the invasion of their territory. In a few days, an army of volunteers would arrive and overturn every lawn, every flower bed, for vegetable plots. When would they ever enjoy this view again?

'Mr Pirazzini died this morning,' she said at last. 'Did you know?'

He stiffened. 'Yes. Yes, they telephoned me at the Bank. I was frightfully sorry to hear it.' He turned to her. She looked washed out, dishevelled. 'I'm sure you were a great comfort to him, Evvie.'

She trained her gaze on him. 'Why do you say that?'

'Why do I say what?'

'That you're sure when you're not sure at all.'

'I'm sure he was lucky to have you visit as often as you did.'

'Geoffrey, every ounce of Mr Pirazzini's luck left him the day he was taken to the Camp. Has his wife been informed?'

'Why do you ask,' he said, 'when you know the answer?' She blamed him. Never mind Government policy. She was making Mr Pirazzini's fate a consequence of his actions or inaction, or possibly both. But today, unusually, her resentment didn't rankle. The new feelings he had – of discovery, of life and appetite – insulated him from whatever hostility lay between them. They made him feel compassionate and undefensive. He felt a curious lightness of the soul; a silken sense of something wider. More than ever, he wanted his wife to have what she wanted and to be released from the anger that was exhausting her.

He wanted, too, to tell her that something strange had happened:

that he had fallen in love, or into a passion at least, and that the woman was a Jewess, or at least she gave him to believe she was a Jewess – and that it didn't *matter*. He couldn't explain it. Perhaps he didn't actually love her, perhaps it was her exoticism, but he was, against all expectations, chiefly his own, in the grip of something. A fascination, a sense of – he didn't have the words – of being *alive*.

Even now, ironically, impossibly, Evelyn was the person he longed to tell.

She crossed her ankles and turned her face to the setting sun, closing her eyes to him, and to the world bearing down.

He rolled up his shirtsleeves. He could almost feel Leah's long, beautiful fingers once more on his shoulders, on the back of his neck.

Evelyn's mind wandered back to the Camp.

When she'd been quite sure that Otto had fallen asleep, she'd surprised herself by standing and walking around to the other side of the screen. Suddenly she had wanted to make a gift of *The Waves*, to leave it, with the page marked, on the washstand beside his bed. It made her feel glad, a little thrilled even, to imagine his delight when he awoke and found it.

He was sleeping on his stomach. In the sweltering heat he wore only the bottoms of his regulation nightwear, and the sheet with its official four-digit number had slipped down his back. She drew closer. His ribs stood out like the staves of a ruined barrel. But his back . . .

Her hand flew to her mouth. She'd had to look away to get her breath.

She'd picked the book up again, slipped it into her bag and walked away as noiselessly and quickly as she could. She'd had no right.

High above the terrace, the canopies of the golden acacias were drenched in the light of early evening. They rippled in a breeze she could see in their leaves but could not herself feel. Such heat, even at this time of day. She thought of him up at the Camp. When, she wondered, would he see so much as a tree again?

'Evvie, listen.' Geoffrey's voice made her start. 'Simply tell me what it is you would like. If it will make you happy, I'll give you the grandstand itself.'

The grandstand. She smirked. None of his words these days seemed like his. Her husband was an imposter.

'And if you want to continue your efforts at the Camp, I'll speak to the Head of Patrol,' he said.

'I would simply like to read to the other man in the infirmary. His name, I believe, is Otto.' She knew it was. 'I realize of course that the barracks, when he returns to them, won't be appropriate but surely there is somewhere –'

'I'm afraid not.' He rose from his chair. A shaft of evening light shone broad and mellow on the trunk of the old beech tree. He had to shake himself, focus. 'Otto Gottlieb isn't entitled to privileges.'

She shrugged. 'I've discovered he likes to read. He likes books.'

He could hear something more in her voice. The man, his plight, had touched her in some way.

'Choose anyone else.'

She blinked and smiled falsely. 'I don't understand.'

'Otto Gottlieb is a Category A.'

'Goodness. He's too thin to do anyone any harm – except himself of course, as we know already. Do you feed them up there, Geoffrey?'

And still the man's voice was in his ear: *I daresay it's also rare to meet a Superintendent who takes so great an interest in his prisoners.*

'He came to us from a camp in Germany. He's no stranger to trouble. He's not worthy of your efforts, Evvie.'

'An hour or so, perhaps once or twice a week. What's the harm?'

I am being accurate, not insolent, Superintendent.

'We searched his bed in the barracks yesterday.' He heard the words leave his mouth and he marvelled at his own speed of thought. He'd never been a liar.

'Why? He's still in the infirmary.' Then she realized. That was the point.

'The Head of Patrol had no choice but to confiscate what he found.'

'For goodness' sake. He's a man who tried to kill himself. Surely, with all those hundreds of prisoners, there are more urgent matters?'

'It was contraband, Evvie.'

She batted at a wasp. 'Cigarettes? A bottle? I hardly think it's –'

'He arrived in this country with cash, all of it counterfeit. Nevertheless, the authorities accepted his story and granted him asylum, subject to a tribunal. The tribunal designated him Category A but he was granted the right to stay. He drifted from London to Brighton, for no clear reason. He has no family here; no contacts, or at least none he would name. That said, his sponsor was the Bishop of Chichester. He's here, in other words, on Christian charity and British goodwill. Yet when the internment arrests were made – all Category A, B and C aliens – the police found more forged notes in his lodgings. He was living off the stuff. Now' – he rubbed the bridge of his nose – 'we've discovered still more of it stuffed in his mattress. It beggars belief.'

Somewhere in the Park, a child was wailing. *All's lost*, she thought. *All's lost.*

For Philip's eighth birthday, Geoffrey had taken their son to see how sterling was made at the Royal Mint. A man's wage packet, a person's bank book, a country's currency – all represented something fundamental to Geoffrey. If he had a deep faith of any kind, it was in a work ethic. The sight of unemployed men, men thrown from the path of their lives, as if by some dark, ungovernable horse, haunted him.

He glanced back at her. She was still brooding on it. She hadn't given up the idea. 'There's more, I'm afraid.' He gripped the terrace's low balustrade.

'More money?'

'More reason not to cater to him: black-market activity among the interns.' He bowed his head. 'We strongly suspect he's behind it.'

She sat up, blinking. 'Of course he's not –'

'Evvie, I don't think I need to convince you how low and despicable a thing it is to profit from desperate men.'

She felt winded, dizzy. She would have put her head between her knees were it not for a fear of looking overly affected by the fate of a Category A prisoner. 'Have you reported him to the police?'

He turned, finally. His pulse twitched at the corner of his eye. 'I'm Camp Superintendent.'

Yes, he was saying. *Of course I have.* Counterfeit cash, for Geoffrey, was not merely a crime, it was a profanity.

A part of her brain still worked in its habitual way: how had he gone an entire day with his shirt misbuttoned? The other part reeled. *Was* Otto Gottlieb a conman?

The fact that he enjoyed books was neither here nor there. Even conmen might read – and paint. He'd said he was a painter. Even conmen might be sensitive, thoughtful, aware. No one was *one* thing. After all, she was, she knew, a snob, a regrettable product of her class. She both clung to and despised most of the things it stood for. And Geoffrey – Geoffrey was a man respected for his sense of fair play,

177

for his decency and good sense, yet he harboured an irrational contempt for an entire race of people. Casual hatred required neither examination nor confession. Many of the best people hated casually enough.

How sheltered she'd been. Perhaps conmen were *more*, not less, sensitive than most. Had Otto really kept vigil over Mr Pirazzini's body or had he simply told her he had? A confidence trickster had to . . . gain one's confidence. And he had. Clearly her ability to read people, to read situations, had failed her. She'd lost her bearings.

Damn Geoffrey, damn him. And damn herself.

Their evening passed in its ritual tranquillity. Dinner unfolded without Philip, a novelty which made the meal both easier to bear and more awkward. Then came the washing-up; the *Evening Argus* for Geoffrey; Evelyn's dutiful check on the vacant houses of neighbours; the hanging of the keys; the closing of the shutters; the buzz of the wireless. Finally, it was the book in her lap and the start of an hour's uncomfortable silence while they waited for the news.

When the knock at the door went, just after eight, 'I'll go,' he said. It had to be Philip, back from Tubby's – early. It hadn't yet gone dark.

When Geoffrey didn't reappear, she opened a shutter. A bobby stood on the doorstep, his face downcast and his helmet in his hands. Geoffrey was nodding, his features sombre and heavy. She could hear the low rumble of their voices but not the words they spoke. When he stepped inside again, it was only to ask if she would dash upstairs for his suit jacket and tie.

'Is it about the Category A man?' She brushed down his jacket, miming wifely duty.

'I'm afraid so,' he said.

178

The point, he told himself grimly, was to spare her the facts: Philip, roaming the town with the Dunn boys again, and now frightened out of his wits in the lock-up like some little ruffian.

It was a collateral stroke of luck that Evelyn had assumed the Constable had come to the door to follow up on the case of Otto Gottlieb.

'Can't it wait until Monday?' She made herself say that much. Whatever the man had done, he was still recovering from surgery, although the image that flashed through her mind was, not of his shoulder, but of the scarred landscape of his back.

Geoffrey resolved he would add nothing to his lies if he could help it. He ignored the question and checked his wristwatch, holding it up to his ear, as if it, like him, were losing time. 'As I'm out, I might as well return via Tillie's and collect Philip.' He sounded off-hand enough.

'Geoffrey?'

He hovered at the threshold. His jaw flexed softly, like a well-oiled trigger.

Who are you? she wanted to ask. *Who are you now?* Somewhere within her, the words were pushing, pushing.

'Shan't be long,' he said. Then he kissed the top of her head and shut the front door, too hard, too quickly.

Bang.

24

Summer was ending, Tubby was forbidden, and Orson, it seemed, was nowhere. Philip pulled hard on the bell at Hanover Crescent.

'Sorry, Mr Stewart-Forbes. I thought you would be Ivy.'

'I am not usually Ivy, Philip.'

'Could Ivy please call Orson down for me?'

'Ivy is not with us today.' Mr Stewart-Forbes always spoke slowly, as if each word had to be released from a stone paperweight.

'That's all right. I can go up and knock on his door myself.'

'Orson is not at home.' Beneath Mr Stewart-Forbes's cardigan, the aged slump of his shoulders straightened.

'I haven't seen him all summer. Is he sick?'

'He's in Steyning, at his grandmother's house.' Mr Stewart-Forbes's eyes were clouded and rheumy. 'I will tell him you called.' Then he nodded into the distance – 'On your way now' – squinted briefly into the sunshine, hoisted his trousers, and closed the door.

Only Clarence remained. When Philip spotted Mrs Dalrymple at her window that overlooked the Park, he ran across their terrace at Number 7, into the Park, and up the stairs to her terrace at Number 6.

But: 'No, I'm afraid Clarence cannot come out to play, Philip Beaumont,' she declaimed from her window. 'He is unhappy. He is hiding somewhere – out there!' She gestured with her gnarled, bejewelled hand. Even as they spoke, the Park's lawns were being turned and tilled by a team of volunteer intruders. 'The war effort, the bloody war effort,' she railed. 'It's the new religion!'

'We're Church of England, Mrs Dalrymple,' he offered feebly.

The gold in her teeth flashed. 'Vegetables! Victory! It's claptrap and rot. Clarence has been off colour ever since this lot marched in like evangelists ready to dig for Jesus – or Churchill, or whoever's leading the charge this time. In six months, you watch, they'll be digging just as zealously for Hitler.'

'Do you think Hitler *will* come to Brighton, Mrs Dalrymple?'

'Who can say? He isn't one to leave a calling card, is he?' She put a withered hand to her mouth and cooed over the Park. 'Clarence . . . Clarence . . . Come home, sweet boy!' Then she dabbed at her eyes with the tip of the foxtail she wore, even in summer, over her nightdress.

Philip cooed too.

25

Could she do it?

She had seen the police constable outside their front door. She'd heard the low, urgent tones, but still it didn't make sense. A man who is about to kill himself does not wheel and deal on any black market. A man who wants to end his life does not bother to hoard cash.

Wednesday was Geoffrey's half-day at the Bank and his weekly trip to London.

She could hear him upstairs, shaving, dressing. In a moment or two, he'd come dashing down the stairs, the bloodied specks of tissue on his face a testament to his impatience to be gone.

She reached up to the key board, took down his set, and prised the two shiniest keys from the fob.

It was the child he saw first, or rather the child's hoop, just visible from his office door. He remembered it suddenly, sticking out from beneath Leah's bed. Yellow, if his sense of colour could be trusted. Now, here it was, out of place, like a sickly detail from a dream.

The boy, who could only have been three or four, stood very still in the Bank's panelled hush. He was dressed in grey woollen shorts, a matching school blazer and tie – cast-offs that had been hastily tacked up to fit a boy too young for school. When he discovered Geoffrey studying him – a tall man, a wooden pillar among the

Bank's wooden pillars – he stared back intently, with the eyes of the man in the photo.

Why was Leah here of all places? She should have been at her window, on the sill, lifting her face to any breeze; turning languorously as he entered the room; stubbing her cigarette out in the Eiffel Tower. She was in his Bank, not that she had any notion that it was his Bank or even that he was a banker. From his office doorway, he could hear her smoky voice and halting English, though she herself stood just out of view.

He risked it. He let himself be drawn. From a few feet away he noticed, with a barb of both concern and embarrassment, that her arms were bare. The marble white of her flesh glowed too obviously in the Bank's half-light. He could see the scar from the gas ring on her forearm. Her dress was simple and dignified but it was obvious even to him that it had been made at home. She had neglected to wear not only a summer jacket, but also a hat and gloves, and from behind, he could see that the heels of her court shoes were worn down to their shafts.

She was explaining to his clerk that she would like to open an account; yes, she was a legal alien; here were her papers to prove it, and her Identity Card; no, she had not realized three signed references were required. She could assure him she had funds for the account.

She remained composed as always, but he could hear the suspicion rising in her voice, and no doubt Matthews could hear it too. It wasn't difficult to understand. She feared the paperwork was a ruse to keep foreigners out, and in truth it was.

She glanced over her shoulder to check on the boy, looking without seeing anything other than his obedient grip on the hoop. He stared solemnly at his mother's back, and in the discreet gloom, amid the restrained queues and the penumbra of the counter lamps,

Geoffrey drew closer, close enough to see, in the pool of lamplight, that the notes she presented to Matthews were large.

The question cut through him. Paid to her by whom?

From a few feet behind, over the wooden slats of the grille, Geoffrey caught the clerk's eye and nodded his sanction. A benign gesture, Matthews would have assumed. An official pardon for non-Englishness. Then he smiled tersely at one or two clients in the queue, appeared to check his wristwatch against the clock on the wall, and withdrew to his office, his heart banging like a bull at the gate of his chest.

It was, she thought, as if all the world were parched. The soil of Race Hill lay cracked and pale. Flies quivered over dried-out piles of dung but there were no sheep left, for there was almost nothing to graze. She strode higher, towards the course, watching her step as a matter of habit, on the lookout for the wild orchids and moon daisies of late summer, but only the rangy husks of toadflax clung on.

(*Is your journey really necessary? Think before travelling!*)

Occasionally the ground crumbled away as she walked; not even that seemed solid these days. Beneath the soles of her summer shoes, she could almost feel the chalky scarp rising through the turf, like a skeleton, bone-bright. The hill, that August, no longer knew bees in its wild thyme, or the blue flashes of butterflies, or skylarks lifting off from their nests. Everything was burned out. Yet the day was as muggy as a Turkish bath.

She had submitted to the morning's knitting circle and the end-lessly patient clacking of all those needles. She had procrastinated, queuing for fresh plums and blackberries, only to leave the grocer's with half a dozen bruised cooking apples for which she'd paid a fortune. She hadn't believed she would actually go that afternoon until she started the climb up Elm Grove.

It was Wednesday. Geoffrey was certainly on his train to London; there was no risk of discovery or of him telephoning her at home. Still she'd hesitated. How could she bear to return to the Camp? She wanted only to forget the sight of Otto Gottlieb's ruined back, for what could she do, even had she any energy left to think about it? What's more, there was Geoffrey's warning of Otto's criminal history; a cautionary tale told for her benefit. Yet that didn't render it untrue. In any case, it was impossible now to visit the man, whoever he really was, and she no longer had the desire. Desire for almost anything was leaching away. These days, her plans and hopes seemed only to point towards her own foolishness. Better to forget. Better not to want.

Yet here, once again, she was climbing Race Hill, and as the white roof of the grandstand came into view, she stopped, panting for breath, and turned to look back over the town. She could change her mind. There was no requirement to carry on. Indeed it would be sensible to turn back.

A heat haze had settled over the bowl of Brighton, a yellowy fug of smoke and steam that rose like a stale sigh of purpose from, she supposed, the station, the munitions factory and the ack-ack guns. She turned her face skyward. Above her, above the hill, a sparrow-hawk rose, its wings outspread as if in an act of will over gravity. She shielded her eyes and squinted.

A lone female. She could see the bars on its breast.

She fumbled for the two keys in her pocket – still there, jingling on the loop of twine she'd cut as soon as he'd left the house.

She had come this far.

*

The humidity aside, it was good, he thought, to be out, good to have departed the Bank and its stately gloom. He took long strides, out-pacing most of the lunchtime wanderers on the Queen's Road. His travel pass and Identity Card were safely stowed in his breast pocket, his attaché case was in one hand, and he clutched his newspaper gamely under his arm. The platform for London would be Number 4 as it was always Number 4. First Class would be empty at this hour, which meant that the journey would be time to gather his thoughts over a cigarette or two, and to clear his head of the morning's visit-ation by Leah and her child. Why feel jangled? She had a right to go about her business; to shop; to post letters; to present herself at a bank.

He picked up speed. Somewhere on the far side of the station, on the shimmering tracks ahead, whistles were blowing and a Klaxon sounded. He'd been warned there were delays. Up the line, hun-dreds of burst tins of jam were wreaking havoc following a hit to a freight container in the early hours. Still, delay or no delay, he would board a train as he did every Wednesday. He would watch the tawny fields of Sussex flicker past his window and, thirty minutes from Vic-toria, he would cast his eye over his weekly report for Head Office.

Only he didn't. At the end of Queen's Road, he carried on walk-ing, head bowed, past the station, making the steep climb up Terminus Road. He passed the camouflage factory where the girls spilled out for lunch, green-handed and green-faced; then the Water-loo Arms where sawdust for the floor was being delivered and spread for the day.

There would still be time to make his train if he chose to, par-ticularly given the delays. He had only to turn around and revert to type. There would then be no need for a telephone call to Seymour-Williams first thing tomorrow. No excuse to be made (the *jam*, the ridiculous jam). But when he looked up, blinking himself out of thought, he discovered he was already standing in the road where Number 39 stood back from the other houses, like a plain girl at a dance.

She wasn't expecting him.

Evelyn stood once more at the mouth of the tunnelled entry. At least she and the young sentry had grown accustomed to one another. They exchanged a few words, then she followed him up the corridor of wire while a fighter plane chugged overhead. 'No books today?' he asked without waiting for her reply. He turned his raw, boyish face to the sky, squinting at the vapour trail through the criss-crossings of wire. 'Ours,' he said. 'Not to worry, Mrs Beaumont.'

'I just need to collect a few of my things from my husband's office.'

She followed him up the hill and out the tunnel's other end, where he quickly assessed the grounds for her benefit – 'All right from here, Mrs Beaumont?' – and returned down the hill to his post.

The first of the two keys turned cooperatively in the lock, and the relief was immense. How easily she was in, through the stable-style door of his office. In the previous life of the racecourse, this room had actually been the VIP cloakroom. She had a vague memory of passing her fur across it to a smiling attendant one cool spring evening and asking Geoffrey to keep the ticket safe in a pocket. 'Don't dare lose it, will you now, duck,' the woman had said to her as she admired the fur, 'or I'll be looking the business mesself next Saturday night.'

Evelyn eased the door shut behind her, seated herself in her husband's chair, and allowed herself simply to breathe. She considered the room. The HQ. The Superintendent's office. The rows of coat rails were long gone of course but, even given its functional history, the room was a place of comparative privilege. The furniture, firstly, wasn't nailed to the floor. On the far wall, the King looked out in stern endorsement from a huge framed photograph. The walls had been freshly painted in a creamy white, and there were two windows, each of which, she could see, opened perfectly well. One window presented a view of the sea; the other overlooked what had been, in another lifetime, the square of the racecourse. The light bulb had a proper shade and was not dimmed with offensive orange paint. There was a washbasin on the far wall, a bar of Imperial Leather soap, and a clean hand towel, where presumably, each Monday evening, before leaving, her husband washed his hands of it all.

If she were a man in Geoffrey's position, would she be any different?

She didn't know.

The desk was bare save for a plumbing invoice on a steel spike and a stack of manila files in an 'out' tray. She shuffled through them: Brandt, Frankel, Ganz, Montefiore, Oster, *Pirazzini*. There he was, his name in green ink, while at the bottom, in a mimeographed box, someone had rubber-stamped the file 'Closed'. Inside, clipped together, lay her old friend's passport, his Identity Card, and the record of his brief appearance before the Enemy Alien Tribunal Board the year before. The paperwork was minimal. *The less said.* On the final page, two neat sentences in black ink stared back at her: 'Death by natural causes. No reparations due from War Damages Commission.'

The man she shared a bed with had written one sentence after the other, tidy as sums on a balance sheet. If she felt a jolt of contempt for him, she felt only slightly less for herself. She should have insisted that Mr Pirazzini be moved to hospital. That would have been a far more valuable show of friendship than her determined efforts to read to him. Otto Gottlieb, conman or not, had been right to laugh at her.

She rattled one of the deep steel drawers – locked. As was the next. And the third. The second key on her loop of twine opened nothing. Her hunch had been wrong. The gamble of the journey had been pointless. Outside the pot-brush head of the Head of Patrol passed the window, and she sank low in the chair. The ridiculous truth was that she had no idea what she'd imagined she'd find.

Geoffrey knocked a second time, and a cow-eyed girl of about sixteen opened the door, peeping over her duster as if it were a feather fan and she a showgirl. 'Are you inquiring about a vacancy, sir?'

She yelped as he brushed past her and sprinted up the stairs, two at a time. 'Leah, it's only me,' he said, speaking through her door.

There was a long, sickening pause.

'I am with someone.' Her voice was low and heavy.

It was early, just past midday. Yet – *someone*. Like a kick to the groin.

But if he was here, why not another? His mind skidded.

He had started back towards the staircase when he heard the key turn on the other side of the door. *Christ*.

What choice did he have but to recede back up the corridor and allow her guest to beat his retreat down the stairs? Who wanted to see another man here? To imagine. He disappeared around a corner and sank back into its shadows, willing the moment to pass. The carpet smelled of mildew. A plate with bread crusts sat outside one door; a stained teacup outside another. The walls were crammed with faded pastoral scenes of happy shepherds and shepherdesses. He shouldn't have come.

Unbearable minutes passed. She didn't call to him. When he finally risked a return, he merely found the door open.

He hovered in the doorway, noting the cheap flowers that stood

stiff in a vase on the dressing table. Were they red? He could distinguish neither reds, pinks nor greens, but it hardly mattered.

The dress she'd worn earlier in the day, at the Bank, hung on a
wire hanger from the curtain rail. Now she wore only her dressing
gown and her leather mules. She was spraying the room with its mist
of scent. The smell, as always, was clean and crisp; lemon and cedarwood. Evelyn had never worn scent, and the discovery of it on
Leah – on her neck, at her cleavage, her collarbone, behind her
earlobes – had, in itself, been enough at first.

What *was* this thing that had happened to him?

The Experiment, as he had once laughingly described it to her,
had been short-lived. The 'cure' had been quick and decisive. Whatever it was that had followed – love, lust or some wordless
fascination – whatever it was, it had taken possession of him quickly.
He had expected to feel queasy, remote, those first few times, there
with a stranger whom he would pay within the hour. This wasn't the
43 Club, after all, and he wasn't twenty-one and numb with whisky.
There was Evelyn; there was Philip. Yet the startling revelation had
been, not how mechanical the experience had felt, but how
intimate.

Had he deluded himself? He lingered now at her threshold, painfully aware of the reason for the scent; of her back to him; of her
silent displeasure and her interrupted appointment; also, of the picture on the shelf of her husband or lover, once again not turned to the
wall. Why had he come? Why hadn't he caught his train? The sight
of her with that shiny silver atomizer revolted him. A gift, a gift, but
from whom? Across the room, the window was open, as ever and, as
the curtains lifted in the breeze, the dress on the rail rose too, reveal-
ing what she'd assumed she had managed to hide: her son, curled
small on the windowsill, clutching a yo-yo.

I am with someone.

If the boy recognized him from that morning, he gave no sign.

On Geoffrey's office wall, George VI gazed down at her from his vast loneliness. *It is time for you to go, my dear*, he seemed to say. The midday sun had passed overhead, and the room had started to grow dim. She stared ahead, trying to determine in her mind the moment to leave, the moment when she might cross the grounds and draw as little attention as possible. What had she supposedly come to collect? How foolish of her not to have planned her subterfuge better.

Even as she reproved herself, her mind was idly wondering how Geoffrey, a man impatient with shoddy workmanship, could tolerate the crack that ran up the far wall of his cloakroom-cum-office right beneath the picture of the King. It was unlike him not to insist that the wall be replastered.

She stood and walked slowly across the room.

She reached up and removed the King from the wall.

The crack wasn't a crack but a groove.

Of course.

The wall wasn't a wall but a door. Nailed to it was an engraved plate. VALUABLES. At eye level, a brass key-cover glinted.

He removed his hat and, from his awkward seat on the edge of her bed, watched her wander over to the dressing table and pour water into a pot. The kettle on the gas ring was whistling a fury. 'Why come? Is not your time.'

Her directness, so entirely un-English, embarrassed him. He felt his throat tighten, his mouth dry. 'Forgive me,' he said, but he didn't offer to leave.

He'd been trying to make light of his unscheduled visit, smiling at her son; teaching him, as he'd taught Philip, how to 'walk the dog' and how to put the yo-yo 'to sleep'. But the boy had only scowled and refused to tell him his name. Nor did Leah insist.

'I am sorry,' she said flatly. 'His English, not good. And he is too young for such tricks. Also, if you row with wife, you cannot stay here. Is against rule.'

'I wouldn't dream –'

'Tea?' she said, looking past him.

'If it's no trouble.'

She rolled her eyes, then reached for two cups from the shelf, and poured, before the tea had had time to steep. She passed him his cup and seated herself on the bed beside him, where they sipped in silence. Her beauty mark, he noticed, was missing from her left cheek. Her back was poker straight. The boy had retreated again to the window-sill, and now she spoke gently to him in their own language.

Geoffrey listened and watched, feeling a foreigner's sense of exclusion. The boy nodded with a gravitas that was disconcerting, almost unpleasant, in so young a child. Above them, the man in the photo watched from the shelf, disapproving and severe, and in that headlong moment, Geoffrey understood what it was that had impelled him past the station and up the soot-stained hill of Terminus Road to her door. After seeing her in the Bank, after watching her smooth out those notes so painstakingly on the counter – after imagining their source – he'd needed to lay claim to her again. To make her his own. It was a sort of fever. He knew it was. But the truth was, there on the edge of her bed, no matter how casual he endeavoured to seem, he felt like a gun about to go off.

He reached across the gap between them and, out of view of the child, gingerly stroked the side of her thigh.

She set down her tea, rose, and moved to the window. 'He like trains, don't you, Misha? He watch that bridge on and on. Some time he forget to eat! Me, I no want trains. I want sea, ocean. I come to Brighton for *sea*, as when I am small child. A window by the sea. But trains, trains, trains! And now, beach closed!' She ruffled her son's hair. 'But he happy, and I thank God. And now, we sleep only to noise of trains at night. If no noise, if too quiet, we wake, eh, Misha?'

She scooped him into her lap, perched herself on the edge of the sill, and spoke to the window. 'Out there, trains and aeroplanes are toys . . . Everything, simple. This is why I come here. So he have simple. Me, when child, *not* simple. I am born in Odessa. On Black Sea. A resort. Like Brighton but more, much more beautiful. In Odessa we all think, ah, I am in Italy. You should see our buildings. And *everybody* is in Odessa. Is port. How you say? *Free* port. Turks, Russians, French, Germans, Armenians, Tatars, Jewishes, Polishes. They come, they stay. Yes? My father is Jewish, my mother is Russian Orthodox. In Odessa, this is nothing. No . . . is *good*. They meet in orchestra of Odessa Opera Theatre. Very famous theatre. My mother, on violin. My father, piano. He is from old family in Odessa. Important family. He study at Conservatoire with Witold Maliszewski – yes?' She turned.

Geoffrey smiled weakly. 'I am a philistine. You must excuse me.'

'I am five years old when Revolution come. Is very bad for my father. His family, too old, too much money. He is a . . . ? How you say?' She took aim with her finger.

'Target.'

'Yes. His brothers are shooted into holes they must dig first for their own bodies. Go, go, go, everybody say to my father. So he go then, fast, to Poland. I am too young. Four years my mother wait in Odessa. Is terrible. When I am nine years old, at last we travel with Maliszewski himself to Warsaw. On train, in compartment, I ask him

193

why we must go, I do not want to go, Warsaw has no sea, and he tell me that Red Army men not like music and better we go where people like. My mother tells me *Ssh, ssh, Leah*, but Maliszewski smiles into his old, yellow beard and commands for me hot chocolate. Funny, yes, I remember? Then, when I am twelve years old, I study with him, like my father before me, only now at his Chopin Music School in Warsaw. When I am fifteen, he make big *konkurencja*. Many students. Many countries.'

'Competition.'

'Yes. Competition. I am good. Not best. But *good*.'

And he thought again of her long fingers, of the unexpected elegance of her hands, of their expressiveness – their touch.

He shifted on the soft edge of the bed and looked again at the face of the man in her photo. 'You haven't mentioned your brother.'

'No,' she said. 'No brother. No sister,' as if she had forgotten entirely the import of the question and her previous lie.

She set Misha on the floor and reached for her tea. 'Then, *all* change again. You understand me? Suddenly, am I Jew? Am I not Jew? In Warsaw, quickly they want to know. Like you here first time. Why this question? For me, for people from city like Odessa, this is like *game*, as if you demand: are you more or less than five feet five inches in your height? As if everyone pretend, with hard faces, but soon they will say, *Ha ha, joke, of course joke! What! You believed us? You were frighted?*

'My father dies one month before Misha is born. Is terrible to bury father and have baby in such days. My mother, as I say, is Russian Orthodox. I tell her, good, bravo, *I* am Russian Orthodox, and if I am, Misha too. But my father is known in Warsaw for many years. My mother say, *Leah, if there is any question, there is no question. You, Misha, you are Jewishes.*

'And so, England. In London, I try for teatime orchestra in this Boots and that Boots. But no job. I try pubs, too many pubs, but no one want me for piano. They say, my English not good. True, I say, but music speaks, not me. Yes, they say, but no one need Chopin in England when war come. The Red Cross in London has too many peoples. So we get train, to Brighton, the sea' – she turned back to the room – 'to here.

'Bad, you think. *Yes*, bad. Of course, bad. Every day I hate it. I miss my mother. And my piano. But is not for ever.' She searched his face. 'Understand me, there is worse. There is very much worse.' She gathered Misha to her.

He nodded but, suddenly, her gaze oppressed him, like some dimly remembered hot towel thrown over his head in a childhood illness. Her gaze, her voice, the detail – it was all too much. The more she revealed, the more he felt trapped in that small room with the weary rhythms of her voice and the misfortunes of her history. It was shameful but undeniable, and in spite of himself, in spite of his efforts to blink the image away, he saw her once more, pressing and smoothing those large notes on the counter at the till.

On the window seat, Misha was cupping his mother's ear and whispering something to her, in Polish, Geoffrey presumed. She smiled quizzically, first at her son, then at him. 'What mean this?' she asked, her face as unguarded, as trusting as she was confused. 'Misha say you live in the dark house. Today, in this morning, he call bank "the dark house".' She bounced Misha on her knee and smiled. 'I don't understand.'

26

Did it make it better or worse that he emptied his wallet on her dressing table before fleeing Number 39? The entire episode was his fault. He knew it. He couldn't help but know it. Wasn't this the time-honoured way in which men betrayed women? He imagined it was. At the moment a man finally gained a woman's trust, he ran. He felt smothered. He discovered the bounder within himself. And if he did manage to stay, he forever reserved the right to show her his complacency or disdain.

For years, Evelyn had been the exception. He had wanted her truly; had needed her truly. Then the war had come and that weight of need had shifted between them. He'd outgrown her, against his every expectation – it was a relief, it was a bereavement – and, in a way that they both seemed powerless to stop or explain, she'd grown smaller, angrier and more anxious. They moved these days in their own spheres. Because what could either say?

And Leah? She was a remarkable person. If he had sensed that before, he knew it, clearly, today. He even suspected he loved her and that he would miss her dreadfully. She had simply said too much; she had *revealed* too much. How ironic that her first real words to him were the proof of feeling he had secretly craved from her for all these weeks. Yet once they had come –

He glanced back to see her, poised and inscrutable at her window.

Obviously the boy *had* remembered him, at the Bank. But it was utterly unthinkable that Leah might come to know a single detail more of his real life. He couldn't expose Evelyn and Philip to that kind of embarrassment or risk. There wasn't a decision to make. He walked briskly on.

His train from London wouldn't pull into Brighton for another four hours. At the usual time, he would join the shadow of his former self at the station's exit, remember who he was, and turn left on to Trafalgar Street, just as he did every Wednesday afternoon. He'd recover his equilibrium as he fell in with the other commuters. However, until he did, he felt exposed and sick with himself. What's more, he couldn't be seen, at a loose end, about town.

On Terminus Road, the public bar of the Waterloo Arms was hushed and dank. He knew better of course than to ask if there was a saloon, while to inquire about a snug would have been tantamount to asking to be taken out back and beaten till his brain bled. The publican stared. The men at the bar stared. They'd been eating from a tray of winkles, prising the creatures from their shells with pins and catching them fast between their teeth. At the sight of Geoffrey at the threshold, the oldest, a man with a silver-and-black widow's peak, sighed, pushed the tray to one side, and slid a misshapen parcel beneath his jacket.

It was a stagey gesture. They were on 'Brighton business', and they wanted him to know it. What other kind of men were without work in the middle of a summer's afternoon with a war on? Since the closure of the racecourse, most of the betting, the loan-sharking and the black-marketeering had moved into pubs of this kind, off the beaten track. Only last month, a determined police sergeant had taken a punch, immediately below the chin – the cleanest way to snap a man's spine.

197

Geoffrey removed his hat and bent low, grateful for both his size and the distraction of his newspaper. The day's sawdust was still fresh but the musty sweetness of a century of spilled ale, tobacco smoke and woodsmoke clung like tar to the walls. The blackout curtains were two-thirds lowered, even at this time of day, and overhead, the ceiling bulged like a tumour.

He made his way to the bar, knocking his head against a beam and swearing softly. His eyes were slow to adjust. The drinkers remained silent, apparently uninterested in either him or the reason for his intrusion. The air was thick and tacky, as if suspicion and casual rancour mingled with the dust. The publican and his stomach leaned corpulently over the bar, resenting the irritation of a new customer with a good fedora and a leather case. In a low voice Geoffrey ordered a stout, lit a cigarette, nodded to the winkle-eaters, and made a show of glancing at the headlines. Only as his bottle hit the bar did he reach for his wallet.

His face must have betrayed him.

Beside him, a man with small, rabbit eyes laughed into his beer. 'She must have been very dear, sir!'

A roar went up. The joker's hand rested lightly against the bar. A razor blade was taped to his finger, snug as a wedding ring.

A joke, Geoffrey told himself. A lucky guess. They were always going to have their fun.

'May I interest you in a *loan*, sir?' It was the oldest man, the one with the lumpen parcel. 'I dessay you must be feeling *spent* this fine afternoon.' He raised a winkle to him, caught the soft dead thing on the end of his pin, and tongued the end of it in a grotesque pantomime. Another boom of laughter rang out, and Geoffrey took in the hard, glittering eyes and the brilliant white rose in the man's buttonhole. Only now did it occur to him. The house for 'Gentlemen

Lodgers' was just half a mile away. For what other purpose did men like himself appear in this part of town?

'I should be fine, thank you,' he said to the widow's peak. Then he flashed the publican an unsteady smile while, behind the cover of the bar, his fingers scrabbled furiously in the depth of his pockets.

Three shillings delivered him.

A raucous cheer went up.

Thank God he'd left her when he had.

It was as if, Evelyn thought, she had stepped into some deep pocket in the lining of the day.

She propped the door open with the picture of the King, and in the vague light, could just make out shelves to either side and, to the right, what might have been a coat rail. She could find no light switch, and the storeroom only grew darker as she edged her way up its length, the smell of mothballs and dust catching at the back of her throat. She stifled a cough and narrowly avoided something large on the floor – a gramophone, could it be? – only to crash into a metal filing cabinet. Was the Head of Patrol still outside?

She edged her way down the length of the room. A slim chain knocked cold against her cheek and she cried out, like a child walking into a cobweb. *Quiet*, she told herself in her mother's sternest voice. *Quiet*. Then she reached up, yanked, and the room flooded with light.

At one of the only two tables, he sipped his stout and lit a cigarette. Four hours to kill. He had loose change enough for one more bottle. Both it and his paper would have to last. He smoothed out the front page and, at the window next to his table, he eased up the blackout curtain by inches.

'We Shall Come! Says Hitler'.

He sighed and turned the page.

> On the weekend, the German bombers over London mostly flew at a very great height and dropped their bombs at scattered points with no apparent plan. It can only be assumed that the object is to terrorize the civil population, and those targeted are best able to judge for themselves how completely these attempts fail. The destitute awaiting money after raids remain very cheerful.

Somehow, he doubted it.

At her feet, towers of cigarettes: Du Maurier, Three Bells, Player's. Viceroy. Pall Mall. Woodbines. German brands. Russian words. Contraband. An Aladdin's cave of it.

On page 3, 'Parliamentary Debate'.

> In the House of Lords, the Lord Bishop of Chichester petitioned for the release of internees in the nation's labour camps. 'Do you know, my Lords, that Jews and non-Aryan Christians who have been brutally imprisoned in camps in Germany or expelled, individuals who are not regarded as Germans at all or as human beings by Hitler and who cannot possibly be a danger to England, form the great majority of the internees?'

He drew hard on his cigarette. He had the Lord Bishop of Chichester to thank, he thought bitterly, for the fact of Otto Gottlieb. According to the tribunal notes, the Bishop had arranged for him to be released from a German camp just days before war was declared. Now Bell was denouncing Britain's labour camps too, and the scandal was growing.

*

She could hardly take it all in. *Suits*. Some beautifully made. An entire rail. Shirts of every size. Three dinner jackets. In the pocket of one, an engraved silver flask. On the shelves overhead: vodka, gin, whisky, Caribbean rum. Neat rows.

He checked his wristwatch and surveyed the situation at the bar. No change there.

> Churchill tells the House of Commons: 'Our people are united and resolved, as they have never been before. Death and ruin have become small things compared with the shame of defeat or failure in duty.'

Yet below . . .

> Reports from public shelters in poor crowded districts suggest that harsh lighting, inadequate clothing, cold concrete floors, and the noise of crying children fray people's nerves. Public disorder and arrests grow more frequent.

On the lower shelves: a box of wristwatches. Here at the Camp, time no longer moved. A chessboard. Notebooks. Cigarette cases. Letters, tied with string. Framed photos – each face, an innocent unaware of this place in which they'd landed.

And books. Dostoevsky. Dorothy L. Sayers. Flaubert. Kafka. *Best Jewish Jokes*. The Waverley novels. A monograph: 'Einstein's Special Theory of Relativity'. Agatha Christie. *The Confessions of Saint Augustine*.

He sipped his beer and tried to stretch out his legs without drawing attention.

In Folkestone last night, German bombers swooped out of the sun and people saw the bombs leaving the racks as the raiders dived to within a few hundred feet of the roof tops. Fatalities were few. Three laundresses are reported dead.

He thought of Tillie. How was she these days? he wondered fleetingly.

She'd come full circle, it seemed. At her feet again: the gramophone. Phonographs, too, piled on the shelf above with sheet music, an accordion and a mouth organ. In the corner, a cello case leaned like a woman against the wall. Three violin cases were propped alongside.

At the cabinet, she riffled through the files. Fender. Finke. Gabbler. Gas. Glick. Golden. And there: *Gottlieb*.

She opened his passport. Its front page was stamped with the word 'Entartete'. Meaning? She found his Identity Card; glanced at the record of his tribunal – 'Sachsenhausen', 'counterfeit', 'Category A', 'Intern No. 6031'. She lifted out a single sheet: 'Record of Contraband and Confiscations'. The list was long and careful. She knew the hand.

> oil paints
> watercolour paintbox
> stolen butter knife
> oyster shell (paint palette)
> pencil
> quill pen
> three brushes
> lumps of chalk, removed from grounds
> charcoal, stolen from Camp laundry

strips of wallpaper – stolen from former lodging house,
 found in lining of jacket
Images 1 to 3 on wallpaper: sea through wire; sheep
 through wire; Gypsy boys through wire
Images 4 to 7 on card: internee body in watercolours.

She rummaged among the boxes and shelves till she found it: a brown-paper parcel at the back of a high shelf.

She ripped the string with her teeth. The pictures were fragile in her hands: small paintings on the card backing of a soap-flakes box. Sea, yes. Sheep. Children, yes. Barbed wire, everywhere.

Then, as she'd dreaded: Mr Pirazzini, haggard and yellow with death, his eyes open in surprise. Two images.

On the edge of the blanket near his shoulder, the artist had captured the stamp of his four regulation digits. But there was something else, something less defined. His face, though emptied by death, had been softened. The watercolours had rendered him transparent, translucent, as if he were already dissolving between worlds. It was a release, she thought. Freedom. That's what Otto Gottlieb had tried to give him.

He must have got hold of his paintbox on the night of Mr Pirazzini's death. He must have bribed someone to bring it to the infirmary or traded some risky IOU for it. One could work quickly in watercolour. She knew that much from her own primitive efforts as a girl. One trusted as much to chance as intent.

Otto Gottlieb's shoulder had been bandaged, the bullet only just extracted, and a nerve in his arm damaged, yet he had managed this much before he was discovered.

The third was a study of Mr Pirazzini's hands, folded on his chest, their blue veins swollen, their liver markings more vivid now than the flesh they marked. The fourth, the fourth was simply the stub of his finger, pale, waxy, yet here, in Otto Gottlieb's vision, not incomplete, not unsightly, but precious.

She had to look away, bow her head, take a breath. It had taken her until now to believe what Otto Gottlieb had tried to tell her, to reassure her of, that afternoon from the other side of the screen. Mr Pirazzini's death – his life, rather – had not passed without notice.

She returned the paintings to their parcel paper and reached blindly for a novel from the storeroom shelf. Agatha Christie.

She would feign ignorance of the ban; she would go to the barracks door and insist on delivering it herself. Who would argue the point with the Superintendent's wife?

'Thank you,' she would humbly say to him.

27

Three years before, in a different lifetime, on a spring afternoon in 1937, Otto Gottlieb, in a jacket and tie, his nails scrubbed clean of paint, sat down to tea with his elderly neighbour, the former silent-film actress Klara Klein. In the inner courtyard at Number 142 Auguststrasse, both turned their faces to the first of the year's careless, unstinting light. 'Bliss!' breathed Klara. 'What a suntrap!'

The mildness of early April was a balm after Berlin's long winter and its privations. From Klara's little table, through the open windows, they listened to Harman the Pedlar climbing the long, broad, stone staircase, flight after flight, shouting his wares more and more impatiently as he climbed. They were amused by the novelty of their first outdoor tea of the year, by the spectacle they gaily presented to any neighbours who stared from their windows and balconies, for life at 142 Auguststrasse was, they knew, unfailingly communal.

At the struggling outset of his career, Otto's parents had tried to persuade him to take a studio in West Berlin, closer to them and the fashionable area in which he'd grown up. His mother had even found him a studio apartment off Potsdamer Platz, with views over the elegant roof garden at Wertheim's, but he had gently refused. Instead he had chosen the Ostjuden district, or the Barn Quarter, so called because, before the Yiddish from Eastern Europe had made its dark jumble of streets their home, it had been the location of the city's stables and cow sheds.

But that afternoon at 142 Auguststrasse, the weekly laundry of the residents made bright bunting across the six storeys of balconies, and both Klara and Otto looked up from the courtyard, taking a wordless pleasure in the sight. Above them, Frau Nagel smiled down and kindly refrained from beating a rug. Herr Wexler opened his book and pretended to read as he eavesdropped. Fräulein Weiss carried her geraniums on to her balcony after their long confinement indoors, and somewhere on the top floor, two women argued audibly about the dishes they would use for Passover. All the while, the sun winked in Klara's tabletop mosaic of shiny blue and red tiles. She poured. Otto cut the strudel. Had time accommodated their respective births differently, with fewer decades between them, they would have been lovers, so sparkling and deep an affection did they share.

He must, she said, tell her everything; how it had come about; who would be there; which of his models he had fallen in love with, for she had seen several women coming and going on the stairs. 'Naturally I am wildly jealous,' she said, and she smiled mischievously over the teapot.

After more than a dozen years painting, Otto Gottlieb was to have his first solo exhibition at the end of June in a small, avant-garde gallery in their district, and Klara had bought Ceylon tea and freshly baked apfelstrudel to celebrate. He chatted. She advised, running her hands through the ferns that uncurled in the pots around her table, and when he'd finished his tea, she took his cup, reversed it, turned it three times in his saucer and lifted it up once more.

She pushed a shining silver lock of hair from her eyes, raised the pince-nez she wore on a green ribbon around her neck, and peered. Ever an actress, she raised her free hand to call for silence from the non-existent crowd and, coincidentally, Harman the Pedlar stopped shouting and even the arguing women went quiet as she studied the dregs of the leaves. At that moment, she looked less like the Romany she was by birth than a steely-eyed biologist examining a culture on a slide.

She looked up, her eyes glittering over her specs. '*Well . . .*' she declared.

'Doom?' he grinned, and helped himself to a second piece of strudel.

'On the contrary. *Many* will see your paintings. Indeed' – she paused for dramatic effect – 'the leaves say the *nation* will see your paintings!'

He laughed into his tie. 'Then I must paint you, Klara! *You* must sit for me!'

She demurred, covering her smile with freckled hands and shaking her head. 'My dear Otto, come, come. Do you think I could bear for the *nation* to see me like this, as I am now, a ruin in a house-dress?'

'A ruin! How you tease.' He craned towards her. 'And who said anything about a dress?'

Her hands rose once more, this time in a silent-film display of shock. He reached for them and kissed them.

Otto Gottlieb's first triumphant review arrived on the 3rd of July, in the Saturday edition of the *Berliner Morgenpost*. Klara rejoiced. His parents rejoiced. His neighbours were amused. He was relieved beyond words.

Its retraction was published the following day. In it, the young reviewer declared his regret for his 'inexperience and haste'. He had failed to note, he explained to the *Morgenpost*'s readers, that Otto Gottlieb was not an accredited member of the Culture Chamber, and he apologized both to his readers and to his editors for his 'lapse of critical and moral judgement'. The views he had expressed in no way constituted those of the *Morgenpost*.

Even so, the young critic would not save his job, and in the days to come, he would be required by the Reich Culture Chamber's Deputy for Visual Culture to account for his 'unaccountably Jewish-Bolshevist' taste in art. It would take him three days to persuade the Deputy of his regret for his actions and his renewed determination to reject 'perversity'. During his time at the Culture Chamber, he was denied his wristwatch, sunlight, sleep, and the use of a lavatory.

Otto Gottlieb's paintings, a series of oils depicting life in the Barn Quarter, were confiscated. The small, heretofore unknown gallery was closed. Its owners were bankrupted; its doors kicked in. Later, someone would smear human excrement over its windows.

His canvases were loaded into a windowless van. They took his Hungarian women in their Shabbat shawls, *shpitzels* and aprons. They took the buxom dancers of Clärchens Ballhaus, sickened, it would seem, by the women depicted in the extremis of the dance. One assiduous officer produced a Swiss Army knife and scratched at the impasto and its stippled surfaces, as if to expose, in the welter of bodies, planes and perspectives, an especially dangerous form of perversion. Then they turned their attention to the nudes.

A year before, in the sanctuary of a local church hall, Otto had discovered, quite by accident, actors who had been cast out of the Neues Theater following its transformation into the German National Theatre. Offering what little he could as a fee, he began a series of female life studies. In his modest studio on the Auguststrasse, he worked almost obsessively with model after model, fascinated by the physical intelligence of those women; by their ability to communicate small profundities through the fluid line of an arm, in the arching of a back or in the attitude of a pair of hands. In every gesture, a story.

He began with charcoal on canvas, sketching impulsively before slathering on the pigment, mixing it at times on the canvas itself, trying both to get the life of the flesh and to see through the flesh to the essence of the sitter, to the spirit. He worked unhindered by either faith or doubt in what he was doing. Neither was relevant, he told himself, for he himself was not relevant, or was only inasmuch as he, the maker, needed somehow to become the subject he painted. Boundaries disappeared. He could feel the moment an image took life. 'Yes,' he told the young critic, 'I think that is fair to say. One is always, also, painting oneself. It's inevitable, though one's focus is necessarily trained upon the subject. I suppose all of life, whether off the canvas or on it, is made from' – he'd allowed himself to smile carelessly for the first time that opening night – 'the intercourse of two things.'

He hadn't realized his words would find their way into the *Morgenpost* review. He had never dreamed there *could* be a review in any national paper. He'd had wine. He'd relaxed at last that evening. Now in print, he sounded like one of the so-called louche intellectuals from the days of the Weimar. 'Regulation' beauty bored him, he'd been foolish enough to admit. He couldn't paint it. It depended too much on smoothness, on symmetry, on stillness. What did anyone know of those things in the Barn Quarter, there in the hubbub of its narrow streets?

It hardly mattered that the reviewer went on to praise his work for its invention and technical bravura. It was only a matter of time before the Culture Chamber took a devastating interest in his work.

So it was that, just two days after his exhibition opened, his Yiddish women, his dancers and nudes were slashed free of their frames.

He was provided with a receipt for his work, though no value was assigned to any of the three dozen paintings. He was informed he would hear more in due course. Later that day, when he found his studio ransacked and his paints and remaining canvases removed, he knew, before opening the chest of drawers, that his passport, too, was gone.

He did hear more. All of Germany heard more, as Klara had unwittingly predicted. The *Entartete Kunst* – or Degenerate Art – Exhibition featured the work of more than a hundred artists denounced as Jewish-Bolshevist in their work, whether Jewish by birth or not. Over five thousand paintings, including Otto's, were seized in the first of the raids. They were hung without frames by fraying cords. A commentary, daubed on the walls in crude letters, accompanied each painting. Otto's Yiddish women were 'An Insult to German Womanhood'. His Ballhaus dancers demonstrated how 'Madness becomes Method'. His nude actresses illustrated the Jewish artist's attraction to 'Cretins and Whores'.

The exhibition toured twelve German cities for over four months and attracted more than two million visitors. Its popularity ended only when the Berlin Fire Brigade was enlisted to burn the majority of the works.

Watching the bonfire from a second-storey schoolroom, a twelve-year-old boy called Theo would be the last person to contemplate Otto's Yiddish women before they and the great golden dome of their synagogue collapsed into the flames.

His passport was returned eventually, bearing the new, oversized stamp of 'Degenerate', a designation that made escape to Switzerland impossible. And like all degenerate artists, he was forbidden to paint.

For nearly a year, Klara travelled in secret to a small, little-known art shop on the west side of the city and bought him supplies in discreet quantities. The journey required four tram rides each way and took the better part of a day, but she would not be dissuaded by Otto from her mission. In time, however, even her determination was thwarted. The following spring, when the windows of their building were once more opened wide on to the courtyard, their neighbours smelled the odour of the oils, and a small delegation from Number 142 Auguststrasse presented itself to the local branch of the SS.

The Black Maria arrived later that day. As Harman trudged up the broad flight of stairs, and as the women on the sixth storey argued once more about Passover food and dishes, Klara sat in silence at her table, her back to the courtyard, her face covered in tears.

28

Moments before locking her husband's office door, Evelyn tried to formulate a plan. She would scribble a secret note on the Agatha Christie's title page. 'Dear Mr Otto Gottlieb, Please rest assured that your paintings are safe. Yours sincerely, Mrs Evelyn Beaumont.' But even that posed too great a risk. She would shake his hand and murmur her thanks for his work. The rest would have to be understood.

In the distance, she could see a mirage of boiler suits. Was he among them? She squinted into the day. The men were working in teams, hauling oversized sandbags, sledge-hammering stone to dust, and stirring huge vats with long spades and shovels. Cement. Always more.

As she skirted the edges of the parade square, her head held high in a pose that belied her nerves, she passed the windows of the main barracks and slowed her pace, marvelling. Into their blue paint, graffiti had been faintly scratched. On the first was a doodle of a naked woman. Further along: names and words, some in other languages. Then, a drawing, like a child's, of a ship foundering at sea.

She walked, clutching her stage prop, the novel. Another sketch – a lover's arrowed heart – appeared at the next window. Her own knocked at her ribs. Which guard would she encounter at the barracks door? Her performance had to convince. And how had life been reduced to *this*? Otto Gottlieb wasn't a conman. Her husband was.

Even that morning she wouldn't have believed him capable of blackening another man's name. And for what? To keep her away from this place, from its grim truths at the edge of the town.

A Government White Paper had been published at long last in the wake of all the controversy surrounding the camps. She'd seen it reported in a remote column of *The Times*. If a prisoner could demonstrate his 'usefulness' to the war effort, citing skills in one of eighteen categories, he could make a case for his release to the Camp Superintendent. Artists, writers and musicians were excluded from consideration, apparently because of their inherent uselessness.

An information leaflet had been prepared and distributed to all internees. Out of more than three hundred men still interned on Race Hill, her husband had released just six. The need for cement was, he'd explained to her, acute. In Brighton, there were few priorities greater than gun emplacements and public shelters. How could he justify the loss of labour at such a time?

She looked up at the windows of the barracks again. What was it like to have to scratch crudely towards the light? She stopped to squint, to wonder, for at the next window some kind of mathematical equation emerged strangely from a rectangle of blue while, on the final pane in the row, someone had scratched bar after delicate bar of music. A composition in a labour camp. And she saw again in her mind's eye the instruments Geoffrey had locked away in his secret room: a cello, violins, an accordion, each confiscation recorded in a file in his own hand. 'Contraband'.

How dare he?

Unfortunately, the guard at the barracks door was less daunted by her arrival than she'd hoped. 'If he doesn't want the book, Private, he may cut it up for cigarette paper if he chooses. But I promised the man a book and, trifling though it is, I am duty-bound. If you would summon him, I would be most grateful.' She heard her mother's icy tones.

'With respect, Mrs Beaumont, we don't have an allowance for books, and even if we did, Gottlieb's not here.'

'He's been released?' But how could that be? His operation had been on Friday. Today was only Wednesday.

'Back to the infirmary. That bullet op of his didn't go too well. Blood poisoning now. Could be curtains.' He paused and smiled shyly. 'I dessay you'll think I'm fishing, Mrs Beaumont, but I'm partial mesself to a good Agatha Christie . . .'

Did she even reply? She remembered only breaking into a run – down Race Hill, through the corridor of wire, past the empty Gypsy camp, down Elm Grove and towards the square towers of the Crescent that rose up from the town like beacons of a certainty she would never reach.

Home, he thought, as he turned the key in the door, home, and the familiar overwhelmed him like a gift. The floorboards creaked reassuringly beneath his feet. Even the sight of his own sitting room felt like a reprieve after the hours spent hidden in the pub between its sweating walls. He could breathe once more. Evelyn's cardigan trailed over her chair, and he caught it in his fingers. The noise of the trains no longer rumbled in his bones. He laid his hat on the banister knob. Next door, through the common wall, he could hear Mrs Dalrymple's wireless and the booming of the BBC's programme of organ music. How lucky he was. How lucky. 'Evvie?' he called, dropping his case, slipping off his jacket. 'Philip?'

He found her in the kitchen, reaching for a jar on a high shelf, and on impulse, he bent low, circling her waist with his arms, holding on even as she flinched, as if to say to her, *I will not let you go*. He'd made up his mind. When he sacrificed Leah, he'd made up his mind. He'd given up Leah, though he loved her, because he loved his wife more. *Evelyn*. Because he loved Evelyn more. He knew it now. He would never not know it again.

She turned to him, her face cold, waxen.

'Evvie?'

She shrugged herself free of his arms. 'I can *smell* her on you, Geoffrey. I can smell her.'

It was like a punch to his lungs.

The atomizer, Leah's scent. It had survived the smoke and stink of that pub. The possibility had never occurred to him. Her lipstick, yes. The sweat of them, yes. He'd always washed quickly at her basin. But not that, not her scent. Say something, he ordered himself. Say something. 'What on earth do you –?'

'Go back to London, Geoffrey. Go back to her.'

'Evvie . . .'

She refused to look at him.

I've given her up! he wanted to yell. *I've given her up for you!*

'There is no woman in London,' he said coldly.

Seated on the highest stair, Philip felt the reverberations of his parents' row rise through his tailbone. He clutched Clarence on his lap. Mrs Dalrymple had given him permission to tortoise-sit during her late-afternoon nap, and, as his father's voice boomed in the kitchen below, Philip wished he too could retract his head into some dark, sheltered place.

When the doorbell rang, he didn't move. The knocker started up, knocking inside his head. It was Mrs Dalrymple come to shout at them about the shouting. His parents had woken her from her nap.

He descended the staircase unsteadily. He pressed Clarence to his chest, as if to make of his friend a living shield. But when he'd braced himself and heaved the door open, it wasn't Mrs Dalrymple in her nightdress and foxtail. It was a shorter, fatter figure.

'Orson!'

Orson had never visited his house; he, Philip, had always gone to Orson's. But here, now, after an entirely Orson-less summer, stood Orson. Except his eyelids were puffy. His nose looked red and raw. Even when bullied at school, Orson had never cried. The most upset he'd ever been was the time Mr Stewart-Forbes had told him that the Stewart-Forbeses were not distantly related to royalty after all. Orson had taken the news badly.

'I thought you'd never come home from your grandmother's.'

Orson stared, his eyes pale and watery in the bouncing light of August. The blue blaze of them had gone out.

'My parents are having a row,' Philip added, to fill up the silence between them.

Orson's face was hard like old putty. 'You have to come,' he said.

29

'Say hello,' said Orson.

'Hello,' Philip whispered. Whenever Orson bossed him about, he felt a strange kind of obedience come over him.

'Hal's a hero,' Orson continued in his queer voice. 'Shake his hand.' On the other side of the room, Orson was lowering the needle on the Oswald Mosley phonograph.

Philip approached Hal's chair and tried to look him in the eye – but which eye? His right was fixed and dead, and the left rolled in an orbit of its own.

'Hal's home on leave,' Orson said, even though it was clear for anyone to see that Hal, the real Hal, would never come home again.

As if he'd overheard Philip's thoughts, Hal's mouth started to flap like a fish on a line.

Philip turned, eyes wide. 'What did I do?'

'Nothing,' Orson said. 'It's just what he does sometimes. Here, Hal, listen to this. Here's our man in Worthing.' Orson ran back and seated himself on the edge of the bed, grinning as the cheers from the crowd went up and Mosley's euphonious tones filled the room. 'He likes this bit' – but Philip couldn't see that Hal liked anything at all.

'How do your parents get him into his chair?'

'They pay a man to come twice a day. He's very strong and he has a dog called Dirk. It was easier at my grandmother's cottage, because the staircase wasn't high, but my mother said we couldn't carry on living on top of one another like that. On weekends the man comes more often. Then we wheel Hal about the lawns out back or sometimes as far as the Pavilion. When Hal's hungry or thirsty, he moans a bit. When he needs the loo, he bangs the arm of his chair and we run for the bedpan.'

Philip blushed for Hal. 'What happens if there's an alert?'

'He has to stay up here and take his chances because there's no getting him down without the man to help my father. My grandmother, who's entirely batty now, said a direct hit would be a blessing, and that's when my mother started to cry and said we were moving back to Brighton.'

Orson jumped up just as suddenly as he had sat down, dashed to Hal's desk and started to rummage. Now that the secret of Hal was out, he seemed as giddy as a girl. It was as if he were showing Hal off, like an exotic pet from the *Wonder Book of Exotic Creatures*. Hal was a capuchin monkey sitting up in a chair, or a ghost-faced lemur who had travelled in a cage from Madagascar.

He started waving a photo in Hal's face. 'Here's Jane, Hal. Remember Tarzan's Jane? You like her, don't you, Hal? Look, isn't she nice? And here's your Troubadour's Cup. "Half a league, half a league,/Half a league onward,/All in the valley of Death/Rode the six hundred!"'

'He's starting to cry, Orson.'

'No, he just needs his drops. The doctor told us his tear ducts aren't right because the bullet went right through the bridge of his nose. Lucky for him he can still see well enough through one eye. They had to leave the bullet in his brain because it was too dangerous to take out after all, but at least his hair's grown all the way back, hasn't it, Hal?' He leaned towards his brother's ear and shouted. 'I say, Hal, your hair's grown all the way back!'

Philip wasn't sure how he preferred Orson: quiet and sad, as when he'd appeared at the door, or oddly cheerful as now. 'Don't you think he's tired, Orson? He looks tired to me. I should go.'

'Don't be a clot, Beaumont. He always looks like that, and you've only just arrived. Besides, Hal doesn't get many visitors.' He ran to the card table, lifted the needle on Mosley, and threw open the ward-robe's doors. 'Here! Look. Hal says you're allowed. You can pop the special belt. Remember?'

He remembered. But when had Hal said he was allowed? Hal wasn't saying anything now, and, as Orson dangled the belt, its lea-ther gleaming, its buckle shining, Philip knew it was wrong to take it, with Hal propped up in his chair and his arms and legs all wrong like a starfish.

'Go on,' said Orson. 'Have a go.'

The steel of the buckle was cool in his hand. 'I like your belt,' Philip croaked, and as he pressed the button on the back, he felt the pleasure of the studs as they popped at his will.

'Now, Beaumont. The belt is yours for today. And this is mine . . .' He bounced the silk stocking with the foot full of crushed glass. 'Hal gets this.' He popped the old Luftwaffe helmet on to Hal's tipsy head. 'Righty-ho.'

'Righty-ho?' said Philip.

'*Righty-ho*,' said Orson. 'Hal gets to go first.'

Geoffrey stood at the kitchen door, blowing smoke into the evening air. The long shadows of the trees in the Park were melting into twi-light, and as he looked out, he could almost see it: innocence, the last of their innocence as a couple, slipping darkly, abjectly, out of the day. 'I've ended it. I don't know how many times I can say it.'

'It's not only what you've done . . . It's what you *won't not* stoop to do.' She listened to herself. How impassioned she sounded. Yet it was only a line she had rehearsed in her head weeks ago. She didn't care, she didn't care. In truth she felt only a cool, hard resignation. 'Are you sure the ambulance is on its way to the Camp?'

'He will get hospital treatment tonight. Rest assured there will be no distinguishing Otto Gottlieb from one of the noble wounded. Now let that be an end to it.'

His tone brought her round, sharp as smelling salts. 'Good God. This war, this wretched war, has gone to your head.'

'Perhaps you would rather I'd buried it in the sand.'

'Everything has been taken from those men, and yet you lock away instruments and . . . and books! What end could that possibly serve?'

He dropped his cigarette outside the door and turned to her. 'It is a labour camp, Evvie. A *labour* camp. I am not proud of it. I dread the days I have to be there. But you know as well as I do that I don't make the rules.'

'No, you only follow them, slavishly. What possible reason could there be to —?'

'Are you in love with him?'

She turned, aghast. 'So inquires the man who keeps a mistress in London!'

'Keep your voice down.'

'You're ashamed!' She could hear herself, acid and shrill.

'Of course I'm ashamed! And Philip is upstairs.' He slammed the back door and dropped into a chair.

'I have to leave . . .' she heard herself say.

'Whatever are you talking about?'

'Leave. I have to leave here.' She spoke – or rather the words emerged from her – but inside she was dumb and reeling. Because it was with her still, that smell, the woman's scent on his jacket, in his hair. And the pills . . . buried just outside. Foul treasure. The bodies, she'd heard, exuded the smell of bitter almonds.

'I'll sleep at Number 5 tonight. I have the key. It's straightforward enough.' Did the war taint everything finally, everything, even this little life?

'Do I so repel you?'

'I shan't leave of course until Philip is in bed, and I'll be back in the morning before he wakes. If the alert goes, I'll come back for him immediately.' Would she go? she wondered. Perhaps. Perhaps not. Nothing really mattered. That was the truth of it all. Everything these days was words, words. And lies.

She looked up and called through the ceiling – 'Philip!' – for there was still the faint, almost illusory notion of dinner to see to; of hands to be washed; of his uniform to be tried for the new term – 'Philip!' Of this little life.

Orson squeezed himself into the space beneath Hal's desk. 'Right,' he ordered, 'now push Hal's chair in front of me so you can't see me at all.'

'I should go home . . .' said Philip, wheeling Hal over to the desk.

'Can you see me at all?'

'No.'

'Is the handbrake on?'

'Yes.'

'And the helmet? Is the helmet still on Hal's head?'

'Yes.'

'Then we can begin.'

'My parents don't know I'm here.'

'Excellent.' He peered out from behind Hal's chair. 'That was me speaking, incidentally, not Hal. *Now* it's Hal.'

He cleared his throat and deepened his voice. 'It is a sunny day when I'm decorated for bravery on the Pavilion lawns under the big bandstand. Hitler pins the medal to my chest. Then he pounds me on my back, and all the people clap, and I am wheeled inside the Pavilion. There are musicians and servants and drinks trays and flowers everywhere. Oswald Mosley is there already and Lord Haw-Haw. Everyone shakes my hand, then we drink Pimm's and stuff ourselves with cucumber sandwiches and –'

'Orson.'

'*Hal.*'

'*No*, Orson.'

Orson's head appeared. 'What?'

'Hal's eyes are leaking again.'

Orson crawled out from the desk space and looked into his brother's face. 'Hello, old egg. Everything all right?'

But things weren't all right and they never would be again. Hal was moaning and beating the arms of his chair.

'Does that mean he's hungry or that he needs the loo?' whispered Philip.

'Hal, quiet now . . . Ssshhh . . .' Orson murmured gently, more gently than Philip would ever have thought possible. 'It's all right. I'm here. I'm here, Hal. Me. *Orson.*'

Hal's starfish legs started to kick and spasm, and if Orson's face had ever had any natural colour in it, it left him now.

'What is it, Hal? What is it?'

But Hal was in the grip of something dreadful, an arm-to-arm, leg-to-leg combat with an invisible enemy.

'His lips are turning blue,' breathed Philip. 'I'll call your mother.'

'Don't,' Orson said in a steely voice. 'She'll just cry. That's all she does. He goes like this sometimes. Almost never. But sometimes.' He swallowed hard, got hold of one of Hal's shaking, man-sized hands and pressed it tightly between his own. For long, shuddering minutes, he held tight to his brother's hand until Hal's tremors subsided. When he finally let go, he went on trembling for a moment himself, as if caught by the tail end of Hal's storm.

'Would he like a glass of water?' whispered Philip.

'We have to make Hal happy,' Orson said, and his voice went queer again, as if he were speaking from inside a dream. 'We really do.'

Philip pushed his fists deep into his pockets. A sadness like he'd never known was inching up inside him, little by little, like water in one of Houdini's tanks. He felt for Hal. It was terrible to be somebody who only made your mother cry. He thought he understood, and that paralysed him even more.

'You have to help, Beaumont.'

He wanted to help. 'Let's push his chair to the window. Let's get him some air.'

But Orson didn't release the handbrake. 'He doesn't want air. Hal is a Second Lieutenant. He saved an entire rifle section of men in France. He doesn't just want air.'

'What does he want?'

'Want?' Orson turned the word over in his mouth. 'Why, Hal wants a Jew, of course.'

The sadness was filling him up. 'Don't be daft.'

But the spell of Orson's voice wouldn't stop: 'That's what he wants . . . We have to get Hal a Jew.'

'A Jew for what? I don't know what you mean and, besides, I have to go home now.'

Orson was wiping Hal's face with his hankie. 'If it weren't for the Jews, there wouldn't be a war, and if there weren't a war, Hal wouldn't be . . . this way.' He turned slowly back to Philip. He was crying now, from inside his dream. Snotty tears were streaming down his face. 'Tell Hal you'll help.'

'Get one how?'

'You have to tell him.' Orson wiped away his tears and turned to his brother.

'But I don't know what you mean.'

'Will you help or won't you?'

The helmet sat jauntily on Hal's crooked head. The secret belt and the stocking lay at Philip's feet. He looked at the ceiling, then at the door, then at Orson. His heart was balled up like an old sock in his throat.

He looked into Hal's fixed blue eye and nodded.

30

Across Brighton, the raids had quietened and, by late August, life seemed almost languid again. Men played patient rounds of cricket on The Level, couples lounged on the Pavilion lawns, and a weekend parade of elephants marched up Grand Parade led by waving, sequinned girls.

Philip was eating a plum at the table on the terrace. His father was at a meeting at the Camp. His mother sat beside him, with her cup and saucer, her book, and his name tag to stitch to his new school blazer. Plum juice dribbled pleasurably down his chin. The sky over the Park was a ribbon of blue and, at first, it was only as if pins had pricked the fabric of the day. Tiny marks. He shielded his eyes to stare. Then a column of planes burst out of the sky.

He stumbled to his feet, knocking his mother's cup to the terrace where it smashed, but his mother was stuck to her chair, her astonished face turned to the sky. Plane after plane after plane. A swarm of fighters and bombers. The roar of their blaze filled the world.

Why wasn't she moving? They needed to run down the terrace stairs, through the scullery door and out the other side to the coal cupboard beneath the street. But his mother only stared as the enemy planes sawed the air overhead, splitting the sky so fiercely in their flight it was as if Heaven and all of its dead would come falling through.

She pulled him close to her. Her cheek was wet against his. 'Poor London,' she murmured, and he looked up too, marvelling, trembling and willing all at once. *Yes, keep going, keep going, get London, not us.*

Day after day, twilight came, the gulls went mad and, within minutes, the planes appeared, roaring over the cliffs of Sussex like grievous angels.

Life was a long, clenched vigil; a shuddering climax endlessly delayed. In *The Times*, Anthony Eden warned that the threat of an invasion by sea was 'acute'. In Germany, Radio Bremen reported that 'Hitler may at any hour give orders for the invasion to begin.' On the six o'clock news, Churchill himself reported that invasion plans were moving steadily forward. There were rumours of an invasion attempt withstood at sea, though Geoffrey's own sources couldn't agree the location or the number of ships involved. The following week, it seemed they were spared again; the invaders, they were told, had turned back for the coast of France after encountering high winds in the Channel.

The beaches were only as ready as they would ever be. Army wagons rumbled up and down the Lewes Road, day and night. Geoffrey had his military travel pass and papers on him at all times, for any day now, at any moment, he might be required to leave. A packed suitcase waited under his desk at the Camp; another sat behind the door of his office at the Bank; a third in the under-stairs cupboard at the house. He and his small team at the Bank had rehearsed their departure each Tuesday for months, and he had long ago resigned himself to that dreadful day – to the slow tolling of the church bells and the agony of departure, to the panic on the streets as he made his way to the station. But now, little by little, in one form or another,

Evelyn was leaving *him*. He had prepared for every eventuality but that.

What was worse, he had no idea what to do or how to bring her back. And so, in spite of every plan, he could no more contemplate leaving her than he could erase his memory of the first time he saw her, under that paper lantern, her eyes brighter than he'd known eyes could be.

Of course she was no longer that girl. He was no longer that unhappy young man who'd felt redeemed by her arrival that summer's night. A single moment couldn't ultimately matter. What was it compared to the span of a marriage and its undoing? Yet there in the dark of his office, on the grim edge of a camp dedicated to the manufacture of gun emplacements, with the sickening drone of the first planes of the night already in his ears, that thin, fleeting, first moment overwhelmed him again. He'd risked too much to be with Leah, more than he'd dared imagine. But in the moment he'd given her up, the knowledge of what he stood to lose had suddenly loomed. If he lost Evelyn, he'd lose his world.

AUTUMN

In those weeks, bombs dropped like the leaves of autumn. Edward Street was hit. The Lewes Road. The streets of Whitehawk.

Yet, after the nightly pounding of London, these attacks were afterthoughts only. Leftover bombs were surplus weight to be tipped by enemy pilots before the long journey home.

For those on the ground, week after week, sleep was fitful and the days were drowsy. Then, on a golden afternoon in mid-September, the Odeon Cinema took a hit in the broad light of day. The town staggered.

From every side of Brighton – north, south, east, west – people gathered on The Level to hear the reports. Tins rattled for donations. The muffin men called. A man with a sunburned face declaimed from the Book of Revelation. Gypsies read palms by the public loos. It was a morbid, confused carnival, and the tattered news of the day blew in like litter across the green.

A matinee. Dozens dead. Fifty dead. Hundreds dead. Many more injured. Children. Their parents. Gone. All before Saturday teatime.

The projectionist had been blinded by flying glass.

It had taken an eternity for anyone to find the lights.

The screams, they said, were heard as far as the seafront.

St George's Road, Lavender Street, Essex Street, all along to Bed-
ford Street – wrecked.

Philip and Orson were meandering through the crowd, marvelling at calamity, when Philip's heart jumped.

'Frank!' He couldn't help himself. 'Frank! Frank, it's me, Philip!'
He sprinted away, running after a tall, lanky figure in the crowd.
Orson squinted after.

At the boating pond, Frank Dunn stopped at last, but his eyes
couldn't seem to focus.

'Frank, it's me, Philip.'

'Phil?' he said, blinking.

Should he say . . . ? 'You have blood on your jacket, Frank.'

'Tubby's mate?'

He nodded, braced for Frank's anger because he'd left Tubby
without a good friend in the world. But Frank didn't look angry. He
looked busy. He kept reaching for something in his pocket over and
over again.

'Are you bleeding, Frank?' he tried again. 'I thought you might be
bleeding.'

Orson came up from behind, grinding a blackjack between
his jaws. 'Orson Stewart-Forbes,' he said, offering the cornet of
sweets.

Frank stared over their heads, searching the crowd.

'This is Frank,' Philip said to Orson. 'Frank Dunn. Tubby's –
Norman's – brother.'

'Ah,' said Orson. 'Yes, I remember . . .' He looked at the state of
Frank's shirt. 'A jolly good thing your mother is a laundress.'

Frank had dark rings under his eyes and his skin was grey like ash.
'We ran out of room, Phil.'

'Ran out of room where, Frank? Have a sweet. The pear drops are nice.'

'Sister said we had to take 'em out by trolley, tip 'em on to a stretcher in the mort, then plant 'em in the barrow out back in the yard. But the barrow was filling up and the ambulance wasn't coming, and that first one, bloody hell, she was heavier than she looked. 'Cos I've only ever carried the sick, haven't I? Not the stone dead.' He started turning his pockets out.

'I had the legs end and me mate, 'e had her head, but the blanket kept slipping. "Don't look down," 'e said, like you tell someone when they're standing on a ledge. 'Cos her legs, she had no stockings on, and they were pale. All pasty coloured. I never seen a colour like that.'

'Frank works as a porter at the Royal Sussex,' Philip added for Orson's benefit.

'The back part of her left leg was shattered at the knee. It was –'

'Horrid,' said Orson.

'Meat,' said Frank. 'Just meat. Then we nipped back inside, stuffed some corpses closer together on the floor and cleared up to make room for the others that were coming in. But nobody comes for a while, not after the first rush, and a sort of disappointment hits us. We're pacing up and down in the yard, getting hot and bothered, and the more bothered I get, the more I think about Lorraine, my girl, and wonder where she is, 'cos her ol' gran lives that way, on Lavender Street, doesn't she, and I'm wondering if she, Lorraine I mean, is okay. Except the truth is, I'm not worrying 'bout her, Phil, not like I should be, I'm imagining her looking like those people, like Lorraine, but like Lorraine as meat, and Phil – Phil? – be a good lad and go pinch us a gasper.'

Philip and Orson stared. Frank's hands were trembling like some-one had them on strings.

Orson made a sharp movement with his head, which meant, *Leave him now*.

'I have to go, Frank. But would you say hello to Tubby for me?'

'Tubby's in hospital.'

The bottom fell out of Philip's stomach. 'Right now?'

Frank nodded and looked away, and it all came rushing in. Tubby had no one. Tubby had had to go to a matinee on a Saturday instead of stopping out to play. If it hadn't been for the Pier that evening, thought Philip, and the lock-up and his father forbidding him from seeing Tubby, and him agreeing because he didn't want his father to tell his mother, Tubby would never have been at the Odeon, watch-ing that film. They would have been out together, like every Saturday before.

'He's going to be okay, isn't he?' He waited for the answer like a fist to his face.

The muffin men were shouting. Up ahead, a woman was sobbing. Philip opened his eyes at last and saw Frank's eyes trained on an old gent who was lighting up a few feet away. Frank spoke too slowly. 'Should think so, Phil. After he's scrubbed down . . . Caught it in the shelter, the quack says. Scabies.'

Orson leaned in close, so close Philip could feel his breath against his ear. 'See?' he said. 'What did I tell you? Dirty, *dirty*.' In his eyes, the blue gaslight flared.

32

The nights were drawing in. It had taken an age to come. October the 16th. Now, at last, over three hundred men gathered in the stands. Most of them hadn't seen moonlight in months, except through painted windows, but that evening, the full moon over the Camp seemed bigger than the blackout. He'd timed it right.

I'll give you the grandstand, he'd said to her once, and tonight he needed his plan to work, more than he'd ever needed a plan to work before. He escorted her from his office at the last possible moment. 'Is it bad news?' she asked him. 'Has something terrible happened?' She hated the place. She'd refused at first to go. 'Why? What is it? What aren't you telling me? Has another man died up there, Geoffrey?'

Earlier that day, he'd thought they'd never get the Steinway up the hill but somehow it had been accomplished. A few of the men had knocked together a rough stage. A piano-tuner had appeared. New turf was laid over the finishing straight in front of the grandstand. There was no rain in the forecast. Even in mid-October, summer hadn't released them from its hot grip.

They took their seats. A gull let out a long, plaintive cry overhead.

When the first notes from the piano spilled into the atmosphere, her eyes still hadn't adjusted, and she couldn't see the source. She turned to him, helpless, bereft, at the adagio's slow lament, as if he, Geoffrey, were taunting her in some way; as if it could only be a trick, a phonograph, a bone to a dog.

Then the marbled clouds drew back to reveal the moon, and the piano itself seemed to rise, like a black, white-capped wave. A refugee called Eli played tenderly, in spite of a hand damaged by frostbite. In the wide night, there was only the full moon, the grave piano and, minutes later, the reprieve of the violins. Two prisoners from Italy bowed the darkness.

In the stands behind them, the prisoners went still.

Evelyn gasped, craning forward. Nor did she flinch as he reached for her hand, and he felt he might have wept.

All the while, far below, the sea hypnotized the stony shore and, in the rear of the benches, Otto Gottlieb – returned from hospital and from death a second time – let his eyes linger on the sight of her.

Her arms were bare and, leaning forward as she listened, she stroked her forearms and idly touched her own cheeks and lips in the way women often do at the theatre, lost to the world around them even as they draw the attention of it. Her hair was pinned up. The nape of her neck was white and fine in the moonlight. He heard again her reading to him through that screen, the beautiful resonance of her voice . . . How rare, though, were glimpses of her face.

He'd seen her properly on her first visit in July, as she'd stood at the end of Mr Pirazzini's bed, though the sight of her there, that day, had irritated him, and he had deliberately looked away. Later during her visit, she'd pivoted on her chair, apparently affronted by his smile, and the indignation of her face had been, he'd convinced himself at the time, unattractive.

At the standpipe, on the day of Mr Pirazzini's death, he'd been granted her profile only, a glimpse stolen. Literally, stolen . . . Otherwise that day, he could only curse the screen that concealed her.

Turn, turn, he willed her now. But she didn't turn, nor did she at any point that evening. Of course she didn't.

He saw the Superintendent reach for her hand, and closed his eyes, breathing as if music were air.

To every man and woman listening that night, nothing had ever sounded sweeter or more stark. It hollowed them out. It recast them. As the nightly procession of planes stormed in off the Channel, Beethoven's 'Moonlight Sonata' climbed high into the atmosphere over Race Hill.

Only much later, as the men filed back to their barracks, did Geoffrey lead her up, up, up through the stands to a narrow side staircase and from there, through a hatch on to the grandstand's roof.

Its expanse lay incandescent beneath the moon. A breeze stirred the night. The music still conjured their senses. On top of that grandstand, on top of a sea-lit cliff, it was as if they floated peacefully in a phosphorescent tide, he in his pale linen suit and she in a light summer dress she hadn't yet packed away for autumn.

Otto turned back, hearing voices as though from another plain, and, peering into the moonlight, saw them.

He stopped. His heart stopped. It broke in his chest like a wave on the stones below.

A few of the other prisoners turned also, wondering what had brought him up short and half expecting to see a stray plane emerging from the night sky. Instead they discovered the Superintendent and his wife hand-in-hand on high, like immortals, beautiful and remote.

33

In November, the bombs got bigger. A crater smoked in the Pavilion Gardens at the heart of town, and hundreds gathered. One hundred and ten pounds of high explosives had detonated, miraculously, below ground, but wet clots of earth and turf landed up to a mile away on windowsills and chimney pots; on the frozen horses of the carousel and on the great bronze wings of the Angel of Peace on the prom. The town grew strange to itself.

At its highest and furthermost edge, Race Hill lay churned to mud. The wind off the sea had teeth. To look at the place – the grim blue windows, the men hunched in their donkey jackets – who would have believed a concert had taken place there in the moonlight just a month before? Yet it had been worth the effort, Geoffrey told himself. The men's morale, if not high, was not as desperately low. More crucially, Evelyn had not moved out to sleep at Number 5. She was still in their bed. Some nights, she allowed him to press her feet between his, to warm them in the chill of their room.

He dreaded the invasion less for its obvious catastrophe than for the time it could steal from him. If he were required to leave Brighton before he could put things right with her, they would never be put right again. In the meantime, in their day-to-day life, she was suspicious of anything that smacked of grand gestures, anything at all.

At the Camp, though, regulations were loosening up. Every week there were new memoranda. Routine decisions were increasingly left to the discretion of camp superintendents. It was an unspeakable relief to empty the contraband cupboard and to order, almost on a whim, the conversion of a stable block for R&R for the prisoners three evenings a week. It wasn't freedom for them but it wasn't misery either.

He could say nothing to her of these changes, for he had no right to boast or make claims. Things would have to take their own course. But there was one further thing he would risk.

His motor was delivered on time to the Camp from the lock-up where it had been sitting uselessly for months. In the transport shed, he filled a jerrycan with Army petrol and recorded the quantity in the accounts ledger.

He'd never enjoyed the forty-mile journey from Brighton to Chichester, in spite of the beauty of the views: the golden fields near Amberley, the silver sweep of the Arun River, and Arundel Castle, ornate and majestic above it all. His childhood dread had never fully released him.

When he was three years old, his father had, with the heaviest of hearts, committed his mother to the Graylingwell Asylum in Chichester, the best institution of its kind in Sussex by all accounts, so that she could be made to live. His father had expected her home in a month, perhaps two. She never returned.

Neither of them had ever been able to understand why she wouldn't simply put the food in her mouth and chew. She had wanted to come home to them; she swore, always in tears, that she longed to be home. At times over the years, he'd thought the frustration and grief would kill his father, but rather more predictably, she had died first, in the year he went up to Oxford. It was both desperately sad and a great relief. His mother had died. Among his university friends, at last, nothing more needed to be said. How much easier than in his schooldays, when he had never found an adequate enough lie to explain her vast absence from their home and their lives.

The asylum's façade had been grand, he remembered: bright red bricks, endless Georgian windows and a benign clock face at the top of a high central tower. But inside, on a seemingly endless corridor, her room had been austere, without even pictures on the walls. Typically she was dressed in the regulation blue cotton dress and a bib stained with soft food she refused to take from her nurse's spoon.

He was relieved to speed past the old turning into the grounds and to drive instead in the direction of the spire, to the centre of the small cathedral city.

George Bell, Lord Bishop of Chichester, was one of those men – short, slight, smooth-faced – who had the look of a middle-age schoolboy, yet already in this war, he had gained a reputation as a thorn in Churchill's side. Bell had long been a fierce critic not only of National Socialism in Germany, but also of the German Church's acceptance of Government doctrines, on 'Aryan' superiority, for example. The problem for Churchill, however, was not Bell's challenges to the German Church, but the eloquence of his articles in *The Times* and his arguments in the House of Lords. The problem was all that humanity.

Bell denounced the 'indiscriminate' bombing of Berlin, adopting the German phrase 'terror-bombing' to describe the unofficial tactic employed by both sides. 'Night-bombing of non-combatants is a degradation of the spirit for all who take part in it.' He challenged official British propaganda and encouraged his churches to do the same. He pleaded the case of the Jews in Europe and that of Jewish refugees. He denounced Britain's labour camps.

It was never destined to be the easiest of meetings but Geoffrey seated himself in the Bishop's reception room and accepted, from the man himself, a cup of Indian tea and a slice of lemon. George Bell wore shabby leather carpet slippers and splashed the tea liberally as he poured. But his recall was sharp. 'Gottlieb, yes. I first heard the name from a German church colleague who'd been barracked with him at Sachsenhausen; a colleague we got out in '38 with the help of our German counterparts.'

Through the Georgian windows, past garden beds bare with November, Geoffrey looked across to the ancient cathedral cloisters, where a group of churchmen hurried in their cassocks. He shifted on the narrow sofa, readying himself to make the case, but the Bishop hadn't finished.

'Coincidentally, and not long after Otto Gottlieb was mentioned to me, I received an anonymous letter with a newspaper cutting, an old review of his first exhibition in Berlin.

'The letter was written in a woman's hand. Elderly, I should think. Her English was quite good. She had, I believe, once been an actress or a singer, I can't recall which, and she had travelled widely abroad. Before the war, she had, she said, read a piece of mine in *The Times* in which I noted my interest in modern art in general and new German art in particular. I am, you see' – waving a hand at the hotchpotch of the room – 'something of a collector, and that detail lingered in her mind, apparently because she thought it odd for a bishop to be keen on modern art. In her letter, she provided a character reference of sorts for Gottlieb and begged me to intervene at Sachsenhausen.'

Geoffrey sat back with his cup and saucer and feigned neutrality. 'He's a lucky man.'

Bell paused to study him. 'Of course, if there is any case that *can* be made by the Church for a man there, any man, it is incumbent upon me or one of my colleagues to make it. In this instance, it took the better part of a year and delicate diplomacy, but in the end, I was able to plead his artistic reputation to the Home Department – although, in fact, I'd never heard of Otto Gottlieb until I received the woman's letter with that one review. When the cause is right, Mr Beaumont, I am only too willing to deceive with the best of them.'

Geoffrey smiled obligingly, glanced at the Bishop's walls and privately wondered that his housekeeper, not to mention the Church, tolerated his so-called art collection.

'I had expected he'd stop in London, once he was past the tribunal, but he said he was keen on Brighton; he wanted the sea light. Brighton, as you know, is part of my diocese. I managed to find him some work painting sets for one of the theatres. Nothing steady but it seemed enough. He found digs, and that was the last I heard, although later, sadly, I was able to imagine the rest.' He sighed. 'Speaking of which, Mr Beaumont, I'd hoped to visit your camp, but as you may recall, you replied to my letter only to say that visits were not advisable.'

His gaze was stony over the rim of his cup.

Geoffrey straightened and returned his cup and saucer, like an offering, to the table. 'I apologize, Your Grace. Until only recently, I was bound by regulations and a shortage of manpower. Naturally you are welcome at the Camp at any time, and if useful employment for Gottlieb may be found, I am only too happy to give my consent. As you'll know better than I, artists may now, finally, be considered for release, though we still must argue every case on utilitarian grounds. I've come today in the hope that you might have work of some variety here in the Chichester area for Mr Gottlieb, as you were his sponsor.' He smiled wryly. 'Unfortunately, when Mr Gottlieb was asked to produce a list of the practical skills he could contribute to the war effort, he insisted he had none; that he is able only to paint. I'm afraid his official records cast some doubt upon even that.'

'Excellent,' declared the Bishop, ignoring the intended barb. 'I have a church in need of a mural painter, and people at war need churches. The mural will be in the modern style. A fresco. I am sure we can agree it will be eminently useful. Is there anything else, Mr Beaumont?'

Geoffrey flexed his hand. 'Forgive me, but I feel I should remind you that Gottlieb is not only an enemy alien. He is also Category A and a Jew. Your parishioners might not –'

'I hope he is good with heights. I shall arrange the scaffolding and meet him there tomorrow for a preliminary look.' George Bell rose from his chair, and Geoffrey understood what it was to be one of his own clients at the Bank, courteously but summarily dismissed. The Bishop extended his hand. 'At midday, shall we say? St Wilf's in Elm Grove. It's not far from your camp, as I recall.'

He smiled and shook Bell's hand. 'Not far at all. Just a mile or so away.'

At the back of the Lewes Road and just minutes from Park Crescent.

The harder he tried, the closer Gottlieb got.

34

The meeting was an unusual one: a Lord Bishop and a 'degenerate' painter. The breath of the two men hovered in the frozen air of the church as if the words they spoke trailed ghosts. Finally, at the foot of the scaffolding, Otto Gottlieb thanked George Bell and said, regretfully, that he would have to decline the commission. He was sure His Grace would find another artist eager to take it on.

Sunlight streamed from the tower, the silence of the nave seemed to beat with each man's heart, and George Bell experienced a peculiar sense of loss.

Outside, the tyres of the Black Maria that had delivered the painter from the Camp were spinning on a thin sheet of ice. George Bell could only stare, lost for words, as the man dashed out the door, slipped on the ice and stumbled to catch the van before it set off back to a labour camp that had already stolen six months of his life.

That day at Sachsenhausen there had also been ice – on the boot-testing track – and it had seemed to Otto that he were falling for whole, long moments while the watchtower rose higher and higher, the sun spun in the grey sky, and the heavy pack on his back pulled him down. Before he passed out with the pain, he felt his ankle twist and snap.

When he came to, his foot was resting on a pillow at a sickening angle. He felt his stomach heave. The nurse explained that the bones had been weakened after the many previous sprains; his ankle had multiple fractures, and surgery would be required to realign the joints. He could expect a plate and screws in his foot, and a leg cast for three to four months.

She was the nurse with the pretty doe eyes and the voice like honey. He started to scream.

There were men in the ablutions block, their testicles burned and swollen; others, castrated. Some, from the Jewish barracks mostly, were dying slowly from injections or so-called racial investigations. The cellar below the pathology room was an open secret, a room stuffed with bodies.

It took two SS guards to hold him still long enough for the nurse to administer the needle. He wanted to never wake up.

Yet he surfaced from the anaesthetic to see it was as the nurse had said. They had operated. His leg was suspended in a short cast. More strangely still, as soon as he could sit up, she brought him a watercolour set and a large sketchbook. She smiled and said they were interested in seeing his work. 'They?' She reminded him, with a knowing wink, that they favoured a naturalistic style. He would be permitted to paint the other men in the infirmary providing he attempted no interpretation. He must be accurate and accurate only. Did he understand? *Of course*, he said. *Yes*. What was happening? What trick was this? He opened the paintbox. Burnt Sienna. Cadmium red. Cerulean blue. He hadn't seen colour in over a year. He'd thought he would never see it again.

That night he dreamed of the nurse's breast in his mouth and her hair falling across his face. Someone was amputating his leg from the knee down. It was torture, but necessary because freedom, he understood in the dream, came at a terrible cost. Without the leg in the cast, he was maimed but untethered and free. Even so, it was hard to turn from her soft doe eyes and her breast with its sweet morphine drip. When he woke, his face was covered in tears and he'd come in his sleep.

A week later the sketchbook and his paintings went missing from his bedside table. He was given crutches and told to report to Room 51 in Barrack RII. He hobbled across the parade square, assuring himself that they wouldn't dispose of him if they had just taken the trouble to operate.

The room stank of bleach. It was windowless but brightly lit. A steel table served as a desk, and was bare save for a clipboard, a box of sharpened pencils and, unbelievably, a large clear jar of boiled sweets.

Against the far wall stood a filing cabinet and four wooden chairs in a row. The centre of the room was dominated by a short examination table. In the middle of the tiled floor ran a gutter with a drain.

A man in a lab coat and civilian clothes stood by the filing cabinet. Otto watched him open a drawer, close it, and turn, holding his sketchbook to his wide, soft stomach. He introduced himself as Dr Metzger and began to talk, immediately and at speed, of art – of Rembrandt of all people – of that artist's remarkable powers of observation, of his unflinching eye for detail. Otto blinked. He couldn't keep up.

'Do you know *Bathsheba at Her Bath*?'

He shifted on his crutches and tried to look the man in the eye. 'Indeed. I saw it at the Louvre years ago. It . . .' Did he dare say it? 'It moved me profoundly.'

'He gets the deformity right. That is the thing. He sees like a scientist. How many artists manage that?'

'The deformity?'

'In the left breast. It is perfectly rendered. That is the power of Rembrandt. You may take a seat.'

Otto lowered himself on to one of the wooden chairs and rested his crutches against the wall.

'You have a dilemma, Mr Gottlieb. You find yourself in a labour camp and yet you are unfit for work.'

'This is only my first day on the crutches. I will improve.'

Dr Metzger approached, picked up the crutches, and removed them to the far side of the room, smiling. Then he seated himself on his desk. 'I am involved in anthropometric research, cranio-facial studies mostly. Deformities. Sometimes, cranio brain ratio work. Head injuries are a growing area of interest. I require good records, accurate records. You are very lucky, Mr Gottlieb. I can no longer carry on doing the work, not at this rate, and documenting it myself. The fact that I cannot has probably saved your life.'

He looked up. 'I am very grateful.'

'I work with children, local Jewish, Roma and Sinti children specifically. Mongoloids when we can get them. Twins of any variety. Sometimes I work with the same children for up to a year, depending. They will change considerably in that time. Your paintings must be in watercolour, for the sake of speed, and they must be anatomically correct. You must be able to work with the measurements and proportions I give you. You must be able to scale up or down as requested.'

'I can do that. I trained initially as a draughtsman.'

'You must be able to produce records both before and after.'

He felt something grip the back of his brain.

Dr Metzger reached for a sweet in the jar. 'Before, after and, in some instances, during the surgical interventions.'

Otto stared at the table, at its straps and stirrups. 'If I may, Dr Metzger, what is wrong with these children?'

'You mean, what is wrong when they come to Sachsenhausen?'

Otto nodded.

'Race aside?' The sweet bulged at his cheek.

'Yes.' He made himself say it. 'Race aside.'

Dr Metzger glanced at the clipboard, turned back a page, and was distracted briefly by a detail there. Then he looked up and leaned across, proffering the jar of sweets. Evil was mundane, not monstrous. 'Nothing, Mr Gottlieb. There is nothing wrong with the children when they arrive.'

When the Superintendent first told him of the Bishop's need of a mural, a fresco, he'd felt life surge within him for the first time since that June morning when he had swum out too far. The space of the church would be his, the Superintendent had explained. It would be closed for services for the duration of the renovation work. He would have to report to the local police station once a week but, otherwise, he would be a free man. He would be paid modestly for the work upon completion. In the meantime, he would need to find other temporary work to keep himself. Did he feel capable?

In that moment, Otto had liked the man.

Entirely modern, the Bishop had said. Nothing sentimental. A single fresco spanning the three walls of the Lady Chapel.

But that morning in the nave, when the Bishop had announced to him the subject of the commission, the words had closed on him like a trap. 'Suffer the Little Children'.

Just months ago, he'd thought he'd go mad with it, Room 51, the memories. Any decent human being would have killed himself long before he tried.

The Bishop offered to find child models from the parish.

He fled the place.

Later that same November day, summoned to the Camp's HQ, he found, not the Superintendent and his disapproval, but the Bishop alone at a salt-smeared window, taking in the view. 'Is it a fear of heights?' he asked, without turning. 'The dimensions are for you to say. It is for you to decide how to use that space. If not the Lady Chapel, something less large scale.'

If he knew, Otto thought, *he wouldn't let me anywhere near his church.*

'Perhaps it's the location? A church? I assumed you were a secular Jew, but if I have offended –'

He shook his head. 'It really isn't a matter to concern –'

'Then it can only be the theme.' Bell turned. 'I chose it for the Lady Chapel because St Wilfred's is a parish with many young families. It is the moment of course when Christ says to the Apostles that the children gathered must be allowed to go to him; that they mustn't be kept away. No doubt you know the story. But you must name your subject.'

How could he say that there was nothing more he could actually say? He thanked the Bishop again and turned to go.

'Mr Gottlieb, *please*. I need an artist, and I believe you need not to be smashing limestone over a long winter. I ask you to put whatever reservations you have aside. You owe me absolutely nothing but –' Here, Bell produced an envelope, a single sheet of notepaper and a yellowed newspaper cutting from his pocket. He laid all three on the desk. 'But I believe the author of this letter took considerable risks – considerable personal risks – to send it; to ensure, not only that you would live, but that you would paint. The letter was opened,

249

Mr Gottlieb, and resealed before it left Germany, which is troubling of course.' He looked him squarely in the eye. 'I feel we must both persist for *her*. I feel you must accept this commission for her.'

Klara.

And again he was at the table in the courtyard at 142 Auguststrasse, the sun on his face and her aged, girlish laughter sweet in his ears. He wanted to rail at her for mixing her fate up in his. He wanted to take hold of her hand and kiss it.

'There must be *a* subject, Otto – if I may? Some Old Testament story you would like to reinterpret, to make your own. I'm only a churchman, not an artist, but I refuse to believe there isn't *something* you wouldn't like to paint. *She*' – and he tapped the letter on the desk – 'she refuses to believe there isn't something.'

And he saw her once more: the Superintendent's wife at the standpipe.

She hadn't been well that hot August day. She'd only just discovered the tailor's deathbed. The heat had been stifling. Her voice had grown fainter. They had been talking through the screen when he heard her, retching suddenly on the other side. She'd run, stumbling from the infirmary, and he'd managed to heave himself from his bed.

When he looked down the slope at the back of the hut, he saw her, rinsing her mouth at a tap and spitting, over and over again. The infirmary was isolated, at the far end of the Camp. There was only the ocean behind her, and he was, as far as she knew, in his bed, behind a screen. Water pooled over her shoes. He heard her swear. Then she unbuttoned her blouse hurriedly, cast it to the ground, and pulled her slip down as far as the band of her skirt.

He watched her splash water over her throat and chest. Her back was vulnerably pale in the afternoon light. He could see the labour of her ribs; the curve of her neck as she lifted her hair; the small of her back; her breasts, delicate as blossom. She bent low to the tap and let the water run down her face, and finally, he made himself turn away.

When she returned, he was where she expected him to be. She sounded fragile but better. 'Please, you're quite welcome,' he called, 'to pull your chair to this side!' He'd tried to sound offhand, carefree, but he'd felt his eyes screw up tight with hope. His heart ticked. *Would* she stay? He almost thanked God, a god, some god, when he heard her chair scrape across the lino – though she would come no closer than the other side of that miserable screen.

He hadn't seen her since that afternoon, not unless he counted the glimpses of her at the concert over a month ago – in their grandstand box, craning forward to see, and later, on its high white roof with her husband under October's full moon. It had run him through.

Now, in the Superintendent's dingy office, he met the Bishop's eye. 'The choice is mine, you say . . . ?'

'Entirely,' said George Bell, 'though if you could rule out the story of Sodom and Gomorrah or the Four Horsemen of the Apocalypse, I'd be most grateful.' He smiled. 'I'll need to approve the sketches, but that is all.'

'Bathsheba,' he said to the Bishop. 'Bathsheba, David and Uriah.'

George Bell picked up Klara's letter off the desk and passed it to him. His features softened. 'I believe she approves.'

David, King of Israel, arose from off his bed, and walked upon the roof of his house: and from the roof he saw a woman washing herself; and the woman was very beautiful to look upon. And David sent and inquired after the woman. And one said, Is not this Bathsheba, the daughter of Eliam, the wife of Uriah the Hittite?

It was all there between those lines, Otto realized. Bathsheba's beauty had seduced King David, he would seduce her, and life would never be easy again.

The fresco would be monumental but intimate. Familiar but dreamlike. Of the moment but – could he do it? – timeless.

And it came to pass in the morning, that David wrote a letter to Joab, and sent it by the hand of Uriah. And he wrote in the letter, saying, Set ye Uriah in the forefront of the hottest battle, and retire ye from him, that he may be smitten, and die.

He could still see *Bathsheba at Her Bath* on the wall of the Louvre. King David's letter lay in her lap. In Rembrandt's story, it has travelled first to her. He has altered the story in this one aspect. So too did his countryman Govert Flinck in his version. She contemplates the letter as she bathes, and in this way, is implicated. Half guilty. She loves her husband but, week after week, he will not go to their bed. He sleeps among servants rather than go to her. She loves him but now, she also loves the King, whose child she carries.

She does as the King asks. She seals the letter and passes it to Uriah to pass to Joab. Unwittingly, Uriah will deliver his own death warrant. In her heart, full and heavy, Bathsheba wills him leave her. She wills him to war.

In this century, Otto told himself, Bathsheba's bath is a rough standpipe on a mean slope. It *can* only be a rough standpipe on a mean slope. She is beautiful but small, slim – 'rationed' rather than full-figured. A half-nude in profile. He can see the composition fully, blazingly, in his mind's eye. On the central wall, Bathsheba has pulled her slip down as far as her skirt. Her skin is pearly, lustrous. In the sky overhead, fine vapour trails loop madly with razor wire. To her left, on the adjacent wall, David, the King of Israel, is a Jewish prisoner. He is wounded. His king's cape is a regulation blanket clutched across emaciated shoulders.

The war has never stopped, Otto told himself. It is only our parts that change without reason or warning.

On the third wall, to the right of Bathsheba, Uriah, her husband, stands tall in a linen suit on the roof of the grandstand – for the high roof belongs to him and not to David in this century. The letter of war peeks out over his breast pocket. In the lower foreground, small groups of his prisoners smash limestone. He watches a dogfight in the sky overhead through binoculars, but he is looking in the wrong direction. He does not see his wife washing at the standpipe. He does not see the man who watches her.

Each of their three faces is turned from view or obscured.

Only the light off the Channel, he thought, *forgives them.*

35

Sylvia's mother-in-law's house was tucked away in a secluded valley in the North Downs. 'Come!' Sylvia had insisted. 'We'll have the run of the place. Martha is doolally and with us in town these days, but Tom still can't bear to part with the old heap. I expect that when London is lost, he'll insist we maroon ourselves out here.' She raised an elegant eyebrow. 'I'll kill myself, *of course*.'

It was dark so early these days. How long, Evelyn wondered, had the two of them been sitting there in what Sylvia called 'the nook'? The teapot was cold, the spiky heads of the teasels in the vase on the hearth seemed to be blackening with the heat, and little by little, the fire and the spectacle of each log's collapse was overcoming her like a drug.

'You do still love him, Evvie . . .'

She couldn't be sure if Sylvia was asking her or assuring her, and for a fraction of a moment, a moment that arrived like an illicit gift, she felt the relief of simply giving up. *Love whom?*

When she looked up, Sylvia was beating back her mother-in-law's Pekingese with the fat roll of *The Times*. The dog would neither stop begging nor yapping, yet she felt strangely, pleasantly detached. She watched as Sylvia bent down and surrendered to the thing an entire plate of biscuits. 'Fortnum & Mason's,' Sylvia declared. 'That should shut it up.'

'She'll be sick.'

'Well, it's either that or ring that nice man the taxidermist.' Sylvia gave a nod to the stag's head on the wall, threw another log on the fire, and sank back in her chair. 'Do you still love him, Evvie?'

She blinked, shaking out her hair, as if she'd been caught in a sudden shower. 'I must . . . Or I will again.' And she meant it. Since the concert in the Camp and his small displays of tenderness, something – a warmth of some kind, or the memory of it – had been restored. She no longer seemed to recoil at his touch, and not only because she was too weary to sustain any pitch of feeling. No one belonged only to themselves, after all. Compromise made life possible.

So why then at night did her thoughts bolt? *It is too hard between us, Geoffrey. You don't love me. Not truly. Roll up the razor wire. Roll back the oil drums. Let them land on the beach. Give every invader a stick of Brighton rock and a souvenir postcard. Get the orchestra back on the West Pier. Muster up a fanfare and go. Go off to your war . . . Because it's time. Surely for the two of us, it's time.*

Over the ruins of their tea, Sylvia lit a cigarette and chattered on. She and Tom had been at the Café de Paris the night before. Vivien and Larry were out and married at last – no longer a scandal. 'So *that* was dull. But Vivien had the appetite of a wolfhound. Who would think to look at her? She ate oysters by the plateful and then an entire Steak Diane. When the waiters flambéed the thing at their table, you'd have thought it was Atlanta burning all over again. Why, I've never seen such shameless over-acting.' Sylvia tapped ash into a cut-glass vase. '*Someone* had to upstage her.'

Evelyn smiled. She felt herself coming to. 'You are incorrigible.'

'Me? I simply danced a dance with a beautiful woman in a dinner jacket, and it seems that no man there, including Olivier, could take his eyes off us.'

'Tom included?'

'No man except Tom of course. He removed himself to the Gents, where he read his daily stack of memoranda, I expect. He loves and deplores the bohemian in me in equal measure. But he always forgives me, because that is what we *do,* isn't it, darling girl?' She drew hard on her cigarette. 'Now tell me, who was Geoffrey's woman?'

'I don't have the faintest,' she said. Her own voice sounded strange to her. 'Someone in London.'

'No.' Sylvia stabbed at the fire with the poker. 'Tom would have said. He and Geoffrey have their drink every Wednesday at the Traveller's Club, on The Mall, then Geoffrey goes direct to the station.'

'Tom wants to spare me, I imagine.'

'Possibly, but he wouldn't spare me. There wasn't a woman in London, not unless Geoffrey was suddenly taking a later train home. There wouldn't have been the time, not between the Traveller's and his arrival back to you.'

'Well there *was* a woman. He confessed as much.' *Brighton then.* She had to shut her eyes, force the images back – and the smell of that scent.

'Evvie, darling' – Sylvia pushed the tea things out of the way with one sweep of an elegant arm – 'these things mean nothing, you know.' She leaned across the table. '*I mean,* they mean nothing to *them.*'

She felt the line of her mouth harden. 'Of course not.' It wouldn't do to sound like a child.

'So you've forgiven him?'

She forced a laugh. Then suddenly, overwhelmingly, she understood. For all of Sylvia's displays of nonchalance and unconventionality, she was on a mission. She had commiserated. She had displayed indignation and sympathy. Now she was telling her, in the tone of her voice, in the blue-grey slate of her gaze, that it was time to accept. To behave. To toe the line. That was why it had had to be a weekend visit. In the country. With neither escape nor diversion. 'Do you think Sylvia might have a word?' Geoffrey would have said to Tom. 'Darling' – Tom to Sylvia – 'would you mind speaking with Evelyn when the time is right?'

'*Have* you, Evvie? Forgiven him.'

'I haven't sued for divorce yet, if that's what you mean!'

Sylvia eased herself back in her chair, removed a book from the bookcase, and withdrew a slim bottle of gin. 'Sweetie, you know very well that's not what I asked.'

The Unit had had to burn out all vegetation and roots before digging the shafts down. Now, only the white wooden marker of the UXB cross remained, ghostly among the blackened stumps of the trees and hedges.

It was one of those November days, Geoffrey thought, when the sun was destined never to appear. A staff sergeant stood solemnly at the opening to the main shaft, intent on his listening equipment. Geoffrey, an official observer, stood at the edge of the blighted field as the Lieutenant updated him. It was day three. They'd located the thing at last. The sterilizer was on standby. A block and tackle had been slung over the joist of a neighbouring house. They had their removal lorry at the ready – a cattle truck the Army had comman-deered. Early that morning, as they'd driven it through the town, the men on the squad had poked their heads through its bars and mooed at the Saturday shoppers. Now, in the gloom of Shaft 3, forty feet underground, two of them were trying to fit a clock-stopper to the belly of a bomb.

It wasn't only a matter of extracting a ticking fuse, which was hellish enough, said Lowell. Now the fuses themselves were booby-trapped with wire-sprung switches. Even if their clocks were stopped, they could still blow if moved. In one test, a pencil tap on the bomb case had set the thing off.

Every house and shop within a radius of eight hundred feet had been cleared. Traffic had been stopped. The depth of a bomb, Lowell mumbled, depended on the soil. Clay offered greater resistance to the bomb but it also made 'the dig' more difficult. If the disposal crew weren't blown sky-high, they could still be buried alive.

The Army was low on timber for shoring up the shafts. They'd had to forage in bombed-out houses for floorboards and doors. Worse still, the war effort couldn't spare trained sappers. Lowell had to make do with retired soldiers, young men deemed unfit for ordinary duties, a watchmaker and a pair of gravediggers. They worked in relays of two for twenty minutes apiece to minimize the risk. Remarkable men, Lowell said.

The month before, he'd lost ten in one blow. Bomb Disposal Section 28. He went to check the time on his right arm, then remembered it wasn't there. His sleeve dangled uselessly. 'Almost dark and not yet half past three.'

Those who waited their turn to go into the shaft seemed neither white-faced with nerves nor grim with resignation. Geoffrey watched them. They didn't appear to be gathering up memories of a first kiss or their father's hands or a child's sleeping face. They looked bright-eyed; their pupils were wide, their cheeks ruddy, like men in love. Like men on the edge of something.

He envied them that. In their company, he felt inert and unformed, a cipher, while they moved through the November gloom and across the wasted field with a strange grace, like men half made of light.

*

Orson came up with the plan. They were to meet in the Park on the Saturday Philip's mother was away in the country and his father was out on Army business.

Philip scooped charcoal out of the Park's bonfire pit. Orson arrived with a mortar and pestle and the two packets he'd lied for at the chemist's: flowers of sulphur (for his brother's boils) and salt-petre (so his mother could cure a side of pork). Philip fetched his father's box of matches from the mantel. Orson produced the special ingredient: cordite strips extracted from bullets and sold for tuppence a piece behind the bicycle shed at the Grammar.

The case was a sardine tin. Orson had soaked the fuse in saltpetre overnight.

The day was overcast and grim. The Park was empty. No one was about. Clarence was asleep in his annual hibernation.

Orson examined him. 'His shell is as good as a bunker. Besides, all his bits are tucked in.'

Philip agreed that they were. The idea was to measure Clarence's flight-path.

It was louder and brighter than they'd expected. The horseshoe shrubbery exploded, and it seemed like a dream. Then Clarence was in pieces, Philip was crying, and Orson told him there wasn't time for that. Nothing made sense. Orson started to run. Philip had never seen him run before. When he returned, it was with the box that had been Clarence's bed. It always sat next to Mrs Dalrymple's scullery wall.

Orson started to dig in the ground with his hands.

Philip shivered. 'That's the turnip plot.'

'So?'

'So people will dig for turnips.'

Back on the Beaumonts' terrace, Orson pointed to the spade that was stuck upright in the soil. 'There,' he said. 'Deep enough so your parents won't find it.' But Philip didn't move – he couldn't make himself – so Orson sighed and reached for the spade himself. When the spade hit metal, his eyes popped behind his glasses.

MCDOUGALLS SELF-RAISING FLOUR. FOR PASTRIES, CAKES, SCONES, PANCAKES & BOILED PUDDINGS.

Philip took it from him. 'It's not yours.'

'Then you open it.'

He met Orson's eye. 'You killed Clarence.'

'So did you.' Orson nodded at the tin. 'Are you going to open it or not?'

They had to bash the lid against the terrace table. Then Orson's hands plunged in. 'Money,' he said.

'You can't have it.'

Orson fished at the bottom. 'What the . . . ?'

'You're not allowed.'

Orson lifted the flap of the envelope.

Philip peered in. 'Medicine?'

'No . . .' Wheels and sprockets spun behind Orson's eyes.

'Sweets?'

'Definitely not sweets . . .'

'My father will be home soon.'

Orson slipped the pills into his shirt pocket.

'What are you doing?'

'I might need them.'

'What for?'

'For Hal. If he doesn't get better.'

'You said they weren't medicine and you said Hal won't get better.'

'Happier. If he doesn't get happier. He might not *want* to go on if things stay like they are. He hates it. The bedpan and the sponge baths and Mother dressing him. He *hates* it all. And her kisses before bed. And the way she cuts and combs his hair. And that phonograph . . . I told her, "You're making everything worse!" I said, "You're nasty, Mother! He doesn't *belong* to you!" and Father locked me in the telephone cupboard all night as a punishment.' He fixed Philip with a wild stare: 'Remember . . . You promised. You promised you'd help.'

Orson had said nothing of it since that summer day but now he was saying it – he'd remembered – and worse still, there was a dirty old tin buried in his garden, and a pair of bright pills in Orson's pocket that didn't make anyone better, and worse than everything, worse even than the broken mess of Clarence, was the promise he'd made to Hal that day . . . *We have to get Hal a Jew.*

Orson chose a spot, among the dead stalks of autumn, for Clarence's grave. 'It's jolly good the Park is empty today,' he said. 'If anyone asks, say you heard the blast and it was a lorry backfiring.'

Philip's teeth chattered. The force of the blast still trembled in his jaw. A cold drizzle fell. 'I *killed* him,' he whispered. Because Orson was right, it was his fault because Clarence had been his friend, not Orson's.

'He died in his sleep,' Orson said. 'That's the best way to die.'

'I killed him.' How Mrs Dalrymple would hate him if she knew.

Orson checked the pills in his shirt pocket and buttoned his coat. 'Never mind. I won't tell anyone what you did.' His eyes were sticks that poked.

36

She stepped inside, stamping the sleet from her boots, and walked into the nave where two small paraffin stoves coughed out more stink than heat. Frost dimmed the inside of the stained-glass windows. The altar was covered in dust sheets, and the long red carpet that ran to it had all but disappeared beneath the mud and damp.

'Ha!' he called out merrily from the scaffold. 'You've come to read to me while I teach myself how to mix plaster! Splendid!'

She smiled and unbuttoned her coat. 'I'm afraid not! You're no longer a worthy cause!'

She walked up the centre aisle. She was only passing, she said. The other week, when she'd learned that the Camp had been closed at last, she'd almost cheered. She'd asked her husband what had become of the last of its residents and was thrilled when she'd learned about his commission.

'Yes! Your husband arranged it,' he said. 'He spoke to the Bishop last month.' He glanced back at her. 'I am in his debt!'

'Not at all,' she called, taking a seat in a middle pew. She felt an involuntary flickering of pride. Geoffrey had said nothing of it to her until she had asked, and now, now she was moved to see Otto Gott-lieb dashing about this space, between ladders and arches, juggling trowels and brushes, free at last. For the first time in months she felt a force of feeling for her husband, like a hidden spring pushing hard, painfully, behind her heart. For the first time in more than a year, she looked forward to getting home; to telling him she'd popped into St Wilf's and she knew, she *knew* now, that the commission had been his doing.

Like her husband, Otto Gottlieb was a changed man, or so it seemed. His hair had grown thick if rather wild. He had blood in his cheeks and had put on weight, or at least he appeared less thin under the bulk of various jumpers. But how did he work in such temperatures? It was even colder inside than out. Her breath made wreaths in the air. She couldn't bring herself to take off her gloves or hat.

He was hauling a heavy bucket from the chapel into the nave, so she wouldn't have to call around the corner. 'Apologies!' he said. 'Plaster needs constant attention or it gets lumps. This is yet another trial batch.' He rolled his eyes at his own poor showing.

His dark hair was flecked with silver. A pencil sat behind one ear and a cigarette behind the other. His eyes were wide and deep-set; his face, pale, angular, almost Oriental across the cheekbones, and in need of a shave. He had bad teeth but a charming smile, and he was tall, not as tall as Geoffrey but tall – *for a Jew*, she heard herself think, and she wondered that her mother could still sit, ensconced, at the back of her mind.

He was handsome, in an uneven sort of way, she decided.

Handsome for a Jew, her mother-self added.

Perhaps she *had* caught it, the vileness, from her parents. Once upon a time, Geoffrey had been her shield; her guarantee of immunity from their views. She'd shaken off their habit of contempt like an infection. She and Geoffrey had lived altogether differently. He was a man committed to fairness in all things. That was their story. Only now she knew he'd let her down from the start – from before the start in fact – shamelessly goading a Jew at a Midsummer Ball. Perhaps she'd always sensed it. Perhaps she had intuited more than she'd ever admitted to herself.

The hairline crack in the man's monocle.

His glowering stare.

The split in the seam of Geoffrey's jacket.

The man's sudden departure at the sight of them a year later at the theatre.

Hadn't she disliked him at first sight? Wasn't that the truth? *Foreign*, she'd decided as she passed him at the ball. She'd noted his hot, ugly stare. The discourtesy of it. The affectation of his eyepiece. The lofty intelligence of his face. His small, silly neck in white-tie. Put him next to Geoffrey or Tom, and he was a clockwork, wind-up toy of a man. A man who'd snubbed the man with whom she had – already – fallen in love. She was eighteen years old, ignorant, and everything about him had unnerved her, through no fault of his.

In their life together, had Geoffrey disguised his true opinions less for himself than for her? Was it the unspoken condition of their marriage? Did her own rot run deeper than his? Would it – had it – spread to Philip?

Otto was pulling on another jumper, more moth-eaten than those he already wore, and the memory of his scarred back flashed luridly in her mind.

'You're shivering!' he announced brightly. 'Would you like a cup of tea? I have a kettle to call my own.'

'No! Thank you! I really am just passing.' She looked high into the rafters, avoiding his eyes. 'You don't mind painting a church?'

'Not a bit.'

'Will it be New Testament or Old?'

'Old. I can reveal that much.' He winked.

'A compromise between you and the Bishop?'

'None was needed, I assure you. I was simply very grateful for the work.'

'It's just that most churches tend to find the New a little more . . .'

'Palatable?'

'Yes!' She laughed. 'Easier on the eye!'

Only then did she see, in the pew across the aisle, the crumpled blanket, the mildewed pillow, and the hot-water bottle. His accommodation. A damp, threadbare towel had been thrown across the baptismal font. Was he washing there?

'I trust you're being paid?' she called in an apparently casual way.

'Something up front for the materials and the rest upon completion.'

'And when will it be unveiled?'

'In June, or possibly even May with a little luck.'

'But that's months away! I thought frescoes were high-speed work.'

'Once one can actually begin. But here, the exterior wall needs renovation work first. The pointing between the brickwork is faulty, and the builders are distracted. Bombed houses seem to have that effect. There's water getting in somewhere – can you see all that staining? That must be put right before any new plaster can go up. And until I can get the plaster on the wall, I can't test my pigments. I'll need four or five good tones for each colour. *That* will be the fascinating bit. Watching the colours emerge.'

'Emerge how?'

He looked up from his bucket. 'I work on the assumption that there is a secret chemistry in all art; in this case, a reaction between the pigments, the plaster, the temperature, even the spirit of the building. I tell myself that the colour in a fresco is dependent upon the most minute of things; that it is catalysed by the light of the first onlooker's gaze, by the carbon of their breath, by the speed or calm of their hearts.' He seemed to forget to stir.

'In any case, *first* there are compositional sketches to be approved and cartoons to be drawn – after I find three models, that is – and all this before I can even begin to mix the pigments. *Then* it's a case of fifteen to twenty sections per wall. Three walls. Each section must be painted in a day, because everything's determined by the speed of the drying plaster. A fresco has something of its own mind. One plans every square inch but there remains the element of chance, fate, mystery, coincidence – call it what you will. *Finally* there will be some tempura work for the finer detail at the end – if the shakes in this arm of mine forget to shake,' he added.

He let his eyes take in the loveliness of her once more, but she was distracted, her head turning as she surveyed the church.

'Forgive me. I have completely lost the art of conversation.' He grinned. 'God only knows *how*.'

She suppressed a smile. 'You do well enough.'

'Would you model for me?'

His words took even him by surprise.

'Clothed,' he added.

Did she blush, she wondered, out of pleasure or embarrassment? 'Are you in the habit of painting naked women, Mr Gottlieb?'

'Otto.' He shrugged and smiled. His stir-stick was in motion once more. 'I am, rather. But that won't be required.' For he would not forget the perfection of her naked back in the sunlight. It was emblazoned in his memory, on his heart.

'Clothed?'

'Rest assured.'

She narrowed her eyes. 'In that case, my answer is' – her mouth twisted impishly – 'no!'

266

He looked crestfallen, and she clapped. 'Apologies!' she laughed. 'I couldn't resist. And please, call me Evelyn.'

'Evelyn — are you sure you won't consider it? I have two male models, men from the Camp as it happens, but I need —'

He had pushed too far.

She started to button her coat. Her smile was still warm but faltering. 'I'm afraid it won't be possible.' She was withdrawing into a married woman's respectability, straightening her hat. He'd lost her. In the tower over their heads, winter gusted.

'Otto, tell me, where is it you are living these days?'

She was Lady Bountiful again.

When she had insisted he meet her outside the Salvation Army on Park Crescent at half past four that same afternoon, he'd imagined she was about to introduce him to the local soup kitchen, which he would be too ashamed to say he knew well already. Instead, in the gathering dusk beneath the grim Christian fortress, she passed him a set of keys. Number 5 Park Crescent, she said, nodding to the town-house across the street. A neighbour was away for the war. At Numbers 4 and 8 too. It was a scandal that such large houses should sit empty. Her gloveless hand touched his. The keys, when he took them, still held her warmth.

He glanced up. An old lady at Number 6 watched them from a high window and then was gone. The November sky was pewter. The first snow was falling, falling, muffling the world. Only her eyes were bright.

She was talking. He made himself listen. Others on the street would not be 'of the same mind', she said, but Number 5 was neighbourless on one side — that was to say, Number 4 — and on the other, it shared a wall with one elderly neighbour only at Number 6. He was on the verge of saying he'd just seen her, but Evelyn hardly paused for breath. She was sorry but the shutters would have to remain closed at both the front and back. It would be for the best if he slept in the study and lived on the ground floor only. There was bedding in the linen cupboard and a servants' loo in the scullery. He would have to rely on the gas heaters since chimney smoke would arouse curiosity, but even so, the house would be warmer and more comfortable than a church pew in winter. He would have to enter and exit the house at the back, via the Park, keeping to the far perimeter path. 'If anyone should see you and ask, you are to say you're visiting friends at Number – and here,' she said, 'your memory should fail you. Please say as little as possible. Please sound as English as you possibly can, and please be discreet. Mr Beaumont, incidentally, is often in the Park on weekend afternoons with our son when the weather is fine. You won't be using the front door, and I must, in any case, hold on to that key. But the big one on your chain is for the Park's gate and the little one is for the kitchen door, which you should lock from the inside when you're there and obviously from the outside whenever you leave.'

'This is enormously kind,' he said.

She pressed her collar to the white of her throat and bounced briefly on the balls of her feet. Then she extended her arm, smiled broadly, shook his hand, and wished him well. She would very much look forward to seeing the mural in the spring.

She was making herself a stranger again. Her words and tone made it clear: she hoped not to bump into him on the Crescent.

The sky had deepened to night. The wind had come up, and the flurry of snow was blowing harder now, stinging their eyes and cheeks. He wanted to draw her to him and wrap her in his ill-fitting coat. 'There's just one further thing, if I may,' he said.

She huffed on her hands. 'Geoffrey will be home shortly and I really must –'

'It's only that I still find myself in need of a female model, and, as you'll appreciate, I've not been in much of a position to meet women of late. Nor is it a request one can simply put to a woman standing at a tram stop. In spite of my impropriety earlier' – he grinned his charming best – 'I understand your position entirely. But I wonder if you or your husband might put me in touch with the other woman who attended the concert at the Camp that night. Or better still, per-haps you or your husband might intercede on' – he raised his eyebrows comically – 'the Artist's behalf.'

'The other woman . . . ?' she said.

'At the back of the stand that night . . .'

But women weren't permitted at the Camp. Geoffrey had made that point more than once. No female visitors, no female staff.

Otto let his eyes linger over the detail of her: the lustrous brown top of her head; the berry red of her coat; her small, bare hands; the bright energy of her in the snow-shaken night. His heart would have to survive on such details, like a wretch thieving food. Yet the bleaker he felt at the imminence of her departure, the jollier he sounded. 'In the row just ahead of me. I assumed she worked in the laundry or the cookhouse? Whatever the case, she had exceptional posture. Those benches left much to be desired but that woman's back never slumped once throughout the concert. *That*, you see, is an underrated quality in a model: a sitter who can actually sit! And while hers isn't the sort of figure I actually require for the mural' – his gaze sharpened – 'it is always good to draw from life, at the start of things at least, and in any case, I need to – what is the phrase? – limber up.'

She was grateful for the blackout, for the darkness that covered the tumult of her face. Even as she listened, nodding, hardly hearing what he said, her world was plummeting, like a gold-caged lift down a dark shaft.

'I'm sorry, Mr Gottlieb. I'm afraid I couldn't say who she was.'

It was all she knew, all she could hold in her head: Geoffrey had not given her up after all.

That day, he'd smelled it, even before he'd looked up from the contracts on his desk: cedarwood.

He'd winced as he stood. His secretary had hovered. Would they be taking tea? Leah had shaken her head, embarrassed, and removed her gloves. He'd walked around to the front of his desk, held her chair, and longed for the weight of her in his lap.

'How are you?' he asked. 'How are you both?'

'Yes. Well.'

She looked pale. Her coat was too sober a blue – it aged her – but her beauty spot was in place, and her lips were slick with colour. She sat, her face lowered. The silence was painful.

'Is it money?' he said finally. 'May I help?'

'*Yes*. Money. Exactly.' She laid a manila envelope on the desk and slid it towards him. 'You left this at mine when you . . . when you went.'

He met her eyes. 'When I fled.'

'Yes,' she said, 'when you fled.'

'It was a . . . gift.'

She looked past him, her eyes cold.

'An apology, rather.'

She reached for her gloves and stood.

'Keep it, Leah. Do please keep it.'

'It is not mine.'

'Keep it for Misha, then.'

'Keep it for you, you mean.'

'For me. Yes. Please, keep it as a favour to me.'

'I don't need to make you feel good, Mr Beaumont.'

She knew his name.

'Is not my job any more.'

He felt the heat in his face. 'No.'

'I have new job.' Her back was rigid. It was hard to imagine she'd ever lain soft in his arms. 'I play organ at cinema. Is not Chopin, but Misha gets to push the pedals and he loves it.'

He blinked hard. 'You deserve more.'

'Yes,' she said with a shrug. 'I do.'

'I am . . . very grateful to you. Not just for . . . but because I believe you changed me somehow . . .' His throat was tightening. He had to turn to the window. 'Leah, I can't tell you how much I –'

'No,' she said firmly. 'You cannot tell me, can you?' She rose from the chair.

Did he dare? 'There is a concert, an outdoor concert, weather permitting. On the evening of the 16th.' He plucked at his cuffs. 'At the top of Race Hill. The old racecourse.' It was the last risk he'd take. For her; he'd take it for her. 'I'm afraid I cannot arrange a box, but I would see to it myself that one of my staff collects you and returns you safely home.'

At the door, she hesitated and the line of her shoulders relaxed.

'I am told that the pianist once played for the Tsar.'

Her hand hovered over the knob.

WINTER & SPRING

37

Snow fell through December, dimming the town. Pipes froze. The
clock in the Clock Tower stopped. The power failed. Hearts failed.
Dogs drowned, surprised by the icy sea. Still Brighton braced itself
for disaster, for enemy ships on the horizon. The wait was a cold
fever. Dread flattened hope like a late frost, and its residents stifled in
the cold as they had stifled in the heat.

Outside Mrs Dalrymple's bedroom door, in the hush of a shadowy corridor, Evelyn knocked twice, and, hearing nothing, entered
with Philip. It took a moment for her eyes to adjust; for her mind to
navigate a path through the intimate gloom. The room smelled of
candle wax. Its windows were covered with a heavy maroon
brocade.

The details separated themselves only reluctantly from the
shadows. Mrs Dalrymple's foxtail stole hung limply over a gilt
screen. Her rings lay scattered across a rosewood *poudreuse*, their
sparkle all but lost to a chaos of puffs, powder, pots, gap-toothed
combs and yellowing brushes. A tall taper was lit at either end, while,
across the room, on a chest of drawers, a Christmas hamper stuffed
with biscuits, flowers, cheeses and imported fruits rotted fragrantly.
The room was part boudoir and part mausoleum.

A fortnight before, Mrs Dalrymple had formally taken to her bed
for no apparent reason, although she still received occasional visitors

beneath its silk canopy. Three days before, she had announced to Philip from her window that she was dying. He had run in from the terrace to inform his mother, and now Mrs Dalrymple lay in state, propped, haggard and wan against fat bolsters, and covered in an eiderdown of pale gold satin.

Evelyn envied her neighbour the privileges of age. There were dark mornings these days when all she could hope for was more sleep and a delay to the tyranny of the new day. Sometimes she wandered out to the terrace for air and found herself staring, mesmerized by the spot where the tin and its two terrible pills lay buried.

After everything that had been said, Geoffrey had not given the woman up – Otto's inadvertent comment had made that clear – and yet here she was, playing her part of the dutiful wife and neighbour. Why, she wondered, do we seem unable to speak of the things that matter most?

I am alone, she wanted to say. *I am so alone.*

The old lady opened one eye and looked past her. 'Is that you, Philip Beaumont?'

'Yes, Mrs Dalrymple,' he whispered from the gilt shelter of the screen. He turned his head away, but it was no good. In the reflection of a speckled looking glass, her bloodhound eyes were drooping lower than ever.

'I hope you're not growing up, Philip Beaumont.'

'I'm not trying to, Mrs Dalrymple.'

'What is it I've told you?' she creaked.

'Men,' he repeated balefully, 'are execrable buggers.'

'I should like it very much if you would wind up my music box. It is here on my nightstand and plays "Für Elise" rather charmingly. My late and wayward husband bought it for me in Switzerland as a token of his undying guilt.'

'Is there anything else we might get you, Mrs Dalrymple?' said Evelyn, seating herself gently at the edge of the bed. 'A glass of water or tea or a hot-water bottle? A book perhaps?'

The old woman arched a frayed eyebrow and expelled a sigh. 'Clarence used to nestle here, right here beside my hand.' Her gnarled fingers groped the air uselessly.

Philip approached the bedside table, took the miniature music box in his hands, wound the tiny handle, and laid 'Für Elise' close to his ear. But it was no good. He could still hear every mournful word.

'I cannot imagine what variety of *animal* would make off with Clarence.'

He wound the handle again.

'Philip, please. It's very delicate.' His mother patted the edge of the bed. *Pat, pat, pat.* He'd never known so dreadful a sound. 'You miss Clarence too, don't you, darling? Come and tell Mrs Dalrymple about your birthday.'

He nodded, pale as the white Christmas rose withering in its vase on the nightstand, but he didn't move.

'Philip turned nine last week, didn't you? He had sponge cake with jam and a trip to the cinema.'

Mrs Dalrymple knew. He knew she knew. His innards were jelly.

'And did you *enjoy* yourself, Philip Beaumont?'

He nodded quickly and whispered in his mother's ear: 'May we leave now? I don't feel well.'

'It's rude to whisper,' she chided. 'Wait for me in the hallway, please.'

Outside Mrs Dalrymple's door, the shadows swallowed him whole, yet even in this other dimension, every word rang out.

His mother: 'Are you quite sure you wouldn't like Geoffrey to send for our family doctor?'

Mrs Dalrymple: 'I am better left to die, Mrs Beaumont, without being *bullied* on my way by any doctor.'

'Yet if you're not feeling well –'

'If one is dying, one is generally not feeling well, and that is also why the last thing I need, incidentally, is *noise*.'

'Noise?'

'Nois*es*. Plural.'

'From the Park?'

'Through the walls.'

'I'm not sure I understand.'

'I hear noises through the common wall.'

Evelyn shook herself. 'Ah! So sorry. I have asked Philip not to tramp down our stairs but I will –'

'From Number 5. Odd little sounds. I don't like it. I don't like it at all.'

'Naturally.'

'You must ask your husband to investigate.'

Evelyn smiled as convincingly as she was able. An eyelash fell into her eye and she tried to blink it away. 'I'm sure it's nothing to worry about. Mice, I should think, or a bird in the chimney.'

'I'm not sure you understand me. Kindly remember, Mrs Beaumont, that we must *all* keep our eyes and ears open these days.'

Was it a warning?

'Yes,' she said, slowly and in the correct tone. 'We must all be vigilant.'

Remain alert.

Train yourself to notice the exact time and place where you see anything or anyone suspicious.

Make certain that no stranger enters your premises.

38

Father Christmas was not put off by the Luftwaffe. He left a boy-size RAF helmet and goggles, a card game called 'Vacuation, a box of pencils, a new sketchbook for Philip's aeroplane drawings, *The Wonder Book of Science*, an orange from Spain and a diablo.

From his parents, Philip had a knitted hat, a pair of red mitts and a shiny half-crown coin fresh from the Royal Mint. He gave his mother a bookmark and a box of lilac-coloured notepaper that his grandmother had helped him to buy. He'd chosen lilac because lilac was his mother's favourite flower. He gave his father a shoehorn and a shoe-polish kit. His father gave his mother a box of soaps and a new nightdress that was, he told her, the latest in parachute-silk couture. His mother gave his father a blue silk tie and a matching blue handkerchief for his breast pocket. 'Ah!' he said, 'a colour I can correctly name! Excellent.' He folded it Fred Astaire-style and popped it in his pyjama shirt pocket.

His mother smiled but not with her eyes. Later, she came in from the Park with red, raw hands and brussel sprouts that were solid with ice.

After morning service at St Peter's and a long visit at his grandmother's house, Philip investigated, for the first of several times, Mrs Dalrymple's suspicions about Number 5. He pressed his ear to its back door and ate his entire Christmas orange on duty, but he heard nothing at all, neither gull, mouse nor ghost.

When he gave up and went back indoors, he found his father in his chair, blowing smoke at the ceiling, and his mother in her chair with her chapped hands folded in her lap. He strapped on his RAF helmet, spread out on the floor, opened his new sketchbook and tried again to draw a Spitfire that actually looked like a Spitfire while the King's voice rolled gravely on. 'If war brings its separations, it brings new unity also, the unity which comes from common perils and common sufferings willingly shared. To be good comrades and good neighbours in trouble is one of the finest opportunities of the civilian population . . .'

His mother sighed and reached for her book. His father glanced at her, frowning, and asked Philip if he liked his new coin.

Then New Year came and fireworks weren't allowed, but Lord Baden-Powell died so they made do with that instead as Scouts from all over Sussex gathered on The Level for a mournful jamboree. Philip watched it all from Hal's window through Orson's new Christmas binoculars. Hal's man was there to dress Hal and carry him from his bed down the stairs to his wheelchair, which waited outside on the drive. Hal's man was called Marion and had arms like oil drums.

Marion buckled Hal in and heaped rugs over his legs. He pushed his hands into mitts and placed a sheepskin cap over his head. Then he whistled for his greyhound, who was called Dirk. Orson said that sometimes on their walks, Dirk towed Hal's chair down icy streets, and Hal's face lit up with what everyone agreed was happiness.

'Coming, Beaumont?' said Orson. He pushed Dirk's lead in his pocket, in case Hal fancied a tow.

Outside, Marion let Orson and Philip push Hal's chair, one at each handle, until they reached the frozen boating pond where Marion told them to wait while he and Dirk nipped up the road to put a bet on. Then he disappeared into the crowd, with Dirk trotting to heel.

On The Level, thousands of Boy Scout legs were turning blue in the cold misery of the day. Grown-up men in Scout uniforms boomed out prayers and hymns through loudspeakers. Orson complained about the obstruction to Hal's usual route. Philip peered through the binoculars.

'Tubby! Look! There's Tubby!'

It had been months.

Orson put on his specs.

Tubby was taller but as thin as ever. 'Poor Lord B-P,' he said after he'd escaped the ranks of boys. His knees knocked.

'Tell him,' said Orson, although they stood together in a huddle, 'that he may borrow one of Hal's blankets.'

Philip gawped. 'Crikey, thanks, Orson. Thanks, Hal.' He laid one of Hal's blankets across Tubby's shoulders, Red Indian-style. Orson passed his cornet of sweets to Philip, and Philip passed it to Tubby. 'Ta very much, Orson,' said Philip.

'Ta, Phil,' said Tubby, 'it's my lucky day,' and Philip felt something warm and sweet buzz through his chest.

Orson stowed the cornet in his pocket. 'Right,' he said. 'Are we ready?'

'What about Marion? He told us to wait here.'

Orson took up position behind Hal's chair and nodded at Philip to do the same. 'Is Norman coming?'

'Are you coming, Tubby?'

''Course,' said Tubby. 'I'll help you push.'

The sun was falling fierce and red by the time they made it to the promenade. Behind them, the windows of the Queen's Hotel were on fire. Before them, on the derelict beach, a roll of razor wire blew past like tumbleweed. Tank-traps rose like dark, squat lookouts. The wind was up. The tide was swollen with winter.

Orson parked Hal at the railings. 'What larks!' said Tubby.

They eased themselves through a small gap in the fence and made a dash down the beach, weaving their way through the anti-landing spikes as if the entire beach were an obstacle course and this was Sports Day at school. Orson waved them into the shelter of the Pier, out of the roar of the wind. Tubby was still smiling when Orson gave him a sherbet lemon, told him to sit down, took Dirk's lead from his pocket and strapped him, looping the lead round and round his middle, to a steel pile.

Philip felt strange. Orson hadn't said anything about a game.

Orson turned to wave cheerily at Hal on the prom.

'I'm It!' Tubby laughed.

'Yes,' said Orson. 'You are. So close your eyes and count to two hundred.'

The sea hissed up the beach. Seaweed lay rotting everywhere and, not far from the Pier, the carcass of a dog rolled in the surf. Philip stared at Tubby, transfixed by the dream of what you could do if no one was looking.

'Fifteen. Sixteen. Seventeen . . .'

Orson tugged hard on Philip's arm. 'Come on.'

'Twenty, twenty-one, twenty-two . . .'

'The tide's on its way in, not out.' But already he could feel himself succumbing to the spell of Orson's orders.

'Hurry, Beaumont. Hal's all by himself.'

Philip turned, trudged back up the beach, and was halfway to the prom when he stopped. *Was* it a game? He looked from Tubby to the waves to Orson and back again. Then he remembered Clarence.

The stones crunched loud beneath his feet as he ran. 'Tubby's not a Jew!' he panted at Orson. 'I told you before!'

'You don't know what one is.'

'We can't leave him down there.'

'He's a good pretend Jew.'

The sea churned. Tubby's count was growing fainter. When they reached the prom, Hal was trembling in his chair.

'Hal, look!' sang Orson. 'Can you see the little Jew? He's going to have a wash.'

'Crikey. Hal's having another fit.'

'No he's not, Beaumont. He's shivering and he's sad. You can't just forget your promise now that we're here.'

Philip felt his brain go limp. Hal was shaking, Tubby was on number one hundred and forty-three, and the sea was already lapping at him like a tongue.

He shook himself and turned.

'Where are you going?' Orson hollered. 'I haven't said it's time!'

Philip was running and sliding back down the shingle, the stones turning underfoot. 'Tubby doesn't understand!'

'Traitor! You traitor, Beaumont! You're no friend of ours! Not now you're not! Do you hear me?'

He wobbled into a run. Clarence was dead, Tubby was still forbidden, and now, Orson would hate him for ever because that was how much he loved Hal.

39

In the solitude of his kitchen-turned-apartment, Otto didn't hear the
footsteps on the terrace, and as the door creaked opened, tea from the
pot splashed and scalded his hand. He'd forgotten to turn the key in
the lock.

The brown top of a head appeared, then a small face. The boy
could have been the ghost of another.

'I heard someone,' the boy said. 'Are you a tramp?'

Otto looked and then quickly turned away. The boy's arrival was
a shock in his afternoon, but even greater was the shock of the
resemblance.

At Sachsenhausen, Dr Metzger had rigged up a mechanized hammer that could deliver a blow to the head every five seconds. Before
he died from his injuries, Jakob – a bright-eyed boy who'd once lived
with his mother, his baby sister and a pet goose called Gigi – went
insane.

'Am I a tramp?' He ran cold water over his hand. 'No . . .'

'You look like a tramp.'

'That's because I am a painter, and the two are easily confused.'

'Why does your hair look like that?'

'Like what?'

'Like it does.'

'I cut it myself. I'm getting quite good. I don't even need a mirror.'

'You *do*,' said the boy. 'You do need a mirror.' He peered into the kitchen, observing its odd state: the table pushed up against the wall; the mattress in the middle of the floor; the vegetables and drawings that littered the countertops.

'Have you stolen those vegetables from the Park?'

'I have.' His heart was leaden. *Go, go*, he wanted to say. But he lowered himself to his haunches, and met the boy at eye level.

The boy stepped past him. 'Why do you keep your shutters closed?'

'You know already: I am a shameless vegetable thief. This said, I would be grateful if you didn't tell anyone I was here stealing vegetables because the police would lock me up.'

Philip didn't want to say that he, too, understood the fear of prison. 'Are you foreign?' he asked.

'Do I sound foreign?'

'You do a little.'

'Well, that's because I'm Welsh.' He clapped his hands together. 'Now then!' He went to the sink and rinsed out a second cup. 'Tea?'

Philip nodded. Tea was foul but no one had offered it to him before in a grown-up way.

The following day, three cheery taps sounded on the door, and he appeared again, bearing his sketchbook. 'Father Christmas brought it,' he said, and, in that moment, something crossed his face. 'Were you here on Christmas Day?'

'I was,' said Otto.

'Alone?'

'I'm rather good at being on my own.'

'Without any goose or presents?'

He smiled. 'I am Jewish, you see, and we have different holidays.'

'You're a Jew?'

'Yes,' he said. 'A *Welsh* Jew.'

'A Welsh Jewish painter?'

Otto nodded. 'A Welsh Jewish painter vegetable thief.'

'Why do you say "Velsh"?'

He could see the boy trying not to laugh at him. 'It's the vay ve speak in Vales.'

'I don't believe you.'

'Truly. For example, you and I would say "Paris", but Parisians themselves would say "Paree". It is the same only different.'

'I can never draw a Spitfire.' He clutched his sketchbook to him.

'They *are* tricky . . . I may be able to assist. But first, you must tell me your name.'

'Philip,' said Philip. He reached into his pocket and held out a boiled sweet. 'Have it. I don't mind.'

And Otto saw again the small red lozenge stuck to Jakob's clenched, dead palm.

The borders of Otto's world were narrow, but he took a grim comfort in that. He travelled only between the Crescent – the back of it – and St Wilfred's, with forays into town to look for work. Employment was the challenge, a greater one than he'd anticipated. The theatre that had once employed him to paint sets was shut for the war. The owner of the camouflage factory had regarded him warily. One of the painters working on the Pavilion, repairing the blast damage, knew that he'd been imprisoned at the Camp. Brighton was a small town. Small towns the world over were suspicious. Small towns awaiting invasion were hostile.

He ate once a day at the soup kitchen. Most days passed in the wide loneliness of the church's nave. Winter eased. Spring took delicate hold. He saw no one except for the boy, who arrived almost daily at the back door with his sketchbook.

She appeared in April.

He was returning after another failed effort at job-seeking and considered avoiding her – turning the corner or dashing across the road – for she seemed to emerge from another realm and the distance between their worlds was painful. How exotic her happiness seemed. How blind. Yet when she spotted him, there on a mundane street, below the brick face of the Technical College, he suddenly felt it was possible to die from the want of her – he who knew death as more than a lover's convention; he who knew its terrible intimacy with life; its brute weight; the body carried from the Camp's gallows.

She wore her hair pinned back and rolled. A small ridiculous hat sat on her head at an unnatural angle, defying gravity. Her hat, her bag and shoes matched. She looked prettily, predictably bourgeois. Something had happened to her. This wasn't a woman who would be seen carrying bags of books or walking up hills to labour camps or stripping off her stockings in the heat of the day. Yet however well she'd disguised herself, she couldn't hide her pleasure at the sight of him.

'Otto!'

He ran a hand through his hair. 'Mrs Beaumont.'

'Evelyn!'

'Of course.' He nodded solemnly. He must have looked to her like a pauper.

'How goes the fresco?'

'Well,' he nodded. 'Yes. Thank you . . .'

Her face was heavily powdered. Her lips were crimson. 'I hope Geoffrey and I will be invited to the private view?'

Was it irony? 'I don't think so . . . I mean, I don't expect there will be one. A church . . . Wartime . . .' He smiled at the pavement. 'A Jew . . .'

'Don't be silly.' She blushed and turned her face to the sky. 'Glorious weather.'

'Yes.' How long before he could take his leave?

'Though the nights,' she added, 'are still very cool.'

The weather. She spoke to him of the weather. Could the injury be any worse?

'With winter past, no doubt we shall have to ready ourselves again.'

'Shall we?' He hoped that was a drop of rain.

'For the invasion,' she said. 'The crossing . . .'

'Of course.' He kept a straight face. 'Those Germans.'

She caught her lip in her teeth and smiled. 'I wonder if you can guess where I'm going.'

'To read at someone?'

She laughed, and he wished that he could pluck it from the air between them, the music of her.

April blossom drifted at their feet. A tram went ringing and dinging past. The silence after it passed left him mournful.

At length, she looked up, as if a decision had been made; a gamble, calculated. 'Tell me, Otto. May I borrow you for an hour or so?'

Inside the lecture theatre, the omnipresent porter motioned them down the steps. The rows of neat heads descended in tiers. The over-sized chart of the Periodic Table was as certain as ever, and their host, once more, presided gloomily.

Mr Hatchett sat midway along. She nodded to him as they passed. 'My butcher,' she said to Otto, and she felt herself thrill to the case of those words and also, to the presence of Otto beside her – Otto who, like her, had loved *The Waves*. She felt slightly giddy at the thought that Mrs Woolf was about to arrive. 'Back by popular demand,' she whispered to him, 'though I don't imagine she gives two hoots for "popular" anything. I'm quite sure she's above all that.'

They waited. The rows of heads waited. Otto's arm rested next to hers on the armrest, and she studied, eyes aslant, the dark hairs that escaped his white shirt cuff. He didn't cede the armrest to her, nor did she move her arm from it and fold her hands in her lap. The pressure of his arm was somehow delicious. He smelled of French cigarettes and carbolic soap. His nails, rimmed in cobalt blue, needed a trim. From the corner of her eyes, she could see fine white streaks of plaster in his hair. She uncrossed her ankles and crossed one leg over the other, gently swinging a foot. Did his eye follow the line of her leg?

Their host, ever gloomier, waited. She turned to Otto, caught his eye, and nodded at the man's misanthropic face. He returned the joke of her smile. The back of his hand brushed hers. She made small talk. He nodded and smiled.

After a full three-quarters of an hour, the porter delivered a note to their host, who approached the lectern and stated the obvious. 'Mrs Woolf has not arrived. Would you please make your way to the exit.'

No apology, no explanation. 'I can't understand it,' she said as they joined the departing crowd. 'Perhaps it's the trains. Trouble on the line from Lewes. I am so sorry. I've delayed you for no reason.'

They moved down the steps and into the brightness of afternoon. The air smelled of fresh rain and wet earth. 'No,' he smiled, 'no apology needed. I'm grateful in fact. You've reminded me I must read her work for myself.'

'Yes! You must borrow my copy of her latest book. I've made a bit of a mess of it, underlining favourite passages and so on, but . . . No "but". I shall drop it through your letter box.'

'Thank you.'

It was the first time that day that either had referred to his residency at Number 5; to the fact that he was still in hiding on her street. All over Brighton, large homes sat empty, and the Corporation had declared war on the 'undesirables' who were finding their way in. On posters nailed to trees, pub doors and public shelters, neighbours were encouraged to report any sightings to the police.

As they walked together across The Level, towards the Crescent, Evelyn tore a poster from an elm, stuffed it in her coat pocket, and nodded at a bench. 'Shall we get a bit of sun? I don't think I've ever known a lovelier April.'

He brushed rainwater from the bench and spread out his jacket. She demurred – was it his only jacket? – then sat and made room for him on it. A current hummed in the narrow gap between their bodies. Their shoulders nudged. She turned her face to the sun. He studied the homeless men under the elms. In that moment, she felt to him like a charm against that fate.

Her questions came, one after another, as if her previous restraint had been nothing more than thin ice on a puddle. Why, she wanted to know, had he tried to drown himself? Why had he been so rude at first? Why did his passport read 'Degenerate'? Why had he been in a prison camp in Germany? Did he have a wife? A family? *Had* he ever been a conman or a spy? Which painters did he admire? Had he truly liked *The Waves*? Had he found other work yet in Brighton? How then was he living?

'You, Mrs Superintendent, are worse than any tribunal.'

Her face fell. 'Please don't call me that.'

'Three final questions,' he said.

Did he despise her? she wondered. She closed her eyes like a sea-side mind-reader and the questions she most wanted to ask came. *Who* did that to your back? How did it happen? But it was a curiosity too far.

'How did you come by the counterfeit money?'

He stiffened. He resented the need to explain, and yet he wanted her to understand; to know that he was not 'undesirable'. 'As I said to your husband, they had – they still have, I imagine – a counterfeiting operation at Sachsenhausen. The plan, at least at that time, was to weaken the British economy by dropping counterfeit notes from planes. When they do, the hope is that those who find it will be greedy enough to use it.'

'Like you were.' She turned to him.

'Yes.' He met her eyes. 'They stuffed me with notes when I left Berlin. It amused them greatly. When I arrived in England, I was desperate. I couldn't find work. I had nowhere to live. For a long while, no one would agree to contact the Bishop for me. I was terrified of being locked up again. I used the forgeries as sparingly as I could – out of fear of being caught, I should add, not out of virtue.'

'And then you were.'

'And then I was . . . ?'

'Caught. Locked up again. By my husband.'

'Yes.' He rubbed paint from his fingers. 'So to speak.'

'Why did you paint Mr Pirazzini?'

He shrugged. 'No death should go unmarked. Countless do.'

'And why did you paint the stump of his finger?'

'Is that your third and final question?'

She smiled. 'It is a sub-point of my second question.'

'Was it wrong of me?'

'On the contrary . . .' She held his gaze. Then, 'He was a tailor. Did you know that? Highly skilled. But I suppose it only takes one careless moment and . . .'

He laughed. His old rancorous laugh again.

She bristled. 'I only mean, Otto, that no one deliberately puts their finger in a pair of shears.'

'No,' he said, 'others do it for you.'

She turned, her eyes wide.

'Mussolini's men stormed his shop in Pisa in '27.'

She bowed her head.

'Why,' he said, 'do you think he and his wife came to Britain?'

Why, she wondered, did she always understand everything too late?

He stood. 'I must go.' The sight of her walking away from him would be too much. She'd smile, of course. She might turn to wave. But even as they'd sat speaking more frankly than they ever had, he blamed her, inwardly and fiercely, for the devastation of his heart, for her blindness to it.

'Yes! Forgive me,' she said, rising, her thoughts reeling. 'I've kept you too long.'

He pretended to assess the sky. 'I'll get a little work done before I lose the light in the church.'

She touched his arm. 'Final question?'

He winced, hardly able to bear it, her touch. Her lipstick had worn off. Her silly hat was askew, or even more askew. Her hair was unrolling in the April breeze and she patted at it anxiously as she felt his eyes taking her in. *La petite bourgeoise.* But she looked – *she was* – achingly lovely. Of course, as chance would have it, she was also the Superintendent's wife, and he was too many things: a Jew, a refugee, an enemy alien, a degenerate and an undesirable. One didn't want to be many things. One was meant to be singular and pure. Any fantasy he might have entertained about her was as banal as it was tormenting. Life, after all, was simply to be endured.

She had only taken a kind interest in his 'case'. She had touched his sleeve and smiled compassionately. But even as he schooled himself in the facts of the matter, a pair of sparrowhawks appeared overhead, and in that moment, as she looked up too, her face alight, he felt the force of their lives tangle.

'Look!' Her hat was sliding off. 'I used to see them over Race Hill on my way to the infirmary.'

The male was roller-coasting on the thermals.

'We have these birds in Berlin too. They're sacred in German myth. They live in the grove of the gods. I used to watch them as a boy. They're the only birds of prey I know of that hunt in the city. He's trying to win the female.'

Fantasy talk, more fantasy. Why did he do it to himself?

'Third question . . .' She picked up his jacket from the bench and shook out its creases. 'What is the subject of your fresco? You never said.'

He looked past her coolly. The old yearning was overwhelming him again. He had to repel her, to undo the force of her. 'Bathsheba.' He tossed the word carelessly into the breeze. 'The adulteress. Quite the subject for a little working-class Church of England parish, don't you think?'

He heard her start to speak, to utter something bland and courteous, but he wouldn't have it. Blood rushed to his head; the old ringing in his ears returned; his shirt clung to him. How pointless everything was. The April sky was crashing in, blue and too bright, and he had to interrupt, to speak over whatever it was she was so decorously uttering. 'Indeed it is astonishing,' he said with determined indifference, 'that the Bishop ever agreed to the idea. You see, Mrs Beaumont, it is not for nothing that my passport is stamped "Degenerate". I have a knack of falling foul of good society. I wasn't made for it. I have no interest in it. As an artist I am drawn to actresses, dancers and whores – the hatless women of this world – and their themes. Women, in other words, who are alive.' He flicked something, a fly or a bee, from his sleeve. 'Thank you for the diversion. As we're nearly at the Crescent, forgive me, but I shan't see you home.'

She stood for long moments and watched him recede, his words scoring the air. She still held his jacket. He had abandoned it to spite. Why had she ever felt glad of his company? Who was he to her?

41

She had put their exchange from her mind. He was no one, she told herself, a stranger, and she, she had grown sensible at last, 'sensible' in the English sense of the word . . . She no longer dwelled. In fact, in recent months, she had succeeded in putting most sensitivities behind her, for what use finally was all that feeling in a war? Who did it help? What cause did it serve? Not hers certainly. She had never felt as low as she had in the past year.

She was no longer the *femme-enfant* of days gone by. That was Sylvia's term of endearment for her. But no more. How exhausting that person had been, for herself and for Geoffrey too. It was as Sylvia had said. Love, lasting love, was based on compromise. On sacrifice. Perhaps his mistress, wherever he kept her, had *saved* their marriage, not broken it. Sylvia said that was often the way. She had to trust in those things, and she did, or she almost did, as long as she didn't *dwell*.

In any case, she was enjoying her new sense of capability. At last she was at ease in the kitchen she had inherited from Tillie – her own kitchen. The WI classes had been a success. A whole chicken lay before her now, plucked and gutted. Her knife slid cleanly through the flesh and bone. She was jointing the bird like she'd been born to it. Even Mr Hatchett had come to trust her at last. He'd promised to set aside the next plump pheasant or duck. They had commiserated briefly over the cancelled lecture, but in truth, she had practically forgotten it already.

Life was busy. She made sure it was. She, Mrs Chavasse and the other ladies of the WI visited the wounded in hospital three days a week, and at last she'd grown used to the blood and the smells and the ravings. She remained bright and cheery through it all. She let no one down. Being cheery for others cheered oneself up. Platitudes saw one through. Little by little, she was remaking herself.

At home, there were also changes. She'd decided to redecorate, starting with the sitting room. There was a great deal to be said for keeping up appearances. Everything was only a matter of outlook. She'd already replaced Geoffrey's wingback chair and its old-fashioned antimaccassar. She'd even bought one of those new coffee tables, though they never drank coffee, and she had had everything painted afresh.

Not by Otto Gottlieb, however. She'd considered it; she'd even told Geoffrey she had. The man was in need of work. That's what he'd told her, she explained to Geoffrey, when she had bumped into him recently by the Technical College. She didn't mention the lecture to Geoffrey — because, after all, there had been no lecture!

She had, she said, considered offering him the work, but in truth, she felt it would be too awkward. He was moody. Some people just tended to make things worse for themselves, didn't they?

How relieved Geoffrey had looked. And how vulnerable. She could see that now. It had taken her by surprise but suddenly she saw it. Even now, he was frightened he might lose her; that she might have eyes for another man; for an artist, a radical, a man who seemed to share some of her own passions. He was afraid, too, that even if she did stay, she would never love him as she once had; that she had come to see too many of his failings.

His face had looked like Philip's when he woke in the night in the grip of a bad dream. Geoffrey had been on the edge of something, his own chalky precipice, and all he could think about – she knew, she could feel it in him – was the need to watch his step; to not put a foot wrong; to love her as much as she would tolerate. It touched some part of her. Surely, if love was love, it didn't end – it could never be put entirely away – and she *had* loved him.

She could feel it again. She was sure. Or a part of her could. So what followed was a harmless enough lie. And only a small betrayal of Otto Gottlieb. 'If I'm honest, I do hope the commission at St Wilf's is completed soon. Perhaps you could help him find some bit of work? To keep him better occupied? I saw him hanging about the Salvation Army the other day. No doubt it was for the evening meal, but I fear he might also be a little taken with me.'

It had worked. Geoffrey immediately said yes, yes, of course he would find him some sort of employment in town, shift work perhaps, a job that wouldn't impede the progress of the Lord Bishop's mural.

If she had belittled Otto to Geoffrey with those comments, she had also looked after each of them as well as she was able. Geoffrey was reassured of her loyalty and soon, Otto Gottlieb would have paid work.

Above their heads, the old blood mark on the ceiling had been convincingly covered at last by the painters. With it, she had also insisted, mentally, on putting the old spectre of childbirth behind her. After all these years, she told Geoffrey she'd decided not to trust in Dr Moore and his doom-laden warnings. She would ask James to recommend someone on Harley Street. They should have had a second opinion long ago. She was thirty-three but children might still be a possibility. It was important to act now, she said, in case he was called away. Other women were falling pregnant, war or no war.

Why shouldn't she? Wasn't that what they had both wanted from the start?

He had kissed the top of her head and taken her on to his lap. 'Yes,' he said. 'You're right. Of course you're right.'

Now, in her kitchen, the chicken stew was gently bubbling.

She had rinsed her hands and was scrubbing her nails at the sink when the telephone went, startling her from thought.

'Yes, Mrs Chavasse . . . Yes, I remember. The Book Tea . . . Well, please don't give it another thought. There's no need to –' She gripped the cord. 'No, I simply assumed . . . Because just last week her lecture at the –' She reached for the banister. 'No, I hadn't heard . . .' She sank to the staircase. 'Mrs Chavasse? Mrs Chavasse, I'm afraid I must ring off because my son is coming through the door from school. Thank you for . . . Yes, sad, very sad indeed. Thank you for ringing.'

The receiver dangled in her hand like something dead; like the chicken with its broken neck, which she'd carried home only an hour before from Mr Hatchett's when the world had still been itself. She sat hunched on the second step. She needed to be small. She needed to be still. She was vaguely aware of a nail on the step beneath her, its sharp tip pushing its way up through the stair carpet into her thigh, but she felt no pain, no sting, nothing but the tolling of her heart.

When Otto heard someone at the back door, he opened it, expecting the boy to enter, the childish chatter always immediate and reassuring

'Mrs Beaumont, to what do I owe –?'

Her eyes were swollen; her face was red and raw. She was clutching the jacket he'd abandoned on The Level that day a fortnight before and she also clutched the book she had promised him,

299

Mrs Woolf's latest novel, *The Years*. He stood to one side and motioned her through. 'Please. Yes. Please come in. My jacket, thank you. How kind of you to bother. May I get you something? A cup of tea or' – he smiled falteringly – 'a cup of tea?'

'Listen,' she said. 'Just listen to this.' Her eyes were alight. She still wore her apron. Blood stained its front. She opened the book and started to read. 'It's Rose and Sara speaking. Rose speaks first. *"'What did you do today?' she said at length, looking up abruptly.*

'"'Went out with Rose,' said Sara.

'"'And what did you do with Rose?' said Maggie. She spoke absent-mindedly. Sara turned and glanced at her. Then she began to play again." She's playing piano,' said Evelyn fiercely, looking up at him. The book trembled in her hand.

He took a seat on a kitchen chair and stared at the linoleum, grave and intent.

She continued: *'"'Stood on the bridge and looked into the water,' she hummed, in time to the music."* That's Sara. *"'Running water; flowing water. May my bones turn to coral; and fish light their lanthorns; fish light their green lanthorns in my eyes.'"* What,' she demanded of Otto, shaking the book, 'what is that supposed to mean?' Tears slid down her face. 'And this. Just listen to this.' She screwed up her eyes and flipped pages. 'It's Sara again: *"'So I put on my hat and coat and rushed out in a rage,' she continued, 'and stood on the bridge, and said, "Am I a weed, carried this way, that way, on a tide that comes twice a day without meaning?"'"'*

She was sobbing. 'Mrs Woolf . . . I can't believe it.'

'I am so very sorry,' he said, for he understood. He understood entirely.

She raised the skirt of her apron and pressed it hard to her face. 'Apparently, children spotted her. In the Ouse. Near the bank, I think.

Can you believe it? They thought she was . . .' She released the apron. Her eyes flashed. 'They thought she was *a log*.'

She looked away, to the ceiling, to the floor, to the mattress on the floor. She kicked at it in frustration. 'What on earth is that doing here? I said that you could sleep in the study. Not in the kitchen. Not on their mattress. Have you *no* regard for other people's things?'

'Forgive me,' he said quickly. 'I'll return it as soon as you go.'

She covered her eyes with her hand, then balled her hand into a fist and hit her head as if to force herself to return to the self who had been calmly jointing a chicken just an hour before. 'No . . . No. Forgive me.' She shoved her hair back and turned her face up, inhaling hard. 'I don't mean that at all. You're trying to live out of just the one room. I know that. It's thoughtful of you.'

He stood and gently removed the book from her hand, and then tenderly, slowly, drew her to him. 'You've had a bad shock.' Her arms were goose-pimpled. She was trembling. His arm hovered in the air near her back. Could he? In that moment it seemed the only thing that was right and good. He rubbed her back, up and down, up and down. Her shoulders convulsed. 'Shhh . . .' he said. 'Shhh now.'

She fell stiffly against him. Her breathing slowed and deepened.

'It's a sad, sad thing,' he murmured. 'It's only natural you're upset.' Up and down, up and down, his palm against her back. She let her cheek rest against his chest. 'Shhh now,' he said.

Neither of them saw Philip appear at the threshold and freeze, like a boy caught in a spell.

Nor did either see him disappear again and race back along the perimeter path, across the terrace, up the staircase to his bedroom, where he opened his sketchbook and started tearing it apart.

She raised her head and wiped her eyes with her fists. 'I am so sorry.' She pulled a hair from her mouth. 'You must think me mad.'

'On the contrary. I thought you a little mad before. Today I think you're really quite sane.'

She smoothed down her apron, then her hair. She was returning to herself. Soon she would leave. This wouldn't happen again – he knew that. He braced himself for the emptiness of the room after her.

'I'm very grateful,' she said.

Her composure had returned.

'Whatever for?'

She mustered a smile. 'May I ask a favour?'

'There's no need,' and he smiled. 'I will say nothing to anyone. Please don't worry about such things.'

She shook her head, impatient – with herself. 'It isn't so much a favour as a question.'

It had only entered her head as she'd stood, trembling, next to him. Could she say it aloud? Her thoughts were small fires springing up. She'd dampen one down only for another to rise up. *Life, it hardly lasts.* We *hardly last. Fear nibbles away at it, at what there is of it, like fish at the drowned, like worms at the beloved dead. Death doesn't ravage life. It's fear, fear.* And she longed to slide free of its vicious grip.

He could still, almost, feel the warmth of her face against his chest; the dip of her back under his palm. He picked up *The Years* and, once more, saw her hands clasping it in her passion.

'Is it too late,' she began, in the overly modulated voice that came out of her when she was anxious, 'is it too late to ask if you are still in need of a female model?'

He looked up.

'I can sit tolerably well. Deportment classes . . . once upon a time.' She wiped her face again, reached for the book, placed it on her head and started to walk. Then she walked back towards him, book still on head, and smiled without hope.

42

May came helplessly round once more. The horse chestnuts sprang green and full-breasted, the Park was alive with birdsong, and Mrs Dalrymple, true to her word, died of her own accord. On a bright Saturday afternoon, a pair of haughty black horses with plumes on their heads arrived on the Crescent, pulling a glass carriage followed by four men whom no one knew. Her grown-up sons from London, somebody said. Each wore a sleek top hat and a hard face.

Geoffrey had already left for a meeting at the local Army base but Philip and Evelyn came out of the house to bow their heads as the gleaming coffin glided by. Not one of Mrs Dalrymple's sons had knocked on their door to ask about her final days. Not one had invited them to any wake, funeral or funeral tea. They only bore her away.

'Men are execrable buggers,' Philip whispered as they passed, and his mother squeezed his hand. He turned his face up to her. *Don't be stolen away from us*, he wanted to say. *Don't go again to Number 5, to that man.*

Instead he feigned childishness for her. 'Will Mrs Dalrymple meet Clarence in Heaven?'

In those final days, the ordinary world imploded slowly.

At Army HQ, Geoffrey shook Lieutenant Lowell's left hand.

'Plans for the weekend?' asked Lowell.

'Only the usual,' he smiled. He might bowl a few balls with his son. Nine now and growing fast . . .

He couldn't stop turning it over in his mind. Neither a suicide attempt nor a botched operation nor his own subterfuge had resolved the problem of Otto Gottlieb. Now it so happened that the man was frequenting a soup kitchen across from their house. Was there no removing him from their lives?

In one way, he reasoned, it was merely as Evelyn had said: he would be doing the man a favour. Gottlieb was to report for work the following morning at seven. Full instructions were in the Unit's letter, which Geoffrey slipped now into his breast pocket for safe keeping. There were always ambiguities, he thought. Grey areas.

He wanted only for them to be a couple again, for life to return to itself – he wanted it desperately – and now, miraculously, it seemed she wanted that too. Her forgiveness was more than he deserved – sometimes that knowledge hit him like an SC-50 – and as he walked into what passed in Brighton for an Officers' Mess, with that bomb still falling and the letter strange in his pocket, he felt the urgent need of the single malt the Lieutenant was already ordering at the bar.

'Slàinte!' said the Lieutenant. The bottle landed between them on the table.

Geoffrey knocked back the shot and forgot the letter, or, rather, he knocked back the shot so he would forget the letter. No one required Gottlieb to take the job.

'I don't imagine you've heard about Hess?' said the Lieutenant, repinning his empty sleeve. Lowell's diction was strangely top-drawer in that makeshift Mess. He was one of those Edinburgh chaps who'd had every trace of Scottishness knocked out of him at Scotland's best public school.

'The Deputy Führer?' said Geoffrey. 'I've heard *of* Hess. I haven't heard about him.'

Lowell smoothed the tips of his moustache. 'Landed in a twin-engine fighter plane in Scotland on the 10th. Somewhere south of Glasgow. Was flying solo – in every sense of the word apparently. German High Command is furious.'

'Did we pick him up or did he turn himself in?' The whisky burned pleasurably in his throat. He forgot Gottlieb. He forgot that he rarely drank.

'A ploughman arrested him in his field with the help of' – Lowell guffawed – 'a pitchfork. It's classified still of course. The papers don't have it yet. Won't for a few more days, I shouldn't think. He's insisting he speaks to Churchill.' He nodded encouragingly towards the bottle.

'Brave man,' Geoffrey said.

Lowell let out a short laugh. 'Or just plain barking.'

An Army driver delivered him to his front door. In the sitting room, he collapsed into his chair. Where were the old wingbacks? Who'd taken them? He wanted their cover, like a spooked horse wanted its blinkers. He was woozy, unwell. But why spooked? Why jangled? He couldn't recall. Evelyn appeared happy again. Sometimes they held each other in the night. That was something surely. And they hadn't been bombed out of their home. The enemy hadn't landed. His funk was only the by-product of half a bottle of whisky on a Saturday afternoon. In spite of his size, he couldn't handle it. He had never been a merry drunk.

Philip appeared in the doorway and stared at the spectacle of his father slouched in his chair. Cricket was off.

Evelyn arrived with a ham-and-cress sandwich on a plate and a cup of tea. 'Your father is tired,' she said.

Eyes closed, Geoffrey reached into his breast pocket and produced the letter. 'I'll walk this up to . . .' he said sleepily. 'It only needs an envelope.' Where was it to go? His thoughts slipped from his mind like loose change from his pockets.

'A job?' she said, her voice low. 'You've found one?'

And it came to him, fleetingly. 'A *paying* job,' he slurred. 'Army shift work.'

She walked to Geoffrey's study, past their son who hovered, and checked the desk for Bank stationery. None. She returned to the sitting room, opened the drawer in the side table, and removed the box of notepaper that Philip had given her at Christmas. She glanced back at him. He couldn't take his eyes off his father.

'He only needs a bit of rest, darling.'

She read the letter of instruction quickly, hesitated, shook the words from her mind, and folded it into a neat oblong. On the envelope, she wrote Otto's name. It was an odd little pleasure.

'I'll drop this across to the Salvation Army and ask them to pass it to him when he comes in for his meal – this evening with any luck.'

'Good thinking.' He sighed.

'Saves you going up to St Wilf's.' She bent and kissed his cheek. 'Thank you.'

He grimaced drunkenly. 'Let's say no more of it.'

'You haven't touched your sandwich.'

'Did I tell you the latest?'

She smiled and perched on the arm of his chair.

'Rudolf Hess has landed in Scotland. Can you believe it? Last Saturday. The Führer and Mrs Deputy Führer have gone their separate ways, it would seem.' Opening one eye, he winked at her. 'Now he wants to bend Churchill's ear.'

She stroked his cheek and traced his lips with her fingertips. There was no other woman. Not any longer. She knew it finally. They could repair their lives. For Philip, for the family they were, they would.

'Philip, darling? Philip . . .' She pivoted on the chair arm. 'Why don't you play in the Park until –'

But already he was gone.

43

Hanover Crescent was, as always, as silent as it was grand. Philip stood on the wide curving drive and, hand to mouth, called high. 'Orson, I know you're there!'

The sash on the overhead window fell with a clunk.

'I have something to tell you!'

The pane was dark against the light of day but he knew Orson was up there.

'News from Army HQ . . . My father was there this afternoon.'

The sash lifted by inches – 'Bugger off, Beaumont' – and the curtains fell.

It was a full hour before Philip conceded defeat and retreated from the home of the Stewart-Forbeses. He'd reached the end of the arc of the drive when, at last, a voice called out begrudgingly. 'Has Hitler landed?'

He made himself walk, not run, to the front door where Orson's face was a single eye and a slice of cheek through the narrow gap.

'No,' Philip said. 'Not him but –'

'I'm bored of your tricks, Beaumont.'

'Rudolf Hess has landed in Scotland. He's Hitler's next-in-command. He flew in by himself last Saturday. He's on his way south. To meet Churchill. Even the papers don't know.'

'Hess loves England,' Orson declared.

'May I come in now?'

Orson's single eye narrowed. 'You betrayed Hal.'

'But Tubby might have drowned.'

'Jew-lover,' hissed the crack in the door.

And now it was closing. 'Wait.' He felt hot, sick, alone. 'There's more.' A fuse of words was burning through his gut, up his throat and into his mouth.

At last it exploded: 'I know where there's a real Jew.'

The door blew off its hinges.

'Come in,' said Orson.

Upstairs in Hal's room, Orson prepared. He stuffed the glassy stocking deep in his pocket. He gave Philip the belt, and Philip threaded it down his coat sleeve. They were ready, Orson said.

The sky was grey, dirty. Billet's General Store was on the way. 'Sweets first. We need energy.'

The bell tinkled as they entered. The smell of tea and floor wax was reassuring. On every shelf, jars gleamed.

Gobstoppers, sherbet lemons and coconut pips.

Strawberry bonbons, aniseed balls and barley sugar.

Imperial mints, bonfire toffees, bull's-eyes, humbugs, cherry drops, fizz balls and chocolate limes.

The array made Philip feel sweaty but Orson was decisive. The large cornet in Mr Billet's hand was already two-thirds full when Orson spotted a jar full to the brim with red, green and white capsules.

'What are those?' he said, his lips parting.

'New in,' said Mr Billet. His scoop hovered. 'Liquorice torpedoes. Crunchy on the outside, chewy on the inside.' He passed Orson a green one to taste.

44

Otto turned the key and a smile took hold of his face. Evelyn darted into the kitchen and passed him something – an envelope. 'Can't stay.' Her eyes flickered warmly. 'Geoffrey's home. Asleep but home.' She glanced at the countertops and saw, among the clutter, their recent work: three pen-and-ink studies of her face; a charcoal drawing of her head in profile; a pencil sketch of her hands; a water-colour of her reading at his kitchen table.

He wished then that he could turn the key on the door, on the day, on the world.

She leafed through the sketches and nodded at the envelope in his hand. 'It's an offer of temporary work with the Army. Geoffrey arranged it earlier.'

He raised an amused eyebrow. 'The Army uses purple stationery?'

She didn't look up. 'Lilac. I had to put it in something. And I thought you'd prefer me as your courier. Geoffrey was going to find you at the church but I intercepted.'

'Thank you . . .' He reached for the cigarette behind his ear. 'I wanted to stay longer but I was losing the light. I'm almost there. Only the final central section remains. The bit I've looked forward to painting most.'

He struck a match against the range. She wasn't listening.

She studied the profile sketch. She looked up, her face clouded, preoccupied. 'I told him I would deliver it to you via the Salvation Army.'

He tapped his nose. 'Understood.'

'I only glanced at it. It's shift work in town. Please don't feel obliged. If you do want it, they need you to report tomorrow by seven.' She dropped the sketch and started opening cupboards, then his Frigidaire, impatiently. 'Apart from those old potatoes, what do you actually have to eat, Otto?'

'I'm fine,' he said. 'Please don't make yourself late back.'

'You're not fine. You're thin. And you can't report for work hungry.'

'Thank you for this.' He waved the envelope. 'Now go. I'm fine. Truly.'

She blinked something back – a thought, a word, an apology.

He turned the key and bent the crown of his head to the door.

Then, late that afternoon, the three cheery taps: Philip.

'One moment!' he shouted through the door. He gathered up the sketches and stowed them in a cupboard, but when he turned the key once more and opened the door, two boys entered instead of one.

'This is my friend Orson,' said Philip.

'How do you do, Orson,' said Otto. His heart lurched at his ribs.

'How do you do.'

'Goodness.' He forced a grin. 'My kitchen, as you can see, Orson, is a poor place to receive guests.'

'He doesn't mind,' said Philip, walking in.

'Not a jot,' said Orson.

'Should I be expecting any other visitors, Philip?' Otto asked warily.

'I shouldn't think so. I only know Orson. And Hal, his brother.'

'His brother . . .'

'His grown-up brother. But Hal has the shakes and a bullet in his head, so I don't think he'll ever be able to come.'

'I'm sorry to hear that, Orson.'

Orson was looking around the room. 'It must be jolly nice having your own secret place.'

'My friends are away at the moment.'

'I hear you're good at drawing.'

'Philip is very good himself. Which reminds me.' He turned to him. 'Long time, no see, my friend.'

'I've been busy . . .' Philip let Hal's belt slide down his coat sleeve. He felt the cold steel of the buckle meet his wrist.

'Too busy to draw?'

'Yes,' he said, 'far too busy for that.'

'We've had exams,' Orson quickly added, 'at school.'

'Well, I am sorry to hear that too.'

'"Vell?"' Orson repeated.

'He's from Wales,' said Philip dully. He felt odd, unhappy, and he didn't know why. He hadn't been able to eat a single sweet on their way there.

Otto watched the wheels turn behind Orson's eyes. The boy had worked it out, though he said nothing. He was clearly older and more knowing than Philip.

At the table, he served them the rhubarb he'd stolen from the fruit plot in the Park and had boiled up with sugar. In the Frigidaire, he still had the cream top from the pint he'd nabbed off a doorstep that morning.

312

'Hurrah!' said Orson to Otto. 'Aren't you having any?'

Otto shook his head and pulled a cigarette from behind his ear.

Philip stared at his bowl like he might be sick.

Orson smiled as he passed Otto the cornet. 'Here, have one of these. Have as many as you like.'

And still, every time: the jar on Dr Metzger's desk, the children's smiles.

'Go on,' said Orson. 'There's lots. The green ones are nice.'

He reached in blindly. A striped sweet appeared in his hand.

'A bull's-eye,' said Orson. Beneath the table, he kicked Philip's foot and flashed a grin.

'What a treat,' Otto declared and turned away to the sink.

Philip eyed Orson across the table. Then Orson nodded and withdrew, not the stocking from his pocket as planned, but something much smaller: a green pill, one of the pair he'd taken that November day from the buried flour tin. It gleamed like treasure on his palm. Then he raised a finger to his lips, glanced over his shoulder, and slipped it into the cornet.

'Thanks very much for the rhubarb!' he sang out, pushing back his chair.

Philip stared at the cornet that Orson had abandoned in the middle of the kitchen table. He couldn't move. Those pills, he knew, weren't pills that made you better . . . And everything started to spin like a propeller in his head. Otto was showing him once again how to draw two lines for the Spitfire's fuselage; next, at their cross-hairs, a large oval; then, for the tail, a quadrilateral; then two more ovals for the wings; and finally, for the tail fins, two small ovals and a little circle. 'You have to find the secret shapes *inside* the thing you want to draw,' he'd explained. It had been so exciting to see the plane, the real thing, appear on his page at last.

Spin, spin, spin, and Otto was hugging his mother and touching her back, and his father was drunk in his chair and too tired for cricket in the Park.

He and Orson were supposed to scare Otto – with Hal's special belt and the lasso of broken glass. Then he was supposed to say: *Leave my mother alone.*

He was reaching for the sweets – to stuff them into his pocket, to carry them and the pill away – when he saw it. Poking out from beneath the fruit bowl. A lilac envelope with his mother's handwriting.

He had given his mother that notepaper set for Christmas. Now here it was, in Otto the Jew Thief's house. She had written him a secret letter.

He pushed back his chair and almost stumbled over the table leg.

'Yes, thanks for the rhubarb!' Then he ran out the door in Orson's wake and didn't stop until they had crossed the Park.

They stood by the burn pile. 'Will he die?' he panted.

'Maybe, maybe not,' said Orson, wiping the sweat from his cheeks. 'Russian courtiers tried to kill Rasputin with cyanide but he didn't die because they fed him pastries and sweet things by accident. Lots of sugar might stop it. I found a book in the library.'

'Is it painful?'

Orson shrugged. 'First it's hard to breathe. Then you fall unconscious. Then you have a heart attack and your skin turns pink. He's German, you know.'

'Not Welsh?'

'Of course not Welsh. A spy, no doubt. We might get a medal.'

'Orson' – he tipped his face to the sky because tears pushed at the backs of his eyes – 'the green liquorice torpedoes look just like the pill.'

'Yes' – Orson pulled up a sock – 'that was lucky, wasn't it?'

314

45

Twilight came and Evelyn was back at Otto's, edging through his door bearing a dinner plate covered by a pot lid. Heads of lilac poked from her skirt pocket.

'What's this,' he laughed, 'my last meal?'

'My Frigidaire is full. Leftovers. You have to eat if you're working for the Army.'

She spotted it then, the cornet of sweets on the table.

'You've found me out,' he said quickly. 'My sweet tooth!' It would do her no good to learn that two neighbourhood children had discovered him.

She laid the plate on the countertop, and, at the tap, started to fill a milk jug for the flowers.

He reached for the cigarette behind his ear but found only a pencil. 'Forgive the question, but where does your husband think you are?'

At the sink, the water chugged. He supposed they'd rowed. He could sense something simmering within her.

'Checking our neighbours' houses, as I do at this hour. I'm not stupid, Otto.'

'I didn't suggest you were.' He checked his shirt pocket, then a cupboard shelf. But nothing. Only an empty packet.

A tendril of hair fell across her cheek and she swatted at it. The tap was still running at the sink. She was lost in some dark haze of thought.

'What is it?' he said. 'You're not yourself.'

She turned, her words quick as a slap. 'You don't know what "myself" is, Otto.'

She bored herself. She bored him. Why *should* he know who or what she was? But none of this could be spoken. *Fear. Fear. That's what separates us.* From others, from ourselves, from life.

She wanted life, she wanted it badly. She needed the world to burst open. To go up in smoke. She wanted the enemy to invade the shore and be done with it. Fear was exhausting, but nothing tired a body like hope.

She watched Otto ransack his one-room home for a cigarette. He was fine. Free now. Happy as long as he had a sketchbook, a French cigarette and a pencil or a paintbox. He knew what his life was. He knew his mind. What had he told her that day on The Level? *I am drawn to actresses, dancers, whores, and their themes. The hatless women of this world. Women who are alive.*

She shivered. His kitchen was draughty and the week had been freakishly cold.

'I'm wrong for it, aren't I?'

'For what?'

'Your Bathsheba.'

He stopped in mid-motion, his face a question.

'I'm entirely wrong.' She looked at the lino. 'I realized when I saw your sketches earlier. They were here before . . . Did you pitch them?'

'Of course not.' So this was the source of her mood. 'I put them away for safe keeping.'

'I thought you rude when I first met you, but actually, although

316

you hide it well, you are unfailingly polite.' She smiled faintly and turned to go. 'You need someone . . . compelling. I know that.'

'Yes. And that day in St Wilf's, I asked you because I wanted you.'

The tap still ran uselessly behind her.

'No, the woman you actually wanted was the woman you saw that evening in the stands at the concert.'

'That isn't true.'

She turned her face to the ceiling. Her cheek, her chin, trembled. 'She was my husband's mistress, incidentally. Or prostitute. Or whore. I don't know the parlance these days. I haven't seen her myself, but you have, and Geoffrey has – obviously – and she is no doubt . . . compelling. Perhaps she can be located.'

'Stand there, please.' He pointed to the sink with his pencil.

She bowed her head. 'No, really . . . It's too late, Otto. But thank you for trying, thank you for your courtesy.' She nodded, her decision made, and walked to the door.

'Yes,' he called. 'Our work together has been ordinary. I grant you that. It lacks life. I've wondered about it a little myself. But that is the work, and if there is any fault, it is mine. *You* are not ordinary, and I am not ordinary. We are not. Go if you want to go, Evelyn. Tell yourself what you like. Pity yourself as much as you like.'

She was struggling to turn the key. The door tended to swell in damp weather. *She is leaving me*, he thought, *always leaving*.

Something hot burst within.

'Fine. Knit for Britain if you must. Pat the hands of the dying. Wear as many fucking hats as you like. As you felt obliged to remind me a moment ago, you are not stupid. But you know as well as I do that the greatest risk in life is to risk nothing.'

He reached for his sketchbook and clapped his hand against it. 'Now either do as I say or leave and don't come back – not with food,

317

flowers, books, keys, jackets, gainful employment or . . . or any other charitable donation. I may be a lost cause, but I am not the lost person in this room.' He bent to breathe, a hand on a knee. 'Nor, I'm afraid, can you expect an apology.'

'You have nothing to apologize for,' she said flatly.

'Leave if you're leaving, Evelyn.'

She stood, her face impassive, her hands balled at her sides.

He turned and continued his search for cigarettes. At the sideboard, he shook another empty packet and swore in German.

'Right,' he said with his back to her. 'It would seem you are still in the room. Good. But I will not allow a word more. I require silence from a model. Your body needs to do the talking. Go stand over there, stand where you were at the sink. Move the lilacs.' He pointed. 'By "go", Evelyn, I mean now . . . Here, give those to me. No – face the sink, not me.' He squinted. 'Leave the tap on. Turn it fully on.' He took a breath. 'No, *on*.' His eyes were hard. 'Now take off your blouse and roll your slip down to your skirt band.'

'You said "clothed".'

'Bathsheba *bathes*. It's what she does, Evelyn. In my experience, it is difficult to bathe with one's clothing on.'

He bent, reached for a paintbox, and kicked a cupboard door shut.

Searching the house, Philip at last found his father upstairs. He'd fallen asleep in his bed right after dinner. A fug of drink and bad breath stirred as he slid through the door. He shook him by the shoulder. 'It's the blackout. We have to close the shutters.'

His father didn't open his eyes. 'Ask your mother, please, Philip.'

'She isn't home.'

Geoffrey sat up, glanced at the clock on the nightstand and buttoned his shirt. 'No . . . Of course she's not. She's checking our neighbours' houses. Nothing to worry about.' Even in the twilight of the room, still drunk, he could feel the force of his son's frown.

Philip stood at the threshold on the edge of light. How could he say it? He was sure, sure . . . Otto was in Number 5. So was his mother. So were the sweets and the torpedo pill.

'Something's wrong,' he said.

His father was searching the sheets for his shirt. '*No*. Nothing's wrong.'

He wobbled on a loose floorboard. 'Her chain with the keys is still on the key board.'

Geoffrey checked the Park. He walked the Crescent. It was a Saturday evening in the middle of May. Not quite dark. It made no sense. He'd have to walk towards town. Perhaps she'd decided on a stroll while he slept. Perhaps she'd left him. He never seemed to shake the fear.

He told Philip to go to Tubby's. He scribbled a note of apology and told him to give it to Tillie when she answered the door.

'But I can't.'

'Why can't you?' His tongue was thick. His head was cement.

'Tubby's forbidden.'

He lowered himself unsteadily to meet his son's heavy gaze. 'Tonight, he is not forbidden. He is unforbidden. He will never be forbidden again. Now go find your toothbrush, your pyjamas and your gas mask. And wear your coat. It's a cold night.'

At the sink, she clutched herself. 'What are you doing?' She could hear him behind her, shovelling coal.

'Making a fire, a low fire. Otherwise you will freeze. There's no hot water, I'm out of paraffin, and you're shivering already.'

'But —'

'Towards me, please . . . Three-quarters. Untense your shoulders. Let them drop a little. Lift your ribcage.' He double-checked the key, pulled a chair up behind the kitchen door, and hooked one long leg over the other.

'Do I turn the tap on again?' How trite everything sounded. She glanced down at herself. Her breasts were small, absurd.

'Yes — on.'

Water gushed forth like a geyser, icy and sharp, and she bent to it, gasping as she splashed her face, her neck, her breasts. Foolish. She felt foolish. And so naked.

She heard him sigh. She waited for him to direct her or to shout, exasperated. It was a brave effort, but it wasn't working. If it was obvious to her, it was obvious to him. In a moment, he would offer her the towel and be done with it. That would be the sensible thing, they'd admit failure, and she'd be released.

Instead, without a word, he lay his sketchbook on the floor at his feet, stood up, and hauled his jumpers and shirt over his head in one swift motion.

She turned to him.

His ribs stood out like a cage of bone. His skin was pasty; his nipples sunken. Beneath his clothes, his body was older than he was. He turned to lay his clothes over the chair back, and she saw then, once more, the hidden landscape of his back; the scar tissue, red and livid; its sheen ghastly in the kitchen light; the iron stamp of hobnails.

He bent for his sketchbook and took his seat again. 'There,' he said, 'I think that's better. Shall we resume?'

Tears stood in her eyes.

His pencil hovered, and he shook his head, smiling into his page, wordlessly saying, *No need, no need for tears.*

'I'm so cold,' she said, and he rose from his chair and went to her.

Evelyn was nowhere. Geoffrey had walked as far as the Pavilion. She would not have gone further in the dark, not without so much as a torch. In any case, the prom was closed; the beach off-limits. Had she taken a coat? Was she in trouble somewhere? Their neighbours' keys jingled madly in his coat pocket, and he had to turn up his collar against the cold. The sleep after dinner had only made him feel worse, more stupefied, less steady on his feet.

The Crescent's windows and towers were blinded, the night was thick – starless, moonless – and now, as he glanced up, there was something else to mystify him. At Number 5, a thin twist of smoke rose, grey and pale, against the blackout.

Squatters. Perhaps an intruder.

The coal glowed in the grate. Otto led her to the fire, and there, in the squeeze between it and the mattress on the floor, she reached for his hand, clutching at his fingers. Was it pity? he wondered. He couldn't bear it. He couldn't. He'd break her arm rather than suffer her kindness. But when her palm pressed his, he understood.

Her body rose as he kissed her – her breast to his chest, her lips to his neck – and the awareness overwhelmed him. He'd go through everything again to arrive at this moment.

Obscene. An obscene thought.

And true.

He reached out, smacking the wall for its switch until there was only the flickering of the fire in the grate. His lips grazed her throat, the hollow of her collarbone, her nipple, and her hands moved over the ruin of his back, light as a child's.

Years. It had been years since he'd been touched.

As Geoffrey turned the knob of Number 5, he had the uncanny sensation of stepping into his own home. The layout was identical: the vestibule, the staircase to the right, the telephone on the side table, a sitting room to the left; a corridor stretching past the study to what had to be the kitchen. Where the floorboards dipped, he was grateful, briefly, for the upright of the banister. With or without the adrenalin, he was conscious he was still drunk. He turned one ear to listen . . . But nothing.

At the entrance to the study, he picked up a brass doorstop and weighed it in his hand.

Later, he wouldn't remember it falling. He'd remember only the scent of lilac as he entered the kitchen; the unprovoked pleasure of it; the moment's transport to their bedroom, where the heavy blooms spilled over the vase next to the clock.

It would be a long, slurred moment before his eyes adjusted – to the heavy shadows and the flickering light, to the impression of bodies on the floor.

Then the scene exploded: the white magnesium flash of her back and the sight of her body wrapped in another.

He was hardly aware of the commotion of cries as they sprang from the mattress. His stare was fixed and dead. No words reached him but he registered dimly that her voice faltered – with tenderness, with pity. He couldn't hear, think, focus. He could only stumble forward, one heavy arm absurdly raised, like a man playing Blind Man's Bluff as his heart failed.

From The Level, a siren blared, louder than their cries, and its moan seemed to stream from their gaping mouths. The two men locked, lurching into the fire, then separated before Geoffrey lunged again. The jug of blossom toppled. Water streamed. The fruit bowl smashed. The half-eaten stew on the plate flew across the floor. Cutlery clattered from its tray. Glasses shattered. Otto's head flew back against a wall and, only as Geoffrey slipped on the floor, did his hand release Otto's neck.

Each man gasped for breath.

Evelyn couldn't stop shaking; it was as if a current ran through her legs, and she felt herself sink to the floor.

Otto pressed his shirt to his head. Blood trickled down his neck as Geoffrey vomited into the sink, then turned, slow and bewildered.

He rubbed his coat sleeve over his mouth and began to cross the room again, bumping into corners, kicking at the wreckage on the floor. *Thank God*, she thought. *He's leaving . . . Thank God.* Then, at the door through which he'd come, he scooped up the brass doorstop as if it were a cricket ball.

In the grate, the embers of the fire collapsed into a pyre of ash. The two men drew close, magnetized. Each smelled the other's sweat and hatred, and each pressed closer by degree, the brass gleaming, until Evelyn, wild-eyed and pale, forced herself between the two beloved bodies.

Geoffrey wavered on the balls of his feet. He looked down at her, his face clammy and waxen, his eyelids heavy. She could smell the blood on his shirt; the vomit on his breath; the whisky, stale from his pores. The sirens wailed over the sky, the sea, the cliffs, but still she heard him.

'Jew-bitch.'

46

There is no invasion as fearful as love, no havoc like desire. Its fuse trembles in the human heart and runs through to the core of the world. What are our defences to it?

The day broke through a heavy quilt of cloud. Geoffrey opened the shutters. A heavy frost obscured the pane as if to say, *Don't look, turn away, it is better not to see*. He poured water from the ewer and gulped it down, suddenly profoundly thirsty. Blood crusted black around his nose and mouth. He could taste it. They were both still in their clothes. Neither had spoken. Neither had slept.

Beneath the sheet, she was pulling her skirt down awkwardly over her hips. In the thin dawn light, her face was bone, sockets and shadow. Did he feel humbled or sickened? He didn't know.

'Evvie . . .'

She lay her arm across her eyes.

'It was the shock. The whisky. The sight of –'

Her head nodded beneath her arm.

'I never drink like that. It was the . . .' Did he pity or hate her?

She turned on to her side.

'I have no idea why I . . .'

He moved towards the bed once more. Was she asleep?

'Do you still love me?' he tried. The bedsprings creaked under his weight. 'I only need to know that. Then I'll leave you be.'

She listened, eyes closed. Hail, huge pellets, was bouncing off the window. It was lashing the world. *All that new blossom*, she thought. *It won't last. It won't survive the day.*

He came round to her side of the bed and crouched beside her. 'Evvie?'

'Yes,' she replied flatly.

Yes, I love you or yes, leave me be?

'He intrigued you. He seduced you. You were still hurt by my relations with –'

She didn't open her eyes. In the murky light, her lips were ashen.

And Otto was there again – fleeing across the Death Strip in a pair of boots that kept falling off his feet. Earth sprayed up with each bullet from the tower. Pitter pitter pitter. His legs were collapsing, his feet bled, children were crying for sweets as he ran. Then a calm came into his head: 'Modeh ani lifanecha melech chai v'kayam shehech-ezarta bi nishmahti b'chemlah, rabah emunatecha.'

He woke to hail against the window and squinted at the clock. Five minutes past four in the morning.

Chairs lay toppled. Below his back, he could feel shards of glass on the mattress. His pillow was damp with blood. His head ached. Near the range, the brass doorstop glinted like some terrible totem.

I give thanks to God for restoring my soul to my body.

His mother's prayer. It had been almost a year since he'd even thought of it. Now, today, it had returned.

He dressed quickly, shoved his sketchbook down his shirt, and buttoned his coat up to the neck. He read the Army's letter of instruction again, returned it to its envelope, and slid it into a pocket. Key in hand, he realized he was hungry.

He scanned the room. There was nothing for it. He walked to the table and picked up the cornet of sweets. It had survived the eye of the storm.

Three hours later, triumphant, paint-smeared and bright-eyed, he reported to the Army meeting point. From there, the squad was transported to a pasture, a salt-dashed field where you could stand on the high edge of England in the spendthrift light. For the weather had come good, and the sea was vast, alive. He'd never not thrill to it.

The other new recruit, a mechanic called Nick, leaned towards him on the stone wall where they waited. 'Good prospects,' he said with a click of his tongue. 'Life expectancy, ten whole miserable weeks.'

Otto laughed.

The farmer was fuming because he'd painted his herd with luminous paint and still the Huns had dropped their bombs.

'Those Huns,' mumbled Nick. 'Not an ounce of regard for bovine life. They deserve everything we can throw at them.'

'At me,' grinned Otto.

'Yeah . . .' said Nick. 'At you. *Cows*. You barbarian.'

Nick was almost the only man on the squad who hadn't said, 'You're German? Bloody hell. Don't get ideas, will you?'

The glowing carcasses of the eight cows had to be removed before the squad could start, and the day wasn't going to be action-filled. The original plan had been to dig for an SC-500 buried near the swill-yard, but early that morning, the Unit got word of a cluster bomb dropped in the farmer's field. Nobody could say how many 'bomblets' had been released as they fell, and how many lay scattered or buried, still live. They were likely to be fitted with the new trembler-fuses, which meant they couldn't be disarmed. They'd have to be either surrounded by sandbags and destroyed *in situ* or shot by a marksman from a safe distance.

When Otto and Nick weren't heaving sandbags between controlled explosions, they were required only to observe. There would be more legwork, they were told, later, when the field needed tidying. Nick spat over the wall and laughed. 'Legwork!' He lifted up his trouser legs and knocked on his braces. 'Ever get the feeling they'll take any fucker?'

'Polio?'

'Yip.'

'You, a cripple, and me, the enemy,' Otto declared. 'What a team we'll make.' He pulled the sweets from his pocket. 'I lied to the Lieutenant. I'm only here until I have enough for a deposit for a room. A week or two at most.'

Nick tssk-tssked. He plucked a handful from the cornet. Otto did the same. They were sucking noisily when Otto jumped from the wall to his feet. A sparrowhawk – half bird, half memory – was lifting off from the field. It glided over the cliff edge, its wings tilting like a spinnaker to the wind. 'There!' said Otto. 'Do you see it?' But Nick couldn't pick it out against the sky.

The Butterfly Bomb, or bomblet, was a two-kilogram anti-personnel weapon. Its thin cylindrical outer shell hinged open when dropped, giving it the appearance of a metal butterfly as it fell to earth. It was new – only Lieutenant Lowell had seen the diagrams – but the day was an unqualified success. Easy work, comparatively. Dull, largely. At seven, as the others packed up the lorry, Nick and Otto walked the field, scanning it for the unexploded butterflies. 'The duds have no wings left,' Lowell had said. 'They look like ordinary tins.'

Each carried a sling for their collection. By dusk, Nick was limping, but they'd covered most of the field. They made plans for the pub. They met mid-field and popped a few more sweets in their mouths. Yes, Otto said, there was a woman. Or at least, there was now. He grinned at the ground. He needed to find his feet again. This was the start, he said. Her and his painting.

The paint was still drying, he told himself, the colours were emerging; *she* was emerging.

They surveyed the next field for strays, taking a half each. Only a few glinted in the evening light. 'Over there!' Nick called. He pointed to a green edge where field became cliff. Otto jogged easily towards it. The day dropped its cargo of light and the world expanded to the horizon. He felt again the softness of her lips; the press of her palm against his, their fingers laced; the ends of her hair brushing his face; her legs cleaving to him. And that morning, still, he'd felt the fluid lines of her move through him, through his arm, as he finished the triptych in the chapel.

The sparrowhawk swooped again. Was it trying to determine if the shiny butterflies were edible? He felt almost as streamlined as it as he ran, in spite of the sling that bounced at his hip and bit into the tender flesh of his back.

He looked out over the edge. Wasn't that beach the very one where the guards had taken him and the other men to bathe that day last June? The beach where he'd tried to swim out, away from life, and had failed. Or did he only imagine it was?

The horizon dissolved and the world fused in the furnace of the evening. Everything was fleetingly, unremarkably, translucently whole – sea, sky, the bird, the boat rotting on the beach below, the men's voices from the field, the sweet in his mouth. His mind flared. Reality rippled. He felt its flux at his fingertips as he dropped the dud into the sling. He could already see the thickness of paint, its slather and the promise of this, all this, on canvas. He'd got it, it was there, held in his mind's eye when the sea light exploded, the sparrowhawk shrieked and his mother's head turned next to his in the darkness . . .

He could smell the scent of her hair on the pillow, and Evelyn was reading. *The sea was indistinguishable from the sky.* Then Klara laughed, the women argued over their Passover dishes, the hammer whirred towards Jakob's head, his Ballhaus dancers burned, the water spilled over her breast and shoes – she swore *some light shallop had foundered* – the boots stamped on his back, the sonata rose high, and her hands found him –

It was more than an hour before Nick found the path down the crumbling cliff side. He scrambled, falling most of the way on legs locked in their braces.

It was impossible, the Army said, to recover the body before morning.

Night fell. The sea pounded the beach. The wind picked up.

Otto was dead before he hit the beach; dead before the rockfall buried him. Nick told himself that.

He sat by the mound until first light, flouting orders to return to the transport. He couldn't feel his legs. He had no coat. He didn't know Otto's last name but he knew, though nothing had been said, that he had already been alone too much in life. He wouldn't leave him now.

The dew turned to frost, then to dew again.

47

Otto wouldn't have been mad enough, Nick would later tell the Coroner, to pick up the bomb if it had still had its wings – no matter what he had or hadn't attempted in the past. He'd had plans to get lodgings, to paint pictures. There was a woman. He was happy. Christ, he'd had sweets in his pocket.

Of course Otto hadn't shaken the thing, deliberately or otherwise. Of course he wasn't some German saboteur. He'd just dropped the dud in his sling, same as before, when it went off.

After the verdict that day, Nick went for their drink on his own; a lonely, bitter memorial. When had life grown so cheap? Otto hadn't even been allowed his ten miserable weeks.

'Death by misadventure'. The phrase meant nothing. It changed nothing. Weeks later, the official advice on unexploded butterfly bombs would be deemed 'flawed'.

Upstairs, in the heavy hush of their room, Geoffrey left the cup of sugary tea on her nightstand and turned back the bedspread. He removed, very gently, her shoes and stockings. He said she must lie down. But she only sat, rigid on the edge of the bed, watching the steam rise from the tea.

He, too, was in a kind of shock. He didn't know what he felt, not for Otto, not for himself. He could think only of her. And Philip.

He'd deliberately timed the news so that Philip wouldn't yet be home from school.

Rain drummed the roof . . .

He was closing the shutters when he heard her storm down the stairs.

She hardly felt the ground at her feet as she ran. The rain was cold. Otto, she told herself, would turn the key and open the kitchen door as always. He would press her close and weep with her. Something, she would tell him, *something* had gone very, very wrong. How had *this* happened to them? Life didn't sacrifice its lovers. That was the stuff of novels. *What am I to do with you gone from me?*

On the perimeter path in the downpour, she stopped short. It occurred to her only now. Geoffrey had removed her shoes. Her foot was bleeding. There must have been something sharp on the path.

'Come inside, Evvie. Come and get warm.'

He had followed her into the Park.

She was drenched and didn't care. She cared still less about the cut on her foot. The rain would wash it clean. Or not. What did it matter? She turned and took him in, standing tall in the pouring rain, incongruous in his jacket and tie.

'He would have been better for you than me. I know that. He would have made you laugh as you need to laugh.' She was pale, almost translucent, with grief, with the shock of the news. He coaxed her up the stone steps but, halfway across the terrace, she stopped to stare at the lilac bush and the handle of the spade stuck in the ground beneath.

'Evvie, please, let's talk about things inside.'

'You knew,' she said, without turning. 'You knew about that job.'

'He needed the work.' The rain trickled past his collar.

'That's why you got drunk with Lowell. Because you knew. You knew how dangerous it was.'

He laid his jacket over her shoulders and seated himself at the table, surrendering to the weather.

But still she didn't turn. Still she didn't look away from the spot where the tin lay buried. 'And I gave him the letter. I'm the one who arranged it all.'

'You weren't to know. You asked me to find him what I could. And I did.'

'Do you ever think what it would be like to leave all this, Geoffrey?' She motioned vaguely to the Park, to the sky, to the Crescent's solid turrets. She looked back over her shoulder. Rain streamed down her face. 'We seem to make death, you and I . . .'

'That's a nasty cut on your foot. Come inside.'

'You're relieved, aren't you?'

'Of course I'm not.'

'Why not? You found us together. I loved him.'

'Because you love me. You love me *as well*.' His eyes filled.

Her voice was small. 'Death breeds death, doesn't it?' She thought of the pills, just a few feet away. 'First Mr Pirazzini. Now Otto. And still, those pills, just there . . .'

He bowed his head low. 'How long have you known?'

'From the first . . .'

The rain drove at his back. 'I'll dig the things up. I'll get rid of them.'

'No,' she said, 'no, leave them now . . .'

Something in the tone of her voice unnerved him, and he rose from the chair, reaching for her hand. 'It's upset you. I can see it's upset you.'

In the soak of her clothes, she was tiny, frail. Her teeth chattered. Her foot bled. 'No,' she said. 'It's the sensible thing, isn't it?'

Later, after school, Philip would find them together in the kitchen:

His mother, small and wet, curled like a question mark on the lino.

His father, on his knees, wet too and huddled over her, as if the roof of their house were falling in.

48

In June, the German Army turned east. Hitler had decided to invade Russia rather than England. After a year of extraordinary tension, Brighton exhaled.

When she arrived, St Wilf's was still closed for renovations, but a workman smiled kindly and produced a key. It had taken her more than a month to feel capable of this and now, unexpectedly, as he unlocked the side door, she found herself stepping directly into the Lady Chapel.

The stained glass glowed with the morning but the air was cold and stale, the air of a crypt.

Her footsteps rang out in the hush. The gleam of the pews was dulled by dust and fallen dust sheets. The jumper he'd been wearing that night in the kitchen, the one he'd suddenly peeled off, lay now on the flagstones between two pews. His sketchbook sat propped on the font, open to his final study where water from the kitchen tap streamed like grief over her face.

She took a seat in a pew, bent for his jumper, and pressed it to her face. But nothing. No trace. Was that what she'd feared all this time? The final proof of his absence.

Today, she told herself. She would tell Geoffrey today, for how could they go on? The memories – the knowledge – would never leave them, and they could pretend no more.

She turned her face at last to the fresco and felt her own sharp intake of breath. Its scale was vast; her naked back, monumental; her skirt, a dull navy. The crude tin bucket at her feet shone in the light.

He had seen her. That day at the standpipe that terrible day.

She had bent at the waist, just as she bent now – high on the wall overhead. She'd cupped her hands to splash her face and, now, in his painting, the action of her left forearm covered her pendant breast. The point of view was his – or King David's rather – from his position on the slope above. At the standpipe, the water gushed out over her shoes and pooled brightly at her feet. Even that was as it had been that day, for she'd forgotten to kick off her shoes.

Yet he had said nothing. *Why?*

She'd never know.

Each of their three faces was obscured – her profile by the gush of water, Geoffrey's by a pair of binoculars, and Otto's because he stood with his back to the onlooker. *Turn around*, she wanted to say to him. *Turn for me.* He was David, King of the Jews, in a thin MoD blanket. His hair was shorn. His shoulders were bare and wasted. The turf beneath his feet was burned yellow. Overhead, as he watched her, a male sparrowhawk rode a thermal.

In the chapel, the morning's light streamed, and it occurred to her that it was as he'd said: his colours were drawn into life *by the carbon of her breath, by the light of her eye, by the speed of her heart.*

She wanted to say to him, *Otto, my heart is dead.*

On the grandstand roof, above a group of prisoners in grey, Geoffrey as Uriah watched two fighter planes through binoculars. The sky above him was ripped by razor wire and contrails. In his breast pocket, poking out over the top, her lilac envelope waited with the letter of instruction. She could see Otto still, turning it in his hands after she'd delivered it that afternoon. He'd smiled to himself,

335

amused no doubt by the thought of her coloured stationery finding its way into his composition.

All the way across the triptych, the edge of cliff-line made a thin, undulating ribbon of brilliant white, and, suddenly dizzy, as if with those heights, she had to lean forward to rest her head in her hands against the next pew. The cold of the flags rose through the soles of her shoes. She was hungry, and yet, *again*, the wave rolled through her, nausea, grief, anger; anger that he'd left her to *this*, to the loneliness of a stone chapel, to the cruelty of him gone. She hadn't ventured near Number 5. She'd paid a woman to clean his room and take away the wreckage of that night.

She was still light-headed as she rose and walked, eyes straining . . . but yes, there it was, his name on the envelope, just as she'd written it, only painted here in his own hand. *Gottlieb*. It was all that appeared of his name over the edge of Uriah's suit pocket – his only signature on the fresco.

The air in the chapel seemed to surge and crest like a wave in the light that radiated from the three walls, and for a fleeting moment, she felt the massive life of the painting gather her up, as if it had extended itself into three dimensions to absorb her, there in the pew with his jumper in her lap; as if there were no boundaries between her body and his vision; between the present moment and their past.

Was she seeing on these three walls the story of Bathsheba, Uriah and King David or another story, their own, lying in wait within the ancient one, ready to ambush them all: this war, their passion, the Camp's high roof, the mean standpipe, that stray wingless bomb . . . ? In Otto's story, Uriah was sending David to his death. Their fortunes had reversed, and here, Bathsheba's hand was in – on – that letter, for how could the lilac envelope ever mean anything else now?

Time churned. How alive she'd felt in his arms that night, so alive there was no knowing it for the joy that it was.

She turned and walked to the rear of the chapel. She needed to hold the whole of his composition in her mind's eye, as *he* must have done that morning before leaving. His vision shuddered to life on the walls. The colours pulsed. The razor wire glinted. And she saw. The war he'd evoked wasn't this war, their war, it was only *war*; the war that never ended but only began somewhere new, time and again.

Yet the fresco was luminous. Here was every brute evil and loss, but above it, through it, rolled the light off the Channel and its vast reprieve.

She walked to the front again, slipping past the chapel's small bare altar, and raised her hand to the wall to feel him in his work; in the brushstrokes of the hillside where he'd handled the pigment more freely. If only she could conjure the flat of his palm against hers – but again, nothing. Something painful welled in her chest and her heart laboured beneath her ribs, while, unknown, within, at the end of a fine fuse of flesh and blood, life pulsed.

ACKNOWLEDGEMENTS

My thanks must firstly go to the remarkable team of people at Hamish Hamilton and Penguin Books. I am especially grateful for the talent, insights and generous support of my editors Simon Prosser, Anna Kelly and Juliette Mitchell. I'm proud to be with a publisher that champions some of the best literary fiction being written today. Long may they thrive. I'm also grateful to my publicist, Lija Kresowaty, for her energy and skill; my copy-editor, Sarah Coward, for her exceptionally fine eye; and editorial assistant Marissa Chen for her enthusiasm and ready help.

Equally, I'd like to extend my thanks to my agent, David Godwin of DGA, whose passion for literature is always inspiring, and to Heather Godwin, for her kind support behind the scenes at DGA. I'm also grateful to Kirsty McLachlan, Caitlin Ingham and Anna Watkins for their thoughtful words and efforts on this book's behalf.

Thanks are due to my good friends Karen Steven and Hugh Dunkerley. Each read the manuscript at a crucial point in its development, and offered vital perspectives and suggestions. I would also like to thank my friends Theresa Burgess, Rebecca Ford, Jackie Quinn, Adam Marek, Sally O'Reilly and Sue Roe for their good company and generous understanding of the writing life.

In the last six years, Diana Reich, Artistic Director of the International Charleston Festival, has offered me kind support, and that has been a gift. Di Speirs at the BBC has been a warm and generous presence; her interest in my work has been invaluable. Helen Dunmore's encouragement has meant a great deal and is much appreciated. Cathy Galvin, Director of Word Factory, has been another great inspiration.

Funding from the Canada Council for the Arts arrived in 2008, just when I needed it most, and I'm profoundly grateful to the Council and my native land for these lifelines it offers its writers. In the UK, I'm also very grateful for the Authors' Foundation, which offered me generous financial assistance. The lovely people at Booktrust do the most wonderful things to promote writers, and I'm very lucky to have been on the receiving end. I'm fortunate, too, to share in the dynamic literary culture my colleagues and students – past and present – create at the University of Chichester.

My mother, Freda MacLeod, my sisters Kate MacLeod and Ellen MacLeod, and my sister-in-law, Liz Payne, have been unfailingly supportive. The writing of any novel is a marathon of sorts – at times exhilarating and at times gruelling – and it's a process that extends over years. It has always meant so much to me to have their love and encouragement, and never more than during the writing of *Unexploded*.

I am indebted to the work of Virginia Woolf and specifically, to her novels *The Waves* and *The Years*, and to her essay 'The Leaning Tower'. Woolf's life and work have been an inspiration, and I am very fortunate to have been able to cite from her work.

I am also indebted to *Brighton Behind the Front: Photographs & Memories of the Second World War*, which was compiled and published by the ever-impressive QueenSpark Books of Brighton. An account from this book – reproduced with the permission of the Mass Observation Archive at the University of Sussex – is the source of my character Frank Dunn's description of the bombing of the Brighton Odeon on 14 September 1940.

Unexploded is a work of fiction. While great care has been taken to create an authentic picture of the period and place, it is not always possible to serve the literary demands of a narrative and each historical fact in a single work. This novel features major and minor events from the period May 1940 to June 1941. This said, it should not be taken as an entirely accurate historical record of that year.

Alison MacLeod